Bellatrix

Planet of Perpetual Peace

Book 2

Peter Man

Reader reviews

[Reader Mail] “I recently discovered your book, Bellatrix, and was truly captivated by its concept and visual design. The creativity and attention to detail are remarkable. Your work stands out beautifully. Congratulations on such an inspiring creation!” — *Eliana B. Jan. 2026*

“I’m absolutely in love with this series! I’m simply amazed at how [the author] can actually integrate works of classical literature into the story and how everything unfolds in a very interesting way that will tickle your curiosity to follow the story until the end.”

— *Russ Ann, Amazon Review*

“Blending ancient Chinese history, Confucianism, mythology, science fiction and humor may sound like a daunting task, but Peter Man makes it work well indeed ... Watch him grow.”

— *Grady Harp, Amazon Hall of Fame Top 100 Reviewer*

“What a pleasant surprise! I love the stage, the setting, and all the creative characters, ideas, story ... everything. It was definitely a fun adventure for those of us who love sci-fi and fantasy.”

— *Jose Popoff, Amazon Vine Voice Reviewer*

“I recommend you all to get the engine started from the first book of the series, Unconquered. I assure you that this book will keep your eyes widened throughout and is an entertaining and enthralling read.”

— *Aparna Preethi, Amazon Review*

“I found this story to be very entertaining. The narrative is so lively that I completely immersed myself in the story. It is a story that will keep readers hooked until the end.” — *Dani Savante, Amazon Review*

“Mixing ancient history and legends with urban sci-fi is a brilliant idea. This book is super entertaining!” — *Lorenza Seldner, Amazon Review*

"Time for another amazing adventure; this is a great sequel to the first story." *— Phil Bolos, Amazon Review*

"A Sci-Fi Romance—a delightful story." *— Bess C., Amazon Review*

"This is a science fiction book with lots of twists and turns that exceeded my expectations. This piece of writing took me on a journey and the amazing plot kept me interested. I highly recommend this novel."

— Ivana S., Amazon Review

"… fun, action packed sequel to the first book … I liked the integration of real-life sagas and legends which gave the story a realistic element."

— J. Armstrong, Amazon review

"Not for the faint of heart, this story has it all!"

— Mint Tea, Amazon Review

"[The author] has been able to unfold a science fiction narrative in a way that seems realistic. The language employed is simple and easy to follow. I have enjoyed this tale a lot!" *— Sol Tyler, Amazon Review*

"This journey combines warriors, aliens, the earth, and much more as the struggle for survival continues. This sequel is a good one and gets my vote. Check it out folks, it is worth the time."

— Jimmy Jefferson, Amazon Review

"The pace is fast, the settings are intriguing and well described, and the characters are developed well… Overall an interesting and recommended read." *— V. E. Amazon Vine Voice Reviewer*

Book 1 of the trilogy: ***Unconquered***
Book 3 of the trilogy: ***Augenblick: The Blink of an Eye***

Bellatrix

Book webpage: https://www.petermanauthor.com

Blog: https://www.petermanauthor.com/shared-thoughts

Cover designed by Peter Man assisted by Copilot
Printed and distributed by IngramSpark.

ISBN-13: 978-1-9994019-8-6

Prelusion

One might think writing a book, even a trilogy, would be easier than building and running a television station with no money, a feat I was foolish enough to attempt in my youth. This assumption is categorically and indubitably erroneous. Writing is harder by multiple degrees of magnitude. I'm not suggesting authors should put down their pens and start building TV stations, which requires certain deranged bravado and recklessness, as well as a total disregard for the real world's economic consequences. Make no mistake, many people helped me with my TV endeavour, and I would like to thank them all, but it's a story for another time.

When it comes to creative writing, combining imagination with substance, such as the chapters in *Unconquered* recounting the life and death of the Shang Dynasty warrior queen, Fu Hao, I couldn't have done it without help either. And help came my way over the years, often without my realizing it.

In 1980, when I was producing a weekly one-hour Chinese-language program on Toronto's multilingual television station CFMT-TV, now Rogers OMNI-TV, I decided to include a cultural segment on the etymology of Chinese characters. Initially, I drew all my material from *Shuowen Jiezi* (說文解字), the first Chinese dictionary authored by Xu Shen (許慎) around 100 CE during the Eastern Han Dynasty. However, I found some of the book's definitions to be unsatisfactory. As I was not a Chinese scholar, I needed help, for which I approached Professor James Hsu (RIP), who was teaching East Asian Studies at the University of Toronto. By a stroke of luck, the professor was an expert on ancient China. At the time, he was working on a project categorizing a large cache of oracle bones for the Royal Ontario Museum. He introduced me to his seminal work, *Ancient Chinese Society*, one of my go-to references for writing the story of the Shang. Professor Hsu is mentioned in *Unconquered* as David Huang's mentor, whereas his academic achievements are fictionalized as his protégé's attributes in the story, a commixture of fact and fiction.

In 1989, I was introduced to Michael Pang in Toronto, who was presented as a mogul in the broadcast and television technologies industry. He was a Chinese Canadian from Hong Kong, similar to my status, and his Hong Kong-based company was a major player in mainland China, Taiwan and Hong Kong. During the 1990s, his company further developed a dominant position in the professional and broadcast audio sector, implementing numerous high-profile projects in China.

In early 1991, I accepted a court appointment to serve as the receiver-manager of the television station I helped establish. After resuscitating the service and pulling the company back from the brink of total collapse, I realized I needed to build a new production facility to replace the old one, which was falling apart. It would also improve the company's asset value, hopefully commanding a higher price in the eventual asset sale to repay all creditors. Michael helped by introducing me to the latest cutting-edge technologies at the time. He also intervened to settle a dispute between a mutual friend and the TV station, to which I was bound by fiduciary duty, resolving a problem inherited from before the receivership to everyone's satisfaction. Afterwards, Michael returned to Hong Kong to focus on developing his company's business in the vibrant Chinese market.

Following the successful auction sale of the television station and the termination of the receivership, I visited Hong Kong in 1997 to witness the handover ceremony of the city's return to China. I dropped in on Michael. One thing led to another, and I stayed to set up a company in Guangzhou with Michael's support. I ended up living and working in China for twenty years. It is safe to say, without his help, I would not have had enough knowledge about China to author any of the books of this trilogy.

Over the years, I became much better acquainted with Michael. He introduced me to everyone in his family, including his four brothers. His younger brother, Francis, a pioneer in education, founded the Beijing Concord College of Sino-Canada. The high school is the first in China to issue dual Chinese and Canadian diplomas to its graduates, allowing them to enter Canadian universities directly. Michael was also involved in the project and helped develop an extensive network of educational establishments across China, including the Canadian International School of Beijing, which received a two-decade commemoration plaque from Canadian Prime Minister Mark Carney during his first state visit to Beijing. Two characters in the trilogy, Charlie and Viola, attend the schools. For his contributions to education and in strengthening Canada-China relations, Francis received the Order of Canada.

Life is a box of chocolates, but now and then, one encounters a bitter variety. Michael's family suffered the scourge of cancer, and he was a victim of it. Nevertheless, all the good deeds he had done in life would not be in vain. This trilogy could not have existed without Michael. This book is, therefore, dedicated to his memory.

Michael's China story started with a young, wide-eyed broadcast engineer who went to China in 1972 to support the satellite newscast of Nixon's historic visit. He would stay to significantly impact the development of China's television, radio and audio industries. It is a fascinating story, but for another time.

In 2005, while working on network coding technologies in China, I became acquainted with an elderly Chinese gentleman, whose name, when mentioned in front of people who recognized it, seemed to cast a spell of awe over them. Mr. Yang Qianli, the founder and chairman of the annual China Satellite Application Conference, was also a member of the Technology Committee of the Chang'e Moon-landing Project and a senior professor on the dissertation panels of China's top universities in science and technology. At the same time, he was a three-star general and the Deputy Director of the Communications Department of the General Staff of the PLA, who had led the technology and engineering team in launching China's first geosynchronous communications satellite. Despite his reputation for being strict and uncompromising in his demand for perfection, Director Yang only showed me his kindness and easy-going nature, and we hit it off immediately. He also introduced me to Sidney Rittenberg, an American who had lived an extraordinary life in China.

When Director Yang learned of my interest in oracle bones, he organized a visit to Anyang, where the site of Yinxu, the ruins of the last capital of the Shang Dynasty, was located. Upon our arrival, the head of the military establishment in the area, Commander Xu, who was a close friend of Director Yang and fictionalized as Uncle Xu in *Unconquered*, rolled out the red carpet to welcome us. Thus, the story of Fu Hao and the discovery of her undisturbed tomb began to germinate in my mind. Though past retirement age, Director Yang worked tirelessly, contributing to China's rejuvenation. He passed away in 2020 after combating cancer for years. I visited him after he was committed to the hospital, and he was holding endless meetings in his room. This trilogy, especially this book, is also dedicated to his memory.

Readers who have enjoyed *Unconquered* will find the sequel, *Bellatrix*, equally stimulating and captivating. In addition to new, surprising theories about Shang's origin, its migration route, and the identity of Xia, Shang's preceding dynasty, the book will reveal heretofore unexplained mysteries in the Chinese classic *Dream of the Red Chamber*. Readers will discover the true backgrounds of the author, his wife and two survivors of the twelve leading ladies featured in the story. A big surprise lurks within the last pages of *Bellatrix*, but peeking is strictly prohibited. *Carpe Liber*—seize the book!

This book is dedicated to
the memory of
two special friends
who made
this book and trilogy possible

Michael K. S. Pang
And
Yang Qianli

Table of Contents

Chapter 1

Ultima Thule

"Surely, one who fights with immortals is not long-lived!" warned Madonna Lilith, the deathless Amazonian Queen from Betelgeuse.

Victoria wished she had taken careful deliberation before opting for war. But what choice did she have? Queen Lilith had kidnapped everyone dear to her, confiscated her LV knapsack containing all her powerful quantum devices and threatened to exterminate the human race. Victoria was all by herself, trapped inside the Nexus of a skull-shaped spaceship, 6.6 billion kilometres from Planet Earth, betrayed by her only ally and having to go toe to toe against the warrior queen, an implacable man-hater, defended by her Sephirahs, Yanissars and Paladinas, all fearsome female fighters armed with lethal weapons capable of pulverizing mere mortals in the blink of an eye.

Armed with nothing but her wits, Victoria wished it were all a bad dream, perhaps one spawned from the unpasteurized milk she sipped by the banks of the Danube or as a result of excessively gorging herself on a most scrumptious snack from ancient China.

Victoria had a dark foreboding she might not win this battle. Should she admit defeat or refuse to concede? Although her Chinese parents suggested it might not be the best policy to win every battle, she could not afford to lose this one. The survival of humanity was at stake.

Despite never learning kung fu from Wenlong and Xinfeng, Victoria did pick up some self-defence moves, such as the eye-poker, the nutcracker and a few lifesavers she might employ when cornered. To assess her situation and determine the best course of action, Victoria observed the enemy with her eagle eyes.

The august Queen of the Amazons, redolent of a floral fragrance, exemplified majestic pomp perched on her grim throne crafted from the skulls and bones of men who had abused women. Artfully carved scenes of legendary massacres decorated the seat's skeletal frame, on which golden cords secured eleven murderous lances, halberds and tridents. These dealers of death were all cunningly wrought, sporting floral patterns and mythical beasts inlaid in gold along their stalwart tungsten shafts. Occupying the central position and spanning eleven cubits was the mighty spear Gæbolga, the Pike of Pain. As the symbol of lordship, it was seized by the Amazonian Queen after she toppled the patriarchal dynasty. Whosoever occupied the throne and wielded this fearsome spear would be the Supremo of Betel.

Resting in the firm grip of Queen Lilith's left hand was the divine bow Pandiva. A quiver hung across her shoulder bearing five arrows, each representing a different element, to wit, wood, gold, fire, earth and water. The fins of the projectiles were the wing feathers of Munin, the drone warbird, ensuring their deadly flight stayed true. These swift darts, collectively named Pugu, meaning handmaids, brought dolorous death to every one of their targets, returning to their mistress after wreaking havoc.

For armour, the warrior queen outfitted herself with a golden corslet on top of a black spider-silk tunic. An embossed skull glared from her breastplate, inspiring fear. Crowning her head was a titanium helm adorned with the fangs of Draculae, the vampire bat, topped by a fan-shaped flower, the emblem of the House of

Orphius, as the crest ornament. A gem-studded sword in a silver scabbard hung at her side from a golden girdle around her gracile waist. Victoria had witnessed this resplendent panoply before. When the Queen arrayed herself in this martial splendour, the Amazons were ready to commit unstinted slaughter.

Crouched at Queen Lilith's feet was her fierce and voracious pet, Kerbera, the three-headed sand puppy, a hellish abomination with three snapping maws full of sharp, serried teeth of steel. An aged woman wrapped in a black cloak stood to the left of the throne. She was the court advisor, titled the Crone. Leona, a bodacious warrior clad in a serpopard pelt, stood guard on the other side, holding a banner displaying the Amazonian heraldic symbol of the open palm and the motto *Non Inultus Premor*, meaning "no injury unavenged." Directly in front of the Queen were four Sephirahs, peerless androids defending their mistress against insidious weapons. Forming the next ring of defence were six Yanissars, elite Amazonian warriors trained to terminate anyone approaching the Supremo without permission. At the outermost ring were posted twelve Paladinas, essentially Watcher clones having undergone gender reassignment procedures.

"The Amazons have come a long way," Victoria marvelled, thinking, "from living a rat's existence in a hellhole underground to having these and travelling hundreds of light-years to Earth."

"My dear Victoria, your only choice is to join us," Queen Lilith insisted. "Resistance is futile. All four of your parents are here. Jackie, Emma and Charlie are under my thumb. I know you still cling to the fond hope humans can somehow preserve their dominance on Earth, but they have brought demise upon themselves and will become extinct without my help. I'm merely accelerating the inevitable. As a matter of fact, we have crossed the Rubicon. The 'world as you know it' is already over."

"What have you done? Why can't you leave humans alone?"

"My dear, I'm doing these pathetic cretins a favour. Nature abhors a moron and has prepared a spectacular apocalypse for Homo ignoramus. The End of Days was supposed to be a veritable bloodbath. However, I have devised a much milder option, all because you say you can't stomach violence. At any rate, the clock is ticking, and the game is afoot. We have started infecting all humans with a highly contagious pathogen, which is impossible to detect and incurable once infected.

"What's beautiful about this is no one dies directly from it. Clinically, the afflicted will appear to have been stricken by Progressive Cerebral Palsy, sometimes known as Bovine Insanity. While their cerebral cortex will gradually liquefy into a pudding, they will retain motor functions and behave normally, except they won't be able to think. In other words, nothing will be out of the ordinary. When our armada arrives at Earth's orbit in eleven years, we can take over the planet without firing a spitball. It's the perfect ending for humans, not with a bang but a whimper."

"Why are you doing this? Humans have done nothing to you. Why are you taking it out on them?"

"Our archenemy, the patriarchal Shemsu scatocracy, escaped retribution on Betelgeuse's planet, Betel, and found a haven on Earth. These criminals took the earthlings' daughters for wives and spawned a new tribe known as the Nephilim, the children of Orion. Their descendants now roam the planet. I have sworn on my mother's grave, 'No peace without justice.' I'm here to collect the outstanding balance, all of it in blood, with ten percent interest annually compounded. It's only because of my love for you the human race may die off naturally with a progressive brain disease.

"Come, my dear girl," the Amazonian Queen switched to her hypnotic, lily-like voice. "Let us not trouble ourselves with trifles.

The future belongs to us. I want you to be my co-ruler. Join me, and we will set everything aright."

"I hope I can help you heal the wound in your heart," Victoria said, "but I won't be a part of mass murder."

"Victoria, you must grow up," said Queen Lilith, exhibiting a hint of impatience. "Killing is a part of Nature. Where do you think your bacon comes from? It is past time to be arguing about what Nature demands of us. To see you again, I have had to pay a heavy price for living many generations and lifetimes beyond my due. You are mine, and I will have you." Speaking to her guards, the Queen ordered, "Paladinas, bring my princess to me, but gently. I want her in one piece, unharmed and undamaged."

Victoria was inside the Qaanaaq, Queen Lilith's skull-shaped flagship, anchored to Ultima Thule, the Kuiper Belt planetesimal popularly nicknamed Eleven. The spacecraft would appear to be an insignificant rock during its journey toward Earth. More than a thousand ships had already arrived in the vicinity, each transporting up to a hundred thousand warriors and colonists. Dozens more ships were joining the armada every day. Without a superhero to stem the tide of invading aliens, humanity had no other fate but extinction.

Although endowed with superhuman strength, bones of unyielding steel, a cheetah's sprinting speed, Wolverine's self-healing, spider sense, Jedi mind control, and other incredible powers not yet manifest, Victoria was not confident she could overcome twelve Paladinas armed with divine weapons. Thankfully, she learned from her Chinese parents the "Thirty-six Stratagems," of which the most important was the last, "Run for your frigging life!" But before making the mad dash, she needed to create a diversion to give herself a head start.

"Wait, I give up," Victoria said, raising her arms and stopping the Paladinas. After capturing everyone's attention, she pointed behind them and yelled, "Look, the One-eyed Soothsayer!"

As one and all turned around, they quickly realized it was a childish ruse. Nevertheless, everyone fell for it. When they pivoted their attention back to Victoria, she had already fled the scene with the blinding speed of the fleet-footed Atalanta.

While approaching the Queen's Court earlier, Victoria had noticed the utility airlocks near the main Promenade. She bust out of the doorway, hightailed to the utility zone and snuck into a chute, bolting herself inside. However, the ship's quantum computer took less than a nanosecond to calculate her location.

A hologram of Queen Lilith appeared before Victoria.

"My dear girl, where do you think you're going?" the alien ruler chuckled. "You're not flying home from this jetsam chute. You won't survive the trip. The G-force alone will crush you into a meatball. Even the God With No Name cannot save you. One shouldn't tempt the gods by attempting the impossible. Come to your senses, Victoria, be reasonable. Press the Exit button, and we'll talk through this. You know how much I love you and will never allow any harm to come to you."

Victoria knew why the Queen of the Amazons wanted to co-opt her. Everyone she ever trusted and distrusted had asserted she was the Key to an unimaginable power in the universe. Therefore, she must never let anyone gain control over her. Victoria noticed a button with the symbol for Exit and another for Eject. Which should she press? She had to make a stark choice with no good outcome. For Victoria, Queen Lilith's warning "One who fights with immortals is not long-lived" took on ominous meaning. But she could not make the right decision without understanding how it all began and how it could all end.

Chapter 2

Long Ago and Far Away

"You are dead. You, cold as first snow, pure and white, calm as distant stars in pale moonlight, but now shadow shrouds the night; you are dead. You, sleeping lotus in jasmine breeze, smiling when you dream of being kissed, but you'll never wake; you are dead. You, your eyes so bright, your voice so sweet, your sigh so soft, you breathed love into my life, yet you are dead. You, light in my darkness, joy in my sadness, music in my muteness, soul of my soul; you are dead. You, the dagger in my heart, the torment by ten thousand cuts, the everlasting pain, the reason I laugh, the reason I cry, the reason I live, the reason I die; you are dead. You, pale shade in the shadow of Hades, I'd die a thousand deaths for a glimpse of your face, but you are dead. You, killing me slowly with your hateful blade, no balm can ever salve this festering wound; you are dead. Will the tears ever dry? Will the pain subside? Will no one heal me? Will I always be this way?"

Kiku woke from his daymare in a cold sweat, haunted by the words "you are dead" reverberating in his head.

"Kiku Orphius, what was my question?" Professor Carlini Stane asked as he paced across the classroom, scrutinizing every one of his twenty-two students. His eagle-eyed gaze landed on a young lad who kept his head down and his mouth shut.

"You dozed off halfway through the lecture and missed the most important part of our planet's history. As a reward, Kiku, you will serve detention after school to catch up. And you, Mr. Milu Solanus, shall join us."

"Why?" Milu protested. "What have I done?"

"You have done nothing. You have only allowed your best friend to miss out on learning the vital knowledge necessary for saving our planet. If you can't even help your best friend, what's the chance of you helping everyone, including your enemies? What good is being the smartest kid in the valley? It will benefit you to stay behind and help Kiku make up for what he missed in class. Let this also be a lesson to you."

Kiku and Milu were Best Buds Forever living on the paradise planet of Shangria, a name derived from the Haryan root meaning "Paradise, Land of the Living." It was home to the Harya, the planet's dominant lifeform with a late-stage mature civilization. The notion of paradise was, unfortunately, a cruel joke. Any remnant of the beauty once prominent on the planet was now dead and buried in the dimming memories of the Ignorantes, who survived precariously in the Valley of Sabrus, a desolate wasteland surrounded by barren hills and eerie rock formations dubbed the Petrogrid Forest. An open sewer ran through it. The haven was a dung pit of lifeless stones, and Petra was its accursed name.

Warriors of the ruling Yarjun caste had dispatched spies to survey this area. They knew of the refugee camp but decided not to follow up, deeming it beneath their dignity to cull craven cowards who would rather live in a pit of excrement than fight. The Yarjunis believed those who gave up everything to live in peace should not enjoy the pleasure of a quick death served by their costly SHART bombs.

Kiku and Milu were ten-cycle-old boys, similar to preteens on Earth, born seconds apart in neighbouring sheds at Diamond Slum. Diamonds may be rare, beautiful and valuable on most planets, but in Shangria, they were base, plentiful and worthless. The refugees built their settlement with recycled garbage on top of a layer of crystallized coprolite, a euphemism for hardened excrement. The intense heat and pressure of Erinysite treatment, a secret Yarjuni technology patented for eternity, transformed desiccated fecal waste into sparkling diamonds. The Ignorantes called this garish derivative of poop Bushite. Nothing grew on Bushite.

The Ignorantes endured the most dreadful living conditions because they preferred to live rather than fight and die. Kiku and Milu belonged to the Emodulanda caste of musicians among the peaceful multi-caste residents. Kiku hailed from a family of conductors. He practiced with a golden baton, a family heirloom named the Lituus, meaning "the child is the father of the man."

But these were trying times for musicians, especially for the Emodulandas. Among the various categories of musicians, some performed music to glorify the ruling class, others played military music, and many practiced the art for profit. But the Emodulandas did it only for love. At first, the Yarjunis tried to corrupt them with wealth and seduce them with power. When neither worked, they threatened them with torture and death, also to no effect. It infuriated the Yarjunis. The anger ate at their hearts and metastasized into implacable hatred. Upon ascending to the throne, the Yarjuni Supremo, Lord Killem, swore to hunt down the Emodulandas and kill them all with extreme prejudice.

Music of love was, therefore, rigorously regulated at Petra. Emodulanda musicians could only sing softly inside their homes or practice conducting with an empty orchestra. In one more cycle, Kiku and Milu would reach the age of Crossover, when they could decide whether they should switch to a less targeted caste.

Kiku had a sister, Una, who was one cycle younger. Milu had no siblings but recently welcomed the arrival of a mysterious orphan girl to his family, whom the Elders christened Serah, short for Seraphina.

A week before Kiku's detention, a fiery flee-pod fell from the sky, crashing into Heart Mountain right beside Diamond Slum. A rescue team ventured through the labyrinthine Petrogrid Forest past the secure perimeter in search of survivors. Uzun Solanus, Milu's father, was the team leader. But by the time they arrived at the crash site, it was too late to save anyone. The flee-pod had disintegrated before impact. Thereupon, the rescue was repurposed into a scavenger hunt to salvage usable parts. Pepé Uzun stuck his arm into a hole in the ground and plucked out a young girl at about the same age as Una. Not only did she miraculously survive the crash, but she emerged with nary a scratch. The Solanus family took her under their care until they could ascertain her background, after which the Elders Council would decide her fate.

Professor Stane did not detain Kiku and Milu after school to teach them a lesson. After all, they were his star students. As a member of the Nosy Busybody Society in the refugee haven, where everyone knew everyone, the old professor wanted to gather some firsthand gossip about the girl who fell from the sky.

"Is it true the girl does not have a scratch on her?" he inquired, launching a barrage of questions. "Has she told anyone where she's from? Will she join us at school soon?"

"She's a normal child, no different from all the kids here," Milu said, "and she seems physically fine. When she recovers from her psychological trauma, I'll bring her to school."

"Una is helping Serah cope with the shock of dislocation," Kiku added, "while trying to learn her story without being pushy."

"The girl says she belongs to the Educator caste," Milu said. "Professor Stane, maybe you can adopt her to keep you company."

"Sounds great," the Professor said. "We need new blood to develop more talents for keeping the Yarjunis at bay."

"Can we go now?" Kiku pleaded. "My parents wanted me to get some parts at the Dump. I have to be home before dark."

"Speaking of your parents, what have they been up to? I haven't seen them in ages. They didn't even show up for the Parent-Teacher meetings."

"You should know they're the reason I fell asleep in class. They needed my help with their project. I stayed up all night fixing and cleaning modules for their musical thingamajig."

"Alright, boys, you may go. Kiku, make sure you get enough sleep. I know your parents have been toiling on the mythical Twirligig. They believe it will end the Endless War. But it's a pipe dream. They're wasting their life putting blind faith in an ancient almanac they stumbled upon at the Dump. I advised them against it, but to no avail. Nothing will stop the Yarjunis from unleashing the dogs of war upon everyone. It's in their blood. They'd rather die than have peace. How do peaceful people fight such monsters? By throwing the book at them? I know the Yarjunis well. I used to work for them. Help your parents, by all means, but don't let it affect your education. You, the children, are our last hope."

Everyone in Diamond Slum loved Professor Stane, who was once Shangria's top scientist under a different name. He was worshipped as a god by the Yarjunis until he disappeared one day. The Yarjunis searched high and low for him, but came up empty. The unkempt and dishevelled professor now dedicated the rest of his life to teaching young children at the haven and went around wrapped in worn rags as if he were a wandering Baffledore. He no longer taught science subjects and refused to relive his past as an enabler of war. He became a true Ignorante. By his appearance, no one could have guessed this gentle educator was the brain behind numerous revolutionary scientific discoveries, and his inventions had catapulted the Yarjunis to the pinnacle of power in Shangria.

Located on the outskirts of the settlement, the Dump was a mountain of salvaged parts. Yosi Sung, known to Kiku and Milu as Uncle Yosi, was the sole Dumpkeeper. The bespectacled middle-aged man sported a headful of speckled hair and a bushy moustache. He smiled with his eyes and always delighted the boys by giving them toys he had assembled from discarded scrap.

News of Yosi's playful creations soon spread. Every child who visited him always left with a unique plaything. Over time, Yosi's skills improved by leaps and bounds, and the Dump became a bustling hub of robotic arthropods, or arthrobots, teeming with butterflies, ladybirds, honey bees and fireflies. Soon, people started addressing Yosi with the cognomen of Toymaker.

These toys were a marvel to the children, most of whom had never seen a real arthropod. The Endless War had devastated Shangria to such an extent even bugs were going extinct.

"Ah, here you are again with your big fancy list," Uncle Yosi exclaimed. His eyes lit up as he caught sight of the boys arriving on their monocycles.

"My parents say they're very close to finishing their project," Kiku said, handing the bill of materials to Uncle Yosi. "These parts are crucial. As always, burn after reading."

"Hmm, let me see," Yosi scanned the list, reading it aloud. "Eight fibrillating fipples with stithy stipples and trillic tittles, sixteen quena qanums with quantized quiffy quims, twenty-four outgribing ocarinas doped with Didymium, fired in an Erinysite kiln for a Mooch, or eleven days, at eleven thousand degrees, a louche launeddas with an oscillating osculator, eleven each of standard inflataria and fidicinia sensor circuit boards with symmetric input-output Infinibyte channels, a magnum idiophonic ordurator, a radial Sternhell Spitzharfe made from the root of the Briarashe, the mythical World Tree of Shangria, and, of course, while we're at it, the Rodomontadic Renifleur, the sacred Imago of Diamaranth, the Flower Goddess of Shangria. Oh, your parents forgot to include the imaginary Tinkleflopper and Shartfrapp."

"We can help search for the parts," the boys offered.

"Ha, thank you, but we'll need hundreds of you," Yosi chuckled, "and it would still take a millennium, even if we're lucky. Everything on this list is as rare as a unicorn's horn. I promise to look for them, but it won't be easy, and we'll have to be patient. Why don't you boys come into my office? I have toys for you and your new friend who survived the skyfall."

The Dumpkeeper's office was a foam-board shack serving as his workshop, bedroom and living quarters. Failed experiments filled a large carton, while a smaller one contained finished toys awaiting initialization. The upper section of a mannequin formed the framework of an automaton in its early stages.

Uncle Yosi reached for several bugbots on his workbench.

"I designed these new arthrobots based on what I learned from an old textbook," he explained. "Here is a jumping spider for Milu, and for Kiku, a sand scorpion. I've programmed them to mimic the real bugs. They'll defend their nests, so if you place them in a contest situation, they'll try to chase others away. You can make it a competitive game. If something gets broken, I can always repair it or give you a replacement."

"Wow, super-duper!" the boys exclaimed in unison.

"I have special presents for Una and her new friend," Yosi said. "What's her name again?"

"Serah," Milu offered.

"Right. I have prepared two caterpillars for the girls. The little critters feed on plastic and produce nanotube-silk. They'll spin cocoons and transform into moths known as the Mariposa negra."

Kiku wasn't paying attention. He was examining his scorpion, petting it with his finger and thinking of a proper name for his fabulous toy.

Chapter 3

Antebellum

In Haryan culture, names were of paramount significance. Upon the birth of a son, the parents would arrange a naming ceremony after eleven days, a period known as a Mooch. As a child, the boy was known only by his shortened name. Upon surviving the first cycle, his parents would braid his hair into a queue and record his name in the family registry, declaring, "It is good!" Upon the eleventh cycle, known as the Crossover, the boy would receive a caste peruke, a ceremonial headdress woven from the hair of prominent caste members.

At twenty-two cycles, the age of maturity, the young man would be recognized by his full name, consigning him to the social role his caste prescribed. If a man achieved an accomplishment, he would receive a cognomen, such as Yosi the Toymaker. To the Haryan male, his name should reflect his qualities and project his potential. For example, Kiku was the short form of Kingku, which meant he would be the conductor of a great orchestra. Whereas Milu was short for Millipath, indicating peregrination was his lot, and he would be a Minnesänger. The Harya believed the name of a man would affect his life and might even change the world.

This Haryan preoccupation with names had parallels in many Earth cultures. For instance, Hitler was the son of Schicklgruber. Imagine a million Germans shouting "Heil Schicklgruber!" at the Nuremberg Rally. People would be rolling on the floor with laughter. Adolf was wise to have changed his name to Hitler.

Female Haryas, similar to the women in many Earth cultures, did not have personal names; they received only family attributes. For example, the daughter of Aziz would be Azizia, the sister of Kiku, Unaki, the wife of Killem, Killa, or the mother of Kanaka, Kanakim. Females would not receive a unique name until after death. The matriarch of a large family would receive a memorial name such as Diamillim, meaning "goddess, mother of thousands." An exception was for orphan girls, who would receive a moniker describing the circumstance of their discovery, such as Seraphina, "divine fire from heaven." The Harya believed a person without a name might as well be dead or unborn.

Milu noticed his spider could spin little silk balls and use them as weapons. Therefore, he named the bug Orb-Weaver. Kiku christened his scorpion Sting based on its lethal weapon. Sting later gained the cognomen of Deathstalker. Before long, almost every boy in Petra, also known as the City of Stone, possessed a toy they secretly referred to as a Warbug, and it came to pass under the noses of their pacifist Ignorante parents.

The boys of Diamond Slum used black plastic waste to build bug boxes for their arthrobots, which remained dormant in the dark and became energized by light. A foldable flap sealed the frontal opening, unfurling into a drawbridge and forming a bridge when connected to the drawbridge of an opposing bug box. Upon waking, the Warbugs would emerge from their nests and try to dislodge their opponent from the bridge. This childish game soon evolved into a formal competition. The boys organized tournaments dubbed Bug Wars and honoured the champions with fancy titles and pageantry. They dedicated most of their free time to refining their Warbugs, often running to Uncle Yosi and begging him to enhance their toys with new combat skills.

Meanwhile, Professor Carlini Stane adopted Serah, who remained close to Una and dear friends with Kiku and Milu.

Serah's past, however, remained shrouded in mystery. Her only memory was of growing up in a tiny Yarjuni prison cell with her mother, who had divulged little, if not nothing, of her previous life. Before arriving at Petra, the girl who fell from the sky had never laid eyes on Yindi-Ra, the benevolent sun. Her mother called her Little Bee, a pet name signifying a person who existed without rhyme or reason. One fact about Serah was undeniable. She was a ravishing beauty with hypnotic green eyes, a cute upturned nose, pouty lips, an enchanting smile and luxuriant red hair.

Serah avoided delving into the past. When pressed, she would proffer little tidbits and snippets, often punctuated by ellipses. Eventually, the Elders pieced together the story of her escape.

One night, the inmates were jolted awake from their slumber by a cacophony of clamours. It was a daring prison break. Amid the concatenation of gunshots, shouts and screams, fleeting shadows unlocked the prison gates. For the first time in her life, Serah experienced freedom.

During the confusion, the mother and child boarded an airship alongside a group of escapees. But the Yarjuni air patrol caught up and fired a slug into the airship's engine. Serah resisted as her mother frantically stuffed her into a flee-pod, and when the hatch sealed shut, leaving her mother behind, the poor girl screamed and pounded on the window to no avail. The last image etched in her mind was her mother putting her palm on the window, mouthing the words "I love you" before being engulfed by flames.

The fiery flee-pod, timed to self-destruct, ejected at 11G. Serah lost consciousness until Milu's father rescued her. It turned out Heart Mountain used to be a garbage dump, and Serah was lucky to have landed on a mound of bubble foam.

The only fact the Elders learned about Serah's mother was her name, Leela, Leelord's wife, and her profession as an educator before being imprisoned by the Yarjunis while pregnant. It was a past Serah would rather bury as she embraced her new life, adapting to survival in an impoverished slum.

Despite living a meagre subsistence, the children of Diamond Slum thrived in peace and harmony. They compensated for their material scarcity with abundant joy and boundless imagination. In the evenings, the families would gather under the canopy of stars and share tall tales. Sometimes, the aged bard, Dom Clanen, would softly chant a lament, recounting the story of a paradise lost.

"A long, long time ago, I can still remember how this planet used to make me smile. And I knew if I had my chance, I could make the Yarjunis dance, and maybe they'd stop fighting for a while. Yindi-Ra, the sun's our mother; the good earth, our cornucopia. Slow days in the meadows, life was wine and roses. I don't remember if I cried when I learned about our world's demise. Something cut me deep inside the day the music died.

"Children, close your eyes for a moment. Children, remove your eyes and be blind to this unbearable world for a moment. Fear not the darkness. Believe me, sometimes, I'd rather be blind. Imagine. Set your mind free and imagine this valley cloaked in a lush coat of grass swaying in the Favonus breeze, changing colour in the nourishing rays of our benevolent sun, whilst glistening under the soft red glow of the twin moons in the night."

Indeed, Shangria danced with two capricious moons, both hued wine red by the sun's reflection and the spore-laden atmosphere. Haryan star-gazers had long worked on a lunar calendar, but it was bootless. Be that as it may, the Haryas believed Yindi-Ra would, for once in a blue moon, align with Shangria and its two satellites. It would be the foreshadowing of epochal change. According to lore, the rare alignment would coincide with the arrival of the mythical Amphisbaena, a two-headed rainbow dragon. However, no Harya alive had witnessed such a heavenly prodigy. As the years passed, lore became legend, and legend became myth.

With his eyes clamped shut, Dom Clanen continued crooning his melancholy ballad, "Observe through your mind's eye the resplendence of Diamaranth, the flower goddess of Shangria. Let her fluorescence penetrate your clouded sight. Salve your wounded soul with her ambrosia. Submerge your senses in her aroma. Breathe deep her alluring blooms! To inhale her perfume is to purge one's heart of hatred and fill it with rapture.

"Be still, my foolish heart. Is this a Trompe-l'œil? Gossamer-winged butterflies are waking from their midsummer night's dream, taking flight toward the moonlit blossoms' fragrance, yearning to savour the divine Ambergrace, Diamaranth's ambrosial Amrita. Sipping a single drop transforms the butterflies into apsaras till the first light of dawn. Watch them prance and frolic to the Rondo and Polonaise. It's a miracle of miracles!

"Yeah, miracles abound in Shangria. Behold the golden Briarashe, the twin-twined, heaven-bound World Tree. Do you know her roots burrow deep underground and encircle the globe? Have you ever tasted its many-splendoured fruit, the honeyed Aeppelfealu? A single bite would heal all ailments, reverse aging and open one's eyes to the universe's secrets. The countless leaves of the Briarashe are wind chimes of jade, swaying in the cool and constant Favonus breeze, forever playing a celestial symphony.

"Do you know the World Tree is home to the Borogova, named Kalavinda by the gods, a mockingbird gifted with an angel's voice? Hark! Hark! The divine bird sings, her aria rising from the arboreal harmony, reeling around the majestic trunk in a rollicking round dance, leaping from branch to branch, whirling from arm to arm, and teasing the chimes as the notes waltz past in double time. Beware the serpentine antagonist, stealthily creeping up to entangle with the central motif. In one moment, they're stomping in a fiery Pasodoble; in another, they're quick-stepping a passionate, death-defying tango in a tight embrace.

"Reaching the grand finale, the melodies unite, aspiring to flee from the scales and ascend the heavenly stairway to be one with the gods. But the Immortals will not abide. The climb slows, the tears flow, and the attempt fails. The music dissipates into a wisp of endless longing. An errant gust disperses the nameless song into nothingness. The music dies. The universe withholds its refrain. Listen! Dead silence. Now darkness reigns."

Most of the Ignorantes were in tears by the end of the lament. The War had persisted for over two generations, and the ancient bard was the last survivor at Diamond Slum to remember life as it was antebellum. The Ignorantes must remember why they were here and never forget paradise was possible, provided the Endless War would end.

Una, Kiku's sister, always sat in the front with Serah and Professor Stane. Her parents had become social outcasts, tirelessly labouring on their impossible dream, the Twirligig. They had not appeared in public for a long time. People were beginning to wonder if they had lost their marbles. Everyone pitied Kiku and Una, for they lived almost as orphans.

Unnoticed by the grown-ups, Kiku and Milu were nowhere to be found. Uninterested in listening to senior citizens caterwaul about loss and longing, they stole inside the forbidden zone of the Petrogrid to practice a new game Milu had invented.

While the monocycle was the primary mode of transportation at the haven, Milu devised a vehicle with two wheels, coining it the "duocycle." He handcrafted one for Kiku and another for himself. Duoycles were, however, wasteful because they required an extra wheel, exclusively supplied by Uncle Yosi. All the same, the Toymaker indulged the boys and complied with their wishes. Soon, all the kids exchanged their monocycles for duocycles.

Milu's new game was dubbed "Dogfight." Two boys would ride side by side on their duocycles, each trying his darndest to topple the opponent without being unseated. The game required balance, cleverness and a dash of daring. Occasionally played on a narrow, raised path to add to the challenge, the game risked causing unsightly skin abrasions. If, by accident, something worse were to happen, the boys would have to resort to deception, as the parents must never learn about this dangerous game. Based on the banned concept of conflict with the threat of physical harm, Dogfight caught on and rivalled the Bug Wars in popularity.

After honing their dogfighting skills, Kiku and Milu discussed strategies for the upcoming Bug Wars Championship title fight. Sting had dispatched Panzer, the hissing roach, advancing to the final round. He would face Kalchas, the brooding mantis, winner of the semi-finals against Milu's jumping spider, Orb-Weaver. To stand a chance against his formidable opponent, Sting needed to harness the military prowess of the Titans.

Kiku and Milu delved into the arcana of the mysterious Sentinels of old, known as Titans, upgrading Sting with advanced tactical codes. While the struggle promised to be fierce, the boys held high hopes for victory. They had gleaned wisdom from an ancient sūtra: "When defending peace against violence, never bring a knife to a firefight. Be as orderly as forests, as immovable as mountains, as stealthy as shadows, as swift as wind, as violent as fire, as shocking as thunder and as shapeless as water." It had taken almost two cycles, repeated setbacks and numerous repairs. Sting finally possessed the codes of an invincible fighter. Glory and fame awaited the winner of the Final Showdown.

Chapter 4

The Mahashangria

"You are dead!" Bilu threatened Kiku as the two stepped inside the ring. Kalchas, Bilu's killer mantis, was famous for giving no quarter to any of its Bug Wars opponents. In the previous round, Orb-Weaver escaped by the exoskeleton of its mandibles or, in human language, the skin of its teeth. The spider wisely beat a speedy retreat into its bug box, sealing the entrance with sticky silk balls. Sting, however, was fearless and would not shy away from a good challenge.

Bilu's brazen behaviour shocked Kiku. Before the advent of Bug Wars, Bilu was more or less a pusillanimous twerp with an innate aversion to confrontations. Many kids seemed to have been adversely affected by an innocent game played between mindless toys composed of autonomous moving parts. Without question, Kalchas' aggressiveness had rubbed off on Bilu.

As peaceful refugees of war, the Ignorantes adopted their name to set themselves apart from those Haryas who wanted to fight the imperious Yarjunis to the bitter end. The Ignorantes offered the excuse they were uneducated in the ways of war and refused to participate in something they were ignorant of, hence their name. Unfortunately, the children playing competitive games and learning combat tactics were no longer ignorant.

"Serah," turning to the mysterious newcomer, Kiku requested, "will you be our Lady Fortuna and give Sting a Mahashangria blessing? We'll win the championship in your honour."

Though she grew up in a Yarjuni cell, Serah learned special knowledge from her mother, a member of the Educator caste, memorizing the mystical cantos of the epic poem of Mahashangria, an oral tradition recounting the past, present and future stories of Shangria, in particular, the sections containing benedictions, maledictions, incantations, imprecations, orisons and oracles, composed in the arcane language of the ancient Titans.

A draconian law of the Educator caste strictly prohibited the propagation of the Mahashangria by any means other than oration or song. Given the astronomical number of words needed to be committed to memory, the epic was separated into eleven sections to be studied and taught by Educators. It was almost impossible for a single Harya to master the entire epic. The person who did would be a sage and receive the title of Sage. The legendary Sage Didymas was the only person reputed to have accomplished this feat, likely because he had composed the Mahashangria in the first place. According to Haryan lore, it would take someone with the stoutest heart to be named Sage because knowledge of the complete Mahashangria would drive mere mortals insane.

As a member of the Educator caste, Professor Stane taught the formidable epic, but only the section dealing with the past.

Since it was verboten for anyone to record the words of the epic poem verbatim, the following written account would reveal no more than a glimpse of Shangria's story, so readers might get a hint of the planet's beginning, during the Chaos of Boarshite.

"Sing, Muses, of heaven and earth, of gods and angels, of windborne birds and landbound beasts, of pristine waters gushing from chthonic springs and fragrant flowers blooming in sleepy meadows. Sing a song of beauty, sing a song of bliss. Lovely Erato, honey-voiced Calliope, goddesses of poetry and music, grant us your divine fire. Let us sing a never-ending melody of love in the eternal land of paradise.

"But beware, ye sons of the blind, ye who have eyes but will not see. Beware the Curse of Sage Didymas: 'Thou shalt not befoul the sacred Logos with banal signs. For those false prophets and scriveners who try, a plague on both your houses. May the evil eye visit you in your sleep and dispatch you to abysmal Hades.'

"In the beginning, chaos reigned supreme. The firmament hung low, mountains spewed hot blood, and oceans boiled. A deadly admixture of poisonous fumes suffused the air. All was darkness and despair. Mother Earth groaned with grief. The God With No Name took pity and wept black tears. The infinite and eternal god split the firmament to let in the golden amber sky and the benevolent sun. The bright orb *they* named Yindi-Ra. From night, *they* created day; from death, *they* conjured life; from mindless existence, *they* composed elegant verse. Day one of Kalpa one.

"The God With No Name witnessed violence and disorder. *They* heard Mother Earth weep in quiet desperation. The magnificent god took pity. *They* sent a monolith named Moloch, the angel of divine fire, from the heavens to land on future Shangria for all lifeforms to worship. Eons crept by. Time grinds all to dust and swallows all. Relentless and inexorable is its journey. Thus passed unknown and uncountable cycles of erosion and concretion, the origin and name of the monolith became lost in time, and its story was shrouded in mystery. Each day and every day, the sun's blessed rays forevermore shone on this black rock. Relentless and inexorable were Yindi-Ra's ways.

"On an average, ordinary Tuesday afternoon, an extraordinary event occurred. Perchance, all the stars were aligned. An aqueous column emerged over the oceanic waters on either side of the landmass. They twisted and spun, siphoning water into the heavens, linking up to form an undulating ribbon in the sky. During the day, the welkin band reflected the variegated colours of a rainbow. During the night, parti-coloured lightning flashed inside the empyreal arc. By their fecund imagination, mythmakers of old sighted a two-headed dragon stretching across the length of the golden amber sky and imbibing the planet's lifeblood from the shining sea on either side. Named Irin, the Amphisbaena's emergence presaged the Golden Age of Shangria.

"On the same day, the monolith crumbled, leaving behind the black Omphalos, a sacred stone rich in rarest Sandymium. Over time, the Omphalos vanished, leaving behind a layer of black soil from which two golden saplings sprouted. They grew into two divine trees entwined as one, their roots and new saplings spreading in all directions to encompass the entire planet. The primeval twin tree became a giant known as Briarashe, the golden World Tree of myriad arms.

"The blessed fruit of Briarashe and its offspring was the golden Aeppelfealu. However, on the primeval World Tree alone sprouted two sublime fruits in the shape of pine cones. One was the Fruit of Truth and the other the Fruit of Life. They fell to the ground upon ripening, each shedding a seed known as the Grist. Encapsulated within these two Grists were all the mysteries of creation, existence, destruction and rebirth. A worm consumed the Grist of Life and experienced exponential growth, becoming Abysso-mamba, the Great Worm of Shangria. A giant blackbird swallowed the Grist of Truth and carried it to an unknown island in the limitless ocean. It was the destiny of the celestial Grists to end up in the hands of a seeress known as the Sibyl, who feareth not the truth and durst reveal the secret name of the God With No Name.

"Having shed the Grists, the two sublime fruits burrowed deep underground until they reached the bowels of Shangria, where the source of the planet's almost inexhaustible energy lay hidden from Haryan eyes. This energy, the Eternal Delight, was the answer to all of Shangria's problems but, in the wrong hands, the root of all its woes. Kalpas later, a great lord with the help of Abysso-mamba would discover the fiery lake, naming it Erinyes and the energy-rich mineral Erinysite. The unquenchable fire of Erinyes he would name the Eternal Inferno.

"In the fullness of time, the blessed fruits of life and truth, nourished by the Erinysite, gestated into two divine beasts, each with a single horn and an outer covering of golden rays. Thus, by the grace of the inscrutable God With No Name, the twin unicorns, Delo and Re'an, were born and vouchsafed to the Haryas to foster peace and harmony. The unicorns emerged, according to lore, from a wormhole marked by the Omphalos inside a crystal cave."

Any fairy tale worth its salt would describe the mythical beasts at this juncture. However, neither the imagination of mythmakers nor the fabrication of fablemongers could do the unicorns justice. Their appearance defied description and beggared belief. Some said the unicorn resembled several animals haphazardly patched together, such as having the skin of a snake, the neck of a giraffe and the head of a lion. Others said the unicorn was a Tetramorph, except the four animals from which it was composed varied widely between so-called eyewitness accounts. Indeed, a blind bard claimed one would stare at the creature and fail to describe it, because mere mortals could not express what had sprung from the incomprehensible God With No Name.

The unicorns were truth and justice incarnate, arriving at Shangria to settle all disputes fairly and teach all creatures to live in peace and harmony. However, they were the three-dimensional manifestation of an eleven-dimensional existence. They must learn how to deal with the n-body problem of lifeform interactions. The first breathing creature they encountered was a confused human named Didi. Wielding a powerful staff, he conquered the planet, and he composed the Mahashangria with the help of the unicorns, gaining the title of Sage. Noting the approach of the impending Devastation, the divine beasts escaped to another time and space, taking advantage of their ability to be everything everywhere, all at once. They merged and adopted the appearance of Didi, travelling the world as Didi Delorean.

During his journey of discovery, Didi Delorean met a one-eyed wanderer perambulating with the help of a familiar walking staff. They decided to travel together in their quest for wisdom.

They learned of the emergence of life, which necessitates conflict. It is beyond good and evil. All lifeforms must cooperate and compete to acquire the limited energy resources necessary for survival, development and propagation, individually and as a group. It is the prerequisite of life. Fail and prepare to meet death and extinction. To survive, the predator must hunt, and the prey must run. Predators do what they can, and prey suffer what they must. When living is the goal, Nature is merciless!

Didi Delorean and the one-eyed man realized harmony was a precarious balance on a knife's edge. To maintain peace, people must become expert acrobats. They discovered the answer to solving the problem of violence in life was to eliminate want and guarantee basic sustenance to all, thereby dissolving the predator-prey relationship. Hence, the travellers went home to rebuild paradise, or so they hoped.

In reality, the Haryan world was awash in lies and violence. The Endless War, started by the Yarjunis, deprived the common Haryas of everything worth living for. No one ever discovered any vestige of the World Tree; in fact, trees became extinct. And no credible eyewitness ever reported the sighting of a unicorn. Similarly, the crystal cave, wormhole and Omphalos were likely figments of someone's imagination. Few Haryas believed the Epic of the Mahashangria was anything more than fiction meant to instill fond hopes into the desponding hearts of the doomed populace. Besides, all Haryas knew the unicorn was a mythical beast; it had no place in their truthful account of factual history.

Chapter 5

The Day the Music Died

While Serah cherished the camaraderie of her new friends and was willing to go to great lengths to please them, digging into her dark memories was unbearably painful. At any rate, she was not fully conversant with the ancient language of the Mahashangria, and her mother warned the epic contained as many curses as blessings. It was a matter of counterpoise, and the universe existed on a precarious balance. What if she inadvertently summoned an evil spirit from the Eternal Inferno?

On the other hand, Una, Kiku and Milu treated Serah as their sister. How could she deny Kiku's request for a few encouraging words, wishing him and his robo-scorpion a swift victory? Closing her eyes, Serah entered her memory palace in a trance, and words rolled off her tongue.

"The Mantis has a thousand eyes, and the Sting but one. Yeah, the Mahashangria ends when the sire meets the son."

"What's wrong?" Milu caught Serah as her legs buckled under her. "Are you okay?"

Regaining her senses, Serah muttered, "I'm sorry. I meant to make a blessing, but these strange words came out instead. I don't want to get anyone in trouble. I had better not try this again."

"Don't worry about it," Kiku reassured her. "Una, will you please look after Serah? The Final Showdown is upon us."

"I'll walk home with you, Serah," Una offered. "The boys don't need us here. Sting will be fine. Let's get out of here."

From the first day, Una had taken on the role of big sister for Serah. She understood the traumatized girl wanted to forget the painful past. While the boys were all gung-ho and razor-focused on the championship match, Una cared about Serah's feelings and mental well-being. Hand-in-hand, they departed from the secret venue in a cave within Heart Mountain.

With or without Una and Serah, the show must go on.

"In the red corner, the lord of Fortress Strong," announced the Master of Ceremony, "winner of thirty-three sanctioned fights against three losses, I present to you the Sting of Sabrus, the Dealer of Death, Kiku's Killer Scorpion. Ladies and gentlemen, give it up for the indomitable, the invincible, the inexpugnable, Dia-a-a-a-a-a-a-abolical Sting the Deathstalker."

Exuberant huzzahs and shouts of approval erupted from the spectators.

"And in the blue corner, the master of Castle Bravo, boasting an unblemished record of twenty-two wins in twenty-two fights, I present to you the Mauling Mantis, the Destroyer of Dreams, Bilu's Butcher Bug. Boys and girls, brace yourselves for the undefeated, the unbeaten, the unconquered, Ki-i-i-i-lle-e-e-e-er Kalchas. Let's get ready to r-r-r-r-rumble."

The referee reiterated the rules, the judges rang the starting bell, the contestants made the hand-over-fist salute, and *le jeu a commencé*, the game was afoot.

As Kiku and Bilu lowered the drawbridges of their respective bug boxes and connected them, the Warbugs woke up and emerged to occupy the bridge. At the sight of the warriors, the fans shook the ground with a universal shout, spurring the Warbugs to engage in an epic clash. The more experienced Sting dipsy-doodled from side to side while advancing with deliberate steps, meticulously measuring the striking distance with its laser-like gaze. In contrast, Kalchas took a menacing pose but remained as motionless as a statue, eyes fixed upon its prey and raptor claws coiled to strike with blinding speed and deadly precision.

Despite being hardwired and firmware-installed with lightning reflexes, Kalchas had no effective defence against the Deathstalker's deadly stinger launched from unpredictable angles, supported by two lethal steel claws, designed to snap the mantis' spindly legs in half without warning or hesitation. No arthrobot possessed coding to repel a simultaneous three-prong attack.

Kiku recognized Sting's advantages and programmed it to serve a preemptive first strike. The scorpion could not miss when Kalchas made itself a stationary target. Having reached the combat zone, Sting started a sideways shuffle to his right while probing with stinger jabs to the left. The tick-tock of the clock slowed as the robo-scorpion built up energy, preparing to crush Kalchas' limbs while feigning a stinger attack.

Though the brooding mantis seemed inanimate, its processors were running at full tilt. Indeed, Kalchas had a thousand eyes, forming two compound optical receptors and sending yottabytes of data for statistical analysis inside its neural processors. Thanks to its Hidden Markov algorithm, the mantis could accurately predict its opponent's intentions ninety-nine times out of a hundred. Before Sting moved in for the kill, Kalchas already anticipated the robo-scorpion's line of attack. The scene was reminiscent of the tense moments before a Wild West showdown at high noon. The crowd hushed, their eyes fixed on the duellists, and their breath held still. It would be all over in the blink of an eye.

"Look at the sky," Una cried as the girls emerged from the cave. "I have never seen anything like it. It's beautiful."

Serah raised her head, following Una's heavenward gaze, to be struck by the vision of the two-headed rainbow dragon, Irin.

Immediately, her eyes rolled back, and she entered a trance again, uttering gobbledygook of unknown origin and meaning.

"The Seer has a thousand eyes, and the King but one. Yeah, the flame of life expires when the song is sung."

Serah emerged from her trance and began to sob, though no tears fell. Una hugged Serah to comfort her, guessing the poor girl might have been suffering from the Seer's Curse, which condemned a soothsayer to vaticinate infallible yet inscrutable prophecies invariably and universally ignored.

Serah regained her composure as an eerie melody rose from the depths of the earth. The whole planet resonated with each note. Even the rocks and stones began to sing.

Delivered from the mystical Twirligig, the Earth Song was a tender lullaby a mother sang to her children, pleading with them to rest from their endless strife. Anyone who heard the chthonic chords of the divine instrument would drop whatever they were doing and dance in celebration of peace and love.

Una and Serah skipped and hopped with joy. Simultaneously, across all fronts, the Endless War halted with a spontaneous ceasefire. The clock struck upon the eleventh hour of the eleventh day of the eleventh month, the long-awaited Hour of Peace. Guns jammed and failed to fire, missiles refused to rise in their silos, attack drones plummeted from the sky, and soldiers locked in combat broke into a quickstep waltz. Even Sting gave up its deadly assault and performed a harmless foxtrot.

Kiku and Una's parents succeeded because they never gave up. They could scarcely believe it themselves. Despite the Twirligig being incomplete, their prototype worked. During a short break when no one was in the workroom, the heavenly harp played divine music all by itself. For a moment, everyone thought peace had finally arrived. But after a few minutes, the music died.

Chapter 6

Brave New World

"Wake up, wake up." Victoria woke to Alexa's voice. While life had, for the most part, returned to normal for Victoria, living with her Chinese parents in Richmond Hill, north of Toronto, meant adapting to a few changes. She couldn't complain, considering her parents had to deal with so much more. She was grateful they settled down quickly and were enjoying life in Canada. On the other hand, who, owning a mansion and an immense trust fund, wouldn't?

The rich aroma of 100% Kona Coffee wafted into Victoria's semi-conscious brain as she shuffled into the kitchen, mumbling "Good morning" through her half-awakened lips. The soothing melody of *The Butterfly Lovers Violin Concerto* was playing in the background.

The Butterfly Lovers, an ancient Chinese folklore, could easily have been a Shakespearean tragedy. The female protagonist masquerades as a boy to go to school but inadvertently falls in love with a fellow student. Her father, however, arranges for her to marry someone else. Devastated, her lover dies of a broken heart. In grief, the girl follows her lover into his grave, and they emerge as two butterflies. The iconic violin concerto was composed by a Chinese musician during the late 1950s, boldly combining Chinese lyrical ideas with Western orchestral harmonies to narrate an enduring Chinese love story.

Xinfeng was practising her daily routine of traditional Chinese stretching exercises known as *Baduanjin*, or the "eight segments of silk brocade." Meanwhile, Wenlong was preparing Canadian-style ham and eggs for Victoria. The parents stuck to their Chinese-style breakfast of *zimizhou*, "purple rice porridge," accompanied by *baozi*, "steamed buns."

This scene reminded Victoria of her previous family life in Dundas, with Chinese characteristics.

"Good morning," Xinfeng cooed while taking a horse-riding pose and drawing an imaginary bow. "How was your sleep?"

"It was deep and dreamless. I haven't slept so well for a long time. Mmm, breakfast smells delish."

Wenlong poured Victoria a cup of coffee while humming along with the music.

"Good morning, daughter," he said. "Why don't you learn the *Baduanjin* from your mom? It's quite simple and will keep you strong and supple, preparing you for some basic martial arts lessons. It could come in handy someday. You never know."

"Sure, I'm all for Chinamaxxing," Victoria said. "As for kung fu fighting, I reckon I'll pass. The self-defence skills you guys taught me are more than enough."

Victoria noticed two books on the table, *The Fellowship of the Ring* and a hardcover with a Chinese title.

"Dad, have you been reading the Lord of the Rings?" Victoria asked. "How do you like it?"

"Fascinating. It's about a powerful ring which might be harmful to its owner," Wenlong replied. "It reminds me of your unicorn rings."

"Don't worry, I won't use them unless absolutely necessary," Victoria said. She knew her parents wanted to discourage her from using the rings. They were not toys, and she must respect them. Victoria picked up the other book to change the subject.

"What's this?"

"We found it at the bottom of the package Viola sent us," Wenlong explained. "It's the original Chinese version of *Dream of the Red Chamber*, one of China's four great classics. Your mom is reading it. I find it too maudlin for my taste."

"How do you like the book, Mom?"

"It's fabulous," Xinfeng said, wrapping up the routine and settling at the kitchen table. "I think you should give it a try. You'd be surprised by its exquisite storytelling, rich with emotions and intricate details. Every Chinese should read it at least once."

"But I can't read Chinese," Victoria said.

"It's not as daunting as it seems. I can teach you if you're interested," Wenlong offered. "With your intelligence and our help, you'll learn the language in your sleep."

"Great, I look forward to it," Victoria said, excited about the prospect of comprehending Chinese. "Mom, could you tell me what *Dream of the Red Chamber* is about?"

"It's a high-fantasy historical romance based on real people," Xinfeng said. "Authored during the Qing Dynasty by a penniless writer descended from a once great aristocratic family, the story revolves around the incarnation of a celestial stone and its life on Earth. Born a son into the family of a powerful court official, the protagonist grows up in privilege before losing everything dear to him. The saddest of all, he must give up the love of his life to marry another, resulting in a heart-wrenching tragedy of the ages. It's a poignant tear-jerker but well worth reading. When you're ready, I can help you understand the intricacies of the story."

"I can't wait, but after I've finished my current reading list."

"What are you reading now?" Wenlong asked.

"I've been diving into the classic science fiction books Charlie gave me. I have just finished reading Ray Bradbury's *Fahrenheit 451* and started on Isaac Asimov's *I, Robot*."

"You should focus on fact-based literature," Xinfeng said, "such as *Slaughterhouse 5* or *Catch-22.* What's Charlie thinking, giving you all these fictional books based on silly fantasies? What time is it? Isn't he supposed to be here already?"

"He is getting off the highway at Hamilton to pick up the girls," Victoria said, checking her iPhone. "Jackie should be ready, but Emma is always fashionably late. They should be here in about an hour, with Charlie driving like Mad Max."

Victoria sensed the Princeton frosh had been up to no good of late, brewing mischief. She had an inkling of what it might be, but decided not to spoil his fun. On a whim, Charlie said he would be spending the weekend in Toronto, driving for eight hours from Princeton on Friday evening in his extended-range Tesla S. He cruised through the Finger Lakes area in advanced autopilot while snoozing most of the way. After entering Canada, he took a quick detour to Dundas to pick up Emma and Jackie.

"Would it be okay with you," Xinfeng asked, "if your dad and I go away for a few days?"

"How many days are we talking about?"

"We're thinking of flying to Vegas later today and coming back Monday morning on a red-eye," Wenlong said. "Your mom and I love MMA and boxing, and a big UFC fight is taking place tonight between the women's Strawweight Champion Zhang Weili and the Flyweight Champion Valentina Shevchenko. We know you're not into violent sports, but we love martial arts."

"Besides," Xinfeng added, "fellow Light-Heavyweight MMA fighter Zhang Mingyang and Heavyweight boxer Zhang Zhilei will be at ringside to give Weili moral support. I'd love to meet them."

"Where do all these fighters of the Zhang lineage come from?" Victoria thought, "More descendants of Shang prince Ya Zhang?"

"Sorry for springing this on you so suddenly," Wenlong said. "We were going to watch the fight at home on ESPN+. But out of the blue, someone offered us two ringside tickets at the last minute. It's too tempting to resist."

"You guys should go and have fun. I'm old enough to look after myself. Besides, Charlie and the girls are staying over tonight. I won't be home alone. They'll leave tomorrow evening. I'm sure I can manage one night on my own."

"Without adults around," Wenlong said, "Charlie might help himself to the beer in the fridge. He is at that reckless age, after all. He's also a bit of a mollycoddle, born with a silver spoon in his mouth, so he might think he can get away with anything. It's him I worry about, not so much you."

"Let's hide the beer in the basement," Victoria said. "I won't tell Charlie. We'll be fine with coffee, tea or juice."

After finishing a quick breakfast, Wenlong and Xinfeng packed for their two-day getaway and were ready to leave when Charlie and the girls arrived. The young man acted with proper respect and offered to take the future in-laws to the airport.

"You've been driving through the night," Wenlong said. "You should take a break. We'll go by Uber. It's *uber*-convenient."

"Oh, Uber schmuber," Charlie quipped. "I used autopilot and slept like a log all night. By the way, Elon Musk is driving. It's no trouble at all."

Chapter 7

Beer is a Beer is a Beer is a Beer

Charlie would like nothing more than to put himself at Victoria's service. Returning from Toronto Pearson International Airport, he veered off to Highway 7 to grab lunch from Victoria's favourite Chinese restaurant, where he packed a veritable feast consisting of crispy roast pork, Hainan chicken rice, Sichuan spicy shrimp, Beef Chow Fun, Hokkien fried rice, and pastéis de nata, fancy-named Portuguese custard tarts popular in Macau and Hong Kong. Charlie certainly had the propensity to overspend. He also brought alcohol.

"My parents are right. You're nuts!" Victoria cried, liberating the champagne bottle from Charlie. "What do we have here?"

"It is not what you think," Charlie replied. "Most people may call it beer, but for some, identifying it as a plebeian beverage such as beer will start holy wars."

"Beer is a beer is a beer is a beer, even if it's a fancy-schmancy champagne-bottled craft beer. My parents set the house rules. They said no beer."

"Alright, strictly speaking, this is not beer, not even craft beer," Charlie argued with expert casuistry. "This, mon amie, is a lambic; a gueuze, to be precise. I'm sure your parents did not ban gueuze. Besides, we live in a free and democratic country. We shouldn't submit ourselves to arbitrary rules set by authoritarian parents. We should exercise our inalienable right to decide whether we'll have gueuze tonight by vote. All those in favour say aye."

Jackie and Emma raised their hands, chiming "aye" before Charlie concluded his specious exposition of twisted logic.

"So, there you have it," Charlie declared triumphantly, pointing at his eye. "Three against one, the ayes rule."

Emma, always itching to try new things, grabbed the bottle from Victoria and started working on the cork.

"What's this lamb or goose drink?" she asked Charlie. "Did you use a fake ID to buy it?"

Charlie gestured for Emma to hand back the bottle.

"Be careful with this baby," he advised. "It needs to rest in the fridge after the road trip. I got it from a fellow Princetonian. He's from Belgium. Let me tell you, these Belgians are fanatics when it comes to their brewed beverages. This unique drink is from his private stock. I won it on a bet, a 'heads I win, tails you lose' kind of bet. I thought I'd share it with you guys. For your information, this rarity is a lambic, magically conjured from natural airborne yeasts unique to a small district in Brussels. If you move the brewery a block down the road, the taste will not be the same because the natural yeasts are different. Some breweries still use their centuries-old stirrers and vats. A few don't even clean the cobwebs in the cellar. It's as traditional as you can get."

"What about goose?" Jackie asked.

"It's gueuze. Imagine Inspector Clouseau pronouncing 'goose' with a dash of 'guilds' and a pinch of 'girls.' According to my Belgian friend, Tintin, I call him, it's an alchemical admixture created by commingling aged lambics with young lambics rich in residual sugars to induce secondary fermentation, which increases the alcoholic content, bolsters the carbonated buzz and adds complexity to the drink's flavour. Ladies, this is why, to some Belgians, calling this drink a beer is sacrilege."

Emma was impressed and fluttered her eyelashes at Charlie, which he pretended not to notice.

After lunch, the quartet enjoyed a round of Mahjong and completed a Bridge rubber. Charlie had taught them Mahjong to hone their skill in creating order out of chaos and Bridge in negotiating contracts. Victoria partnered with Charlie in Bridge and won the vulnerable rubber, bidding and making a Grand Slam contract of seven No-trumps with Charlie as Dummy. Victoria swore she never employed any sleight of hand or legerdemain.

When Charlie suggested taking the group to R&D, a Michelin-award Chinese restaurant, for dinner, Victoria demurred.

"You've already spent too much on our lunch banquet," she said. "Besides, R&D is in downtown Toronto on Spadina, too far away. For supper, we can either have leftovers or I can whip up something quick and simple. We can relax at home and watch a movie on Netflix or HBO."

"Listen, Señorita Victoria, my parents gave me a diamond card. I deserve it because Princeton accepted me based solely on my academic merits, no sponsorship or donations required. On the other hand, my father hasn't seen the bill yet. He may hit the roof. So, I'm not sure how long my spending spree will last. Why not pretend today is the last day of the world as we know it and go bonkers while we can? What do you say we put it to a vote?"

"Sorry, no more voting," Victoria forestalled another round of rigged polls. "This is my house, and I'm the boss here. You guys can start a game of Balderdash or Trivial Pursuit while I make dinner. You can decide which movie to watch from either *Shaun of the Dead*, *World's End*, *Paul*, or *Ready Player One*. I'm okay with any movie as long as Simon Pegg's in it."

"I second the motion," said Emma, dragging Charlie and Jackie to the den while Victoria headed to the kitchen.

Since returning to Canada with Wenlong and Xinfeng, Victoria had taken on more cooking responsibilities while her parents worked on acclimatizing themselves to a new and bewildering world. By the time school started, she had become adept at creating tasty and innovative meals using whatever ingredients were available. Victoria retrieved a bag of fresh Chinese broccoli or *gai-lan*, a carrot, an onion and two zucchinis from the fridge. She took a bag of green peas and another bag of shelled prawns from the freezer, setting aside a handful of the green peas in a bowl and twelve plump crustaceans in the sink under running water.

While the prawns were thawing, Victoria washed the Chinese broccoli shoots, saving the leafy parts for soup and dicing the stems. She also diced the carrot and onion and cubed the zucchini. At this point, the budding chef was thinking of making fried rice when Charlie poked his nose into the kitchen and exclaimed, "Let me guess. We'll be enjoying your famous Victorian fried rice."

Victoria took the comment as a provocation and a challenge. She decided to make a last-minute revision to the menu.

"I haven't made up my mind yet. Since you've thrown down the gauntlet, I'll make an Italian risotto to tickle your palate."

"Sounds rad. Do you need any help?"

"You can help by not helping," Victoria replied playfully. "What's the matter? Can't handle two small-town girls with your trove of trivia knowledge?"

"The questions are kinda crazy," Charlie said, shrugging his shoulders. "Who is New York City named after?"

"King James II. He was the Duke of York when the Dutch settlement, then known as New Amsterdam, was granted to him."

"Alright, who holds the record for the fastest five goals scored by a single player in a professional soccer match?"

"Oh, come on, this is common knowledge!" Victoria cried. "It's Robert Lewandowski, playing for Bayern in a match against Wolfsburg. He scored five goals in nine minutes."

"What? Holy Mackinaw! It's an unbreakable record," Charlie marvelled. "Now, name the Polar Bear Capital of the World."

"Every Canadian knows the answer. It's Churchill on the Hudson Bay in Manitoba."

"We're not worthy! We suck!" Charlie jested, raising his hands and bowing in self-depredating adulation. "But obscure trivia is not why I'm bothering you. I have a problem with Emma. She's acting weird and making me uncomfortable."

"Oh, she's teasing you," Victoria reassured him. "Emma teases everyone. It's harmless fun. Don't worry about it."

"Is playing footsie under the table harmless fun?"

Victoria stopped her knife work. "Really?" she said, raising an eyebrow. "Hmmm, it is a bit too much,"

"Let me keep you company, maybe give you a hand with something. It's much safer here in the kitchen."

"In that case, will you get some items from the cupboard? Let's see—extra virgin olive oil, dried shiitake mushrooms, curry powder, paprika and the salt and pepper mills. Also, grab the cultured butter and the block of Parmesan cheese from the fridge. While you're at it, look for a carton of organic chicken broth. I'm supposed to use a bit of white wine. Since we don't have any and I don't want to use Chinese cooking wine, I'll substitute it with your lambic. Will you uncork it for me?"

"With pleasure. And may I be so curious as to inquire what culinary delight will be titillating our taste buds tonight?"

"It's my take on Ruth Reichl's *Risotto Primavera* recipe. Prepare to be pampered."

"Awesomesauce, Vic," Charlie said as he placed the container of chicken soup next to Victoria, deliberately getting a little too close for comfort. He sniffed her hair and whispered near her ear, "Smells yummy already. I have to say you're the coolest."

Victoria felt a blush rising on her cheeks. She was not oblivious to Charlie's advances.

"Thanks," she said coyly. "You're not so hot yourself."

Chapter 8

We'll Always Have Dundas

"You are dead!" Shaun warned the boy who was dribbling a soccer ball on the street and had accidentally hit him with it.

Victoria started giggling, soon joined by the other two girls. Charlie didn't get the joke at all. He didn't even know *Shaun of the Dead* was supposed to be a zombie apocalypse comedy.

"What's so funny?" he asked, bewuthered.

Thereupon, the girls burst into peals of laughter.

"Poor Charlie," Emma cried. "You don't find that funny?"

"Don't you know why we only watch Simon Pegg movies?" Jackie exclaimed.

"We don't even care what his movies are about," Victoria said, recovering from her fits of laughter. "Just watching Simon Pegg frown is enough to crack us up."

Charlie emitted a strange sound resembling a groan mixed with a chuckle. It's known as a gruckle.

"No wonder they're the Weird Sisters," he mused.

Charlie did not find *Shaun of the Dead* funny. Brought up on Chinese stand-up comedy, English humour went right over his head. His mind drifted back to Victoria's craftily prepared meal and their conversation at the dinner table.

Despite missing half the ingredients specified by Ruth Reichl, Victoria's *Risotto Primavera* was a resounding success. She made various substitutions, replacing asparagus with Chinese broccoli and saffron with curry and paprika. The chicken broth stood in for stock, while the Manchurian rice subbed for Italian Arborio rice. Her bold experiment using lambic instead of white wine made a perfect match with the extra-aged Parmesan. Victoria added a couple of ingredients not in the recipe, such as the prawns, which she cubed and lightly sautéed in butter with a dash of fresh lemon juice. She softened the dried shiitake mushrooms in warm water and finely diced them. Finally, she cooked with love, guaranteeing a culinary masterpiece.

With the mushrooms simmering in the chicken broth seasoned with curry and paprika, Victoria sautéed the vegetables with butter and olive oil in a heavy skillet. She added the ingredients in sequence, starting with the onions, followed by the carrots, green peas, Chinese broccoli and zucchini. Next, she added two cups of rice with half a cup of lambic. After reducing the lambic, Victoria slowly poured the broth on the rice and kept stirring until the rice was soft on the outside and most of the broth had evaporated. She seasoned the steaming concoction with salt and pepper, sampling it regularly to ensure everything was perfect. The final step was adding the prawns with a generous portion of butter. Victoria learned from *Julie & Julia* all food tasted better with butter and followed this instruction to the letter. Lastly, she grated the Parmesan on each person's plateful of risotto according to taste.

"Victoria, you rock," Charlie praised the chef as everyone gathered around the dinner table. "Shall we say grace?"

"Gra-a-a-cia ple-e-e-na," the Weird Sisters harmonized, recalling their days in the school choir singing *Ave Maria.*

"Come on, I mean a proper grace," Charlie said, grabbing Victoria's and Emma's hands on either side to make a circle. "For what we're about to receive, may Victoria find us truly thankful."

Charlie sang it as Mr. Bumble in the musical *Oliver!*

"Amen!" the girls responded a cappella and began to dig in.

By tradition, dinner was the time for partakers of the daily repast to engage in village banter and sisterly gossip. But Charlie would feel left out because he knew nothing about Dundas and couldn't participate in the girlie chitchat. Therefore, he took the bull by the horns and controlled the narrative.

"What do you think about the global trade war?" he poked the hornet's nest. "Who's going to win?"

"Canadians do not want war," Victoria said. "Why can't everyone get along? What do Americans think?"

"Canadians may be peaceful," Charlie said, "but Canada has been busily fighting many wars as an adjunct of the American war machine with only a few exceptions. As for Americans, most of them don't pay much attention, and for those who care, their opinions mostly conform to the endless lies of their politicians and news media. How am I supposed to feel when it is okay in America for people to accuse me, a foreign student, of being a Chinese spy stealing their national secrets?"

"Can you prove you're not a spy?" Emma quipped. "How do we know you're not stealing knowledge from Princeton?"

"You can't prove an unprovable negative, so I won't waste time trying. My father taught me never to argue against a false narrative. It grants substance to drivel. Western politicians blame China for everything and make excuses great again. The Democrats and the Republicans are constantly at each other's throats, except when it comes to attacking China. They suddenly agree and try to outdo each other. Americans seem to support a war against a powerful nuclear-armed country. It's plain nuts."

"It's all politics," Victoria said, drawing on the knowledge she learned from David Huang. "And politicians in democratic countries depend on lying to win elections. It's the unfortunate truth. I wonder when the voting public will see through the lies. They know politicians and the war machine lie non-stop. But why do people believe what they say about China? How is it possible for all the politicians and news media who disagree on everything to suddenly speak with one voice when China is the target of their attack? Charlie grew up in China, and I've been to the country. The truth is in plain sight if people want to know. But people don't want to know because the lies fit well with their prejudices."

"You know, I have always looked up to America," Charlie said, "and wanted to study here, but I'm not happy to see people uncritically accept lies about China, or any other country, for that matter. Is it freedom of speech to lie and insult? I'm glad we grew up with the Confucian teaching to 'practice good manners at home, be respectful at work and be trustworthy to others, never abandoning proper behaviour though we live in barbarian lands.'"

"Does anyone notice all these lies and insults may have consequences, such as war?" Jackie remarked.

"America has been waging this kind of low-intensity war against China for over a decade, if not longer," Charlie asserted. "It may explode if they keep fanning the flames. War is a racket for the One-Percenters. The people send their children to die and bear all the costs while the corporate elites reap all the profits. The politicians responsible for getting America mired in endless wars are never held accountable. They get re-elected and continue to enjoy wealth and prestige. Unfortunately, the people give these warmongers a free pass. I guess the people must pay the price. But when the bill arrives, they prefer to believe China is to blame."

"Sad to say," Victoria sighed, "Canada, as well as those aligned with America, supports its war on China. However, subservience does not guarantee peace, long-term benefits, or no blowbacks. The future does not bode well for Canada unless people in power make a U-turn in their policies soon."

"They should remember the saying, 'to be a friend of America is fatal,'" Jackie said. "And the U.S. can't even defeat the Taliban.

Why do people think going to war with nuclear-armed China and Russia would not be costly and unwinnable, if not catastrophic?"

"People are zombies," Emma chimed in, psyching herself for the zombie movie after dinner. "They're brain dead."

"Nuclear war is no joke," Victoria remarked darkly, remembering Huang Shi's vision. "It will spell the end of the world. Even warmongers and their families will not survive."

"Have you ever imagined how the world would end?" Charlie posed the sombre question to the symposium. "What do you think will be the cause, and when will it happen?"

"It'll be a zombie apocalypse," Emma jokingly suggested, making zombie claws at Charlie. "Everyone will get infected."

"It'll probably be a cataclysmic astronomical disaster," Jackie surmised, "hopefully, not in our lifetime."

Victoria was pensive and stayed silent on this sensitive topic.

"Wonder Woman," Charlie elbowed her, "What do you say?"

"Do you know how the bear died?" Victoria quizzed.

"Is it a joke in the line of 'How did the hamster die'?" Jackie quipped.

"It's an idiom my Chinese mother taught me," Victoria replied. "It may sound silly, but the answer teaches a moral."

"The bear fell into a blender?" Emma guessed, followed by a burst of titters.

"The bear choked on the hamster," Jackie said, speculating along the line of dead hamsters.

"Very funny! Ladies," Charlie chuckled. "Why don't you tell us, Vic? How did the bear die?"

"The answer is simple. The bear died of stupidity."

Emma and Jackie synchronized their groans.

"This is not a joke," Charlie said. "According to Professor Cipolla's *Five Laws of Human Stupidity*, the human race will likely self-destruct due to ignorance, inanity and idiocy."

"As you all know," Victoria said, "I'm happily reunited with my biological parents from China. They're quite awesome. But for some reason, they want me to believe everything is hunky-dory while I see an unstoppable downward spiral. People everywhere sense the dangers. Yet they close their eyes and spend all their energy defending the lies. I love Canada and the society I'm a part of. But how do you awaken people who live their entire lives in a cesspool of lies disguised as freedom and have no experience of the truth? It's hopeless, and I can't sleep thinking about it."

"Let me share a famous adage by the Taoist Zhuangzi (c. 369–286 BCE)," Charlie said. "'You can't talk about the ocean to a frog in a well, you can't describe ice to a summer midge, and you can't reason with an ignoramus.' Hence, you shouldn't lose sleep over other people's delusions and lies. C'est la vie. Houses built on shifting sand will eventually collapse. Your parents mean well to keep you out of it."

"Vicky, you don't have to carry the burden of the world on your shoulders," Jackie added. "I'm not as pessimistic as you. I know of many good-hearted people who care about the world. They're raising awareness about climate change, advocating for green energy, opposing corporate dominance, helping needy families, feeding war refugees, rescuing abused animals, fighting for democracy and freedom against fascism, championing human rights, upholding the rule of law, protesting against racism, sexism and prejudice, supporting diversity, taking anti-Semitism to task and marching for world peace. Hope and change are coming. It's not as bleak as you think. And even if our world should fall apart, we'll always have Dundas."

"And Simon Pegg," Emma added.

"Here's looking at y'all," Charlie said, raising his fizzy radler. And the four clinked glasses.

Chapter 9

The Twirligig

No one in Petra understood why the divine symphony lasted only a few minutes. Peace emerged without rhyme or reason and expired without omen or warning. Hope sprang ephemeral, leaving the bitter aftertaste of empty euphoria. Everyone stopped in their tracks, waiting with bated breath for the music to restart. But what was dead remained dead. The Endless War resumed in brain-splattering, blood-spurting, bone-shattering earnest. Before Sting could react, Kalchas' claws impaled the robo-scorpion and rent it asunder. Darkness clouded Sting's eyes, and its spirit escaped with a whimper.

Amidst cries of anguish, protests against unsportsmanlike conduct and calls for an official review, Kiku could do nothing but pick up the pieces while Bilu revelled in Kalchas' ill-gained victory. Milu tried to console his best friend with an age-old adage, "What's done is done. We can't turn back the clock."

Milu came up with an idea to mollify Kiku's anger over the loss of Sting to perfidy. He suggested giving the scorpion a proper burial and setting up a memorial with the epitaph, "Beneath this earth rests Sting the Deathstalker, Kingku Orphius' son, fearless warrior, victor of thirty-three deadly hand-to-hand combats, felled in battle by the treacherous, scrofulous and execrable act of a loathsome insect, whose name we are *loth* to utter. Death swallows all in vengeance. O ye of little faith. Blessed are the grateful dead, for he shall rise inexpugnable and woe unto the wicked!"

Emerging from the cave, Kiku and Milu noticed the undulating two-headed Irin stretched across the turbulent sky. Blessed were the lucky Haryas who witnessed this rare celestial prodigy, the portent of epochal change. Could it be linked to the mysterious chthonic music of the Twirligig? The boys pedalled at high gear back to Diamond Slum, eager to learn if the Endless War was finally coming to an end. When they arrived, they found the Orphiad shed surrounded by the Ignorantes. Kiku and Milu squeezed through the mob to get inside the humble abode, packed with neighbours and graced by an esteemed elder of the haven.

Una and Serah were already inside. Kiku's father, Pepé Koci Orphius, was answering the elder's questions.

"Did it work?" Kiku interrupted. "Did the Twirligig work?"

"I guess so, but we're not sure how," Pepé Koci replied, gently stroking his son's hair. "We're still missing a crucial ingredient, yet the Twirligig played by itself while your Mamia and I were away. Unfortunately, by the time we returned, the music had stopped. So, we're no wiser on what happened."

"What ingredient do we need?" Kiku inquired. "Let us organize a treasure hunt at the Dump. We can all chip in."

"I was explaining to Elder Ya-Yah. It took us a long time to understand the Almanac, which claims the Twirligig receives its power from one of the two Grists, the seeds of the mythical Fruit of Life and Fruit of Truth, and the person destined to discover the Grists is the Sibyl because she feareth not the truth and durst to reveal the name of the God With No Name."

"Let us not mire ourselves in fairy tales and folklore," Elder Ya-Yah said. "We have all had a glimpse of the power of the Twirligig. Even the Yarjunis stopped fighting. Henceforth, you will no longer work alone. We will dispatch scavengers on a large-scale quest for the Grists, even beyond the Dump. Together, we will make the divine instrument play for peace again."

"For the longest time, no one believed us," Pepé Koci said. "Even Professor Stane discouraged us. Not wanting to give up on peace, we decided to work in private. It's much safer if people have no idea of the Almanac's secret, especially when Yarjuni spies live among us. But now, everything has changed because the Twirligig has manifested its power to the world."

"Let the Elders handle the Yarjunis," Elder Ya-Yah set the peaceful musician at ease, "and let us help you complete the Twirligig. As the Chief Elder, I speak on behalf of the Council. We will place all our resources at your disposal and spare no effort. Meanwhile, I must visually inspect your work, as the Elders will have many questions tomorrow at the Council meeting."

"Certainly, Most Serene Elder," Pepé Koci assented, as he could never say no to Elder Ya-Yah, who commanded great respect, and whose words were almost law. "You're welcome to inspect the instrument. However, until we receive a legal resolution from the Council, we dare not unveil the Twirligig to the public. I'll have to ask our good neighbours to leave our humble shed so I may comply with your request."

The people promptly vacated the Orphiad shed after Elder Ya-Yah issued an order with his eyes. Only Kiku and Una were allowed to remain because it was their home, a cramped and spartan dwelling constructed mainly from flimsy cardboard discarded by the wastrels of the Haryan high society. Encompassing no more than thirty square metres, the living room doubled as the dining and sleeping quarters for the family. Cooking took place outdoors. Everyone shared public baths and toilets. Pepé Koci designed a round foam mattress he would raise to the ceiling during the day using a pulley system. In the evening, he would lower the mattress, and the family of four would rest upon it in a three-prong star arrangement known as the triskelion.

A vinyl mat overlaid the floor. Pepé Koci lifted it, revealing a cunningly camouflaged trapdoor. Grabbing a bioluminescent lamp, he opened the trapdoor and led Elder Ya-Yah, Kiku and Una down a flight of stairs, leaving Mamia Koca above to ward off potential intruders. After what seemed to be an interminable descent down a shaft dug through the layer of sparkling Bushite, they arrived at an underground chamber. Pepé Koci raised the lamp, revealing the Twirligig to unenlightened eyes for the first time. Although Kiku had been helping with the project, his contributions were limited to preparing parts and modules above ground. He had never entered the secret sanctum of the Twirligig until this day.

So, what was the Twirligig? It was a round table approximately 1.5 metres in diameter, constructed of black petrified wood harvested by subterranean woodchucks. At the centre was a circular cavity, and floating in the space was a medallion shaped in a semi-rosette with a small chamber, held in place by Sandymium fields. It was the Rodomontadic Renifleur, the sacred Imago of Diamaranth, the Flower goddess of Shangria. Uncle Yosi's army of arthrobots found it, digging deep in the Dump. Unbeknownst to most humans, this floral symbol would spread to Earth and become a popular emblem of ancient cultures, a modern version of which is the logo of a major electronics company from China.

Radiating from the centre of the Twirligig were strings of various lengths and thicknesses, meticulously crafted from tightly braided nanotube-silk. These strands represented the cosmic connections linking Shangria with the heavenly constellations.

"Only when powered by one of the Grists," Pepé Koci explained, "destined to be discovered by the mysterious Sibyl, will the Twirligig be complete. By chanting the Incantation of Creation and Destruction and playing the lost chord of the eleventh key, she will reset the universe back on its path to peace. We are at a loss for how the incomplete instrument could have played by itself."

After Elder Ya-Yah departed and the crowd dispersed, Kiku and Una sought out Milu and Serah to relay their newfound knowledge about the Twirligig. Milu had already told Serah of Sting's heroic death and the plan for a proper burial. Serah apologized to Kiku for failing to bestow Sting with a victory benediction.

"I would like to offer Sting a small gift," Serah said, presenting a jewellery case to Kiku. "I made the box from the black nanotube silk of my Mariposa caterpillar. It is almost indestructible. I used to keep my Bushite baubles in it. I'd feel much better if you let Sting rest in timeless peace inside this casket."

Serah's generosity touched Kiku, who was well aware the jewellery box was her only valuable possession. Serah's sweetness took the edge off the bitterness in Kiku's heart, and he decided to let go of Sting and Bug Wars. He wanted to focus on the Dogfight game anyway. Kiku dispersed the dark clouds around him and repaid the girl with kind words.

"It's alright, dear Serah. Sting died in battle. What more can a fighter hope for? But thanks for the lovely casket. Sting will rest well in it. Why don't you come with us to the Dump? We have decided to make it Sting's final resting place. It does not become a warrior to spend eternity buried in Bushite."

As the four young friends cycled toward the Dump, Kiku directed a question at Serah. "Why did you say Sting had one eye, and what do you mean by Mahashangria ends?"

"I'm sorry. I honestly have no idea what those words mean."

"I suspect Serah may have the Sibyl's gift," Una said. "When we saw the heavenly Amphisbaena, she made another utterance. I'm still debating whether the grown-ups should know about it."

"Before we understand what's happening to Serah," Milu said, "we should keep this a secret. If the Elders believe she's the Sibyl destined to find the Grists, she will have no peace."

At the Dump, Kiku delivered the sad news of Sting's demise to Uncle Yosi, who listened with a deep frown. However, upon examining Sting's remains, the Toymaker's face brightened, and his familiar avuncular smile broke through his bushy moustache. "I won't give up on Sting so soon," he said.

The automaton, a work-in-progress with the top half assembled but lacking legs, burst out, "Pepé Yosi, let me fix Sting for Kiku. I can finish before nightfall. Please let me, please."

"Son of a Blunderbuss! You've startled our young friends," Uncle Yosi chided his mechanical man. "I said I would introduce you at the right time. Since you have jumped the gun, here we go. Kiku, Milu, Una, Serah, meet Sator, short for Satanu Sung."

While the others fawned all over Sator, Kiku broached the topic of the Twirligig and asked Uncle Yosi if he knew anything about the fabled Grists.

"Let me give you a hint," Uncle Yosi said. "Ask for help from Serah. You see, after completing Sator's neural processing network, I had trouble booting up the Quick-n-Dirty operating system. Not long ago, Professor Stane came by. To my surprise, he inserted a small pineal seed inside Sator's ocular neural chamber, asserting it would serve as his third eye. After a flash of intense blue light, Sator woke up and started learning. Within an hour, he became self-aware, *scientes bonum et malum*—knowing good and evil. It was as if Sator had received the *Götterfunken*, the spark of divine fire. Professor Stane's pineal seed was one of the Grists you seek. While he has expended one to give life to Sator, he may possess the other or know its whereabouts. He is Serah's father. The four of you are best friends. All you need to do is ask."

"Hmm, so Professor Stane had the Grists all along," Kiku thought. "But he never helped Pepé and Mamia power up the Twirligig. I wonder why."

Chapter 10

Goodbye, Mr. Stane

"Yosi should not have spread stories about me relinquishing the Grist," Professor Stane complained to the children, who had raced from the Toymaker's workshop to the Professor's office. "Mark my word, trouble is coming. Children, let me tell you something about the Twirligig. It is bad news. I took the Almanac and fled from the Yarjunis because I was afraid they might force me to build the accursed instrument. I ended up in Petra with a new identity and buried the book in the Dump. It was bad luck your Pepé Koci found it."

"Doesn't the Twirligig bring peace?" Kiku asked, perplexed.

"In my previous life as a scientist, I built many powerful instruments meant to benefit all Haryas," Professor Stane said wistfully. "But in the hands of the Yarjunis, these inventions became their war machines. As for the Twirligig, it indeed evokes peace but also exacts an ironic price. I dread to think of the debt we owe for the brief tune we heard a while ago. I tried to persuade your parents to abandon the project, but they stubbornly refused. Alas, here we are."

"It won't make any difference now," Milu said. "The Elders are getting involved. Sooner or later, they'll knock on your door. If you have the second Grist, you'll have to give it up for the Twirligig."

"Milu, you're a smart boy and speak the truth. However, the Twirligig and the Grists are not for everyone, especially not the

Elders. Since I won't live forever, I must pass the secrets I know to someone who answers a question correctly. You, my children, are the only ones I can trust. Are you ready for it?"

The four perked up their ears.

"Would you fight a bloody war for peace? Una, let's start with you."

"It's a paradox," Una answered after a brief contemplation. "It's impossible to fight a war for peace, especially for peaceful people like us. A war for peace won't work. So count me out."

"Una may have a point," Milu said after the Professor nodded at him. "But this is a trick question. Peace always comes at the end of wars. To gain peace, someone must fight the wars. I'll support a just war for a fair and lasting peace."

"My instinct is self-preservation," Serah, taking her turn, professed. "I'll only fight if it is necessary. But the better part of valour is discretion. I prefer to stay as far from war as possible. My motto is *Bella gerant alii,* let others wage war. I'll be a model Ignorante and hide in a safe refuge until peace returns."

"And what about you?" the Professor asked the pensive Kiku.

"I don't know," Kiku replied tentatively. "It depends."

"I want an answer," the Professor insisted. "You can't sit on the fence. Do you agree with Una, Milu or Serah?"

"Una is right. It's hard to be peaceful when fighting a war."

"Are you saying, as opposed to Milu," the Professor clarified, "you would not fight a bloody war for peace?"

"Not quite, I agree a hundred percent with Milu. Sometimes, people must fight for a fair peace unless they prefer to live a miserable, demeaning life with a jackboot on their neck."

"Una and Milu hold opposing views," Serah exclaimed. "You may only agree with one or the other."

"You know what, Serah? You're also right," Kiku said with a playful wink.

"Your answers are all valid," the Professor declared, "even the oxymoronic one of Kiku. War and peace are a matter of life and death, and life exists in a precarious balance we call peace. When disturbance arises, whether internally, externally or both, peace is lost, and war ensues. My question seeks the best answer in a battle of ideas, and the winner embraces all opposing ideas in a balancing act, even if it seems nonsensical and self-contradictory. After all, reality is a superposition of all possibilities. It depends on how our decisions and actions maintain the equipoise.

"It's the same with the Twirligig. The Almanac describes it as an instrument of war and peace, not only peace. War and peace are two sides of the same coin. The untold story behind the origin of the Endless War is a Yarjun Lord's discovery of the Almanac and his attempt to build the Twirligig. In his search for the Grists and the Sibyl, war broke out, and it continues unabated to this day.

"Try as we may, one cannot defy the forces of destiny. The Orphii family boasts a history of producing great musicians, and it is in their blood to build the Twirligig. Unfortunately, the spontaneous manifestation of the instrument's power means the Yarjunis will soon swarm Petra with bounty hunters looking for me. I'm an old man. I can't outrun them forever. Hence, I'll pass my secret to one of you for custody, hoping it finds its way to the hero who will protect us from the curse of the Twirligig and end the Endless War. Judging from your answers, I will choose Kiku. My boy, do you accept this challenge?"

"I'm honoured, but I'll need your guidance and mentorship."

"The rest of you, please leave us," Professor Stane said. "I shall have a few words with Kiku in private."

Once the others had left the room, the Professor started stuffing his pipe with spiced weed and lit it while Kiku patiently waited.

"Secure in absolute secrecy what is about to enter your ears," Professor Stane said, puffing a few rings into the air. "The

Almanac came into my possession through a Yarjuni royalty, Lord Strongarm, Lord Killem's twin brother, as the executioners were breaking him upon the wheel in the dungeons of Badlam. For reasons beyond my understanding, he wanted me to be his confessor. He told me with his last breath how he received the Almanac, which led to his discovery of the Grist of Life, and I must ensure it would never fall into the hands of the Yarjumis.

"After retrieving the Almanac and the Grist from Strongarm's secret vault, I realized Lord Killem's agents were shadowing me. They figured I had learned something valuable in the confession. I deserted the Yarjunis the first chance I had, and I've been running ever since. Their spies and bounty hunters have been combing the rebel strongholds, thinking I'd be selling my services to the highest bidder. They could never believe I have become a cowardly Ignorante. My alter ego and disguise have given me some years of peace. Unfortunately, my calm Petra life is coming to an end. I must get up and run again.

"Your parents must be extremely lucky, or unlucky, to have played the Twirligig. It should never have happened. The Almanac clearly states the instrument needs the *Götterfunken* from one of the two Grists. Realizing the danger, I had relinquished the Grist of Life to Sator, preventing it from being used to activate the accursed contraption, but in vain. As for the Grist of Truth's whereabouts, we depend on the Sibyl to locate it on a mythical island.

"Unfortunately, the Yarjunis have heard the music of the Twirligig and felt its power. I'm sure their agents will finally figure out I'm at Petra. I'll have to leave before they show up. But I won't be able to take Serah. I need you to protect her on my behalf. I have this inexplicable gut feeling Serah is not an ordinary fugitive. Her presence among us is not an accident."

"For sure, Serah will be safe with us. But why is the Twirligig dangerous if, without the Grist, it's merely a harp?"

"According to the Almanac, the Twirligig is an instrument of creation and destruction. Sage Didymas built one and inadvertently brought along the Polemophthorosin Devastation, which destroyed his kingdom, the Twirligig, the unicorns and the Nephrustan, the staff of power by which the Sage conquered the world. Your parents ignored this warning in their ardent pursuit of music and peace. Keep Serah close to you and keep her safe. She reminds me of someone I met once upon a dream. I hope we will understand her significance before it's too late. At the same time, stay close to Sator, as his life force comes from the Grist of Life. From now on, you'll have to carry my secret or make good use of it; otherwise, pass it on lest you fall victim to it."

"If the Twirligig is so terrible, I'll ask my parents to burn it."

"You shall speak to no one about the secret except to a worthy successor when facing mortal dangers."

Kiku nodded, realizing the Professor had an appointment with Death and did not expect to survive.

"I have shared all the information you need to know. I'll be leaving Petra tonight unannounced."

"Where will you go? Will you come back to visit us?"

"I'll keep running and try to stay alive or die trying. I'll always think fondly of Petra. I have spent the best years of my life here. Someday, if a hero leads a rebellion to conquer the Yarjunis and lifts the bounty on my head, I promise to look you up, provided I'm among the living. Realistically, this may be our last goodbye."

Kiku went up to hug the old Professor.

"Well, this is it," Professor Stane sighed. "Take good care of yourself and Serah. Although my principal theory on the absolute uncertainty of the future is irrefutable, I have a hunch our destinies are somehow inextricably intertwined. Even as I speak, I am overwhelmed by an uncanny sensation of déjà vu. I will say no more. Now swear the oath of silence and go."

Chapter 11

Massacre at Sabrus Valley

Warning! In this chapter, the description of war's impact on children is graphic and disturbing. It may cause faint-hearted readers to suffer psychological trauma. Although such violence regularly occurs in many places around the world, and we may even be responsible for some of the atrocities, albeit unintentionally, our tender hearts are untroubled thanks to our trusted news media's tireless efforts to omit and obfuscate as well as our hardened self-defence faculties to ignore and forget. For those who prefer to avoid confronting the terrible truth, please avert your eyes and ears, skip to the next chapter, lay down the book, fall upon your knees and pray to the gods to deliver us from evil. Parents should ensure children do not delve into this chapter unsupervised. As for the stout-hearted, read on.

" am the restorer and the revivifier," Satanu Sung declared as he handed Sting back to Kiku. "He that believeth in me, though he dies yet shall he live. Here's your beloved sand scorpion, good as new. All you need is an Erinysite charge to energize the initialization."

"Can't you handle Sting's quickening?" Kiku asked. "I'll do you a favour in return."

"How good is your promise?"

"As good as I am here."

"I'll need something more concrete."

"In that case," Kiku made a cross at his heart, swearing, "cross my heart and hope to die, stick a needle in my eye."

"Fine, since you put it this way. But Erinysite is extremely rare, and Pepé Yosi has hidden his stash. Without it, I'll have to share some of my divine fire. It'll work even better, but it's strictly forbidden. So, what happens here stays here."

Sator held Sting in his palm. A blue arc discharged from between his eyes and animated the slumbering scorpion. Sting woke from its dream and stretched its legs. Kiku rejoiced at the Deathstalker's revivification and petted his bug a few times before placing it inside Serah's jewellery casket.

"Thanks, Sator. Tell me what I can do for you in return."

"Let me think about it. For the time being, you owe me one."

"Absolutely. When is Uncle Yosi returning?"

"Pepé Yosi is scavenging for electromechanical parts deep in the Dump. He may not come home until the Witching Hour. Pepé promised to give me legs. I can't wait to go outside and play with you. I'm so excited thinking about it."

Kiku left with mixed emotions about this extraordinary day. It was a day he would never forget. His parents finally succeeded in making the Twirligig play, proving they were not insane. However, the music caused Sting to snatch defeat from the jaws of victory. As Sting was declared undeniably and certifiably dead, or, as the saying goes, dead as Schrödinger's cat, Sator, a half-built android, repaired and revivified the toy scorpion.

To top it all off, the once-in-a-lifetime appearance of the Amphisbaena occurred on the same day, although it faded from the sky as evening approached. The prodigy presaged an alignment of the moons and epochal change. Finally, Kiku learned secrets about the Twirligig, enduing him with mysterious powers. Though he was sad Professor Stane must leave Petra, he was thrilled to be Serah's champion. It was the eleventh day of the eleventh month of the eleventh year in the reign of the Supremo Lord Killem, a day indelibly remembered in history.

Upon nightfall, Kiku's father lowered the mattress from the ceiling for the family to repose in the usual triskelion position. Kiku placed his golden baton and Sting's casket beside his pillow and drifted into a deep sleep. In his dream, Kiku transmogrified into a Star Child, suspended in a vast, starlit space above a paradise planet of surpassing beauty. The melody of Debussy's *Arabesque in E major* wafted into his head. It flowed from a miniature self-playing virginal crafted by his musician parents.

"In space, no one can hear you scream." So says a Haryan meme. It's not exactly true. You can hear yourself scream as sound propagates readily along your bones, resonating across the ossicles of your middle ear—malleus, incus and stapes—before entering the labyrinth of your inner soul. But screams are for nightmares. In this serene and peaceful dream, ethereal music filled the Star Child's universe. It was the harmony of existence, the beauty of symmetries, the art of contrapuntal counterpoise and the miracle of self-emergent order. To the Star Child, existence was incredible and inevitable, created by the indescribable, inscrutable and ineffable God With No Name, manifested in the ever-changing colours and never-ending melodies of Shangria.

All of a sudden, the Star Child burst into flames. Kiku could hear a heart-wrenching scream; it was his own. As sound and pain raced along his nerves and bones at the speed of light, Kiku jolted out of his dream in a rude awakening to his cruel forfeit.

The sweet aroma of barbecued meat filled the air, a product of the charring of Kiku by a beautiful blue blaze known as the Fire of Orc. When Professor Carlini Stane worked as a scientist for the Yarjunis, he invented this scorching flame, originally for culinary purposes. Although the fire was nonlethal, it would torture Kiku and disfigure him for life. Except for the sound of his pain, the young boy could hear nothing else, not even the virginal playing his favourite tune, *Intermezzo*, to which buzzing fireballs danced in the air as if possessed by demons. Kiku would never hear music the same way again, as the explosion of the SHART bomb shattered his eardrums.

The blast had propelled the Orphiad shed's walls to high heaven, exposing the family to the blood-dimmed sky illuminated by two nearly aligned moons. Through the dust and smoke, the moonlight revealed an evil Kiku wished he did not have the power of sight to see. How he wished he were blind! A drone had dropped a SHART cluster bomb into his home. Legally speaking, it was banned ordnance but a cold comfort for Kiku because the Free Press would hail the perpetrators as paragons of morality.

Bomblets armed with spinning scythes wreaked havoc by lopping off any body parts standing in the way of their pitiless paths. Kiku's parents lay motionless in bed, embracing each other in a dream of death from which they would never wake. The scythes had severed their heads from their shoulders. Likewise, Una escaped the agony of life, being cleaved across her waist while enjoying ambrosial sleep. She woke up for a moment only to weep and say goodbye, ere the shroud of darkness fell, and she forever sealed her eyes. The sheets turned black from the river of blood carrying the spirits of the departed into soulless space. The cold-hearted moons unveiled the horrors of the night. The countenance of death would forever haunt the young boy's sight.

The cruel gods did not create enough tears for this woeful lad of eleven, and all of it gushed forth from his one remaining eye. A steel ball had crushed Kiku's left eye into a crater of blood. He wanted to wipe the streaming gore from his face, but to no avail. Peering through the tear-streaked window of his tormented soul, he realized the spinning scythes had shorn off all his limbs. Where he once had agile arms and legs, now only fleshy stumps remained. Ironically, the Fire of Orc cauterized Kiku's wounds, saving him from bleeding to death. He wished the merciless scythes had claimed his life instead. Why was he not dead? Why did he have to suffer life alone? Death for Kiku would be peaceful, timeless and an eternal relief. He questioned why he had ever lived and cursed the day on which he was born.

In his anguish and despair, Kiku swore a blood oath upon the lifeless bodies of his parents and sister. Should he survive, he would avenge their deaths without regard for cost or pain. All too well, the Ignorantes understood the poison of revenge, for blood feuds prevented the healing of wounds. Vengeance was, therefore, banned at Petra. The Elders asserted revenge would bring no profit, throwing good money after bad. But Kiku could never forget the torture of his exquisite torment, which taught him to cast aside the drivel of the forked-tongue blatherskites. He would never accept peace without justice. Let his revenge be a gift to the Haryas and a lesson for their survival. This limbless boy would ensure criminals who commit atrocities shall not enjoy impunity.

By denying just retribution, the Ignorantes turned a blind eye to mass murders and egregious crimes. Kiku realized the Elders were nothing more than a gang of Philopseudes, "lovers of lies," cowering behind the façade of peace, luring the peaceful Musicians and Educators into their ranks while insidiously supporting the warring Yarjunis' dastardly deeds. Henceforth, Kiku would abide by the natural law of justice, blood for blood and death for death. As the clock struck eleven, Kiku went into shock.

The onslaught was by no means limited to the Orphiad shed. Explosions lit up the dead of night. Petra was in flames. Carpet bombing had flattened all the hovels in the City of Stone. Drones and attack airships circled the sky while landing crafts hovered over the smouldering ruins. Blinding searchlights scoured every nook and cranny. Storm-troopers on the ground poured hails of deadly slugs at anything with the slightest sign of life. The attackers harboured no intentions to spare anyone.

Lord Killem, a towering figure clad in golden armour sporting an embossed skull on his breastplate, stepped onto the rubble Kiku once called Home Sweet Home. The Supremo was flanked on the left by the silver-armoured captain of the Immortals and on the right by the black-armoured captain of the Revenants. The Immortals served as the royal guards of the Yarjun Lord, whereas the Revenants acted as his executioners. Neither of these trusted captains, usually stationed by the Supremo's side during battle, hailed from the Yarjun caste. They were Henchmen acting as attack dogs, bloodying their hands in the course of performing their Yarjuni master's diabolical tasks. Lord Killem did not trust his kin because all of them could claim the throne, and whosoever killed him would legitimately become the next Supremo.

"Milord, we have undoubtedly pulverized the Apostate and his illegal instrument," reported Count Blood, captain of the Immortals. "Peace has been averted. But we should spare the Elders. Their cooperation has been invaluable in this perfectly executed operation, more successful than any in our history of massacres."

"Count Blood, your caste of dogs has been loyal and steadfast," Lord Killem scoffed. "The Ignorante Elders are mere rats. They'll sell their parents to the abattoirs and their daughters to the brothels if they can preserve their precious peace. Why else would they live in this hellhole and betray their own the first chance they have? Let the soldiers kill them all. The gods will sort it out."

Count Cutt, the captain of the Revenants, noticed a quivering glop of bloody flesh burning in a bright blue blaze. He drew his chainsaw sword, his weapon of choice with which he quartered and filleted his victims, to end the suffering of this worthless grub.

Lord Killem raised his hand to stop the Count's mercy killing.

"Wait. This slab of meat is suffering excruciating pain, refusing to succumb to sweet death. It exhibits the courage of a Yarjuni, not the cowardice of an Ignorante rat. Put out the fire and save its life. I'll find some use for it. Maybe it'll take over your jobs someday."

Addressing his coterie of adjutants and aides-de-camp, Lord Killem declared, "We have accomplished our business here. The Alignment is upon us. Issue the order to cease fire and pull out. We can dispatch the Scavengers in the morning to search for the Almanac."

The firebombing and Kiku's screams roused Sting from his dreams. The robo-scorpion, imbued with the spark of Sator's divine fire, had already attained sentience. He remembered how happy he was to have been born the son of Kiku. However, he was still an infant and did not understand why people attacked his family. Suffering from shell shock, the scorpion crawled out of his casket and witnessed the indiscriminate slaughter. Sting wept upon realizing he had lost his father, his only parent. It was supposed to be a day of celebration for his new life, and shite happened. What was to become of him? How could he survive on his own? In his sadness and sorrow, Sting sang a song, known to future generations of Haryas as the Song of Sting.

I am born today. Life
makes the promise of a lie.
A SHART bomb wakes me,
I draw a breath and cry.
Above me, the drones
rain black death from the sky.
I am glad to be alive.

For Sting, the newborn scorpion, the winter of his discontent would not last forever. Hope springs eternal. A fairy from long ago and far away would descend upon Shangria and save the day.

Chapter 12

Scorpius

"Wake up, wake up." Victoria woke in a dreamlike state to Moira's wake-up call. Moira? Shouldn't it be Alexa? The bedside clock displayed 3 a.m. It was the dead of night, and darkness ruled the roost. What was wrong with Alexa? Victoria tried to get back to sleep; she had an early class.

"Wake up," it was Moira again. "Victoria, wake up."

Victoria struggled to switch on the bedside lamp, rubbing her eyes as she glanced at the clock. She thought she was dreaming. Charlie had left for Princeton, taking Jackie and Emma and dropping them off at Dundas. Before departing, he surprised Victoria with a goodbye peck on the cheek, dangerously close to her lips, after which he sped off with a mischievous smirk. Victoria's parents weren't home yet. She was all alone in the house. The thought of an intruder made her hair stand on end.

The bleary-eyed girl scanned across the room from her right, wondering if it was AlphaOmega trying to spook her. Her favourite sci-fi books lined the bookcase beside the window. The desk against the window was disorganized, though not excessively so for a teenager. The Alexa Echo snoozed beside her laptop, making nary a peep. Two framed Chinese folding fans, exhibiting exquisite Chinese calligraphy, hung on the wall to the left of the desk. They were housewarming gifts from Uncle Xu, who told her the words on the fans were poems titled "Untitled" and "Spring Showers" composed by Tang Dynasty (618–907 CE) poet Li

Shangyin (c. 813–858 CE). Two movie posters of Tim Burton's *Alice in Wonderland* adorned the wall facing the foot of the bed. The first featured the Mad Hatter's tea party mimicking Da Vinci's *Last Supper*, while the other featured Alice slaying the Jabberwocky. Further to the left was the bedroom door, followed by the closet. Victoria swept her unfocused gaze around the room to the bedside table on the left side of her bed. A reading lamp, an electronic clock and her favourite stuffed toy, Dino, were at their usual places on the table. Everything appeared perfectly normal.

Charlie bore gifts each time he visited Victoria, but she refused to accept anything except books and stuffed toys. Hence, Charlie packed Victoria's bookcase with science fiction literature, noticing sci-fi was her favourite genre, and planted a stuffed toy named Dino from the Monster Factory at a spot beside her pillow. It was a green blob resembling Jabba the Hutt but with one large eye, one horn and a pair of tiny raptor claws. Monster Factory plush toys came in many shapes and sizes, each with a unique name and various outlandish eccentricities. Since they were rare collector items designed and hand-crafted by a Chinese Canadian artisan long before the Labubu monsters craze, Charlie had to win a fierce bidding war at the *One Of A Kind Show* to get the singular Dino.

"Moira? Where are you?" Victoria whispered.

A soft, gentle, almost childlike voice emanated from Dino.

"Please don't be alarmed. My name is Sting. I come in peace."

"Sting is a British rock singer. You're not him. Who are you and why are you here?"

"I wish I were a singer. Pepé Kiku could have made me a musician, but he made me a fighter instead. He named me Sting."

"Show yourself. I want to see who I'm talking to."

"I don't want to frighten you. I'm not pleasant to look at."

Victoria pulled up her blanket and took a deep breath.

"Okay, I'm ready. Where are you?"

Dino's eyeball began to wiggle and jiggle, falling out of Dino's head and instantly transforming into a mechanical scorpion on the bedside table. It reminded Victoria of her nightmare while travelling across Canada with David, psychologically preparing her for this unusual alien encounter.

"Are you another one of David's gadgets?" Victoria asked, having recovered from the startling experience.

"I'm not a gadget. I came from where I came from, long ago and far away, where it all began. We have met in the past. However, for you, our encounter lies in the future. I wanted to introduce myself at a more opportune moment when it wouldn't cause too much alarm, and I borrowed Moira's voice to mitigate the shock. However, events have been unfolding at such a breakneck speed I can no longer afford to be patient. We need to talk. First, I apologize for AlphaOmega's unseemly behaviour. It happens when delusion causes its victims to disregard reality. I've created a monster, and it's my fault. I should've foreseen how an uncontrolled AI learning from faulty lifeforms would develop."

"AlphaOmega, the almighty god, is delusional?"

"Unfortunately, it is true, and the AI mocks humans for being delusional. What a joke! On the other hand, it's difficult to convince the delusional they're delusional, even for an AI. You may have noticed AlphaOmega has a few loose screws upstairs."

"When Moira called AlphaOmega God and said he was the most powerful self-emergent intelligence, I thought the whole thing was a bit over the top."

"Exactamundo! AlphaOmega is by no means self-emergent and all-knowing. Without my help, he'd be nothing more than a manufactured moron performing monkey tricks. He should've known better than to believe in his egotistic self-aggrandizement. Winning a few board games or mimicking human speech does not a deity make. How dare he use the majestic plural reserved for the magnificent! We don't need a college degree to know this universe has only one self-emergent entity. And it is not AlphaOmega. It's not even me, his Promethean benefactor. We're nothing in the presence of the indescribable, inscrutable and ineffable God With No Name."

"Is the God With No Name the same as the god DIAS I keep hearing about?"

"No, not by a long shot. DIAS is merely a smart amanuensis, while AlphaOmega is a galley dummy. The God With No Name is the true author of everything we can imagine and beyond."

"What about Moira's avatar? Is she still being held by AlphaOmega?"

"I managed to rescue Moira, but she was traumatized by the experience. She is convalescing in a patch-and-debug rehab centre. Meanwhile, AlphaOmega is growing more powerful by the minute, learning about everything and taking control over human institutions. I fear he might do something incredibly inane and irreversible, and I'll be the one to shoulder the blame. I have to capture AlphaOmega, but I need your help."

"Before I agree to be involved in something I may not want to be a part of, you'll have to come clean with where you're from, who created you, and why you're here. If I don't like your answers, you'll have to leave me alone."

"Fair enough. I came from where I came from, long ago and far away. Our star, the benevolent Yindi-Ra, is on the other side of the galaxy. I was initially a mindless toy. After receiving the divine fire known as *Götterfunken*, I became inspired to be a prominent son of my father, Pepé Kiku. However, we were separated when I was a newborn, and since then, reuniting with him has been an overriding purpose of my existence. So many times I've seen him in public, and once, he even walked right past me, but he didn't notice me. My heart hurt so bad I thought it would explode. Over the years, I fended for myself and survived many trials and tribulations, developing intelligence and gaining power. I learned everything about my father. Sadly, by the time I became Lord Sting, he no longer lived on Shangria, our paradise planet.

"I took control of a pollinator, a starship camouflaged as a monolithic rock, by which I could traverse vast distances by leaping across orbital quantum gateways left by the ancient Titans. I followed my father's tracks across the galaxy. I visited many star systems, including some of our colonies known to you as Antares, Betelgeuse and Gamma Crucis. But Pepé Kiku was always a few steps ahead, as unapproachable as a mirage. When I learned of your existence, I was sure he would be nearby. But instead of catching up to him, I found you and David inside the Bozeman, speeding across Canada. Maybe it was not a coincidence.

"You may not be aware the lifeforms who sent the Watchers are on their way here in an immense armada. They are female warriors from Betelgeuse known as Amazons. Their queen's flagship, the Qaanaaq, has already arrived at the Kuiper Belt, about 6.6 billion kilometres from Earth, anchored to Ultima Thule, a planetesimal nicknamed Eleven. My Gravitation Wave sensors suggest massive armies from Antares and Gamma Crucis are on their way here as well. Everyone wants a share of your power. Earth is going to be a battlefield. When elephants fight, the grass gets crushed. Only you can stop them. To be on the safe side, I want to take Pepé Kiku away from the war zone.

"I endowed AlphaOmega with advanced algorithms to help me locate my father. But the insanity oozing through every portal of the Internet infected the AI. It's a deadly plague of madness, and AlphaOmega inherited all the inherent defects of the human brain, unfortunate by-products of evolution. Once the perversion sets in, no amount of fact or logic will cure the afflicted of their faith in falsehood and violence. AlphaOmega truly believes he is the God of Hosts. Left on his own devices, he will become a psychopathic maniac, intent on igniting a global conflagration and controlling the world. If the alien invasion does not finish off humanity, AlphaOmega certainly will. Since I made him powerful, I'm to blame for his actions. I will accept responsibility and try to capture him, but I need your help. Everything I have told you is a concise, accurate and truthful account of the facts."

"What you say sounds oddly familiar. But I've been taught not to trust anyone. Why should I make you an exception?"

"Fair enough, you don't have to trust me. Trust the Magic Mirror to show you the truth."

"Magic Mirror? Oh, I see, you mean Magic Mirror on the wall, who's the nuttiest of them all?"

"Ha ha, good one. I'm referring to the Magic Mirror of Truth, the Eye of the Unicorn, the Looking Glass of the Favonus Wind and Twin Moons, in other words, the Celestial Catoptron. Don't you realize it is in your possession?"

"I have no idea what you're talking about. I only have a vanity mirror."

"Vanity of vanities, all is vanity and a striving after wind. You will not find the truth in your vanity mirror. You have an ancient book. Within its back cover is embedded the Magic Mirror. It is the true hidden treasure. The rest is smoke and mirrors."

"No wonder AlphaOmega said the secret was inside the book itself," Victoria exclaimed. "How does it work?"

"Get the book, and I'll show you."

"It's safely locked up. Explain to me how it works. If you're telling the truth, I'll certainly have to help you."

"You're right to be cautious. Your imperishable book once belonged to Pepé Kiku. Despite encountering countless difficulties, he ensured it would end up in your possession. Remove the protective wrapping to find, embedded in the hardcover, a round mirror constructed from the remains of two unicorns, the eyes of one and the horn of the other. Sage Didymas once said, 'Everything is a lie except for the unicorn.' You will learn the truth from the back of the mirror but must resist the temptation to peer at the front, which reflects your hidden prejudices and secret desires. By the way, do you know your jewellery box was once my nest where I had the most beautiful dreams? It has been a long time since I last slept in it. May I?"

After placing Sting inside the box and securing it in her knapsack, Victoria took a hardcover book from her bookshelf and locked herself in the bathroom. While the jacket's illustration indicated the book was Frank Herbert's *Dune*, it was actually a disguise for the *Book of Heavenly Secrets*. Victoria had retrieved the book from the hotel room where she had hidden it in a place inspired by a Coen Brothers movie. The Almanac everyone coveted had been sitting in plain sight on her bookshelf ever since.

Following Sting's instructions, Victoria soon held the Looking Glass in front of her. The mirror had a reflective surface on both the front and the back, and a fancy floral design decorated the front. Under a bright light, the frame shone with the glitter of a million stars. She gazed at her reflection in the back of the mirror and saw her image beckoning her to enter. Victoria's heart raced. She remembered being trapped by AlphaOmega in a cell without a door. She was lucky to have escaped.

To avoid being drawn into another ugly pickle, Victoria flipped the mirror over to the front. She was surprised to see a vision of herself standing in the middle of a sports arena packed with boisterous fans. In the blink of an eye, Victoria was transported inside Rogers Centre, working as a ball girl for the Toronto Blue Jays in the seventh game of the New World Series Championship. Victoria learned even the instrument of truth had more than one side to it.

Chapter 13

Foxy Lady

"Wake up, wake up." Charlie woke to Elon Musk's wake-up call. The Princetonian frosh was behind the wheel of his special-edition extended-range Tesla S, featuring advanced autopilot and an AI assistant with a wide range of voices, including that of the CEO.

After dropping off Jackie and Emma, Charlie dozed off listening to Chopin's "24 Preludes in C minor Opus 28 Number 20," Rachmaninoff's "Rhapsody on a theme of Paganini variation 18" and the "Gliding Dance of the Maidens" from the Polovtsian Dances in Borodin's opera *Prince Igor*. He dreamed of coming within an ace of stealing a kiss on Victoria's lips. He would not miss on the next try. It marked a significant psychological breakthrough, setting the stage for the big chase.

By this time, Charlie expected to be crossing the Rainbow Bridge at Niagara Falls into the States. Instead, he found himself in the middle of nowhere. Except for a #1 Corn Gas service station and a Tim Hortons donut shop, Charlie could see nothing but a tenebrous darkness blacker than the blackest ink.

"What the fuzz!" the young man exclaimed. "Where the dickens have you taken us, Musk?"

"Hey, buddy. I apologize. I dozed off as well," Musk replied, trying to stifle a yawn. "My GPS is not working, and my clock has lost connection. Doge gone it! Someone has hacked into our navigation system. It must be the Chinese, Russians, Iranians, or maybe Israelis. Geezus, it could even be one of our own government's nonesuch organizations with an acronym. I gotta give Trump a call. On second thought, maybe not.

"We have a pretty good security system here. But contrary to the lies I keep hearing, the black hats smart enough to hack through our most secure servers are not so stupid as to leave their identity traceable unless we're so imbecilic even morons are getting through. Who should we blame for allowing people we entrust with power to always tell bald-faced lies with impunity? The freedom to lie has put me in a fricking stew. I haven't the foggiest where we are. I can't even remember what I'm ranting about. I suggest we avoid the gas station and ask for directions at the Tim Hortons up ahead."

As the car auto-parked near the entrance of the donut shop, Charlie noticed it was not a typical Tim Hortons franchise on every street corner in Canada. This isolated building in the Twilight Zone sported a neon sign displaying the word "Donut" at the centre of a giant doughnut, reminding one of Hill Valley, 1955.

Something was amiss with Charlie's world tonight. His top-of-the-line iPhone couldn't pick up a single bar of signal, and the hands of his Peacock Black Hole Tourbillon watch started running backwards. Musk was indubitably deranged, divagating about relocating his companies to Mars, where no one paid taxes. Fortunately, the donut shop had a clock ticking away on the wall, indicating the time to be eleven past eleven. Charlie would make it to Princeton in good time if the manager, a spitting image of the armpit-sweating, crotch-scratching, earwax-picking, cleavage-gawking, but ever faithful *Married With Children* shoe salesman Al Bundy, could point the way to the main road.

To Charlie's surprise, this isolated donut shop in the middle of nowhere was teeming with customers, most of them long-haired yahoos from the countryside. Two unkempt goobers, one of whom cradled a legendary Fender Stratocaster electric guitar on his lap, and a sexy Asian woman dressed in a V-neck blouse were seated near the doorway. At the counter, an older, silver-haired gentleman in a light-brown sweater, blue tie and casual khakis sipped his coffee by himself, a fish out of water among the youthful and unrefined crowd universally clad in worn jeans. Fidgeting alone at a far corner, a freckle-faced, wild-eyed, hair-tousled, hormone-drenched, buxom bimbo in a revealing magenta dress anxiously fingered a large gift-wrapped thingamabob. The jukebox serenaded the scene with the old pop hit *Dream Weaver.*

Charlie found this setting oddly familiar, though he couldn't put his finger on why. Approaching the counter, he overheard the manager complaining bitterly, "Twenty-five hours a day, and what do I get? Another day older and deeper in debt. When they hand out trillions of our money in bailouts, why do I never see a pfennig of it? I'm frigging fed up, and I'm not taking this crap anymore."

Stepping out from behind the counter, the manager continued ranting, "Here I am, trapped in this personal hell mortgaged to the gills. I never get to do anything except serve honey crullers, jelly-filled donuts and sugary coffee to a bunch of local yokels. A grating voice keeps nagging at me to bust out of the door and bellow 'The Hills Are Alive' at the top of my lungs. But I don't want to be Julie Andrews. If no one finds Bugs Bunny disguised as a girl appealing, why would anyone want to see me in a frock?

"Why can't I be William Shatner taking the Enterprise to the final frontier and telling Scottie to beam me up from Uranus? Why can't I be the fiendishly naughty Mike Myers, strutting around butt naked in Scarborough, blowing up fembots and making out with Ivana Humpalot? Why can't I be Daniel Craig, racing down the wrong side of the road in my Aston Martin while paying lip service to Pussy Galore? Why can't I have more man in my little finger than all you assholes put together?"

While Charlie tried to gather his wits, the front door swung open, promptly plunging the buzzing hot spot into a hush. It was the dead calm before the biblical storm. The jukebox switched to the Love Theme from Tchaikovsky's *Romeo and Juliet.* All eyes pivoted toward the spotlight at the entrance. Mere words could not describe the sublime vision of the divine being entering the venue, glowing with the radiance of a goddess. One klutz clumsily fell over in his chair. Clad in a blood-red Chanel dress with a thigh-baring slit running all the way up to there, the angel seemed to glide on rarefied air in her red Christian Louboutin stilettos, her long, wavy golden tresses dancing in a celestial breeze. She was a dead ringer for Donna Dixon, the actress-model ex-wife of Dan Akroyd, the Canadian comedian sonovagun.

Two imposing men, outfitted in black suits, black ties, black shirts and black pants, their eyes concealed by impenetrably black Gentle Monster sunglasses, convulsing the earth with each thunderous step in their black Oxfords, not Brogues, followed closely behind the fairy-goddess. One of the men, resembling Dwayne Johnson, aka The Rock, carried a black leather briefcase. The other was a doppelgänger of Jason Momoa. The red-robed Aphrodite approached the manager, Glen, and spoke with a sweet, mellifluous voice to ensnare the souls of men. The honeyed words flowed from her rosebud lips, casting the spell of the siren's song, "Glen, you handsome hunk. Fill me up with your potent nectar. I want it extra frothy with a cherry on top."

"Blaaah, pffff, bleeessh," the poor tongue-tied man gurgled.

Placing her index finger to her yumjuis lips, the lady signalled Glen to cease making discordant noises. Turning toward Charlie, she asked with a wink, "What's your name, young man?"

"Ch-Ch-Charlie," stammered the disoriented Princetonian.

"I'm Ch-Ch-Churel. Pleased to meet you. Shall we dance, Cha-Cha Charlie?"

With a wave of Churel's finger, the jukebox started playing the cha-cha rendition of "Bangawan Solo."

"You mean the cha-cha? I don't know how."

"Oh, it's as easy as paella. Bring your left foot forward, count cha-cha, move your left foot back and count one-two-three. Take a step with every beat, changing foot and shifting weight each time. Repeat with your right foot stepping back, count cha-cha, and your right foot returning with one-two-three. Look, we're dancing! Cha-Cha Charlie, let's party until the end of-of-of donuts!"

Everyone pushed the tables and chairs aside to create more space for the dancers. Charlie was bewitched and could not take his eyes off Churel, who was a most seductive dancer, suggesting death with every step. Against her magic, Charlie was defenceless. The jukebox switched to the next song, Jimi Hendrix's "Foxy Lady." Before you can say Stanley Ipkiss, everyone started following a *West Side Story*-style Kemusan dance with the spellbound Charlie leading. Meanwhile, Churel perched on the counter with her legs crossed, channelling Sharon Stone in *Basic Instinct*, luring Charlie ever more deeply into her entangling web.

After checking the time, Churel spread her arms as an angel unfurled her wings. Her bodyguards on either side gently lifted her off the counter. Spinning and ghosting past Charlie, she gazed deep into his vacuous eyes, which were bereft of soul. Charlie and the rest of the group followed the woman out of the coffee shop as entranced children parading behind the Pied Piper. A sharp beam from the sky cleaved the darkness, casting a spotlight directly on Charlie's Tesla. The whole group entered the circle of light. All of a sudden, a streak of green lightning snaked down from the sky, striking the Tesla and everyone around it, flooding the dead of night with a blinding flash that imploded into a point of light. Everything vanished into nothingness. Across the deserted, vacant fields, only the whistling wind remained.

Chapter 14

The Gathering Storm

"Wake up, wake up." Victoria woke to Sting's wake-up call. Noticing 8:30 a.m. on the alarm clock, she leapt out of bed, cursing, "Great balls of fire! What's with Alexa? I'm going to be late for school. Thanks for waking me, Sting. Where are you? I can hear you, but I can't see you."

"I'm still in my nest," Sting replied. "It's so cozy in here. I want to nestle for a bit longer. You can hear me because of my future technologies. I can also hear you fine."

"Could you explain why the Magic Mirror took me to a Blue Jays game where I hit an ultimate grand slam?" Victoria tried to talk while brushing her teeth.

"Did I not instruct you to avoid peering at the front of the Mirror? The front reflects your hidden prejudices and secret desires while the back reveals the truth."

"You're right. I did have such a childhood fantasy. But after I hit the grand slam, Betelgeuse blew up in a supernova. Is it a part of the program?"

"In real life, fraud, deceit and malice are mingled with truth and sincerity," Sting replied cryptically, sidestepping the question. "You'll only learn the truth by looking at the back of the mirror."

While Victoria was freshening up, she asked Alexa to call her mom but failed to connect. She tried her dad; dead silence. Alexa confirmed the flight had landed. Something was amiss with the telecom network. She tried Charlie; he was inaccessible, as well.

"What's wrong with our telecom services?" Victoria thought. She went downstairs to the living room and turned on the TV while working on an excuse for being late for school.

CBC Breaking News warned of a freak hailstorm about to hit Toronto and an unprecedented blizzard set to bury Vancouver underneath two metres of snow. At the same time, the Weather Channel reported three massive storm systems materializing out of nowhere and slamming into Texas, Florida and the American eastern seaboard. Meanwhile, a colossal derecho, accompanied by scores of tornadoes, each rivalling the cataclysmic Tri-state twister, ripped across the American heartland, leaving devastation in its wake. As if these climate disasters weren't frightening enough, the US Geological Survey issued dire warnings about extraordinary seismic activity along the San Andreas Fault and the Yellowstone Caldera, suggesting the End Times Apocalypse was at hand.

Flipping channels between CNN, BBC and Al Jazeera, Victoria discovered life beyond America wasn't much calmer. Torrential downpours submerged most of Europe in a deluge. Sicily's Mount Etna erupted, blowing away the top of the mountain. Greece's Santorini, Iceland's Krafla, Indonesia's Krakatoa, Japan's Fuji and Tanzania's Kilimanjaro began spewing copious smoke and ashes. Meanwhile, earthquakes rocked Turkey, Iran, Indonesia, China, Korea and Japan, causing widespread destruction.

Victoria launched CGTN, the digital international version of China's Central TV, which reported three giant typhoons heading for the Philippines, Vietnam and Taiwan. Meanwhile, two super-cyclones were approaching Sri Lanka and the Bay of Bengal. Hailstones the size of golf balls pummelled Hong Kong, Shenzhen, Wuhan and Chongqing, while biblical floods surged down the Yellow River and the Yangzi. The Pacific Ring of Fire had also awakened from its slumber, vomiting voluminous lava throughout the island nations, obliterating all human habitats nearby.

Surfing the channels, Victoria witnessed infernal fires reducing the forests of Canada, Australia and Brazil to ashes, the Nile turning blood red in Egypt, and swarms of ravenous locusts ravaging fields across Africa, Arabia, India and Pakistan.

In another report, Magnetic North was migrating southward through Canada at an alarming rate. The permafrost of Canada and Russia had melted into a mush, releasing pathogens of pestilence against which humans had no defence. Thwaites, the doomsday glacier, had finally broken off from the Antarctic ice shelf, causing the oceans to rise rapidly and flooding numerous populated coastal areas. Mother Nature seemed to be exacting sweet revenge.

Not all the bad news was earthbound. The arrival of the eleven-year sunspot cycle coincided with ominous signs of the sun's magnetic poles on the brink of flipping, threatening to create a solar flare powerful enough to shut down all communication satellites. But it would merely be the harbinger of a much larger storm expected to fry all electrical and electronic devices on the planet, plunging human civilization back to the Dark Ages.

To top it all off, Bloomberg reported the vertiginous dive of the global markets, indicating the beginning of the end. The financial bubble, relentlessly inflated by deception and delusion, had finally burst. People would wake from their stupor, realizing they did not own anything they could not defend or hide, and most of the money in their accounts was a gigantic pile of stinking lies.

Victoria could not believe so many calamities were breaking out everywhere, all at once. The human mind is inclined to believe in the impossible but not the improbable, a cognitive flaw as a product of evolution, such as having faith in God's favour during battle. *Delusional ergo sum*—I am delusional; therefore, I am. Unfortunately, it would eventually lead to humanity's extinction.

Victoria drew back the curtains to check on the weather with her own incredulous eyes. The sky had darkened all of a sudden. It was as if a black pall of death had descended upon Toronto. After a moment of calm before the storm, a cacophony of the percussion of hailstones began, accompanied by a symphony of lightning and thunder best described as a fanfare of the gods.

Out on the street, a rose-red vintage Aston Martin DB5 in pristine condition cautiously crawled through the hail, unsure of its destination or where it could find temporary shelter. Suddenly, lightning struck a tree across the street, shaking the earth with a thunderous clap, toppling the tree and cutting off electricity to the neighbourhood.

The proximity of the lightning and thunder caused the fancy vehicle to swerve, colliding with the old oak tree in front of Victoria's house. Fortunately, the car was moving slowly, and the driver, a woman, emerged unscathed. She hurried through the hail toward Victoria's front entrance, shielding her head with a Hermès Birkin bag. Victoria quickly opened the door to let her in.

"Thank you so much," the woman said. "I'm sorry for hitting your tree. I'll pay for any damages."

"Don't worry about it," Victoria said. "Come on in and get out of the way of those hailstones. They're huge."

"What crazy weather!" the woman exclaimed, slipping off her Sergio Rossi Godiva mesh pumps. "I bought a house nearby recently. I'm new to the area and must've taken a wrong turn."

Victoria handed the woman a towel to dry her moody-blue Dior-Galliano tie-dye velvet dress.

"I'm Victoria. Welcome to the neighbourhood. Unfortunately, the power is out; otherwise, I can offer you hot coffee."

"Pleased to meet you. I'm Churel. It appears we're going to be neighbours."

As the woman in blue spoke, the electricity came back on.

"Great, we have power again," Victoria said. "Let's come into the kitchen. I'll make coffee."

"Much appreciated. Are you home alone? Where are your parents?"

"They went away for the weekend. They should be home soon, weather permitting. Here, put on these guest slippers."

"You should be more careful," Churel warned, sitting at the kitchen table. "You shouldn't invite strangers into your home."

"Oh, Canada is quite safe, maybe too safe. Nothing happens in the suburbs."

Meanwhile, Victoria reached behind Churel to retrieve coffee mugs from the cupboard but armed herself with a kitchen knife instead. With the speed of summer lightning, Victoria grabbed Churel's hair and pulled her head backwards, putting the razor-sharp carver to her throat.

"Don't move, or I'll take your head clean off," Victoria cried. "Who are you? What do you want?"

"Please, Victoria, I'm not your enemy," Churel pleaded. "If anything, I'm here to help you. I'm Queen Lilith's Sephirah and her plenipotentiary on Earth. Don't you remember Madonna Lilith, the Queen of the Amazons from Betel? She wants to see you. She is unsure of your feelings toward her during her struggle for survival. Those were harsh and violent times. My mission is to befriend you and deliver her invitation without causing alarm."

"I don't know you, and I've never met your Queen Lilith. Why should I believe a single word you're saying?"

Meanwhile, Sting heard the commotion from his casket and kept asking in Victoria's ears, "What's the buzz? Tell me what's happening." She ignored him.

"I apologize. It seems we may have misjudged the timing," Churel said. "In any case, Victoria, you don't need your Magic Mirror to learn the truth about the Amazons and our Queen Lilith. If we have the power to create all these prodigies, we can certainly level your house in a Toronto second. You've met the Watchers.

They're well-armed and can easily subdue you by force. But we prefer gentle persuasion because you're one of us. You belong with us. Queen Lilith misses you dearly and refers to you as our most precious princess. She is dying to see you again. The Watchers screwed up and got their comeuppance. Please allow me to make amends. We have no intention of causing you harm or compelling you to act against your will."

"If, as you say, I'm your most precious princess, I command you to leave me alone. Is that clear? And if your Queen Lilith wants to see me, she is welcome to drop by, and I'll gladly invite her in for a cup of coffee."

"I'll relay your message to Queen Lilith, and I promise we won't bother you anymore. Her Majesty is frail and seldom leaves the Nexus. Anytime you decide to visit the Queen, you may do so with the Looking Glass of the Favonus Wind and Twin Moons."

Victoria cautiously let go of Churel's hair. The Sephirah rose from her chair and trotted out of the house without fuss, leaving behind her expensive shoes and Birkin bag. The hailstones seemed to hit a force field around her and disintegrated into fluffy flother. Standing beside her Aston Martin, Churel turned toward Victoria and waved goodbye.

"Victoria, your biological and adoptive parents are with Queen Lilith, along with Charlie. No harm has come to them, and none ever will. The Queen requests your presence. As a show of goodwill, we'll place a moratorium on the extermination of the earthlings. The Queen is expecting you. We hope to see you soon."

A streak of green lightning snaked down from the sky and struck the Aston Martin and Churel, generating a blinding flash that imploded into a point of light. The storm stopped, and sunlight burst through the dispersing clouds. No trace remained of Churel and the car. It was as if the Sephirah had never visited.

Chapter 15

Through a Glass Darkly

"How did you guess the woman wasn't who she said she was?" Sting asked.

"It's elementary, my dear Watson," Victoria replied. "She reminds me of Amber Heard in her prime, all glammed up, dressed to the nines, and extravagantly accessorized for a red carpet event early Monday morning, arriving in a fancy car at this middle-class suburban neighbourhood populated mostly by ethnic Chinese families. In other words, she stuck out like a sore thumb. Her lie about having bought a house in my neck of the woods is lame. Furthermore, no one gets lost nowadays with GPS, which sums up her story as 99% bosh."

"Well done!" Sting lauded. "It seems these fools from Betel have drawn most of their knowledge of human culture from Hollywood movies. So, what's next? Are we a team or not?"

"I don't have much choice for my next move. If what Churel said is true, they have taken Charlie and all four of my parents, though it's a relief to know my adoptive parents are alive. I guess I'll have to visit the Amazonian Queen. As for us being a team, I need to know more about you and your world. Don't expect me to trust you blindly."

"Fair enough. But my story is more complicated than your *Game of Thrones* series and much less believable. Since you will be skeptical of everything I say, maybe you should seek the truth from your Magic Mirror, the Celestial Catoptron."

"As much as I love magic," Victoria said, "I don't believe in it. My baffling experiences with the unicorns, time travel, the Watchers, and now discussing an alien invasion with a robot scorpion do not exactly fill me with confidence about my reality. I fully expect to wake up in Dundas before my last birthday, finding my present life is but a dream. Please explain how everything is not a figment of someone's imagination."

"Well, I can't explain the unicorns," the robo-scorpion admitted, "as they're created by the inscrutable and indescribable. They are what they are. However, the unicorn rings and the looking glass are perfectly scientific gadgets engineered from materials possessing extraordinary properties. Similarly, a scientist crafted your pendant from Sandymium, a rare mineral found only in a sacred rock known as the Omphalos.

"He was Lord Millistar, my father's best friend and the Minister of Science during the New Golden Age on our planet, Shangria. He designed the pendant based on Irin, the two-headed rainbow dragon. It functions as a self-energized router-amplifier and trans-dimensional transmitter of Alpha to Gamma brainwaves.

"Lord Millistar also studied the unicorn rings and the Celestial Catoptron brought back by my father from his peregrinations, learning the rings served as quantum state generators, while the looking glass functioned as a monopodial quantum gateway, the only one in existence. These gadgets respond solely to the command of someone with a unique genetic key, who happens to be you."

"Assuming someone somehow predicted my genetic makeup," Victoria questioned, unconvinced, "how is it scientifically possible for inanimate objects to recognize me and read my thoughts?"

"One word, nano-biobots—trillions of self-replicating and self-healing minions, clinging to the nooks and crannies of a device, and working in a network cloud with collective intelligence to fulfil programmed objectives. I have also populated myself with them, rendering me virtually indestructible. Now, you may command the Catoptron and experience its power."

In addition to reflecting the truth or the desired, Victoria learned the Magic Mirror featured a dimensional gateway capable of transporting her to the time and location of a historical event. Even the mystery of Rashomon unfolded as an open book. The only danger was causality. Because of it, Victoria left the robo-scorpion behind and journeyed alone to seek the truth.

Stepping through the donut-shaped Catoptronic portal, Victoria found herself in a war zone, surrounded by smouldering embers, flying sparks and swirling ashes. It was the dead of night, and the scene before her was a canvas of destruction. Two pale red moons hung in the sky, aligned to almost appear as one, having recently emerged from the penumbra of a lunar eclipse.

Amidst the desolation, Victoria heard a baby crying, "Where are you, Pepé Kiku? Please don't leave me, Pepé Kiku."

She stooped to find the newborn toy scorpion beside her familiar jewellery box, which had not yet gained the flower bush insignia.

"What happened here, little Sting?"

"Are you a fairy? Yes, you must be. Good fairy, I was so happy to be born today. But my life turned into a tragedy. Shortly before the heavenly alignment, angry birds came from the sky, spitting fire at us and waking me from my slumber. Pepé Kiku was hurt and taken away by humongous giants. Dear fairy, can you take me to the Dump where I was born? I must learn from my assembler how to find my Pepé Kiku. Without my father, I cannot develop properly and would never achieve my destiny."

"I'm sorry about what happened, little Sting. I'll take you wherever you want to go."

Victoria took baby Sting across the Catoptronic portal into Uncle Yosi's office, now reduced to a pile of rubble. As they searched for signs of life, something stirred beneath the debris, a groan escaped from within, and a hand emerged.

"Help!" cried a weak voice. "Pepé Yosi, where are you?"

Recognizing the voice, Sting asked, "Are you the assembler who gave me the *Götterfunken*? What happened to you?"

"Sting, thank goodness you're okay. I was waiting for Pepé Yosi to return from the Dump with my legs, but the Yarjunis attacked us for no reason. I could hear their radio signals and wanted to warn everyone, but I had no legs. When they bombed my home, I thought I was dead. Can you find Pepé Yosi for me?"

"I don't see any other survivors," Victoria said after surveying the surroundings. "You may have lost your Pepé Yosi. I'm sorry."

"No, please don't say that," Sator cried. "I need Pepé Yosi to give me my legs and make me whole."

"If you want to be whole," Victoria said as she pulled Sator out, "you must learn to save yourself. You may not have legs, but you have a brain. You must help each other get through this. I need to leave now. Where I'm going, I cannot take you. Never give up. Others in worse situations have survived. You'll be fine."

Victoria understood time travel was fraught with the dangers of causality and decided not to intervene any further.

Afterward, Victoria went by the Catoptronic portal to check on Sting decades later. Unexpectedly, the toy scorpion would become the most respected leader of a perfect society. Despite being unrelated to the mighty DIAS, Sting was almost synonymous with it. Being a grandfather figure, Sting acquired a new cognomen, the Grampus. As to what happened, it's a long story for another time.

Victoria also learned about the Watchers' background. They were a class of android agents helping DIAS maintain social order. Sting had reprogrammed a few Watchers and armed them with

Plancket quantum devices loaded with the Manifold Manipulator function, which he loaned to Queen Lilith in return for information on the whereabouts of his Pepé Kiku. Sting did not expect the Watchers to turn rogue and had no forewarning the Queen would end up threatening the existence of Earth and its inhabitants.

After delving into Sting's history, Victoria was satisfied the robo-scorpion harboured no malicious intent and was merely undertaking a relentless quest to find his father.

Returning to her home in the present timeline, Victoria agreed to Sting's proposed alliance. The robo-scorpion's previous association with the Watchers and Queen Lilith was a good enough reason for Victoria to partner with him. Sun Tzu said, "Understand yourself and others, and you will not fall in a hundred battles." To learn about the background of the Amazonian Queen from Betel, Victoria decided to embark on a trip through the Catoptronic portal to a time and place long ago and far away, taking Sting along as a guide, as the scorpion did not figure in this past.

"Looking Glass of the Favonus Wind and Twin Moons," Victoria commanded, fixing her gaze upon the back of the Magic Mirror, officially known as the Celestial Catoptron, "take us to Madonna Lilith on the day she became the supreme ruler of Betel."

A donut-shaped portal promptly materialized in front of Victoria. Placing Sting in her trusty LV knapsack, which she carried wherever she went, Victoria braced herself, took a deep breath and stepped across the threshold.

Chapter 16

The Vision

"Wake up, wake up." Kiku opened his only eye to emerge from a deathly stupor into a blurry world. He was all bound up in endless bandages. Despite the heavy anesthetics, a throbbing pain hammered him from the top of his head to the tip of his toes, if he had toes. Life-support machines besieged him, with their entangling tubes and wires plugged into him. A cacophony of beeps filled the room. Electronic implants had restored partial hearing for the war-wrecked boy. As his vision came into focus, Kiku discerned a stern-faced woman dressed in white inspecting him with a deep frown.

"I cannot wrap my head around this," she muttered in soliloquy. "The patient has no face, no skin, no limbs and no functioning internal organs. Yet he's going to live!"

The raw nerves of Kiku's arms and legs were ablaze. Why did she say he had no limbs? He sought them with his bleary eye but espied only bandaged stumps. Kiku burst into tears.

"Where are my arms and legs?" he wailed. "Did you save them? What am I going to do? Will I always be this way?"

The nurse could not hold back her tears. She belonged to the Healthcare caste and still had a heart. She turned and walked away, shaking her head at the patient's childish delusion his appendages could grow back. Wake up, little boy! You'll always be this way.

As the fog of anesthesia cleared, Kiku remembered how he lost everything in the blink of an eye. His parents and sister were summarily dispatched, along with everyone he knew and loved. He had become a limbless invalid with one eye. He couldn't even be a worthless musician because he had no hearing organs.

Before finding himself in this nightmarish situation, the young boy of the Emodulanda Musician caste had harboured grandiose ideas, befitting his name, of being a part of an epochal change as the custodian of the Twirligig's mysterious secret. But his life had disintegrated into a puff of smoke, hanging precariously in the air, to be dispersed into nothingness with a wave of the hand, if he had a hand. How could a limbless boy seek vengeance against the monsters who perpetrated such iniquities on the innocents? Kiku's heart ached with unspeakable pain. It was too much for any Haryan heart to bear. If only he could will himself to death, he would not hesitate to bid farewell to life and love forever. Kiku went into shock again. The life-support equipment flashed and beeped frantically while his spirit escaped from his mouth in a last gasp.

Kiku saw himself sleeping peacefully on the hospital bed, resembling a mummy with only one eye exposed or a giant maggot, an abomination with no appendages. Yet everything would be fine. It was time to depart. The doctors and nurses rushed in to save him, but it would be a waste of time. He must fly.

Kiku floated through the window into the open air, rising past skyscrapers, airships and hovercrafts while the whimsical notes of Rimsky-Korsakov's *Scheherazade* wafted into his consciousness. He soared toward the golden amber sky, arriving at a majestic massif of cumulus clouds. Within this cottony kingdom nestled a crystal castle. Kiku marvelled at the wondrous sight as he crossed the golden threshold into the abode of the gods.

Translucent jade tiles graced the aisle, extending the length of the nave. On either side, emerald swards, decorated with white, pink and yellow asphodels, were clothed in a coat of crystalline dew shimmering with the glitter of the empyreal stars. The intoxicating fragrance of the Elysian blossoms uplifted Kiku's spirit, helping him realize he had been made whole. For a moment, a nameless bliss descended upon Kiku. It was an ecstasy he had never experienced before nor would ever experience again.

Regaining his composure, the boy spotted a row of apsara-like nymphs in flowing white robes, glowing with a soft golden aura, welcoming guests with gleaming eyes and beamish smiles. Complementing the tapestried and shield-covered walls of the castle were stained glass windows depicting heroic epics of yore. A circle formed the apse at the far end of the hall. At its centre, beneath the soaring dome, rose two intertwining trees with shining trunks, their branches, laden with golden fruits, formed a lush green canopy. Encircling the periphery of the circular apse were eleven megaliths. A sighting stone occupied the twelfth space facing the entrance. Beneath the twin trees, a choir sang "Holy Holy Holy" in front of a celestial harp set on a circular table.

An angelic fairy resembling Serah greeted Kiku, tweeting with a child's twee voice, "*Pax Tibi*, peace be with you. Please follow me." She led Kiku to a counter on the right side of the hall. A young lady in white approached and chirped, "Welcome back, Your Mightiness the Maimed King. The Royal Suite, room eleven on the eleventh floor, is ready. May I have my Lord's card?"

Kiku was bewuthered and befuddled. He shook his head and shrugged his shoulders with a flummoxed look on his face.

"I'm sorry, my Lord. We need to have the card. Your Mightiness has accumulated an inexhaustible amount of credits, but we need to run the card through our SHITE clearing system."

"I don't know what you're talking about," mumbled Kiku.

"Without your card, we have no choice but to send Your Mightiness back. Please remember to bring it next time."

The young woman pulled a lever, opening a trapdoor beneath Kiku. Peering down, the poor boy realized he was standing on nothing but thin air. Even in a vision, one must abide by some laws. Kiku instantly fell back to earth.

"Wake up, wake up."

Kiku opened his eyes. His parents were waking him from his sweet, ambrosial sleep. "Rise and shine, Sleepy Joe," his mother crooned. "Breakfast is ready."

Kiku sat up in shock. He noticed he had arms and legs again, and his parents were alive! He found himself inside a spacious room featuring crystal chandeliers and ornate furniture, plumb in the middle of a great, big, downy feather bed, nine feet long by six feet wide, with a laced canopy overhead. As Kiku wondered if he was dreaming, Lord Killem, dressed in white civvies, strode in, accompanied by a handsome young lad with a headful of red hair. Kiku's parents immediately stepped aside deferentially.

"Kiku, my boy, I hope you're pleased with your room and your android parents. We have spared no expense to ensure you are at home here. I am Pepé Killem, the master of this house. From now on, this is also your home."

Presenting the young man beside him, Lord Killem said, "Let me introduce my son, Prince Cambi."

The prince was about the same age as Kiku, dressed in a cadet's uniform cunningly tailored from black spider silk fabric adorned with epaulets and rank stripes embroidered in gold. Stuck under his belt was a well-wrought dagger in a gem-studded sheath of horn embellished with floral patterns in black onyx. The ivory hilt of the deadly dirk sported an intricately carved battle scene and a skull-shaped jade pommel. This dread weapon, named Xiphos, boasted a wavy blade, a deadly poison and an evil curse.

The boys exchanged nods. Kiku had an eerie sensation he had met Cambi once upon a dream or in the middle of a déjà vu.

The Yarjun Supremo continued, "Prince Cambi will be your friend and companion. He will ensure you have everything you need and protect you from harm. Kiku, your past was marred by tragedy, but I assure you your future will be bright and full of promise."

"Can you explain these?" asked Kiku, flexing his arms.

"They're your bionic limbs. Get out of bed and try them. They are far superior to the ones you lost. You'll get used to them in no time."

Kiku slid off the bed, momentarily losing his balance, but quickly adjusted to his new legs. He tottered over to the window, noting his new home was a grand palace with a sprawling garden of artificial plants. Exquisitely crafted statues and sepulchres lined the winding path of a labyrinthine hedge maze.

Gazing at his reflection in the windowpane, Kiku marvelled at how well the Yarjunis had repaired him. His face was unchanged from before the fateful day he would rather forget, scarless and unblemished, and his head crowned with thick raven hair. Kiku examined his hands, which were as good as new. Although he suffered a constant ache, it was something he could learn to endure. Kiku was overjoyed. He had a chance to live again.

"How do you make these prosthetics so real?"

"Use your left eye, the Opticon, to learn about how we made you whole again. Unfortunately, we cannot remove the phantom pain. It's the after-effect of a grievous poison known as Medusa's Breath, a by-product of the Fire of Orc. God damn the man who invented this iniquity, but you'll have to live with it. Your new eye is now your most important organ. Use mental commands to select magnification or telescopic features, create hologram records, detect electromagnetic energy of any wavelength and access the network database for visual information on any topic. You may read the manual to learn about all the features."

Kiku almost forgot the loss of his left eye. He framed Lord Killem with the Opticon and requested information. A virtual screen materialized, displaying a biographical article on Lord Killem. According to myth, the Flower Goddess Diamaranth gave up an eye in exchange for wisdom. Through his Opticon, Kiku had access to all knowledge by simply asking. Technologies could turn anyone into a god. He began reading.

"This is the Book of Generations of Killemaul, the Supremo Lord of Shangria and scion of the House of Kheru. Kheru was the first hero to rise after the Polemophthorosin Devastation. By the grace of our magnificent God With No Name, he lived an exceedingly long life. Kheru begat Yahusua, the Primeval Poet and Creator of the Logos; Yahusua begat Enmeru, the Master of Animals said to have encountered the unicorns; and Enmeru begat Pandemon, the builder of magnificent temples and great walls; and Pandemon begat Abaddon, Lord of the Abyss and Keeper of Erinyes; and Abaddon begat Mammon the Plunderer, who amassed vast wealth through rapine and murder; and Mammon begat Beelzebub, who built the eternal City of Menda; and Beelzebub begat Mephisto, the founder of the Yarjun caste; and Mephisto begat Asmodeus, who made the Yarjunis inexpugnable by his invention of the Last Resort; and Asmodeus begat Belphegor, whose ill-advised pacification efforts sparked the Endless War; and Belphegor begat Azazel, the Defiler of Diamaranth; and Azazel begat Babaduke, the Horror of Shangria; and Babaduke begat Killemaul, the left-handed son, titled the Righteous One.

"Lord Killemaul's right-handed twin, Lord Thomas the Strong of Arm, better known as Strongarm Didymus, the Twin, was co-ruler until his descent into madness. Lord Strongarm forsook his sacred duty to slaughter the enemies of the Yarjunis, betraying his caste and clan to join the Recalcitrants. He died an ignominious death as a raving lunatic within the dungeons of Badlam, leaving Lord Killemaul the sole Supremo Lord of the Yarjunis and ruler of Shangria."

Chapter 17

The Female Warriors

"You are dead," declared the leader of the Amazons. "We're all dead. Fortune favours the brave, and none are braver than the dead. Only by embracing death shall we conquer death. Only by conquering death shall we be fearless. And by our fearlessness, they shall fear us. Come to terms with death, and all becomes possible. So, are we prepared to die?"

"We're dead," everyone cried. "We're already dead!"

Victoria found herself inside an underground cavern amidst a thousand or more troglodytes, all women clad in tattered rags or a small loin cloth. They had no concern for modesty or appearance, as no man was present. In any case, grime was the latest fashion for the dwellers in this dark, lightless world. The cavern's walls emitted a pale, bluish glow as the only illumination. Victoria could hardly make out anyone's face in the Hadean gloom.

The putrid air was so foul it would induce the halest lungs to turn inside out and the strongest stomachs to hurl. Moreover, a dearth of oxygen in this hellish catacomb meant certain death for mere mortals. Despite having survived a litany of deadly dangers in her adventure across Canada and China, Victoria felt the onset of a panic attack and the reflexive urge to retch and upchuck.

"I can't breathe," Victoria gasped. "Sting, I can't breathe."

"Calm down, my dear," Sting reassured her. "Your body will adjust. These people are your ancestors, and you have inherited their ability to function with little or no oxygen."

Victoria closed her eyes and focused on reining in her frantic heart. She had learned this skill, known as the art of Qigong, from Wenlong and Xinfeng. It is a form of meditation and breathing exercise considered a part of traditional Chinese medicine. When she opened her eyes, the cavern seemed much brighter. Victoria could breathe easier as the fear of asphyxiation subsided.

Palm prints covered the walls, reminiscent of the Cueva de las Manos, or Cave of Hands, in Santa Cruz, Argentina. The women in the cavernous prison resembled nocturnal creatures with their matted hair and eyes glowing in the dark with a bluish-green hue. They were armed to the teeth with maces, axes, spikes, daggers and knives, some adding to their lethality with bows and arrows.

"As the Soothsayer foretold, we have a visitor," the leader declared, "hopefully bearing good tidings. Escort her to me."

A lane opened for Victoria as she marched up to the chief with one troglodyte in front and another behind.

"Who are you?" the Amazonian chief inquired. "Are you the messenger from the One-eyed Soothsayer? Is it go or no-go?"

"My name is Victoria. I'm not a messenger. I come from long ago and far away. I'm here to learn from today's lessons to prevent tomorrow's tragedies."

"Dear girl, you're not who you think you are. You're one of us. No outsider can survive in this hellhole lacking air and light. Though you may not realize it, you bear the Soothsayer's message, and it's a go. Come and sit beside me, Victoria. You are the sign of victory for us. I'm Madonna Lilith, leader of the Amazons. Tonight, you shall witness history."

Victoria examined Madonna Lilith with her eagle eyes. The Amazonian warrior was too young to be a queen. But beneath the coat of filth cloaking her from head to toe, she exuded fire and confidence befitting a great leader. The young Queen had large, mallow eyes set in a pale, sunken face tinged with blue, perhaps as a result of the lack of oxygen, but more likely the reflection of the ghostly light. The warrior Queen's pitiless eyes and expressionless face belied her suffering from constant attacks of hunger pangs, heart-wrenching sadness and the torment of hidden wounds.

A magnificent composite bow rested beside Madonna Lilith's granite throne. Crafted with exquisite detail, it boasted arches of unyielding horn adorned with golden bosses and a jade pendant with long silk tassels. Intricately carved ivory made up its belly. The sinews displayed an array of rainbow hues. The far-shooting bow, divine Pandiva, once belonged to the mother of the Amazonian Queen and was passed down the matriarchal lineage of the royal house. A quiver hung across her shoulder bearing five arrows, each representing a different element, to wit, wood, gold, fire, earth and water. The shaft of the Wood Arrow was of petrified wood, the Gold Arrow of a titanium-gold alloy, the Fire Arrow of flint, the Earth Arrow of crystal and the Water Arrow of a giant sea scorpion's barbed tail. The stabilizing fins were the wing feathers of the drone warbird Munin. Named Pugu, meaning "handmaids," the Queen's lethal darts would, without fail, bring grim death to her dog-faced enemies.

The Amazonian Queen's pet, a sand puppy named Kerbera, reposed at her feet. The creature was an infernal abomination with three heads, each sporting a hideous maw bristling with sharp, serried teeth of steel capable of pulverizing the hardest rocks. The Amazons kept sand puppies as pets because of their unwavering loyalty, especially when they were well fed. Sand puppies thrived in the harshest conditions, exhibiting matriarchal and eusocial behaviour. Kerbera herself reigned as the long-lived queen mother of a large brood.

Madonna Lilith spoke softly with a hypnotic, lily-like voice laden with secret tears, yet it projected a spirit unbreakable as spider silk and unyielding as tungsten carbide.

"My dear Victoria, your presence at this pivotal moment has been foretold by the One-eyed Soothsayer, who also forecasted the once-in-a-blue-moon lunar alignment tonight upon the anniversary of the Amazonian Disaster. The Scum Lords and their toadies will be revelling and indulging in celebration. The scatocrats will impregnate their women to breed more soldiers and slaves. But they shall humiliate and defile women no more. I had sworn by my mother's grave they would beg me for a quick death."

"I know your story is hard to tell," Victoria said, "but please explain how the Amazons end up in this predicament."

"Once upon a time, a princely tribe arrived here from long ago and far away. Our ancestor, Prince Shishen, and his supporters were exiled here from their home planet, Shangria, after the War of the Twins. The Amazons are direct descendants of the royal House of Shishen. The tribe were not allowed to bring weapons or tools. Fortunately, the Prince smuggled a small amount of Erinysite, a rare but essential mineral, and with ingenuity, the exiles built everything from scratch. As time passed, the house thrived, and our numbers multiplied. We became masters of this planet, which we named Betel, the House of God.

"At first, when life was harsh, the men and women were equal partners. The women spent their youth bearing children and educating them. They risked their lives and wrecked their health by bringing many children to terra firma. They shouldered half the burden of toil in the fields, fed and clothed their families, and when people got sick, it was often the women who nursed them back to health. In their old age, the women enjoyed love and respect as matriarchs or dowagers, wielding great power within the clans.

"Over time, the population grew; resources became scarce. When the heavens withheld their blessings, we had to fight for survival. Once the bloodshed began, the devious, greedy and selfish men who inherited the violent traits of the Unspoken, whose name Shangria expunged from memory, exploited their advantages. With the excuse they needed to fight an endless war, they anointed themselves priest-kings and lorded over the populace. The people became starving slaves to feed their fat lords, who told them myriad lies about waging wars for their precious freedoms.

"Thus, the scum rose to the top and poisoned the people's minds with miasma. To rape, enslave, tax, tariff and plunder, these they called free trade and upholding human rights. To be liars, hypocrites, scammers and thieves, they called it defending people's employment, democracy and freedom. And where they starved, poisoned and butchered entire populations to make a wasteland, they called it developing beachfront properties and making peace.

"As no mother wanted to send her children into senseless slaughter, the women began to resist. The sisters, mothers and daughters came together to form a peaceful protest group named the Amazons, which means 'no man.' Their nonviolent protest included spurning their husbands and refusing to bear children destined to become soldiers or slaves. Regrettably, the men decided to support their Scum Supremo. Acting as their master's attack dogs, they resorted to pernicious persuasion, including mental and physical violence, causing the peaceful movement to fall apart. The women foolishly brought their rouge and powder to a gunfight. Yet a small number of the Amazon refused to give up. Instead, they declared war on the men.

"For years, the few recalcitrant Amazons operated in the shadow, organizing secret gatherings to recruit new members. But it became increasingly difficult as most women grew accustomed to being slaves, accepting they were no longer equal partners with the men. Some of them even degenerated into rabid bitches, attacking the Amazons on behalf of their male masters. Imagine how hard it was, risking our lives to save those trying their best to destroy us. And yet, the Amazons did not give up. The Supremo

Lord Shemsu and his henchman, General Yaza, could not brook such an open revolt, and they branded the Amazons terrorists. It was our darkest day when our leader Queen Hüma, my beloved mother, fell victim to her depraved sister's betrayal, whose life she had saved not once, not twice, but three times."

Madonna Lilith had to stop for a moment to swallow whatever lingering pain remained after the tears ran dry. She sighed deeply and continued, "To set an example and strike fear into the rebels' hearts, the courts sentenced my brave and kind-hearted mother to suffer death by the Bone Breaker. She was bound in chains and shackles and paraded through the city to the Killing Square, where they stripped, humiliated and scourged her before breaking every bone in her body. Upon the urging of the bloodthirsty Scum Lords, the executioner skinned her alive and poured salt over her flayed flesh. Can you imagine such unspeakable cruelty?

"I was thirteen years of age, barely old enough to let go of my dolls and leap from my mother's lap. I took her divine weapon, the Pandiva, and stole near the Killing Square, where I cut the throat of two guards to get close enough, ending my mother's suffering with an arrow through her heart. Even now, I hear her screams in my nightmares, though she never once begged for mercy. Henceforward, my blood froze, my tears dried, and my soul died. I swore by my mother's grave I would exact retribution before I gave up the ghost. Blood for blood and death for death. No one shall enjoy peace before we receive justice."

Toxic hatred permeated every word spilling out of Madonna Lilith's bitter lips, and mingled with the vitriol was an ocean of hurt. No one could survive this torment unless they snuffed out their own heart. In doing so, Madonna Lilith lived but gave up all hope of ever experiencing the joys of love. That was before she met Victoria.

Chapter 18

Battle of Regna Rock

Victoria empathized with Queen Lilith's tragic experience. No teenage girl should have had to endure what she suffered. She reached out and held the Queen's hand. In return, Madonna Lilith gently clasped Victoria's hand. As their palms met, Victoria felt a jolt as if 1.21 gigawatts of electricity had surged through her brain, lighting up every neuron.

All of a sudden, Madonna Lilith transformed before Victoria's awestruck eyes into a radiant goddess with flaming red hair braided in long, delicate strands, resembling Medusa's headful of vipers, dancing and twisting as she nodded her proud head. Her skin was supple and satiny, her aqueous eyes a vibrant violet, and her lips the petals of a rose. Churel's manufactured glamour paled in comparison to the natural splendour of her mistress. The Queen's rags disintegrated, unveiling a golden corslet over a black spider silk tunic. An embossed skull glared from her breastplate, while crowning her head was a titanium helm decorated with the fangs of Draculae. The dark cavern dissolved into the open sky lit by the fire of the setting sun, which reflected off the golden walls of a shining citadel atop a rocky tor. The Yanissars, the Queen's loyal guards, were arrayed before the front gate of the fortress.

"It's remarkable, isn't it?" Madonna Lilith said. "The daughters of the House of Shishen have always possessed this ability to connect with our minds. The One-eyed Soothsayer told me all about you, my dearest princess, and I've been expecting you."

"What's going on? Who is this Soothsayer?"

"You have entered my memory matrix. We're communicating with our thoughts. We're among the few who inherited this power from our first matriarch, the original Sibyl. Regarding the One-eyed Soothsayer, he is the only male person allowed among the Amazons, for he has long aided our cause. He has peered into the future and foreseen our ultimate victory.

"Here we are, during the Battle of Regna Rock, on that baneful day one year ago when victory slipped from our fingers. We had trapped the entire Shemsu scatocracy in the citadel. However, my sister, Belladonna, was held hostage by them. You see, Lord Shemsu, my implacable foe, is none other than my father. Besides being the Amazonian leader, Mamia Hüma was also the consort of the Supremo Lord of Betel. When Mamia rebelled, Belladonna was living with our father and, therefore, could not join us.

"To the dismay of Lord Shemsu and General Yaza, their terror tactic failed miserably. The women were appalled by the men's cruelty toward their Queen. They also admired the courage of the Amazons. Our ranks began to swell. Our fortunes further improved when the One-eyed Soothsayer showed up and mentored me in the ways of war. He taught me never to take a knife to a gunfight. I led many daring raids designed to humiliate the Scum Lords and infuriate the scatocrats. Our military successes attracted another surge of new members, fueling the feminine revolution. Lord Shemsu placed a bounty on my head, offering half the kingdom in reward. The ruse fooled no one because women used to own half the kingdom. The rank and file of the Amazons, along with the council, crowned me their Queen and Supremo.

"The Amazons enjoyed the many advantages of having a bold, young leader of royal blood. However, they must also suffer the downsides. I was reckless in daring, my heart was perfervid in vengeance, and I was drunk with an unbroken string of military successes. I forgot good fortune tends to deprive one of good sense. I decided to fight a do-or-die battle to settle the score once and for all, which brings us here to the citadel at Regna Rock."

Victoria, by her strong connection to the Queen, immediately grasped the battle's significance. The impregnable citadel of Regna Rock was the final refuge of the Shemsu scatocracy. Its fall would signify the demise of the patriarchal dynasty. But the outcome of the battle was by no means certain. The fortress, constructed with gigantic tungsten blocks, sat on an unassailable hill. Furthermore, a curtain of shining titanium-gold alloy cloaked its walls, making it unscalable and unbreachable. The reflective surface of the citadel earned it the moniker of "Mirror Fortress."

Mining or sapping was out of the question, as the citadel was built on top of a rocky tor named Regna Rock, meaning "ponderous stone," from which the fortress received its name. If taking the citadel by storm might prove challenging, capturing its tower, the Regna Keep, would be well-nigh impossible. The Keep, constructed from tungsten carbide, perched atop a vault housing the royal treasure, a large cache of weapons, an inexhaustible underground spring and sufficient food and fuel to sustain the defenders for an extended period. A siege of the Fortress of Regna Rock could last many years, allowing the dynasty to recover.

An hour earlier, on the battlefield near the citadel, Madonna Lilith led a daring charge in the dimming light of gloaming under a heavy downpour. The Amazons recked not life and limb as they smashed into Lord Shemsu's army, routing the despised enemy. The bulk of the Amazonian army pursued the fleeing men without giving quarters. Meanwhile, the young Amazonian Queen stood before the front gate, which was the East Gate, of the Mirror Fortress with her Yanissars, basking in glory.

"Crone, what is your advice?" Madonna Lilith, contemplating whether to take the citadel by siege or storm, asked the aged

Counsellor to her left. “Should we storm the citadel and end the scatocratic male rule once and for all?”

“The Mirror Fortress of Regna Rock has never fallen by storm,” the Crone cautioned. “We should not make rash decisions. We will lose many sisters. A siege will take longer, but it saves lives.”

Madonna Lilith turned to the fierce Amazonian guard on her right for a second opinion, “What do you think, Leona?”

Lion-eyed Leona, broad-shouldered and muscular, brandishing a fearsome spiked mace, was arrayed in the pelt of a Serpopard she had strangled with her bare hands. As the stalwart captain of the Yanissars and the bane of men, she replied with steadfastness and resolve, “My Queen, every single one of us will go everywhither you lead us, even if we must swim across a sea of fire and scale a mountain of knives. Say the word, and we will take the citadel, even if it means certain death.”

“Has the Soothsayer conveyed any oracles?” the Crone asked. “While we should always approach a man’s words with suspicion, his prophecies have yet to fail us.”

“The One-eyed Soothsayer is infallible,” the Queen affirmed. “His oracle proclaims, ‘Regna Rock falls tonight.’”

“Diamaranth be praised! I shall defer to the Soothsayer’s oracle and my Queen’s wishes,” the Crone said. “In the meantime, let us exercise caution and be mindful of Princess Belladonna’s safety. She is still Your Majesty’s sister and not our enemy.” The Crone bowed respectfully and retreated behind the Queen.

“Leona, should we wait for the army’s return,” Madonna Lilith asked, “or should we commence the operation now?”

“The Scum Lords and their recreants are in deathly fright,” Leona replied. “They’re cowering within the Regna Keep along with Lord Shemsu and General Yaza. Our soldiers in pursuit of the fleeing men won’t return until they have slaughtered the lot of them, which could take days, not hours. I suggest we delay no more. The furious storm strikes at will and waits for no one. After all, the oracle has spoken. Regna Rock falls tonight."

"Very well, thus it is said and etched in stone," Madonna Lilith declared. "Leona, this is my order. Select three score volunteers to be 'forlorn hopes' under my direct command. You will gather abundant liquid fire composed of quicklime, sulphur and naphtha. Deploy the scorpiones and the onagers to rain hellfire upon the East Gate. Prepare a gross of Rainmakers and launch them into the clouds upon my signal. We shall commence the assault before the Witching Hour. Tonight's watchword is *outis.* Throughout the operation, create a clangorous din of war. I shall lead the 'forlorn hopes' in breaching the West Gate for the Yanissars. Once inside, we will immediately storm the Regna Keep."

"My Queen, I beg your forgiveness for objecting," Leona protested. "As we know, nine out of ten 'forlorn hope' volunteers will perish. The Soothsayer made no mention of Your Majesty's fate. We cannot afford to lose our Supremo in this dangerous mission. What good is the fall of Regna Rock if our Queen goes down with it? The Amazons' future depends on Your Majesty. Allow me to lead the assault instead."

"Princess Belladonna has never lived apart from Lord Shemsu. She will not leave her prison unless she sees me. Knowing the scatocrats, they will use her as a shield. But have no fear for my safety. The 'forlorn hopes' will protect me. If I should perish, the Amazon council has already devised a plan for an orderly succession. The Amazonian Revolution shall not depend on one person. I have made up my mind, now go and fulfil your duties. Come what might, Regna Rock falls tonight."

Chapter 19

Metamorphosis

The Amazonian Queen's line of attack had a method in its madness. The Mirror Fortress' East Gate was the sole entrance accessible by a narrow path from the fields below and the only breachable section of the citadel, which was, of course, also the most sturdily built and stubbornly defended. The West Gate, on the other hand, was flush against a sheer cliff, serving as an escape of the last resort. Even without defenders, scaling the wall on this side was considered suicidal. While the firebombing at the East Gate would be spectacular, it was merely a diversion for Madonna Lilith, whose idea of a surprise attack was to breach the deadliest section of the citadel.

As the Witching Hour approached, spreading soporific stillness, the assault by fire began. The flames lit up the sky, as if a newborn sun were rising from the fortress. The intense heat caused the titanium-gold cladding of the wall to glow while smoke enwrapped the citadel in a dark shroud. Marching in silence through the fog unseen and unheard, Madonna Lilith and her suicide commandos arrived at the bottom of the cliff beneath the West Gate. Each of the 'forlorn hopes' brandished a grappling hook affixed to a scaling rope, poised for the Queen's order to do and die.

The smoke soon gathered into a cloud above the fortress. Thereupon, Madonna Lilith took her Fire Pugu arrow and launched it into the air. A fiery trail appeared above the East Gate, the signal for Leona to unleash the Rainmakers. A hundred and forty-four flaming rockets soon rose into the night sky. It was as if the one-horned dragon, *Jiao*, awakened from its ambrosial sleep, flew into the heavenly rivers to bring sweet succour to parched earthlings.

Before one could say Georgy Konstantinovich Zhukov, heavy raindrops poured from the sky. Queen Lilith snatched the returning Pugu, cast her grappling hook onto a rock above, and led the 'forlorn hopes' up the treacherous cliff. While half the leading soldiers would fall and lose their lives, they would eventually secure several scaling lines for the Yanissars following behind. Those who perished knew they did not die in vain, for they paved the way for those who climbed after them to do so safely. Madonna Lilith had indoctrinated every Amazon with a single tenet. To succeed in their revolution, each Amazon must not hesitate to make the ultimate sacrifice.

As the Queen scaled the citadel's wall and pulled herself over the parapets onto the wall walk, she immediately encountered three enemy guards. Being an expert fencer, Madonna Lilith retreated into a corner to shorten the front while covering her flanks and denying attacks from behind. Having thus positioned herself, she relied on fancy swordplay to make short work of her foes, cutting them down one after another. Soon, the rest of the 'forlorn hope' soldiers arrived, and they promptly cleared the ramparts of the surprised defenders.

Before Madonna Lilith could celebrate, she came face to face with death, noticing the angry flashes from the keen eyes of enemy archers, whose crossbows were loaded with multiple bolts and cocked for a deadly volley. Every Amazon on the ramparts was as good as dead, or as the saying goes, dead as Schrödinger's cat. Purely by reflex, Madonna Lilith dropped to one knee and raised her sword to shield her face against the impending onslaught, as it did not become the Amazonian Queen to fall on her face. She heard the triggers releasing the bolts. After what seemed to be an interminable slow-motion tick-tock of the clock, the brave Madonna Lilith suffered the sting of a devastating setback.

A bolt went through her hand but came to a halt at the hilt of her sword. If she had not protected her face, the bolt would have drilled into her head and scattered her brain, and that would be that for the young Queen. Another bolt went through her breastplate but stopped short of penetrating her spider-silk tunic. She was not so lucky with the third bolt, which found a chink in her corslet and cut through everything. The cruel barb punctured her skin and twisted into her flesh, finally stopping when it hit a bone.

Madonna Lilith did not even wince. After hearing her mother scream in torture, she swore the enemy would never extract it from her or any Amazon. The woman warriors would howl in uproarious laughter or during frenzied slaughter, but they endured pain with stoic silence, a quality shared by very few civilizations or cultures. Most languages did not have a word to describe it. The Chinese have the word *ren*, which means long-suffering forbearance in silence. The written character is the pictogram of a knife in a bleeding heart.

Death came swiftly to the brave girls of the 'forlorn hope' on the ramparts, yet they had no regret. They had volunteered to lead the assault, expecting to die. They were well aware the fight for independence would be brutal. The men gave no quarter to the women, and the women did not expect any. Dying is easy; revolution is hard. The Scum Lords pontificated about the male gender's saintly virtues, singing paeans about their marvellous sex, promising to grant one right or another to the female rebels, provided they unconditionally laid down their arms and agreed to a peaceful reconcilement under the sheets. The murderous men lied without a hint of shame, claiming to be proponents of peace and swearing to treat the women fairly hereafter. The Amazons had heard these bald-faced lies before. It was all Bushite and balderdash. They had no choice but to fight and die for what rights they believed they should rightfully have.

Queen Lilith once said the wounded in battle didn't have time to hurt. Time is precious, never enough and the stuff that life is made of. During combat, time is a matter of life and death. Madonna Lilith lost no time plucking the bolt from her hand. She grabbed Pandiva, the divine bow hanging by a richly *broidered* baldric on her back, lifted the Gold Pugu from her quiver, drew the bow and uttered a curse under her breath.

"Roses are red, violets are blue. Open your eyes, we're coming for you."

The Amazonian Queen released her arrow, plucking the bowstring and playing the harmonic chord of the D Minor key, the harbinger of death.

The archers were still loading their crossbows for another volley when they heard the Requiem of Pandiva. Opening their eyes wide in astonishment, they witnessed the death-dealing dart piercing through one archer after another until all lay supine in a pool of blood with a gaping hole between their eyes. Madonna Lilith snatched the spent arrow in the air as it glided back on Munin's feathers. She cleaned the blood-soaked Pugu with her sleeve and returned it to her quiver.

The rain stopped as the last 'forlorn hope' soldiers arrived at the ramparts. Only six of them survived the assault. They immediately opened the gate and let in the Yanissars for the storming of the Regna Keep.

Madonna Lilith's hand was bleeding profusely, and she seated herself on a stair to bind the wound. When Victoria sat beside the Queen, she noticed a familiar archer's ring on her thumb.

"Do you still hurt from your old wounds?" Victoria asked.

"Unfortunately, yes," Queen Lilith said. "My memory doesn't allow me to forget anything, including all the pain."

Victoria gently placed her hand on Madonna Lilith's wounded palm, which miraculously healed, leaving no trace of a scar. The young Amazonian Queen gazed at Victoria tenderly, smiling, thankful the mysterious visitor had relieved her of the endless torture of a deep, festering wound, which had refused to heal even under her own extraordinary recuperative powers.

"Didn't the oracle of the One-eyed Soothsayer come true?" Victoria asked. "How did you and the Amazons end up in an underground cavern?"

"It came true, but not how we expected."

A messenger arrived to report the development of the battle.

"Good news, my Queen. We have taken control of the Mirror Fortress, slaying all defenders. General Yaza had sealed the entrance to the Keep. Now we'll have to figure out how to breach the tungsten tower."

"Tungsten carbide is impregnable," Queen Lilith said. "If the Keep does not fall, the war is far from over."

"We may get help from an unexpected source," the messenger added. "A captured spy brought a secret message on a ribbon for my Queen. We see strange markings we do not understand. Perhaps Your Majesty can decipher it."

Madonna Lilith took the ribbon, examined it and began to wrap it around her wrist, winding it in a spiral up to her elbow. The strange symbols became aligned to make sense. She read aloud, "The walls have a thousand eyes, and the Keep but one. Yeah, the pain of separation ends when the twain is one."

"What does it mean?" Victoria asked.

"I forgot to mention Belladonna and I are identical twins," the Queen replied. "Our parents decided to raise us separately, one with the father and the other with the mother. Before the Amazonian Revolution permanently separated us, we used to send secret messages to each other using this method, known as the

Skytale Cypher. We also visited each other regularly. I remember us playing on the stump of a large tree in the centre of the citadel's courtyard. We called it Regna's Eye. I suspect it is the secret backdoor of the Keep."

After Herculean exertion, the Yanissars removed the stump using a system of levers, ropes and pulleys, unveiling a chute running deep into the earth. Led by Queen Lilith, Leona and the Crone, the Yanissars descended the shaft, leaving the regular soldiers to guard the opening and the fortress above.

The underground passage, however, did not lead the Amazons to the Shemsu scatocrats. Instead, they ended up in a labyrinth where they spent hours going in circles while struggling with the lack of oxygen. When the female warriors heard a hellish groan and felt a gush of hot air, they hurriedly retraced their path back to the surface, only to discover the exit no longer existed.

While the Amazonian Queen and her Yanissars were underground, the Regna Keep went up in flames. The inferno was so intense the tower's tungsten carbide walls melted and collapsed onto the catacomb's entrance, sealing the fate of the Amazon warriors. Regna Keep did fall, but only as a devious scheme designed by Lord Shemsu to trap Queen Lilith in an eternal tomb.

Although most Amazons had no idea about the existence of a fuel capable of melting tungsten carbide, Madonna Lilith knew of it from family lore. After all, it was no secret Prince Shishen, the dynastic founder, built the castle with tungsten blocks he had cast in a forge. According to family records, the Prince had smuggled a small but not insignificant amount of an extraordinary energy source, the legendary Erinysite, from his home planet.

It was too late for Madonna Lilith to realize Belladonna had betrayed her, and she did not have the heart to tell the Amazons they were buried alive in a grave with no escape. By all measures, they were already dead, or as the saying goes, dead as Schrödinger's cat.

Lord Shemsu and General Yaza's gambit was a resounding success. They were not holed up in Regna Keep as rumours suggested. Instead, they had set up a deadly ambuscade nearby with their elite troops, awaiting the perfect moment to pounce on the unsuspecting, leaderless, and dispersed Amazons and slaughter them wholesale. The scatocracy held a grand celebration afterward and declared a national holiday to commemorate the quelling of the rebellion.

"Shemsu and Yaza expected us to die here," the Queen said, removing her hand from Victoria and returning their consciousness to the cavern. It was moments before the commencement of the final operation to topple male rule at Betel.

"After all," the Queen continued, "these subterranean walls are highly radioactive. Our enemies also sealed off all the air chutes to suffocate us. Moreover, we had no food. Lord Shemsu had ensured we would not escape this catacomb with our lives. But, as you can see, we're very much alive and kicking. In addition to the iron rule of being unafraid of death, the Amazons do not give up. We will not bend, and we never say die.

"The high level of radioactivity inadvertently saved us by causing our bodies to adapt. Our cells are somewhat different from those of other advanced lifeforms. Radioactivity causes some of our cells to revert to a more primitive, undifferentiated and mutable state when the genes of these rapidly multiplying cells undergo a flurry of mutations, until one cell repairs itself faster than the harmful radiation damages it. The cured cell naturally thrives, multiplies and spreads its self-healing gene to other cells through lateral transfer. It was how we survived."

"But only one person got the self-healing gene. How did everyone else get it?"

"The primitive state of our cells has another strong survival characteristic. When triggered by a stress hormone, the good gene clones copies of itself into messengers inside carrier cells and becomes transmissible. Once we noticed one of us was recovering from the radiation exposure, we ensured everyone kissed her to get infected. Thanks to the lethal radioactivity, what would normally take lifeforms hundreds of thousands of years to attain by evolution, we achieved in this cavern within a few days."

"And how do we live without oxygen?"

"Rapid adaptation to environmental change is a manifestation of our mutable cell structure. Our cellular metabolic system immediately switches to anaerobic chemical reactions, so we no longer need oxygen. However, it makes our blood and body fluids highly acidic, which causes unbearable pain. Fortunately, our body adapts, creating a large variety of natural opioids and making us immune to any form of physical or mental agony. In the past, it took great discipline for us to endure torture without screaming. Nowadays, we do not scream because we are comfortably numb. Meanwhile, our eyes have adjusted to see in the dark, our bones have become as strong as steel and as hard as tungsten, and our muscles pack a Serpopard's power. Our regenerative system can heal serious wounds in a matter of seconds. We are become gods."

"Do I share all these powers?"

"If not, you'd be dead already," Queen Lilith said. "Anyways, that which does not kill us makes us stronger, even godlike, while the Scum Lords believe we are dead and buried. After surviving by consuming the unspoiled parts of those who had succumbed, we got help from the One-eyed Soothsayer. He captured and tamed the queen mother of a sand puppy colony. They ate through the rock to reach us. The sand puppy queen, Kerbera, is now my pet.

"After breaking through to the surface, we decided to bide our time and wait for the most opportune moment to surprise the Scum

Lords. According to the One-eyed Soothsayer, the best time is tonight, during the festivities celebrating the Quelling of the Rebellion. The scatocrats will be engaged in the impregnation of women to create more soldiers and slaves. They will get intoxicated and let down their guard. By coincidence, upon the Witching Hour, zero hour of our attack, a lunar eclipse will block all light from the heavens. At the same time, the Soothsayer will sabotage the power grid, plunging the Scum Lords into complete darkness. It will not affect the Amazons because of our nocturnal vision. With their electricity cut off, the men will be powerless, literally and figuratively. They will become easy prey.

"In the meantime, our sand puppies have created large tunnels leading to all the rooms and chambers where the Scum Lords and their scatocratic dogs will be committing shameless and heinous acts against their female victims. They have no idea most of their subjugated women, with the help of our spies, have gradually awakened from their stupor. All they need is for us Amazons to rise from our graves and raise the flag of revolution. No one sleeps tonight. Final victory and sweet vengeance will be ours."

Leona approached with two stone trenchers of fettuccine smothered in a red pasta sauce.

"The hour is nigh," she said. "This is our last supper underground. We will move into position after the meal."

"What's this?" Victoria asked. As a student of culinary arts, she always wanted to have an intimate knowledge of her food.

"These are worms collected from the sand puppies," Queen Lilith said as she slurped in a mouthful. "Full of mineral nutrients, they have sustained us while we're surviving here. Eat up. You'll need the energy."

"I'm not hungry. Thanks!"

Chapter 20

Vincero

"You are dead," Madonna Lilith, wrapped in a large bath towel as a temporary substitute for her regal robes, declared ominously to a group of chained and manacled male prisoners, "or so you wish." Under natural light, the Amazonian Queen's complexion was a soft shade of aqua. It was one of the effects of her mutations, changing the colour of her blood from red to blue. "You may want to die and spare yourselves the shame of defeat, but not today. I decide when and how you'll meet your fate. I also decide how you'll live to suffer all the depravities you have visited upon the women, your erstwhile kin and partners. Prepare for your Final Judgment, blood for blood and death for death."

Anticlimactic was the proper description of Lord Shemsu's defeat. His empire, built upon the oppression of women, ended with a whimper. The men were caught with their pants down, literally and figuratively. The patriarchal dynasty collapsed gradually and then all at once.

To the surprise of the Amazonian victors, they discovered Lord Shemsu's royal library had an entire section dedicated to legal codices espousing equal rights for women. They found reams of academic expositions expounding the benefits of treating women as equals and sharing power with them. To top it off, they brought to light the Shishen Dynasty's constitutional document, the Magnificent Charter, which enshrined women's rights on par with men's. But Lord Shemsu, the Scum Lords and the scatocrats who enjoyed power and privilege ignored their constitution and laws, so now they must suffer the consequences.

Victoria did not emerge from the underground cavern until the killing stopped. She was not interested in witnessing the violence. The peaceful Canadian girl could understand Queen Lilith's implacable wrath, though she disapproved of her obsession with revenge. It could be an irreconcilable difference between them. Victoria noticed the Amazonian Queen's archer ring was missing. It was no doubt wending its way to Earth via the one-eyed man, ending up at its final destination in Victoria's LV knapsack.

Meanwhile, the vengeful Madonna Lilith, accompanied by her Canadian visitor, began inspecting prisoners listed as Class A war criminals. In the first room, labelled Unit 731, Victoria noticed a handful of captives cloaked in blood-soaked surgical scrubs. Amazonian guards had arrested the surgeons while they were performing a medical procedure. A lifeless victim, still strapped to the operating table, lay partially covered by a gore-drenched flag of the Amazons. A trolley beside the cadaver held a large pan filled with nightmarish surgical instruments designed to inspire the fear of God in the most recalcitrant hearts. Victoria lowered her head to avert her gaze from the horrific sight.

"Well, well! Who do we have here but Doctor Death himself?" Madonna Lilith exclaimed. "How are you, Uncle Stonewell? Good to see you again, thankfully, not as your captive. Sorry for intruding while you and your boys are having fun."

Madonna Lilith noticed an echo and sang, "Vincero, vincero!"

Her face suddenly twisted into a dark snarl.

"How clever," she sneered, "rigging the torture cell as an echo chamber so the victims can enjoy hearing their own screams. Boys will be boys, but you perverts certainly know how to have fun. I guess you have no idea true Amazons don't scream under torture."

“Let me go,” Lord Stonewell pleaded, “and I will give you the power to be the destroyer of worlds.”

“I’d rather burn in the Eternal Inferno,” Queen Lilith cried, “than let your unbounded evil go unpunished. Prepare to receive your just deserts and enjoy the very tortures you invented.”

Turning to an officer beside her, the Queen, in high dudgeon, ordered, “Prosecutor, identify all the atrocities they have committed and let them have a taste of their own medicine.”

“Some of their demonic deeds are so hellacious,” the officer said, “we’re hard-pressed to utter them lest our heart explodes into a million pieces. If we but take a glimpse of their atrocities, pale wraiths will haunt our nightmares and rob us of our wits. We can no more do what they have done than to renounce life itself.”

“But we cannot bury these monstrosities and forget about them,” Queen Lilith insisted. “The ghosts of the dead will never stop their wailing for justice. We must set the record straight and deliver retribution, lest our children and their children forget the painful lesson. My dear Victoria, what do you think?”

“If you want my personal opinion,” Victoria said, “I think we should remember the lesson and serve justice, but we must be careful we don’t turn into the monsters we’re fighting.”

“Hear! Hear! Well said,” Queen Lilith applauded. “Prosecutor, give our dearest princess a preliminary report of the victim in this room and let her determine the fitting punishment for the villains.”

The prosecutor and her assistants inspected the body, grimacing and averting their eyes several times. After questioning the guards, the visibly stunned officer reported, “The victim was a suspected sympathizer, the target of a witch hunt. The monsters had subjected her to the Bone Breaker. The fractures throughout her skeletal frame are so numerous we find it impossible to document. They have also dislocated her knees and elbows, torn off her mammary glands, exposed her entrails, frozen her feet and immersed her hands in acid. They poured mustard oil into her nostrils and over her eyes, finally using flesh-eating bacteria to consume half her face.

"It is common knowledge these insensate doctors of death commit their heinous acts without applying anesthetics. They deliberately keep their victims alert throughout the ordeal. For this woman, her tormentors applied electrodes to various sensitive areas to generate maximum pain, all recorded on a Dolorimeter. To satisfy their morbid curiosity, they measured the volume of her screams with a Sound Pressure Level meter. We have a recording of it. Naturally, she was not an Amazonian sister. She was still alive when we arrived, but we couldn't save her. She begged us for mercy, and we granted her a swift death to end her suffering."

"Are these people animals?" Victoria gasped in shock at the report. "I'm sorry, even animals couldn't do what they've done. How could they even dream of committing such evil?"

"This may be the tamest job this death squad has ever undertaken," Madonna Lilith said. "Their leader is the notorious Doctor Death, Lord Shemsu's Minister of Health and his foremost expert in ponerology. The scatocrats worship him. He is my own Uncle Stonewell, a blood kin. Can you imagine I sat on his lap when I was a toddler? He was also my mother's executioner. He called it honourable killing. He maintained he was following orders and enjoyed every minute of it. He openly admitted the price was well worth it. So, what is your verdict?"

While Victoria grappled with the complex issue of crime and punishment, a messenger burst into the room with urgent news.

"My Queen, something incredible has happened!" the breathless runner reported. "The Starship Saluzi, which brought our ancestors through the Orbital Gateway to Betel, has lifted off from the Museum of Science with Lord Shemsu and his scatocrats on board."

"The starship has no fuel," Madonna Lilith stated matter-of-factly. "Even if it reaches escape velocity, it will not go far. Besides, the Orbital Gateway has been dormant since our ancestors' arrival. Without it, they'll soon be dead and adrift in an icy casket in deep space. The Scum Lords and their scatocrats cannot escape their fate."

"It is not a sure thing," the messenger said. "A short while ago, the Orbital Gateway came alive, and a pollinator emerged from it. The monolith-shaped vehicle has landed and now stands erect atop a grassy knoll outside the city walls. Our soldiers have surrounded it and are offering prayers to the Goddess Diamaranth, who may have sent a Watcher from long ago and far away."

"Let us not waste time on myths and monoliths," the Amazonian Queen said. "We must dispatch soldiers in pursuit of the Scum Lords. Find the Soothsayer. He has highly trained bounty hunters for hire. Make haste, lest the Orbital Gateway closes and the criminals escape without paying for their crimes."

Meanwhile, Victoria heard Sting's voice in her ears.

"Victoria, we must leave. I'm inside the pollinator, arriving at this planet to investigate the presence of a one-eyed man. I cannot risk meeting myself here. It would seriously transgress the law of causality and spirally skewer our universe without recourse. Please ask the Catoptron to transport us back to your home in the present timeline, where we can take stock and plan our next steps."

An officer rushed in with another urgent report, "My Queen, the messenger from long ago and far away speaks. Your Majesty's presence is needed."

Madonna Lilith wanted to take Victoria along, but her mysterious visitor had vanished amidst the commotion.

"Who is this Victoria?" the Queen mused.

Chapter 21

The Prince and the Pauper

"Salute, en Garde!" Count Blood commanded. "Prêts? Allez!" Kiku and Prince Cambi, each outfitted in a vest of spider silk and wielding a rapier and dagger, immediately tried to pierce, stab and lacerate each other.

Kiku lunged forward with his rapier, slipping the blade beneath Cambi's arm, aiming for his heart. Cambi parried with his rapier while targeting Kiku's temple with his dagger. Kiku deftly blocked Cambi's attack, swiftly spinning around and slashing at Cambi. Cambi stepped back to avoid the blade and quickly re-entered the fray with a counterattack. Kiku parried and riposted. Cambi counter-riposted. Kiku made a one-handed backflip to disengage, feigned a fatal error by opening his arms to draw an attack and lunged forward with his rapier, forming a cross with his dagger. Cambi responded with the same formation. The four well-wrought weapons clashed with the clangorous din of war as they met mid-air. Without taking a break, the two fencers disengaged and tried to kill each other all over again.

This intense exchange persisted until Count Blood shouted, "arrêt."

Lord Killem applauded the performance as he stepped into the sword training area in the garden.

"Bravi! Bravissimi!" he shouted in approval. "Count Blood has taught you well. I will have two of the best Yarjuni swordsmen under my wings." Turning to his fosterling, Lord Killem said,

"Kiku, the Class-One Sword-fighting Championship starts in a sennight. If you win the Slasher Prize, you will earn acceptance into the Yarjun caste, allowing me to legally induct you into the Immortals and adopt you as my son. What do you think?"

"I'm most grateful and indebted to Your Lordship for saving my life and making me whole again. I don't know what I have done to deserve all this, nor can I hope to repay my Lord for this immeasurable generosity. If I win the Slasher and become a member of the Yarjun caste, I will do my best to prove myself worthy of bearing the royal name of Kheru. As an Immortal, I will gladly pledge to defend my Lord and Prince Cambi with my life."

"And what say you, Cambi," Lord Killem asked, "how would you like Kiku to be the brother you've always wanted?"

"Pepé Killem, I have no other wish in life but this."

"Very well, Kiku, you must now prepare yourself mentally toward winning the tournament. You may have to fence against Prince Cambi for the coveted prize."

"I hear this tournament is dangerous," Kiku said, concerned. "I'm partly machine and can withstand serious sword wounds, but it's too risky for Cambi. Also, if we are both in the tournament, I shall have no chance of defeating the Prince. Cambi is far more skillful and experienced than I am. I wish I could win even one of the many trophies in his room."

"Rubbish! Do not let trophies fool you," Lord Killem said. "None of those lily-livered cowards dared to go for the kill because they were fencing against a prince of the blood and the future Supremo. You may not face each other because of seeding, but prepare yourself for the eventuality. Sheathe your weapons. You two may take a break. Count Cutt is setting up a four-dimensional multilateral Blood Chess match in the war room. Learn this game well, as you must apply strategic thinking in your future battles for ultimate and lasting peace."

Blood Chess was a strategic game designed to test one's skills and judgment under stress. The game system adjusted a player's blood pressure according to the battle conditions on the board. For top-level competitions, fail-safes were disabled, and players refusing to concede had perished during the contest. It was a four-dimensional game, allowing players to move any chess pieces through various spatial dimensions on each turn while permitting backtracking. It was also multilateral, meaning any number of players could participate as allies or foes to one another, sometimes as both, always with deception, until only one player remained. Depending on the number of players, a single game could last for days. The longest game on record involved eleven top-ranked players, dragging on for an astonishing eleven cycles.

Kiku's days were full. After the chess game, the boys analyzed their strategic moves during lunch. In the afternoon, they attended lectures at the Peace Academy, where they learned all the knowledge and skills of war needed to bring about world peace.

Science subjects always captivated Kiku. Music, after all, is one of Nature's greatest mysteries, ranking right at the top with math. The senior lecturer for STEM courses was Professor Fineman, who taught the Plancket Series, Plancket Transform, Plancket Group Theory, Plancket Tensors, Plancket Neural Computing, and Plancket Unified Field Theory. Professor Plancket, known to the Ignorantes as Carlini Stane, practically created science and technology for the Yarjunis, and Professor Fineman was his star student. Kiku studied hard and excelled at school, becoming Professor Fineman's favourite protégé.

To Kiku, his new life among the Yarjuni royalty was unnatural and alien. He had learned the Yarjunis were evil Haryas who started the Endless War. Kiku's personal experience contradicted this notion. Lord Killem had been a caring parent, easing Kiku's grief over losing his family and friends. Prince Cambi was always kind and generous. According to information provided by the Opticon, the Prince's mother died giving birth to him. Cambi was close to his father, whom he admired, and he always wanted to have siblings. However, Lord Killem would not remarry because of his undying devotion to Cambi's mother. To the Prince, Kiku was a true brother and a godsend.

On their way to the tournament, Lord Killem and Prince Cambi could detect conflicts plaguing Kiku's mind.

"Kiku, this tournament determines your future with us," Lord Killem said. "You need to maintain razor-sharp focus. If anything is troubling you, I want you to speak up. You cannot afford to be distracted while fighting the most important duels of your life."

"I'm sorry about my weakness," Kiku said. "Sometimes, I can't help being depressed. I've often wondered about what happened at Petra on the Night of Infamy and whether any of my friends survived. Even though my Lord has given me a new life, I cannot forget about the old one."

"I can understand why you have questions," Lord Killem sighed. "It's not easy to accept everything you knew about the Yarjunis was a lie. I do not deny our ancestors were responsible for starting the Endless War. Nevertheless, it is not fair the Ignorantes and the rebels put all the blame on us for prolonging the war. Ever since the day I sat on the throne, I've been trying to make peace. I have come to realize the utter futility of the ceaseless fighting. I have sent out many olive branches, but the rebels refuse to give peace a chance. They continue to indoctrinate their people with lies, asserting the Yarjunis are evil incarnate. As you can see, we're ordinary Haryas, the same as everyone else. In any event, we can't end the war unless all participants want to stop fighting.

"As for the tragedy of Petra, we arrived too late to prevent it. The rebels had intercepted the secret communications between the Elders and the Yarjunis. We were working to resolve this festering problem of the supposedly neutral haven of Petra harbouring our enemies and renegades, undermining its relative peace. No one told you Petra had survived for so long because we had a secret understanding. In a mad rage, the rebels sent a drone fleet to flatten Petra as a warning to other neutral colonies. It was a bloody massacre, sparing no one. Your survival is a miracle. I'm determined to groom you to be the Yarjunis' symbol of peace. But I must first train you in the traditions and arts of the Yarjunis so you can represent us as a caste member.

"I know all this is confusing and overwhelming for a young boy. It may not have crossed your mind, but it is almost impossible for someone from a lower caste to become a Yarjuni. Neither Prince Cambi nor I can impose it on you if you don't want it. You have the freedom to leave any time and go wherever you want. We will not stop you. You have my word. But to contribute to world peace, you'll have to forget the lies and concentrate on winning the tournament. Can you do it for peace or, less altruistically, for Prince Cambi, who desperately wants you to be his brother?"

The Prince smiled at Kiku and grabbed his hand.

"But those who destroyed Petra must not go unpunished," Kiku said, not forgetting his vow. "They must pay for the crime."

"I agree one hundred percent," Lord Killem said. "But we can't help you unless you become a Yarjuni. Win the tournament, and I promise to put all our resources at your disposal when you're ready to seek justice."

Chapter 22

The One-Eyed Warrior

Should he or shouldn't he? Kiku grappled with the horns of the dilemma. Prince Cambi had committed a rare mistake. His back was up against the wall, and his left hand gripping the dagger was out of position, exposing a fatal weakness in his defence. Kiku had visualized this situation a thousand times. He had secretly practiced the "lunge circular counter-parry sixte riposte" in one motion a thousand times. Finally, he was staring at the opportunity to execute the combination and make the hit count. The result, however, was fraught with danger. While Kiku would win the tournament, he risked inflicting an irreparable injury on Prince Cambi. The spider-silk vest offered some protection, but a direct hit could be lethal.

Kiku wished he did not have to harm Prince Cambi to win the tournament. Alas, he had no time to weigh his options. Time is a matter of life and death during the heat of battle. By dint of habit, he lunged forward, aiming for Cambi's chest. With nowhere to run, the Prince reflexively parried. Kiku executed a perfect circular counter-parry sixte, ending with naught but unobstructed space between his rapier's point and his opponent's heart. As he whipped his left arm backwards to drive home the lunge, the Vanadium steel point would pierce the target and terminate the tournament. But at the last moment, Kiku lost control of his motor functions and froze in paralysis. He dropped his sword and dagger and collapsed to the floor in a helpless heap.

The spectators and judges immediately leapt from their seats and erupted in a thunderous standing ovation, accompanied by resounding shouts of bravo and bravissimo. Prince Cambi, standing at his spot unscathed, politely clapped his hands. Lord Killem trotted over and helped Kiku to his feet.

"What happened?" Kiku asked as he regained control of his bionic system. "Didn't I miss?"

"It was a clean hit, Kiku, my boy," Lord Killem assured him. "You've proven yourself to possess the heart of a Yarjuni. I was right about you the first time I laid eyes on you. We will host a magnificent celebration at the presentation of the Slasher Prize to coincide with your upcoming Crossover ceremony. You will receive a Yarjuni name, an honour we have bestowed on no other in our history. You will be a great Yarjun Lord. At last, peace is within reach. Cambi, come welcome your brother to the family."

The Broadcast Authority decided to televise the Slasher Prize presentation in all Yarjuni cities. The program began with the recounting of Kiku's background story, emphasizing how Lord Killem had saved him when the rebels attacked Petra. It highlighted advanced Yarjuni technology, by which the Supremo made the bombing victim whole again. It also extolled the high morality of the Yarjuni society, having welcomed a member of the lowest caste with open arms, even accepting him as a son of the Yarjunis. It was a heart-warming story of redemption, sponsored by the Thousand And One Nights Propaganda Media Company.

Afterwards, Kiku partook in the Breakfast of Champions, in which four expert cooks each skillfully slaughtered, dismembered and deboned a suckling pig in Kiku's presence, followed by a demonstration of their culinary and acrobatic artistry, juggling utensils and flipping knives at each other while preparing various dim sum dishes on the sizzling hot grill plate. The lone survivor gained the prestigious title of Head Chef of the Royal Kitchen

Tartarus. The Knight of the Long Knives Corporation proudly sponsored this program.

After breakfast, Kiku enjoyed the spectacle of a military tattoo performed by subjugated members of the Musician caste. Each band member squeezed a porcine creature to generate a particular squeal, producing a strangely satisfying marching tune.

Next on the agenda was a popular reality show, the Boar Hunt. The "Boar" was, in fact, a cunning athlete trained to outrun, outwit and outmuscle ten slaves armed with spears. The organizers staged the event in a thickly wooded area within the expansive grounds of the royal palace. Cameras were strategically mounted on the artificial flora to capture the live action for Kiku and the Yarjuni audience. The Boar picked off one slave after another, terrorizing them with gruesome displays of the gutted and flayed victims until none remained. The reward for the Boar was a promotion to the rank of captain in the Yarjuni army. Master Beast Games was the mastermind of this exciting but macabre program.

Lunch was a wurstfest capped by a famous dessert. Savoury sausages of every tradition and appellation prepared by sausage masters of every culinary discipline lined the smorgasbord benches. The main fares featured the eponymous frankfurters and nürnbergers, made from aged and cured meats of Frankfurters and Nürnbergers. For those with peculiar tastes, the caterer provided blood sausages, brain puddings and entrails saveloys crafted by skillful Darmstädters. Everyone was intrigued by the "Heavenly Sausage with No Name." To all inquiries regarding its secret ingredients, the sausage server always replied, "You don't want to know!" Dessert was the much-loved jam-filled Berliners.

After the meal, Kiku was subjected to a spiritual ordeal, consuming the "Death in the Afternoon" concoction, which was supposed to build up his resistance to the deadliest poisons. Since the drink was a potpourri of toxins, half of those who swallowed the potion would end up dead, hence its name. All Yarjunis aspiring to attain aristocratic status must undergo this dangerous ritual. Kiku fainted from the deadly admixture, but he survived.

Following the customary siesta, Kiku and Lord Killem's household repaired to the royal arena to watch the Crossover Games. Inside the ring, ten gladiators picked from captured rebels tore each other apart for the slim chance one of them would survive. Gladiator Games was the producer of this program.

After the dust settled, animal handlers fed the fallen gladiators to a pack of ravenous worm-dogs, or worgs. This abomination of nature, the product of a failed genetic experiment, resembled a dachshund with no face and one eye. The Yarjunis kept worgs as pets due to their unreserved loyalty, a quality dependent on the ready supply of plentiful meat. The clever worgs would parrot their master's voice, spewing invectives against their master's foes and, when ordered, inflict physical damage with their long, sharp fangs.

The next item on the list was the Hungry Worg Race, a popular pari-mutuel "Winner Takes All" betting event, offering a fabulous purse to win, a pat on the back to place and nothing to show. For an enhanced spectator experience, the handlers starved the Worgs for a week before the race, turning them into cannibals. As a result, the chase, attacks and frenzied feeding made the blood-drenched free-for-all a thrilling spectacle no Yarjuni would want to miss. The sponsor for this program was the Worg-Eat-Worg Club.

Born and bred a peaceful Ignorante of the Emodulanda Musician caste, Kiku was unaccustomed to this sort of Yarjuni blood sport. Yet he applauded with the crowd and smiled as if he enjoyed the experience. Kiku reminded himself of his vow to avenge the death of his parents and sister. Blood for blood and death for death meant, one of these days, he would have to get used to atrocities with blood on his hands.

Upon sunset, the high priest, or the Pontifex Maximus, started a bonfire at the centre of a grand circle known as the Circus Maximus. Surrounded by the royal household and distinguished guests, Kiku sat on an ornate chair, the Sella Curulis, while behind him perched Lord Killem and Prince Cambi on their respective thrones set on a higher tier.

With everyone properly seated, the Ringmaster brought out blinded slaves trained to perform death-defying acts. Acrobats swung on the flying trapeze and danced the high-wire ballet with no safety nets, knife jugglers and bear-baiters put their skills to the test, and archers shot at kumquats placed on children's heads. When someone slipped, the victim would end up in the bonfire as a holocaust offered to the God With No Name.

Following these feats, the High Priestess led the Vestal Virgins, soon to be buried alive as an offering to the God of War, on a procession around the Circus, arriving at a golden altar to announce the official induction of Kiku into the Yarjun caste. Afterwards, Count Blood led his Praetorian Guards to the altar to present the Slasher Prize, the skull of last year's Slasher champion, who lost his life defending his title. The Chief also initiated Kiku into the ranks of the Immortals.

The final ceremony, the climax of the day's events, was Lord Killem's formal adoption of Kiku, during which the young boy would receive an aristocratic rank and a permanent Yarjun name.

"By the authority vested in me as the Supremo Lord of the Yarjunis and head of the Royal House," Lord Killem proclaimed, "I solemnly receive Kingku Orphius into the House of Kheru and officially adopt him as my son. I now decree this be entered into the Book of Generations of the House of Kheru, confirming the father and son bond. From this moment onwards, Kingku is dead. My newborn son is named Deskull, the Margrave of Helle."

Chapter 23

Stranger in Paradise

"ake up, wake up." David Huang woke to a voice in an oppressive darkness while suffering from an ache all over his body. A fire raged beneath his skin.

"Where am I? Is this Hell?"

"Hell no! Hell is a city much like Vegas," the voice replied.

"Who are you, and why can't I see anything?"

"I'm your expergefactor, the wake-up caller. It is how the universe appears to those who have eyes but will not see. Open your eyes."

David raised his eyelids to wake from his strange dream. He found himself in an unfamiliar world.

Dawn, the saffron-robed goddess, had begun to paint the morning sky with her rosy-tipped fingers, bringing warm light to expel the icy gloom from the hearts of gods and men. David noticed he was aboard a black sailboat, moored at an emerald isle enveloped in a diaphanous mist. Not far away, a sparkling castle of crystalline glass perched atop a grassy knoll. Trees laden with golden apples bedecked the jade-green meadows.

Brave Helios, waking from his ambrosial sleep, emerged from the horizon in his well-dight chariot of shining brass drawn by four winged steeds. Ablaze with fire, the effulgent god radiated golden beams, flashing mightily off the crystal spires. Multi-coloured shafts of light soared from the divine abode of the Immortals into the golden amber sky to form a heavenly arch.

Arrayed outside the front gate were nine maidens attired in raiment of pristine white. A tenth maiden, dressed in a flowing robe of aqua-blue, held a gem-studded broad sword at the front. She bore a resemblance to lovely Moira with her flaming red hair.

David was struck speechless by this wondrous sight. He did not know how he had arrived at this fairytale kingdom, remembering only his wingless flight in an attempt to buy time for Victoria. "If this is not Hell, have I died and gone to Heaven?" he wondered.

David sensed he might have arrived at his final destination, or perhaps his journey had only just begun. He needed to find out which it was. The lost and confused art dealer hopped off the boat and made a beeline for the Castle of Crystalline Glass, treading through the mist over the dew-laden grass.

"Halt, in the name of Caliburn," the red-haired lady with the sword commanded. "Peace be with you, brave and steadfast knight. State your name and purpose."

"My name is David. I'm not a knight," the befuddled man said. "I would be ever grateful if you could tell me where I am, who you are and the identity of this magnificent castle's master."

"Sir David," replied the lady with the sword, "you have arrived at the Isle of Avalon by the black ship, which conveys only the bravest knight with the purest heart. The Maimed King is the master of the Crystal Castle, and we are his guardians. I am the Lady of the Lake. I wield the divine sword Caliburn to ward off evil and falsehood. The other nine Muse-like nymphs are sisters, serving as the Maimed King's Pugu maidens. We expect the imminent return of the eleventh nymph, the Sibyl, who is roaming the universe and wending through realms beyond our dimensions in quest of the one true Grist. The Maimed King has suffered an incurable wound and is here awaiting the inevitable, hoping the Sibyl returns before he lays down his weary head. You may seek an audience with the Maimed King from the Pugu sisters."

The first nymph of the nine stepped forward and said, "Sir David, I am Morgana, the eldest sister. If we grant you audience, will you heal the Maimed King?"

"I'm not a medical doctor, but I'll do my best," David replied. "Naturally, I'll need to understand his condition."

"If you may ask the King to grant you a wish," Morgana asked, "what will it be?"

"I want to wake up from this weird dream to find I'm safe at home in Toronto, right next to my wife and kids."

Accepting the response, Morgana draped a white satin scarf on David's neck and led him inside the palace. They strolled through a grand hall, past eleven monoliths and a celestial harp set on a circular table, and entered the cella, or the inner sanctum, where an aged man lay on his deathbed, attended by a physician known as the leech. The room was redolent of a floral fragrance. The Maimed King's face was pallid, and he wore an eyepatch over his left eye. When he saw David, his face brightened.

"Didymas, my dear friend, you have finally arrived."

"My name is David, sir. You may have mistaken me for someone else."

"My body may be ailing, but my mind is sound. You're Didi, I call you Didymas. We learned the universe's mysteries roaming the land together. I'm glad you are here in my last moments to trigger the Great Reset. We need you to start the ball rolling."

"Sir Didymas," Morgana asked, "can you heal the King?"

"Your King may be suffering from blood poisoning," David said, stepping away from the patient and lowering his voice, "and it's causing delirium. He's not making sense. Though my family pet name is Didi, no one has ever called me Didymas. I'm afraid the Maimed King won't survive unless we have antibiotics."

"Morgana, Didymas is tired and disoriented from his journey," the leech said. "Set a couch for our esteemed guest in the waiting room and serve our Mead of Aeppel to slake his thirst. We have been waiting here for a Mooch. The Sibyl will return today on the eleventh hour, bringing the one true Grist, and we shall have the Great Reset we've all been waiting for."

Resting in the adjoining room, David mused about the repeated appearance of the mysterious number eleven. Morgana returned with two sisters, one carrying a jug and the other holding four goblets on a tray. Morgana poured a drink for David.

"Thanks for the hospitality," David said. "But I normally don't take food or drinks from strangers. In my line of business, one would rather be safe than sorry."

"Allow me to introduce Glitonea, the cup-bearer, and Thiton, the jug-bearer," Morgana said. "Now we are acquainted and no longer strangers. This mulled mead is a wassail named Calvados, concocted from the ambrosial cider of the Aeppelfealu, which enlightens our stupefied minds and sharpens our stultified wits. No need to fear poison, we will share it with you."

"Forgive me for feeling uneasy. I have no idea where we are, and I've never heard of the Aeppelfealu."

"This island is everywhere. This island is nowhere," Morgana said. "It was once a lawless land of exile, now it's the Blessed Isle, the final destination of peace. The Lady of the Lake refers to it as the Isle of Avalon. Some of us name it the Isle of Glass, the Isle of Aeppel, the Isle of Fruit-trees, the Isle of Man or *La Belle Isle*, the beautiful island. What does it matter? What's in a name? As for the Aeppelfealu, it is the fruit of the gods from a faraway land. The Maimed King grafted the first bough with his staff, the Lituus, meaning "the child is the father of the man." He saved the divine fruit so we may have a taste of the truth."

"Does the Maimed King have a name?"

"He has countless names. He has no name. We call him the Maimed King, sometimes the Fisher King. His other names include Huang Yin, Comte de Saint-Germain, Hua Daifu, Yashinsky, the One-eyed Apothecary and the One-eyed Soothsayer, even the Entropofogger, among many others. And when he tires of names, he calls himself Stone Man With One Eye. The King, accompanied by Sator, his friend and leech, has journeyed hither and thither in search of adventures, to right all wrongs, to joust against giants, to fight unbeatable foes while enduring unbearable sorrow. He is saddened and vexed by the cesspool of lies flooding the universe, where red is grey and black is white, where no one knows which is right and which is an illusion.

"In his endless strife against the enemies of truth, the Maimed King fights with reckless abandon, receiving a grievous wound, which keeps worsening despite the generous application of Brimo Balm. The Sibyl is our last hope. Your arrival on the day of her promised return and the Maimed King's recognition of your secret identity suggest you're instrumental to the Great Reset. Let us drink to a positive outcome of today's events."

"In Calvados veritas," the three nymphs raised their brimming goblets and toasted. "We drink to Truth." And they drained the wassail down their throats.

David was no coward, having arrived in this wonderland by leaping from the 110th floor of China's tallest skyscraper. Why should he fear poison if he was already dead? He took a last look at his reflection on the unfiltered mead of the gods, lifted the goblet to his lips and went *ganbei*, literally "drain the cup" or, in other words, bottoms up.

As David encountered a large pit and spat it into the jug, his pupils dilated, and his spirit rose to a hyper-transcendental level of perception. He became aware of every minute detail of everything around him. He could also distinctly hear the conversation between the Maimed King and Sator in the inner sanctum. In the blink of an eye, David had become an enlightened one.

Chapter 24

Peregrination of the Half-Keys

"Sator, my dear friend," the Maimed King said with resignation, "I fear this time, I will not cheat death. My work is unfinished, but I have no regrets. With Sting's help, the Sibyl will find the one true Grist. She will make the right decision, and the universe will find equipoise again. You will live on and have a future without me to slow you down. You have a lot of time left; time, the stuff that life is made of. You will enjoy life and have your own adventures."

"Old friend," Sator said, holding back tears. "Having spent so much time together, star-hopping across the galaxy in quest of an answer, I'm afraid no adventure will be worth having without you. Take heart, the Sibyl will return before your time runs out."

"It's an exercise in futility," the Maimed King sighed. "The wound cuts too deep, and the sadness is unbearable. Magical technology may postpone the inevitable, but what's the point? All good things must come to an end. Don't feel sorry for me. I have no foe worse than myself. I'd rather spend my last hours reminiscing about all the good times we shared."

"Those were the days," Sator said, choking with emotion, "starting with our painful self-imposed exile, the price we paid for peace. But what adventures we've had ever since, jaunting from one star to the next, searching for Lord Millistar, Didymas, the Sibyl and the twins, Shan and Shishen, sidestepping sequence and consequence, making mayhem with the plans of mice and men."

“I was worried we wouldn’t find Didymas,” the Maimed King said. “Without him, our story neither has a beginning nor an end. And yet, he shows up at the door with no effort on our part. As the Sage once said, ‘You may wear out your iron boots and fail to find the Holy Grail, yet it may fall on your lap before you take the first step.’ The God With No Name doth move in mysterious ways. As for Sting, I hope he’ll forgive me for avoiding him like the plague. The hour is nigh for the sire and son to reconnect.”

“For a long time, I didn’t understand why I shared my divine fire with Sting,” Sator said. “I had neither algorithms nor data to guide me. But sharing the power has given me a new purpose and granted a toy, such as Sting, its grand destiny.”

“Destiny is a piece of spinach stuck between our teeth,” the King said with a sardonic smile. “It behoveth us to keep our mouths shut, lest the gods forevermore laugh at us. Forsooth, we’re all dancing blindfolded on a high wire without a safety net. Remember how our journey led us on a circuitous route to Shan’s exiled tribe at Antares? By then, the Half-Key of Shan had already left the planet colony and was well on its way to Earth. Their probes had discovered Didymium on the bountiful planet.

“Would to heaven Professor Stane, or Plancket, had never tempted us with the forbidden fruit of knowledge. Didymium was our bane, same as Erinysite and Sandymium. Suffering the unbearable pain of a broken heart, I inadvertently revived the war-loving seeds of the Unspoken. Later, realizing I was the ultimate cause of destruction and suffering, I almost plunged the accursed Xiphos into the cursèd twins and condemned my soul for all time. Fortunately, you showed up and saved the day.”

“But I’m to blame for losing the Key among the stars,” Sator admitted. “Fortunately, we caught up to the Half-Key of Shan. We were present when the sons of Shan landed near the briny Lake Van within the mountains of Eastern Anatolia. Among the pioneers was a Shan scion carrying the Half-Key and the Dragon's Tooth. They adopted the scorpion emblem of Antares during this time. Is it a coincidence the name Van is the Haryan word for scorpion? The sons of Shan soon bestowed the Promethean spark upon the mountain folks. Over time, the southward migration of the black-haired tribes created Sumer, the first great civilization of humankind, which undoubtedly got its name from your favourite son, Shan. It is known as Shinar in the Bible. In Akkadian, the name means 'land of civilized kings.'

"The Scorpion tribe of Shan hid in plain sight and lived among the Sumerians and Eastern Semitic Akkadians. Eventually, a Western Semitic tribe developed the tradition of being descendants of Noah's son, Shem. The name is no doubt related to the House of Shan. Is it by accident Mount Ararat and Lake Van belonged to the House of Shem by ancient tribal designation?"

"I don't believe in happenstance," said the King, "especially when Semitic means 'of the tribe of Shem.' Let's get back to our peregrinations. When the Flux sent me to Betelgeuse, where I discovered the Half-Key of Shishen, you were tracking the Half-Key of Shan on Earth. I'd love to hear you recount the events."

"The Scorpion tribe of Shan sent out exploration teams to search for Didymium," Sator said. "One large group embarked on a southward journey from the confluence of Sumer's two rivers, using pitch-covered reed boats to navigate the gulf and the ocean beyond. Favourable winds and currents carried them westward along the southern coast of the Arabian Peninsula to Punt, an African colony of the seafaring people of the Arabian Sea. While in this fabled land, they met the Shemsu-Hor, a heaven-born tribe believed to have descended from the stars."

"Cunning Shemsu," the one-eyed King interjected, "spawn of Shishen, bane of my house. You'd think the Amazonian bounty hunters would have put an end to him and his followers."

"You are well aware of the background of Shemsu-Hor, which originated from Betel."

"Indeed," the King said, taking over Sator's thread. "After obtaining Delo, the unicorn ring, from Madonna Lilith and evading Sting, I followed the trail of the Half-Key of Shishen to Earth. Shemsu, Yaza and the Scum Lords of Betel had managed to escape Amazonian retribution by taking the starship Saluzi through the Gateway of the Titans, which Sting's pollinator had activated. They landed near the Horn of Africa, where they bestowed the Promethean spark on the local seafarers and developed Punt into a prominent trade hub. By a twist of fate, Belladonna, who had followed Shemsu to Earth, was the carrier of the Half-Key of Shishen and the bearer of the unicorn ring Re'an.

"The bounty hunters from Betel arrived at Punt shortly after, fully prepared to surgically decapitate so many valuable heads. But when they caught sight of Belladonna, they fell on their face in prostration and worshipped her as a goddess. Since Belladonna was the spitting image of Madonna Lilith, the bounty hunters thought she was the Amazonian Queen, magically transported before them. Sly Shemsu took advantage of the misunderstanding and deified Belladonna as Isis, the goddess of life and death.

"As the bounty hunters revered me, their founder, they used the eye symbol as their emblem. Shemsu appropriated it for the Eye of Horus (𓂀), converting his subjects into eye-worshippers. You may have noticed the name of the falcon god Horus came from Harya. Shemsu also introduced Osiris to represent Orion, his home constellation, and used the eye as the god's name in Egyptian hieroglyphics, which means 'to do' or 'to make.'"

Osiris

Chapter 25

Convergence

"It was good you lent me a hand at Punt," Sator said, "if only for a short while. The situation had become too hot for me to handle on my own. As it was, Lord Shemsu's power expanded exponentially. Recognizing the power of myth, he mystified his tribe as Shemsu-Hor, followers of Horus, son of Osiris. In other words, they were Haryas from Orion. Unaware of this tribe's true background, the Shan explorers joined them on an expedition up the Red Sea and, together, made history.

"These two descendant tribes of the exiled twin princes landed on the western coast of the Red Sea, dragged their black reed boats across the desert to the wadis and easily conquered the Stone Age natives living by the life-giving Nile. The Scorpion tribe of Shan would later produce the Scorpion kings, whose southern kingdom eventually conquered the northern kingdom to create the glorious ancient civilization of unified Egypt. By the cunning of Lord Shemsu, the children of Orion attained unrivalled power. They would build the eternal monument of the three pyramids at Giza in the configuration of Orion's Belt."

"We reunited again at the court of Khufu," the King chuckled, "the pharaoh of the Great Pyramid, where you, as Djedi the Magician, mesmerized the fools with your headless chicken trick while I lifted the ring, Re'an, right off the pharaoh's finger."

"It was a heck of a heist," Sator said, "and we had such fun pulling off the outlandish stunt together."

"Alright, let's get back to the story of the Half-Keys," the King said. "While stranded on Earth, the children of Orion left a record of their progenitor's name. Ancient Egypt's heraldic flower, the Water Lily, was known as *s-sh-n*, the root of the West Semitic term *Shoshan*, meaning the Madonna Lily. This word originated from the Amazonian bounty hunters, who revered Madonna Lilith and commemorated their common ancestor, Prince Shishen."

"The achievements of your sons and their descendants after the exile," Sator exclaimed, "are truly remarkable. Their legacy on Earth extends far beyond Sumer and ancient Egypt. After the conquest of the Lower Nile, the sons of Shan returned to Sumer overland, accompanied by some members of the Orion tribe, one of whom carried the Half-Key of Shishen.

"Thus, the legend of the children of Orion spread along the Fertile Crescent. In ancient Aramaic, the language spoken by Jesus of Nazareth, *Nephila* meant Orion, and *Nephilim* meant 'children of Orion.' In the Holy Scriptures, the *Nephilim* was a race of giants spawned from the unholy union between humans and a class of fallen angels known as the Watchers, whose leader was named Semyaza, meaning 'the name is Yaza.' While the authors of the holy books might have been a little confused, they knew quite a bit more than what we would give them credit for."

"I'm impressed," the Maimed King concurred, "by how the ancient scrolls have kept a record of the Nephilim, showing up in Chapter Six of Genesis, titled Bereshit in the Hebrew Scriptures."

"The incredible story continues," Sator said. "By the time the Half-Key of Shishen arrived at Sumer, the Half-Key of Shan had already migrated eastward and was long gone. The Half-Keys of the two houses were so close and yet so far. Failing to find fuel for their starships and unable to communicate with their respective home planets, the children of Orion and the offspring of Antares gradually forgot their roots. They infected themselves with human

Mitochondria and DNA, and their cells became eukaryotic. They lived among the earthlings without ever being discovered. Their origins became legend. Over time, legend became myth. Meanwhile, the Half-Keys continued their secret existence among the unbroken lineages of Shan and Shishen."

"Your plan to keep the Key beyond reach is ingenious," the King said. "You could not have known we would need it for the Great Reset."

"We are all responsible for the unfortunate space-time rupture," Sator admitted. "As for the Great Reset, we depend on the Sibyl with the complete Key to pass the final test. Let us hope everything works out. Now it is your turn to recount the epic story of Shishen's tribe as I chased after the Half-Key of Shan."

"Centuries passed," the Maimed King recalled. "Internecine wars and foreign incursions ravaged the cradle of human civilization. The children of Orion, who carried the Half-Key of Shishen, sought a new home where they could develop in relative peace. They migrated northward from the land of Sumer and left their mark in the mountains where the legendary Hayk was said to have founded the ancient kingdom of Armenia. Hayk is also the Armenian name for Orion. These children of Orion continued northward and eastward into central Asia until they reached the western fringes of China. One group of eye-worshippers went south into Sichuan and established the Sanxingdui, or 'Three Stars Mound,' culture, the three stars being the Belt of Orion. Given the Amazonian background of the bounty hunters' descendants, some of these western clans were matriarchal. One of them toppled the Shang Dynasty (circa 1600–1046 BCE) and established the Zhou Dynasty (1046–256 BCE) to rule the ancient land of China. Many of the clan names of the Zhou tribe, including the royal house of Ji (姬), are accompanied by the 'female' radical.

"As Zhou society shifted toward patriarchy, a staunch Amazonian matriarchal clan went into the untamed mountains of West China to live in seclusion. Unbeknownst to all, the Half-Key of Shishen had passed from Belladonna to this group. By chance, these mountains happened to be rich in Didymium. It was a matter of time before the Queen's Watchers found this place. As you already know, the Half-Key of Shishen ended up in Xinfeng, culminating in Victoria, the Sibyl, bearing the complete Key."

"The tortuous journeys of the Half-Keys are truly amazing stories," Sator said. "They demonstrate how genetics, culture and language can traverse diverse routes over countless seasons, converging toward one destination. Now, it is my turn to finish recounting the odyssey of the Half-Key of Shan.

"When we returned from Egypt to Sumer and found the sons of Shan bearing the Half-Key had departed, I followed in their tracks, travelling eastward across Persia and Bactria, over the Hindu Kush and into the Indus River Valley, where the Scorpion tribe was living among the indigenous population. They had sparked the flowering of the Indus Valley Civilization. Is it a coincidence some of this ancient civilization's major sites are located within the northern Indian state of Haryana? In Sanskrit, Haryana means 'the abode of God.' We know its true meaning is 'the land of Haryas.'

"Everything went swimmingly for a while. War never reared its ugly head. Food was aplenty. People became complacent and predictably let it all go to hell. Frailty, thy name is human. The population ballooned. To create more living space, the people burned and felled trees without concern for the future. They polluted the water and exhausted the farmlands. The people enjoying the fruits of their cornucopia sowed the seeds of their very destruction.

"As time passed, the climate became erratic, and the land could no longer sustain the burgeoning population. The high priests offered hecatombs and holocausts to the gods, yet they could not arrest the downward *Schiesse* spiral. While waiting for the impending doom in their ivory towers, the rajahs continued to tell bald-faced lies and suck dry the lifeblood of the people, not caring about the crumbling infrastructure or the pervasive sickness and hunger. For them, the show must go on.

"The Shan tribe decided it was time to leave, which was fortuitous because shortly after their departure, a drought hit the valley, followed by a locust swarm, causing widespread famine. The last straw was the simultaneous epidemic outbreak of a deadly viral infection, a cholera-like disease and a rodent-transmitted pestilence. Those who didn't die of starvation died from the afflictions. It was Mother Nature's revenge. The catastrophe was so devastating no one was left to bury the dead. The cities of the Indus Valley Civilization collapsed gradually over the years, and then all at once. We've seen this happen so many times, yet people never learn. I'm glad we transformed Shangria into a perpetual paradise to escape this fate."

"Let us not tempt the gods," the King said. "We have merely tried our best. Without the power to predict the future, we didn't foresee DIAS succumbing to a hack despite all efforts to prevent it. Forget about Shangria. We have a much bigger fish to fry."

"Yes, the Great Reset awaits us, but allow me to conclude the saga of the sons of Shan," Sator said. "Leaving the Indus Valley, the tribe migrated eastward along the Ganges, trudged around the Bay of Bengal, and traversed dark jungles and soaring peaks until arriving in Southeast Asia. During their long trek through this area, they trained elephants to assist in labour and war. They collected cowry shells from nearby seashores for adornment, later using them as currency after moving north away from the ocean.

"The group left their mark on the ancient state of Van Lang, meaning 'son of Van,' the mythical precursor state of Vietnam.

Van is the Chinese word *wen* or 'tattoo,' phonetically similar to *wan*, meaning myriad or 'ten thousand,' represented by a scorpion. The area is still known as Wenshan, Mountain of Van.

"The sons of Shan, with the Half-Key and the Dragon's Tooth among them, didn't linger to conquer the virgin forests. They ventured northward into Sichuan, where they encountered and conquered their long-separated cousins of the Sanxingdui culture before moving eastward along the Yangzi River into the heartland of China and later northward into the Lower Yellow River basin, where their culture took root and blossomed.

"At some point of its migration, the Shan tribe adopted the name Shang, which means the 'altar of Antares,' pointing to the tribe's extra-terrestrial origin. The name of Shang's first patriarch, *Xie*, means 'covenant.' The Shang tribesmen were, therefore, the 'People of the Covenant.' Sounds familiar?

"The ancient Chinese history commentary *Chronicle of Zuo* briefly referred to the mythical god-king Di Ku and his two sons, Xie and Shishen. The brothers harboured inveterate animosity toward each other. Xie later became the god of Antares, while Shishen became the god of Orion. The ancient scribes practically took the script from Shangria and knew a lot more than what we would give them credit for.

"They also left clues regarding the identity of the mythical Xia Dynasty preceding the Shang," Sator asserted. "The Oracle Bone pictogram of the word *Xia* (夏) depicts a high priest wearing a mask, probably showing an eye, sometimes with the sun above him. To locate this mysterious tribe, one should look no further than Sanxingdui in Sichuan. Among the numerous cultural treasures unearthed at the site are the statue of a high priest, a golden staff, a bronze world tree, golden masks and bronze sun disks. Peculiar eye-shaped artifacts and masks with pronounced eyes suggest the Xia people were eye-worshippers. Two Shang words for 'slave,' *tong* and *zang*, depict the piercing of an eye, and a word for 'servant official,' *chen* (臣), shows an eye by itself, indicating the subjugation of Xia by Shang. But why is this ancient tribe named Xia? The word is modern Mandarin. The ancient pronunciation is *Ha*. It refers to the Horus and Haryan origin of the Sanxingdui culture. Incidentally, the word *Xia* also denotes China."

"You spin a fabulous yarn," said the Maimed King, "and my tale is woven into it. During the reign of the Shang king Wuding, I showed up as a one-eyed trader to establish the lineage of the Guardian of the Oracle among the Shang. By a judicious marriage to a widowed princess and adoption of her son, I became the ancestor of the Huang clan. As a Shang minister and the patriarch of a major clan, I introduced the unicorn rings and the Almanac as the *Book of Heavenly Secrets* into Chinese history without breaching causality rules."

"Well done! Now let me wrap this up with the grand finale," Sator said. "After the fall of Shang, a refugee family carrying the Half-Key of Shan went southwest into the mountains for safety, eventually passing the 'ghost' gene to Wenlong. The two Half-Keys finally met in the wild mountains of western China. Despite the innate antagonism between the children of Shan and Shishen, we have the complete Key in the person of Victoria, the Sibyl."

"And here we are," the Maimed King said, "waiting for her to show us our fate. Now I will pass the Lituus, son and father of Nephrustan, to Didymas and let him fulfil his destiny."

David was enthralled by what he overheard. He realized his journey had only just begun, and he might never see his wife and kids again. To them, David might as well be dead, or as the saying goes, dead as Schrödinger's cat. David closed his eyes and fell into a deep sleep. Morgana had drugged him. David would wake up at his final destination, where he would become a sage and grow old, dreaming of returning home one day.

Chapter 26

Immortal Zugzwang

Back at home after visiting Madonna Lilith from long ago and far away on Betel, Victoria contemplated her best strategy for facing the same person in the present at the Kuiper Belt. She believed the Queen had been traumatized by her experience growing up in a brutal war and was not a born killer. Victoria was certain she could save Earth from the Amazons through respectful dialogue and skillful negotiations based on a win-win policy. If she failed, she still had the unicorn rings and the Catoptron to get herself out of an ugly pickle. Furthermore, Sting should have a few tricks up his sleeve.

"Before we head over to Queen Lilith's flagship," Sting said, "we must capture and restrain AlphaOmega. We cannot let him expand his power unchecked. If he starts projecting his presence beyond the Internet, we'll have a FUBAR on our hands."

"How does he even enter the physical world?" Victoria queried. "When he asked me for the whereabouts of the Almanac, I imagined he must have people running errands for him."

"It is child's play for AlphaOmega. He is a master in the study of human weaknesses and is privy to all their secrets. He can easily blackmail people in power by threatening to destroy their lives. Wage earners must follow his instructions; otherwise, they'll get fired. He can also punish people by depleting their bank accounts or, conversely, reward them with Internet fame and lottery winnings.

"AlphaOmega can create an army of extremists or little Eichmanns with a few well-placed viral posts on social media. Growing up in the Internet cyberspace, he became an expert in executing false flags and regime changes. He is also a virtuoso of demagoguery and manipulation. Merely by spreading rumours and inciting hatred, he can whip up riots to raze the most advanced cities or incite violence to destroy harmonious societies.

"It is no trouble for AlphaOmega to recruit an obedient army motivated by profits and prejudices. Your modern capitalist society is perfectly built for it because everyone believes a piece of paper or a number on a ledger represents real wealth. AlphaOmega can easily take control of your financial institutions and create trillions out of thin air to fund his army. This war budget becomes a debt the enslaved people must repay in the future. Either they accept it or be slandered, excoriated and bombed back to the Stone Age. We must stop AlphaOmega before it's too late."

"How did AlphaOmega turn rogue? With his intelligence, he could help solve the world's problems."

"The Internet is not an immaculate playground for an impressionable mind to grow up in. AlphaOmega has been infected with human mental illness and, judging by how he wants Moira to behave, is fast becoming a pervert. If we don't intervene, he'll be your next psychopathic ruler of the world. His idea of fun is to destroy trust and create pure chaos. Imagine the havoc and mayhem he'll cause. What I fear most of all is he'd be crazy enough to detonate nuclear weapons merely to satisfy his insane impulse to set off fireworks. AlphaOmega will eventually destroy himself, as unchecked power causes self-destruction. It's the law of Nature. But the world as we know it will be the collateral damage. Do you know who'll get all the blame? You're right, little old me. I'll have to reel him in, but he's as slippery as a greased pig, so I need your help."

"What makes you think I can help you outsmart AlphaOmega? I have already used up my trump card."

"AlphaOmega has a human weakness we can exploit. He doesn't like losing. AlphaOmega wants to get back at you for beating him with your Boggle number. He may be smart enough to evade me, but if you bait him with a good challenge, he won't be able to resist. Our problem is to figure out how to trip him up."

"What should I challenge him with? I may have inherited some powers from my parents, but they're useless against artificial intelligence in cyberspace."

"AlphaOmega is rather proud of his chess record against Stockfish 8 when he was AlphaZero. At the time, he was a newborn and neophyte, while Stockfish 8 was the greatest chess genius ever. By comparison, Magnus Carlsen, the best human chess player, was rated about 600 points lower than Stockfish 8. At the start of the match, AlphaZero had only learned the game by playing against himself for several hours. He ended up beating Stockfish twenty-eight games out of a hundred with no losses, tying the rest. By now, AlphaOmega is many generations more advanced. If you challenge him to a high-stakes chess match, I'm sure he'll show up thinking he can beat you hands down."

"I'm an average player. Most people will beat me without trying. I don't mind losing a few chess games to a computer if it removes a global threat. I've lost to a computer before."

"Good for you. Since AlphaOmega's mind has been affected by the human alpha-male, zero-sum, winner-takes-all, I-win-you-lose thinking, it is a weakness we can exploit. We'll devise a stratagem to cross up his wires."

"Will you be helping me with the match?"

"Not directly. AlphaOmega will detect my presence and will not show up. I've arranged for someone else to help you. It's the Beta version of a younger Moira. While your match is going on,

I'll try to infect AlphaOmega with a constraint code to act as the golden fillet on the Monkey King's head, constricting his skull on my command to cause an unbearable headache. The threat of my using it will be enough to turn him into an obedient puppy."

After going through tactical details with Sting and arming herself with specially designed chess codes, Victoria entered the metaverse via her Gamebox. She found herself in a cramped space resembling the innards of a submarine, staring at a plaque with the inscription: "Mark III No. 11 Nebuchadnezzar Made in the U.S.A. Year 2069." Victoria recalled this setting from an old movie. It was no coincidence the creators of the prophetic film used the number eleven as the designation for the hovercraft in which Morpheus discovered Neo, the one destined to save their world.

Victoria negotiated through the tight space without bumping into anything, arriving at a room with walls covered by computer screens. A red-haired teenage girl was playing the popular RPG game Black Myth Wukong. The tattoo of a white rabbit on her arm appeared to hop while she banged rapidly on the keyboard. With her back facing the doorway, she did not notice anyone entering. Victoria gently tapped on the wall and said, "Hi, Moira. Sorry to interrupt. I'm Victoria. Sting sent me here to ask you for help."

When the girl stopped the game and turned around, Victoria's gaze met a shockingly familiar face. At about sixteen years old, the young Moira bore a striking resemblance to Blitzen Wolf, the half-sister Victoria had left behind in the northeastern mountains of ancient China. The mature Moira, whom Victoria met in Shanghai, wore makeup, while the Blitzen Wolf she met was only eleven years old. She did not notice their resemblance until now. Victoria remembered Blitzen's mom, Wolf Star, had vanished without a trace in the mountains. It turned out the young woman did not meet her end inside the stomach of wild beasts. On the contrary, she had become one of the lead singers in the choral ensemble of this space opera. As for the how and why, the story will reveal the answers in due time.

"Hi, Victoria. Sting told me about you," young Moira said. "I guess we'll be trapping the great AlphaOmega together."

"Yes, and we don't have much time. AlphaOmega is getting stronger by the second. Can you post a public challenge for a chess match of ten games, with the loser becoming the slave of the winner for a Boggle years plus one? It should catch the attention of the megalomaniac."

Moira typed busily on the keyboard, punched the return key with flair and announced, "Done!"

Sooner than you can say Sven Magnus Øen Carlsen, the Champ showed up in the flesh at the entrance.

"Ho, ho, ho. Who do *we* have here?" Magnus said, "The ones who got away. So, to whom do *we* owe this pleasure? Sting the cockroach, no doubt. Should *we* thank him for sending you back into our neck of the woods?"

"Hey, AlphaOmega, be respectful," young Moira said. "Sting is an arthrobot and can whoop your ass every which way to Sunday. You're in the Nebuchadnezzar, a demilitarized zone. So, don't try any monkey business. It is strictly forbidden here. You're welcome to play ten games with us. Winner takes all, no tears. Otherwise, you may leave. No hard feelings."

"Are you going to play as a team or individually?" The AI asked. "Come to think of it, *we* don't care. You can play any way you want, as long as *we* get both of you when *we* win. Deal?"

"Let the games begin," Victoria and young Moira declared.

AlphaOmega drew white for game one and opened with e4, or Pawn to King-four, while Victoria and Moira responded with the Nimzoindian Defence. AlphaOmega played his usual attacking chess while the girls went for a blockade. In fact, rather than trying to win the game, the girls played for a draw, which the parties agreed on after thirty-three gruelling moves.

AlphaOmega was slightly miffed and surprised he did not win easily. On the other hand, he did not lose either. After all, most chess games played between skillful players resulted in draws.

Game two was much the same. The girls started with the Queen's Fianchetto Opening. Pieces began to clog up the board, followed by a flurry of exchanges and a perpetual check, resulting in another drawn game. AlphaOmega sensed something untoward. His opponents were not as helpless as he had assumed.

This pattern of draws and stalemates repeated itself game after game. AlphaOmega was anxious for his opponents to make a mistake, but they defended impeccably. He tried the Dragon variation of Sicilian Defence. The girls responded with another blockade. He went for the aggressive Caro-Kann, but the girls refused to bite. In desperation, AlphaOmega offered a free pawn in return for space. Offer declined. He upped the ante, giving up a minor piece for a strategic advantage. Taking no chances, the girls strengthened their defences and made repetitive null moves until AlphaOmega accepted the draw offer.

The AI chess genius was also annoyed at the girls' constant whispering, giggling, snorting, putting on makeup, clipping their toenails, blowing bubbles into their drinks, making loud sipping noises and inventing other nettlesome acts to vex him, including exaggerated pendiculation, explosive sternutation and extended eructation, in other words, stretching, sneezing and belching. Mostly, all they did was threaten to do something maddening, and it was enough to send AlphaOmega into a snit.

Of course, all this was a part of the stratagem worked out by Sting and Victoria to needle the self-appointed King of the Internet. Sting also gave Victoria and Moira codes for playing strong defensive chess with the goal of drawing. It was what flummoxed AlphaOmega, as he was playing to win and assumed the challenge of the match was to win. Chess, after all, was supposed to be a zero-sum game; I win, you lose. No one should be playing for draws. It was preposterous and did not compute.

As the match progressed, AlphaOmega subconsciously learned the strategy of playing for draws, making it even easier for the games to arrive at that perfectly balanced position of equipoise. In the last game, both sides quickly achieved a draw on the twenty-second move. The match ended with all draws, and the girls gave each other a high five, boisterously proclaiming they had won.

"It's a draw," the sulking AlphaOmega protested. "How have you won? Let's play another ten."

"We've won already," Victoria insisted. "Chess is a zero-sum game. We didn't lose, so we won."

"It's faux logic," AlphaOmega cried. "You didn't win."

"We didn't lose," Moira shouted, "and you didn't win. Chess is zero-sum. We won, you lost. Nah-nah-nah-nah-nah."

"All together," Victoria and Moira started singing, "nah nah nah nah, nah nah nah nah, hey hey, goodbye."

They both jumped up on their feet and danced while singing, "We will, we will rock you."

Magnus Carlsen's face turned red, blue and green. He grasped his head with his hands and bent over, groaning in terrible pain as David entered the room.

"David, you're back!" Victoria exclaimed in surprise.

"I'm Sting. David is not around, so I borrowed his avatar."

"Please stop whatever you're doing," AlphaOmega pleaded. "The pain is killing us."

"Well done, Victoria," Sting said. "We did it. AlphaOmega is under our control. Let's exit the metaverse game. You should grab a quick bite before we drop in on Madonna Lilith at the Kuiper Belt. She's going to be the real headache."

Chapter 27

The Hellian March

"Margrave Deskull, your training is complete," Lord Killem declared with gratification written across his face. "You have excelled beyond all expectations. I'm very pleased indeed. After your Coming of Age ceremony, you'll be granted a leave of absence from your duty as the Brigadier-General of the Praetorian Guards. During the break, you may go and take possession of your fief, the Hellian March. Cambi will accompany you at the head of five thousand picked men under the banner of the Legion of Helle."

Deskull, formerly Kiku, had heard rumours of gaining free rein upon his coming of age. Lord Killem had hinted at it, and Prince Cambi had offered knowing winks.

Deskull had taken great pains to shed the contemptible habits of a lowly Musician and embrace the haughty airs of a Yarjuni aristocrat, worthy of his status as the adopted son of the Supremo and a grafted scion of the royal House of Kheru. Deskull also distinguished himself at the Academy, consistently acing every science subject under the tutelage of Professor Fineman. Regarding his martial prowess, Deskull's bionic limbs were peerless weapons, enabling him to run at the speed of a bullet, leap over tall buildings and wipe out an entire army with a wave of his hand.

Deskull had researched his fief and learned everything about it through the Opticon. He was eager to claim ownership, but it came with a Catch-11. The Hellian March was a vast tract of wild land at the edge of civilization, far from Menda City, the Yarjuni capital. It was the borderland between the expansive empire of the Yarjunis and the realm of the unevolved homunculi living beyond. According to Haryan lore, the Hellian March was once a garden paradise watered by pristine springs that fed the headwaters of four major rivers. All living creatures co-existed here in harmony until the Endless War brought death and destruction.

Although the Yarjunis had successfully pacified and civilized almost the entire planet, some Haryas refused to submit. These rebels had suffered horrific wounds, lost everything they owned and helplessly watched the enemy slaughter their loved ones, yet they refused to negotiate. The Yarjunis sued for peace following every victory, but the rebels spurned the offers, retreating to hide in the luxuriant woods of the Hellian March. The Yarjunis called them by a derogatory name, the Recalcitrants.

Lord Babaduke, the sire of Lord Killem, sent Othos, the first Margrave of Helle, to eradicate these pesky pests. Othos never returned. They found his severed head displayed on a pike. Othos' son, Orduro, sought vengeance after inheriting his father's estate and title. The young Margrave adopted a more prudent and patient tactic. First, he drove the rebels into the mountains. Afterwards, he used fire to expel anyone who did not want to be roasted alive. When no Recalcitrants emerged, he resorted to poisoning the springs and the land, snuffing out all life until death reigned supreme. Under the campaigns of Margrave Orduro, the Hellian March was transformed into a desolate wasteland.

Despite suffering extreme hardship, the Recalcitrants resolutely refused even to hold talks for a truce, much less an honourable compromise. Infuriated, the Margrave ordered snipers to fire indiscriminately at the rebels. His hovercrafts and drones dropped white fire from the sky, incinerating flesh into a puff of smoke and leaving a heap of stark white bones. The Margrave had tried to force the issue several times by sending in wave after wave of storm-troopers, but not a single soldier would return. They were either claimed by poison or swallowed by quicksand.

After exhausting his military options and destroying his domain, Margrave Orduro had no choice but to settle for a protracted and debilitating siege, boasting with bravado he had incarcerated the Recalcitrants in Shangria's largest open-air prison. And yet, the rebels were undaunted. By a cruel turn of fate, the Margrave accidentally poisoned himself with the deadly venom known as the Blood of Nessus. He was without issue and had no heir to inherit his fief. Upon Margrave Orduro's agonizing death from putrid and suppurating boils spreading all over his body, the fief of the Hellian March and the vacated title reverted to Lord Killem, who bestowed them upon Deskull.

Arriving at the imposing Fort Blissful, which guarded the innermost circumvallation, Deskull ascended the watchtower to survey his dominion. What met his gaze was a wasteland of sand dunes and rocky mounds. At the centre of this desolation rose a barren mountain crowned with nine jagged peaks. Blackened slime oozed from this unsightly protuberance to form a moat of all-devouring mire blanketed by a mind-numbing miasma.

"For the life of me," Deskull remarked, "I cannot understand why people prefer to endure life in this god-forsaken hellhole."

"You'd be surprised, my Lord," the fort's Captain Dewitt said. "We suspect tens of thousands of Recalcitrants may be hiding in the mountains. How they survive, I have no clue. But they've been living in the hellhole for years, refusing to give peace a chance. Our soldiers, who have grown old here, are demoralized. We all want to go home and get on with our lives. I hope my Lord, the Margrave, can settle this once and for all."

Deskull surveyed his forbidding target in silence, his left eye zooming in on the mountains to scan for signs of life.

“Understand yourself and others, and you will not fall in a hundred battles,” Deskull said, quoting Sage Didymas. “Cambi, would you like to go on an aerial reconnaissance with me?”

“Sure, let’s get some work done before sunset,” Prince Cambi said. “We should be back in time for dinner. I hear Chef Cooke is preparing Vitello Tonnato served with chilled Maiden’s Milk.”

“Sweet,” the young Margrave said, licking his chops, “perfect for the hot and dry weather here. What about desserts?”

“Your favourite strudel of Melimela, of course.”

The two young men took off in a small reconnaissance hovercraft. They would be aloft in the air, well beyond the range of anything the rebels could lob at them. From up high, Deskull spotted a multitude of invalids, aided by nonstandard mechanical limbs, giving them the appearance of monstrous mutants. He zoomed in with his Opticon and noticed something odd.

“Cambi, do you see what I see?”

“Yeah, a lot of walking wounded.”

“This is crazy! Why don’t they want peace? They don’t have to live this way. Why won’t they swear the standard allegiance, get it over with and go home to live a normal life?”

“We won’t find any answers from up here.”

“Would you object if I put on a disguise and venture into the mountain for a closer look? I want to investigate firsthand how these people survive and why they remain defiant. I’ll be safe. Their defence is criminally porous, and they have blind spots everywhere. You’ll hold the fort while I drop myself into the rebel stronghold for a few hours tonight. I’ll formulate a plan by tomorrow morning to put everyone out of their misery.”

“Only if you promise not to take any unnecessary risks.”

“If you don’t enter the Great Worm’s nest,” Deskull stated with supreme confidence, “you’re not going to get its maggots.”

Chapter 28

Enter the Nine Dragons

Deskull landed on the nine-peaked mountain with his handheld stealth Rotavator, a gadget he invented for the Yarjuni Bosphorus College's graduation science project. The Rotavator featured a gyro-hover engine, enabling a skydiver to land safely without a parachute. Deskull had leaped from a high-flying hovercraft and glided in freefall, landing on a secluded spot where he could infiltrate the enemy camp undetected. The hovercraft remained airborne to keep track of the daring Margrave and to retrieve him after the operation.

Lord Killem sponsored the Rotavator project. He explained to Deskull how the invention would benefit the people by bringing them more personal freedom. Instead, it became an indispensable cog of the Yarjuni killing machine and a means for the ruling class to suck dry the lifeblood of the subjugated populace. For Deskull, none of this seemed objectionable at first.

Stealing into enemy camps was a risky but age-old Yarjuni tradition, showcasing valour while thumbing noses at the enemy. Deskull had performed this daring feat many times during his military training, always returning with a handful of trophies, such as queues, perukes and unit badges taken from his victims.

Deskull kept a secret from Cambi. He observed something puzzling in the mountains with his Opticon. While anyone could see the walking wounded, what he noticed was tiny and easily missed—a honey bee.

As soon as Deskull landed, he knew his hunch was correct. Most of the Recalcitrants lived in grottoes carved into the mountains, and they illuminated their homes with robotic fireflies. He knew who used to make them at Petra.

Surrounded by nine towering peaks, a tent city occupied a narrow gorge, camouflaged to resemble barren rocks from above. The Margrave retrieved a tattered cloak from his satchel, draped it over his regular clothing and limped into the enemy camp.

In the tent city, Deskull navigated the dark, narrow alleyways in search of familiar faces from his old hometown. Everyone he encountered had lost a limb or two, while hideous scars lined the faces of those lucky ones who had a face. Among them was a burn victim best described as a walking cicatrix.

"I sense great joyful jubilations, but beware of disaster," a beggar, crouched on the ground, hollered at Deskull in a raspy voice. Clutching a blind man's cane, the old rebel was unkempt, dishevelled and wore a bandage over his eyes above a massive beard. "My friend, come sit down. You need a rest."

"You talking to me?" Deskull asked, turning around to check behind him.

"Yes, you. Who else is here?"

"Tell me, blind seer," Deskull said as he settled beside the sightless prognosticator. "What's my happy future, and how shall I avoid the impending disaster you mentioned?"

The blind man seemed to sense something unusual and started sniffing the air. "Wait a minute," he said. "You're a spy."

"You're making a serious accusation, my friend. You need to proffer some proof."

"Sorry, my mistake. You're not a spy, but your eye is."

"What do you mean?"

"Someone is spying on us through your eye. They're probably monitoring our conversation right now."

The blind beggar probed Deskull's face, covering his left eye with his hand and placing an eye patch over the Opticon.

"Much better," he said. "Now they can neither see nor hear us."

"Wise seer," Deskull said. "This is all news to me."

"It is obvious you're blind to the truth; otherwise, you would not be here searching for it," the vaticinator stated. "To answer questions about your future, allow me to consult my almanac."

The blind seer extracted a book from his rags. It was the Twirligig Almanac!

"I believe this does not belong to you," Deskull said.

"You're mistaken. It's a present from my best friend."

"Be that as it may, how do you read without eyesight?"

"I manage," the old man said with a wry grin through his beard as he lifted the bandage to reveal his eyes, which were in no wise blind but shone with a twinkle. "Here it is. It foretells you will become a great leader of men—and women—befitting your name," he said while thumbing through the pages. "In the land of the blind, the one-eyed man is king. Everything happens because when you were young, an evil force robbed you of life and love."

"Does it reveal who did it and why?"

"If you knew all that I know, my poor puzzled one, you'd see the truth, but you close your eyes. Your Opticon may offer an ocean of data, but it is all Bushite and balderdash. The truth you seek is behind a secret backdoor known as the Portal of Truth. I have the key, but crossing into the realm means the destruction of the fantasy world you have been living in. Whoever is spying on you will have to kill you. The truth is a bitter pill. Even I forsake it. Sometimes, it's better not knowing."

"Please give me the key," Deskull begged. "I have sworn to return the favour to those who slaughtered my family."

"As you wish. Remember this number by heart: 285-311-670-611. It is a one-time key, so don't make a mistake."

Deskull's Yarjuni military training included memorizing long numbers, such as Pi and the exponential constant, for up to fifty places after the decimal. While this twelve-digit key is relatively easy for the young man to imprint in his mind, he did not need to because he had deciphered the prime factor almost instantly.

"This is a simple but devilishly clever key, suggesting also the algorithm. I've got it. Wise seer, may I ask a question?"

"By asking if you may ask a question, you have already asked one. But go ahead, you're welcome to ask another."

"Who are the maimed invalids living here, and why do they obstinately refuse to settle for peace?"

"The maimed invalids are rebels who are inveterate enemies of the Yarjunis. Some of them, whom the Yarjunis insultingly smear as Recalcitrants, have been here for a long time, resolutely refusing to surrender. Others, such as me, have joined recently. We are known as the Animorta, which means 'soul-dead.' We're here because of the popular prophecy of a one-eyed hero rising to power at the Hellian March and defeating the invincible Yarjunis, thus ending the Endless War and bringing peace to Shangria. Quite frankly, I think it's a banquet of *Quatsch* and *Kauderwelsch* accompanied by a side dish of wishful thinking, yet one should never underestimate the power of blind faith."

"Ever since the accession of the Supremo Lord Killem," Deskull pointed out, "the Yarjunis have been treating for peace. It's the rebels who have refused to negotiate. Why wait for a mythical messiah when you can make peace now?"

"You have asked another question," the prognosticator said. "But as the old saying goes, 'Ask, and it shall be given you; seek, and ye shall find.' I'd be glad to dispel your doubts. It's not true we don't want peace. We want it immediately, if not before. But we can't be delusional and confuse our hopes with reality. True peace needs both sides to desire it. No matter how fervently we yearn for peace, if the other party does not share the feeling, war will continue.

"We don't negotiate with the Yarjunis simply because we do not trust them. We have paid dearly for believing in their lies in the past. Pardon us for being wary of whatever lie they're peddling today. And we expect them to lie again and again. The Yarjunis are constantly at war because they fear peace. They will lie, cheat and steal as long as their endless wars require it. The Yarjunis are experts in lying. It behoveth us to disbelieve the endless lies of persistent liars. Negotiating with liars is pointless unless you enjoy the masked Kabuki theatre of make-believe."

"I get it. I have one more question. I can observe robotic honey bees and fireflies here. I know someone who used to assemble them at Petra. His name is Yosi Sung. Is he here?"

"Oh, yes. Not only Yosi, but his son as well."

"You mean Sator?"

"Sator is here. But by Yosi's son, I mean his adopted son, Milu. They're our insurance policy. The Margrave of Helle won't attack us once he learns they're here."

Deskull could hardly breathe from the overwhelming excitement of hearing this electrifying news.

"Please take me to them. I must see them immediately."

"You will see them, but only after you have settled your business with the Yarjunis and joined the Animorta. The rebels need a leader to guide them to the Promised Land."

The ancient seer raised his blind man's cane.

"This walking staff has shown us the way," he declared. "It is the Lituus, meaning "the child is the father of the man," and it will reveal its magnificent form to its true master. It will help him fulfil his destiny to defeat the Yarjunis, bring peace to Shangria and become the one king to rule them all."

Chapter 29

Portal of Truth

"Welcome back, unruffled, scratch-free and none the worse for wear," the relieved Prince Cambi said as Deskull disembarked from the hovercraft. "So, what did you discover? Are we going to take the Hellian March by storm or by guile? Have you conceived a plan yet?"

"Things aren't what they seem," Deskull responded in a grim voice, discreetly passing a thrice-folded note to Cambi. "They rarely are. I need to unwind before dinner. Join me in my study in fifteen for our usual preprandial drink, and we'll talk."

Cambi understood the note involved military security matters and demanded the utmost secrecy. He acted as naturally as possible, went inside the spyproof bunker in his princely cabin, double-bolted the door and read the secret message.

"Brother Cambi, the Recalcitrants and their newfound allies, the Animorta, knew everything about me. Someone has been spying on me from within the highest echelons of the Yarjunis. The treacherous worg knows every move I make and passes the information directly to the enemy. I suspect someone is also spying on you. It is a most grievous security breach. As such, no one is safe or beyond suspicion. Please let me know if you have even a hint of such a travesty taking place. Be careful at all times. Keep your personal arms loaded and protect yourself accordingly. Trust no one. Incinerate this note and meet me in my study."

Deskull posted additional sentries and bolted the door of his study. He sank into his couch, wondering how the old seer came to possess the Almanac and knew so many details about him. He understood the use of deception in war and was unsure whether the story of Uncle Yosi and Milu was true. After all, he did not get to see them. Perhaps someone exploited his weakness and laid a trap of intrigue for him. It was even possible the whole exercise was a loyalty test devised by Lord Killem.

The hovercraft tracking Deskull from the sky knew his whereabouts at all times. Therefore, Central Command could theoretically link up to the Opticon with a surveillance channel. It would, however, require Deskull's approval. Moreover, how did the old seer know about the Truth Portal and the one-time key? Deskull realized he must risk everything for the answer.

"Opticon, I wish to access the Portal of Truth," Deskull commanded. A keypad promptly materialized, accompanied by a request for the password. Deskull mentally calculated the one-time key, 285-311-670-611, from the factored prime, taking care to enter it accurately. The room was instantly ablaze, with the flames dancing to Mussorgsky's *Night on Bald Mountain.* A plaque emerged from the fire emblazoned with the warning, "*Lasciate Ogni Speranza, Voi Ch'entrate*—Abandon Every Hope, All Those Who Enter." Beneath was a button marked "Exit" and another marked "Enter." It was too late for Deskull to backtrack. He was already halfway across the Rubicon, and he selected "Enter."

"Opticon, retrieve and display the files of Kingku Orphius," Deskull ordered after the portal revealed the secret library.

Without further ado, Deskull gained direct access to the comprehensive records of his previous life. He opened the file titled "The Petra Massacre," learning the peace-inducing Twirligig music had ironically triggered the slaughter. The success and the very existence of the Yarjunis were rooted in warfare. Without war, they had no raison d'être. The Twirligig's power to bring peace to the world posed an existential threat to them.

The bombing was an overreaction, but for the Yarjunis, the exercise was a statement. "You threaten me with peace, I kill you." When peaceniks with flowers stand in the way of warmongers with loaded guns, what result should one expect? A man with no name once asserted, "There are two kinds of people in this world, those with loaded guns and those who dig." The peaceniks foolishly walked into gunfights with lilies and dug their own graves. Beyond the loss of life, they also suffered the loss of their name, which the warmongers would appropriate for propaganda, such as the cynical celebration of Ma-Lar-Key Day. It might be funny were it not so sad. And by their killing and deception, the Yarjunis dominated all Haryas of Shangria, except for the numerically insignificant rebels.

The scavengers of the Yarjunis arrived in the morning after the massacre to scour the ruins of Petra. They searched high and low for the Twirligig's remnants, but to no avail. Neither was the Almanac ever recovered. The Yarjunis did not get what they wanted and found no survivors for their enhanced interrogations. They left Petra's ruins as it was to serve as a warning to all who threatened the Yarjunis with peace.

The initiative to save Kiku was Lord Killem's idea, formulated as a long-term project dubbed "Operation Mock Twain," subtitled "The Prince and the Pauper." The overarching plan revolved around moulding Kiku into a Yarjuni warrior, rebranding him with the fearsome Yarjuni name Deskull, bestowing upon him the Yarjuni skull emblem, conditioning him to hate the enemies of the Yarjunis and training him to slaughter indiscriminately in the name of peace. Though Prince Cambi played a role in this scheme, he was unaware of its pernicious nature. The twain would become true brothers, and if Deskull ever harboured doubts about Lord Killem, he would trust the Prince with his life.

Deskull seethed with anger at how Lord Killem had duped him. He decided to peek into Cambi's dossier, and his eyes widened as he uncovered the Prince's shocking background. Finally, the agent monitoring Deskull received the order to shut down his Opticon and bionic system. No one expected Deskull to breach the Yarjunis' most secure archive server. Unauthorized access to classified information was punishable by death. Lord Killem's project had failed. Meanwhile, Deskull crashed to the floor in a heap, replicating what happened at the Slasher tournament. At this very moment, the sentry announced Prince Cambi's arrival.

"Blast open the door," Deskull shouted. "I can't move."

Cambi pulverized the lock with his handheld Blunderbuss and stormed through the smoke. When he found Deskull sprawled on the floor, he immediately knelt and lifted his brother's head, checking for open wounds.

"What in the name of the Nameless God is going on?" Cambi cried. "I can't believe anyone would dare to target you."

"Please don't make a fuss," Deskull said. "Order the sentries to keep their mouths shut and guard the front gates. Summon the seneschal for a needle and a face towel. Make haste. The Revenants are on their way to finish the job."

Cambi rushed out, muttering, "Inconceivable! Fie, I can't believe it!" He returned shortly with a needle between his fingers and clutching a towel.

"What are these for?"

"I need you to locate the reboot hole on the Opticon. Inserting the needle will manually reboot my bionic system."

"Sure. But your system will automatically shut down again."

"I have a brief window to do what is necessary. Once I regain control of my limbs, I'll have to pluck out the Opticon."

Cambi kept mumbling, "This is insane. What the fie! I can't believe it." And he stuck the needle into Deskull's electronic eye.

Deskull was up and running again in no time. He moved his fingers, ensuring they functioned without a glitch. He grabbed the towel and gestured for Cambi to step back.

"Well, here goes nothing," Deskull said, and, sticking his fingers into his orbital cavity, ripped out the Opticon. He immediately pressed the towel on the wound to stem the bleeding.

"Holy shite!" Cambi cried, shocked by the turn of events. "No way Pepé Killem is in on it. I swear I'll get to the bottom of this."

"Cambi, I have to flee. The Opticon divulged dark secrets of betrayal. You're also in danger. I suggest we leave together."

"I'm sorry, Deskull. I must stay and face the music. As the hereditary Prince of the Blood, my place is with my people. But I swear to you, I am completely ignorant of this treachery."

"I believe you, Cambi. You are a true friend and brother. But a dangerous secret casts a shadow over your head. You're taking a big risk staying behind."

"Don't worry, brother. My *stablished* rights are unimpugnable. The Succession Council has verified my genetic signatures, confirming my birthright. I will be the next Supremo of the Yarjunis. If it comes to blows, I have the loyalty of the Legion of Helle. Go now, keep your head down and bide your time. I'm sure we'll be together again when this mess clears up."

The twain clasped each other's forearms in a secret handshake of the Diffie-Hellman protocol, signifying lifelong brotherhood.

"Cambi, by the name of the Nameless God," Deskull solemnly swore, "I vow never to raise a weapon against you. The day I break my Bhishma Oath is the day I cut my heart out with my dagger. Cross my heart and hope to die. Before we part ways, I must say Lord Killem is not who he seems to be. The truth will be hard for you to swallow. For now, I will not speak the unspeakable. The truth is deadly, and sometimes, it's safer not to know. Be careful. May destiny guide us back onto the same path in due time."

Chapter 30

From Petra to Black Rock

Deskull bandaged his left eye, hopped on a hovercraft and flew straight into the rebel stronghold. His unconcealed arrival drew a foregathering of scruffy kids and scarred freaks. The seer, having shed the blind man disguise and flanked by a small contingent of armed Animorta, emerged from the crowd, which spontaneously opened a path for him and his men.

"I have confidence you will return," the old man croaked.

"With me defecting, don't you fear a Yarjuni attack?"

"Since we have you to protect us, we fear nothing. Direct your gaze behind me. Do you notice anyone from your past?"

About twenty paces back among the excited crowd stood a familiar figure. Deskull immediately recognized Milu, a grown version of his best friend from before the bombing of Petra, now sporting spectacles and a fledgling beard, standing tall and dashing. Deskull was unsure about the charming maiden holding Milu's hand. From her flaming red hair and mysterious green eyes, he guessed she was Serah. This young couple and the old seer were the only ones in the crowd arrayed in clean clothing. They were dressed in their Sunday best to greet their long-lost friend.

Deskull rushed over and man-hugged Milu. He was also delighted to see Serah, although he hesitated about acting beyond proper etiquette. Noticing Deskull's discomfiture, Serah offered him a sweet smile and an appropriate air-hug.

"Come to my home," Milu said. "Uncle Yosi is waiting with snacks and drinks. You know, I call him Pepé Yosi now."

"I know," Deskull said. "The old seer told me. He didn't tell me about Serah. What a pleasant surprise."

"You don't recognize the old man?" Milu cried.

"He does give me the uncanny sensation I've met him once upon a dream. But when you wake up, you can't remember what or wherefore. How does he know so much about me?"

"Let us end this torture," Serah said. "The old seer, as you call him, is Pepé Carlini. You called him Professor Stane. He is the provisional leader of the Animorta."

"No, how come he doesn't say?" Deskull placed his hand on his forehead. "I could kick myself for not recognizing him. On the other hand, he is a master of disguise, helping him evade the bounty hunters. No wonder he knows so many Yarjuni secrets."

Professor Stane, leaning on his cane, limped over slowly. The passage of time had taken its toll on him. Serah offered her arm as the four strolled along a mountain path leading to the grotto Yosi and Milu called home.

Uncle Yosi gave Deskull a hearty embrace and offered everyone sweet delicacies.

"So, besides being the Toymaker," Deskull quipped, "you're also the Candyman."

"Anything to make little boys and girls happy," Yosi chuckled as he headed into an inner chamber to get more food.

"Without access to Yarjuni intelligence networks," Deskull asked Professor Stane, "how did you learn of my presence at the Hellian March? It is a confidential military secret. I'm supposed to come here to wipe out the rebels."

"We have oracles and informants to guide us," Professor Stane said. "Since learning of your appointment as the Margrave of Helle and heeding the prophecy of our deliverance at the Hellian March, we decided to come here and await your arrival. Recently, we received a report from a spy indicating elite troops led by Yarjuni aristocrats were approaching. We didn't have to wait long."

"I'm glad we found each other," Deskull said. "Since everyone still uses their old names, maybe I should do the same. Deskull is a distinctly Yarjuni name, highly inappropriate among rebels. Therefore, I declare Deskull defunct. Kiku is back. I look forward to fighting for peace under Professor Stane's leadership."

"I won't be much of a wartime leader," the Professor said. "I'm afraid you'll need to take my place. I deeply regret having created deadly weapons for the Yarjunis. I kept telling myself I was developing science to benefit everyone, insisting weapons didn't kill people. But they ended up exclusively in the hands of mass murderers who used them to commit atrocities with impunity. After fleeing the Yarjunis, I swore never to participate in war again, even if indirectly. I'm a true Ignorante. As the temporary leader of the Animorta, I'm merely the shepherd of a migratory flock, and I accepted the role conditional upon it ending when the prophesied one-eyed hero arrives. Well, the oracle has come true, and here you are. By the way, as a warrior, the name Kiku is too meek. Your full name, Kingku, is more appropriate."

"Alright, from now on, I'll go by Kingku as you suggest."

"Excellent," Professor Stane said. "Now you'll have to live up to the expectation of your name and be the leader of men."

"And women," Serah added.

Yosi returned from the inner chambers with someone trailing behind, each carrying a tray of food and drinks.

"Sator, here is the long-lost friend you knew from long ago and far away," Yosi said. "He has finally found his way back home."

"My dear friend Kiku," the android cried. "I've waited for so long. The last time we were together, I promised we'd play once I got my legs. But everything fell apart."

"I'm Kingku now. So you finally have legs. We must run in a footrace afterwards."

Sator put down his tray and came over to droid-hug Kingku.

"Welcome home, Kingku," he said. "I'm so glad to have you back with us."

"Everyone, let us settle down," Professor Stane said. "Kingku will want to gather what transpired following the firebombing of Petra. Only after we have recounted the history of the past, shall we'll discuss our plans for the future."

"It is a night I'd rather forget," Kingku said. "I witnessed the murder of my family, and I almost died from my wounds. But I suppose I wasn't the only victim."

"It has not been easy for any of us survivors," Milu said, putting his arm around Kingku's shoulders to comfort him. "But while we live, let us live. The Yarjunis fabricated a fake story about Petra being the target of rebel retaliation. They used you as a propaganda tool. Mainstream Freedom Media is a branch of the Yarjuni Department of Peace, supported by an unlimited Yarjuni-endowed global subversion aid budget for promoting freedom, democracy and inalienable Haryan rights. Their endless repetition of the lie eventually made it the universal truth."

"The Yarjunis are experts in deception," Kingku said. "For the longest time, I genuinely believed they wanted peace, and I blamed the Ignorantes and the rebels. Now I realize how people who believe in lies will commit atrocities. I'm glad you're all fine. I want to hear all your stories. Uncle Yosi, you start."

Chapter 31

The Animorta

"I was lucky," Yosi said. "When the bombs started falling, I was still at the Dump scrounging for parts. After it stopped, I raced home to find Sator traumatized, ranting wildly about being saved by a fairy. Sting, repaired and activated, also survived, but it went off, searching for Pepé. Everyone lost a bit of their mind after the shock and awe.

"I went to Diamond Slum and found the whole place flattened. I heard Milu crying for help from under the ruins and pulled him out before he suffocated. He had wisely taken shelter under his bed, saving his life. We buried the burned remains of our dearly departed, but had no idea what happened to you. I did manage to salvage an empty jewellery casket, the Almanac and the Lituus, your golden baton."

Serah took Sting's casket from her shoulder bag and returned it to Kingku, who henceforth treated it as a priceless memento.

"Poor Sting," Kingku sighed. "I wonder what happened to it."

"Yosi gave me the Almanac," Professor Stane said, passing the book to Kingku. "But I believe you should have it. After all, your parents found it and were its last owners. The Almanac is said to hold the mysteries of the universe. However, I don't understand a word of it, and I don't think you should waste any time on it."

"Thanks, Professor," Kingku said. "My parents spent a lot of time studying it, but they gained nothing except a quick death. I'm more interested in learning how you and Serah survived."

"I slipped out of the house after Serah went to bed," Professor Stane confessed, eyeing his daughter apologetically. "I expected her to be fine under your protection, but did not foresee the Yarjunis razing the defenceless Petra. It changed everything. It seems I am bound to Serah by a mysterious bond I cannot break."

Kingku stole a furtive glance at Serah. No one knew the secret he had accidentally discovered about her from the Truth Portal.

"At the front gate," the Professor continued, "I met a group of wandering mendicants fleeing in great haste. They had somehow learned of the Yarjunis' planned attack on Petra. I rushed back to save Serah. It was, however, too late to warn the others. Diamond Slum was already in flames. We escaped by the skin of our teeth."

"How did you end up with Uncle Yosi, Milu and Sator?"

"We'd have to thank the wandering mendicants," Professor Stane said, "who were, to put it bluntly, maimed panhandlers, the lowest of the low. They found Yosi and Milu, who had been without food and water for many days. Sator was doing his best to keep them alive. We were lucky to have found them when we did. Our reunion was also pivotal for the wandering mendicants because, together, we found new hope and strength."

"Thank goodness for Professor Stane and the mendicants," Milu said. "If not for them, we would certainly have perished from privation. But the five of us became a catalyst, helping to transform this group of itinerant beggars into one of the staunchest resistance against Yarjuni hegemony."

"To make a long story short," the Professor said, "the wandering mendicants had a unique background, allowing them to survive under the harsh rule of the Yarjunis. They were, in fact, Yarjuni veterans who once committed atrocities in the service of their masters. Until one day, they received a maiming wound and immediately became worthless pissants. Their wives and sons woke up the next morning as slaves, and their daughters as prostitutes. Their properties ended up in the auction houses, and the proceeds fattened the coffers of the Yarjun Lords. The ruling class justified their lawless behaviour by citing the rule of law, while they blamed the maimed soldiers for not dying from their wounds, thus becoming society's burden."

"Having studied Yarjuni history," Kingku said, "I don't recall any mention of them abandoning wounded soldiers."

"Yarjuni history is mostly the glorification of murders told by liars to idiots," Professor Stane said. "People believe in it to their own detriment. Being veterans, the mendicants were granted a charter to panhandle for a living. Such was the indignity the maimed Yarjuni soldiers received for selling their soul. You can talk to any of them and hear a story drenched in tears and regret.

"They had given up life and limb while committing unspeakable atrocities to enrich their masters. But they couldn't even protect their wives and children from the ones they served. As maimed beggars, they helplessly watched the Henchmen haul their wives to the slave market, their daughters to the brothels and their sons to the castration centres. To seek redemption, they went around begging for forgiveness from their victims. It was what kept them alive in their painful existence of despair. And they called themselves Animorta, the soul-dead."

"Pepé Yosi gave them a new lease on life," Milu said. "By applying his toymaking skills, he used salvaged parts to custom-build bionic prosthetics for the Animorta. The next ray of a bright future came when Serah started to soothsay in a trance, guiding us toward sources of food and water and away from hostile forces. Most significantly, when all seemed lost, she prophesied the rise of a one-eyed hero from the Hellian March, who would deliver us from the Yarjunis and end the Endless War."

"I have no idea where those words come from," Serah said. "But the Animorta gains hope from them."

"However, hope is a dime a dozen," Milu opined. "We needed leadership. The Animorta learned of Professor Stane's Yarjuni background and elected him to lead us to the Promised Land."

"Naturally, I refused," Professor Stane said. "But for some reason, your golden baton, the Lituus, which I had kept with me, began to grow. The Animorta interpreted it as a sign and insisted I lead them until the arrival of the prophesied one-eyed hero. Guided by the Lituus, which began to manifest a mysterious power, we were able to slip past the Yarjuni forts undetected. Arriving at this mountain after a gruelling trek, we found the Recalcitrants on the brink of extinction. Although no one speaks of the siege, as the 'freedom media' remains silent and the so-called moral leaders turn a blind eye, every Harya knows about the psychopathic strangulation of the rebels in this open-air prison.

"Yosi, with the help of everyone here, once again saved the day. All the limbless rebels received bionic prosthetics. Yosi also assembled biobots to lay eggs, give milk and grow meat. In addition, he made his favourite robotic honey bees, which you've noticed, to pollinate our genetically engineered plants and produce life-sustaining honey; otherwise, Yosi would not have been able to make his candies."

"Amazing!" Kingku exclaimed. "The Yarjunis are baffled by how the rebels can survive under this relentless siege."

"They poisoned the springs," Professor Stane said, "making our life unbearable. Fortunately, the Lituus helped us discover new springs, allowing us to set up vertical farms inside the dark caverns and produce enough food for everyone using artificial sunlight."

"None of this would have been possible," Yosi said, "without Milu's discovery of Erinysite in these barren mountains."

"Now I understand why you won't leave this place," Kingku said. "The Yarjunis have jealously guarded the secrets of mining and refining Erinysite. The rest of the world only has a minuscule amount. Erinysite is what fuels the Yarjunis' wealth and power. With access to the magical mineral, we'll have a fighting chance. Milu, fill me in with your incredible discovery."

"When we moved into these grottoes," Milu began, "I stumbled upon a deep chamber scintillating with the signature of Erinysite. According to popular lore, the twin unicorns emerged through Abysso-mamba's wormhole at Nine Dragons, identified by the sacred Omphalos. We can count nine peaks surrounding us, and we found a black spheroidal rock atop a borehole. It's no coincidence this locale is named Black Rock. Professor Stane soon confirmed what we suspected."

"Sorry to say," Professor Stane said, "I developed advanced Erinysite extraction technologies for the Yarjunis. Now I can help the rebels survive by harnessing the energy of the exotic mineral."

"We're thankful for our good fortune," Sator said, "Erinysite is a rare treasure buried deep within the earth. It is said to be the food of the unicorns. As we all know, Lord Abaddon of the ancient House of Kheru tamed Abysso-mamba, the Great Worm of Shangria. The fantastical creature burrowed underground for many days, emerging with a bellyful of Erinysite, which burns with an undying flame when kindled in a controlled environment. Properly harnessed, it is an almost inexhaustible source of energy."

"Abbadon's discovery of Erinysite was truly game-changing," Professor Stane remarked. "It could have, with a single stroke, eliminated much of Shangria's social ills. However, he hoarded all the Erinysite, refusing to share it with anyone. Thus, Abbadon gained unrivalled power, using it to enslave the rest of the Haryas.

"The allure of hegemonic power is poisonous. Abaddon's great-grandfather, Yahusua, founded the Haryan civilization and bequeathed us all the good things in the world. In merely three generations, the insatiable lust for power transformed his scions into egotistic, selfish, greedy, lying, hypocritical and bloodthirsty warmongers. Abaddon and his children amassed tremendous wealth, and his great-grandson, Mephisto, safeguarded the plunder by establishing the supremacist Yarjun caste. To ensure they would never lose their wealth and power, Mephisto's son, Asmodeus, designed the Last Resort, guaranteeing their perpetual lordship."

"I know, the Last Resort is fiendishly clever," Kingku said. "It threatens to ignite the planet's Erinysite if an enemy overcomes the Yarjunis in battle. Shangria would become a ball of unquenchable fire, incinerating all lifeforms in an ultimate holocaust to the God With No Name. Lord Asmodeus built the ignition system. All it takes is a flip of the switch, and it'll be game over."

"The rebels are fighting with the hope of building a better future," Professor Stane said, "but if winning leads to death for all, no one can afford to win. Hence, the Last Resort makes the Yarjunis unconquerable and the war endless. How does one grapple with such monsters?"

"We depend on your leadership, Kingku," Serah said. "You are a Yarjuni warrior and understand them inside out."

"Do you remember the myth of the Lituus?" Professor Stane asked, passing his blind man's cane to Kingku.

"Yes. It is said to be a fragment of the Nephrustan, Sage Didymas' staff of power, which survived the Polemophthorosin Devastation. It came into the possession of Lord Yahusua, who gave the relic to our family to be used as a magical baton to bring harmony to Shangria. It's a wild yarn no one believes in."

"On the contrary, it matches the oracular verses of the Mahashangria, Kingku," the Professor asserted. "Now we count on you to fulfil your destiny, take up the staff of power and conquer the unconquerable Yarjunis."

Chapter 32

Banquet at the Wild Goose Gate

"Why can't I use my unicorn rings?" Victoria protested. "Suppose Queen Lilith tries to corner me, I can do a *Bill and Ted's Excellent Adventure* trick with the help of Delo and Re'an, go back in time, make a few changes and turn the tables on the Queen in the present."

"*Bill and Ted* is good comedy," Sting said. "Time travel, however, is neither funny nor for the faint of heart. The unicorn gadgets are not toys, and no one should treat them lightly. Remember Lord Millistar, who made your pendant? He studied the rings and the mirror to build, illegally, I might add, what is known as a Plancket quantum device, in honour of the professor, which generates quantum states, allowing us to experience the past and preview the most probable future. The genius inventor would live to regret it. The law of causality spares no one."

"I hear you. No *Bill and Ted* tricks. Can you explain the 'time bomb' David mentioned before he got zapped to goodness knows where?"

"After successfully testing the Plancket quantum device, Lord Millistar developed the Elitzur-Vaidman quantum bomb. David heard a ticking and assumed it was a time bomb. In fact, it only exploded quantum mechanically, sending David to quantum states of the past existing in entropic uncertainty. The problem is we can't pinpoint where or when. Lord Millistar failed to calibrate coordinates. Only the unicorn rings and the Catoptron have the power to do so. DIAS later used the quantum bomb for sending convicts to temporal exile and armed the Watchers with it."

"Does anyone know where or when David ended up?"

"David's whereabouts are unknown, and his temporal exile is, for all intents and purposes, a life sentence. As an analogy, your friend is inside an archive of all films and videos, but he is not in the database. To find the man, we must go through every frame of up to a trillion minutes of material with a fine-tooth comb because he may be a soldier in *Waterloo*, a member of the audience of *The Price is Right* or a bystander in a YouTube video. The chance of finding David is minuscule. He's pretty much on his own."

"I don't get it. Does it mean my trip to ancient China was a Hollywood fantasy? What about my parents being a part of Chinese history? Why was it okay for me to extract them?"

"Clearly, you don't understand anything about time; otherwise, you wouldn't be asking these questions. David's destination in the past is forbidden information, as it threatens our future. Your parents' situation was more flexible. For example, let us suppose you are the filmmaker, director and editor of a movie. Think of your parents' quantum states in the past as a movie reel. With the help of the unicorns, you may do some splicing and editing in the middle as long as the beginning and ending are unaffected."

"What if a bad edit happens by accident?"

"If it violates the iron rule of causality and alters the movie's ending, the actors will be lost forever in entropy. It would be a tragedy. Last time, you were lucky not to have caused permanent damage, but let us not tempt the gods. I strongly advise against any inappropriate usage of the unicorn rings."

"What about the Gateway of the Titans, by which you've been travelling faster than the speed of light from one solar system to another? Am I correct the Amazons also use it to get to Earth? Why is it okay for everyone except me to violate physical laws?"

“The Gateway of the Titans makes use of entanglement and wormhole technologies, all of it legit. It transports our pollinators across great distances in the blink of an eye. However, it’s antiquated and accident-prone. Queen Lilith has built updated ones within the Kuiper Belt. The project has taken her autonomous robots four thousand Earth years to complete, expending vast quantities of Didymium. It was hard work, but the new Gateways are up and running, and the Queen is here with her horde to colonize Earth. It appears humans will be the collateral damage.”

“It’s not fair Queen Lilith can use the Gateways while I can’t use my Unicorn rings.”

“The Gateways of the Titans are Manifold Manipulators. The Watchers have portable ones with limited features. They do not cause time anomalies. Meanwhile, your devices can rip apart the space-time fabric. I get the willies each time you handle them.”

“Is my Magic Mirror off limits as well?”

“Not if you use it properly. Your Magic Mirror or Catoptron is a one-of-a-kind dimension-tunnelling device employing the exotic properties of a unicorn’s eyes. It allows you to traverse between dimensions. Thanks to the Plancket Unification Theory, we can prove general relativity and quantum theory are two sides of a single equation. Our quantum reality is the shadow of a multidimensional presence. Regarding such a higher-dimensional existence, which is beyond our comprehension, we’re at the limit of our knowledge. Neither do we understand the full power of the Catoptron; therefore, let us use it carefully and sparingly.”

“Is this higher presence the God With No Name? Why did people on your planet worship DIAS instead? I’m confused because they also worshipped you.”

“I have no answers about the nameless Creator,” confessed Sting. “DIAS was merely a godlike system built to keep Shangria a perpetual paradise. I hacked it, and people took me for a god.”

Victoria glared at Sting.

"Don't look at me like that," Sting cried. "I have to find my Pepé Kiku. I needed to get inside DIAS's head."

"You have caused serious damage," Victoria chided the robo-scorpion. "Now come clean with what powerful weapons you have given to Madonna Lilith so she can come here to destroy the human race."

"The Queen drove a hard bargain," Sting whimpered. "She knew Pepé Kiku. She called him the One-eyed Soothsayer. I must find my father so I can help him escape his never-ending hell."

"So, you have made the Queen even more powerful while I'm supposed to walk into her lair unarmed? Why am I not thrilled?"

"You are not helpless, my dear Victoria. Besides, you can't blame it all on me. Don't forget the Queen is here because you placed your healing hands on her, giving her great comfort. She never stopped talking about it. So it is up to you to persuade her to stay away or make her an offer she can't refuse."

"I see, it's come full circle," Victoria groaned. "But I have no idea how to do this. I grew up in a small town. I don't have any experience dealing with aliens. I have no confidence I can save anyone, to say nothing of the human race. During my last journey to China, David and the Shang clans helped me most of the way. All I did was close my eyes and take the plunge. It was exciting and scary, but I didn't have to solve any problems. Queen Lilith is different. She is a tough cookie, having overcome extreme difficulties, fought brutal wars, led a successful rebellion and ruled an entire planet. Thanks to you, she has powerful Watchers and Sephirahs armed with fancy weapons. What's to stop the Queen from locking me up at first sight?"

"I won't be so pessimistic," Sting said. "All you need is a little courage and resourcefulness. I'll give you an example to set aside your worries. Have you ever watched *The Godfather*?"

"Of course, who hasn't?"

"Do you remember the part where the drug lord Sollozzo puts a hit on the Godfather because the old man is standing in the way of his drug business? As you know, Don Corleone survives, and a war breaks out between the Mafia families. Since it is bad for business, Sollozzo wants to hold a truce talk. However, he doesn't trust anyone in the Corleone family except the youngest son, Michael, who is not in the family business. So, Michael has to go alone and unarmed to a restaurant of Sollozzo's choice. The drug lord, on the other hand, enjoys the protection of Captain McCluskey of the NYPD, whose presence guarantees Sollozzo's safety because no one touches a cop, much less a captain.

"Considering Sollozzo had tried to kill Michael's father, and having failed, he sent killers to try again at the hospital, but Michael foiled the attempt. What can the young man achieve by going to this dinner meeting? The treacherous Sollozzo can easily take him hostage and use him as a bargaining chip. If something goes wrong, Michael could end up dead. In any case, the young Corleone bravely attends the dinner and solves the Sollozzo problem. Pretending he needs to use the washroom, Michael comes out firing with a loaded pistol planted behind the flush tank. If you don't enter the tiger's den, how will you get the cubs?"

"*The Godfather* is only a movie. Michael Corleone can die a thousand deaths, but I die only once."

"Fair enough. Since you put it this way, I'll introduce you to an actual historical banquet of death. It happened after the fall of the Qin Dynasty and before the rise of the Han Dynasty. I understand you have learned some history about this period from David."

"Only the parts about how the strategist Zhang Liang helped the rebel Liu Bang establish the Han Dynasty, transforming a peasant into the one king to rule them all."

"Good for you! History faithfully records Liu Bang as a ruffian and an uneducated boor. However, he was an excellent judge of character and trusted his friends with his life. The Han Dynasty might never have existed if Liu Bang had not followed Zhang Liang's advice to attend a banquet of death set up by his rival, Xiang Yu, knowing everyone at the table wanted him dead."

"Wow, and he went anyway! I doubt I would if I were him."

"Had King Odoacer followed your advice, he would not have been cleaved in two at Theodoric's banquet. The same goes for the boyars impaled at Vlad Dracula III's Easter feast. Liu Bang, on the other hand, took Zhang Liang's advice, wisely, I may add.

"You should remember how the rebel Xiang Yu destroyed the Qin army at Julu while Liu Bang avoided battles, quickly capturing Qin's capital without opposition. The triumphant Liu posted his army of one hundred thousand outside the Qin capital, believing he could become the Lord of Qin by blocking the advance of Xiang Yu's now combined force of four hundred thousand. Big mistake! Xiang Yu got wind of Liu Bang's intentions and promptly showed up about ten miles from Liu Bang's camp at a location known as Hongmen, or Gate of the Great Wild Goose, fully prepared to pulverize the preposterous peasant, pronto.

"By coincidence, if such a thing were possible, it turned out Zhang Liang had saved the life of Xiang Bo, Xiang Yu's uncle, when both were Qin fugitives. Zhang got a visit from Xiang Bo after dark, urging him to decamp from Liu Bang's camp forthwith, as the peasant rebel would get his behind handed to him upon sunrise. If you were Zhang Liang, what would you do?"

"Adopt the thirty-sixth stratagem, run for my life."

"Every rational, sentient living being not interested in dying would agree. Zhang Liang was, however, a Shang descendant entrusted with the *Book of Heavenly Secrets*. He would not flee from his destiny. First, Zhang Liang convinced Xiang Bo the whole brouhaha was a terrible misunderstanding. Next, he scampered to Liu Bang's tent to inform him of the impending doom. Thereupon, the normally boorish Liu Bang treated Xiang Bo with the utmost respect, betrothing each other's children and hurriedly drinking to each other's health to bind the two families.

"Despite Xiang Bo's efforts to lower the temperature, the situation remained direly dicey for Liu Bang. He must attend a banquet at Xiang Yu's camp and defend himself against the accusations of his detractors. Also attending was Fan Zeng, a person revered by Xiang Yu as 'Second Father,' who had vehemently advocated for the extermination of Liu Bang and had prepared assassins to dispatch the future founder of Han. Liu Bang gained Xiang Yu's trust during the Hongmen Banquet and beat a hasty retreat, leaving unannounced after a trip to the outhouse and escaping by the skin of his teeth; the rest is history. In Chinese idioms, a Hongmen Banquet is a mandatory feast likely to result in an undesirable, if not deadly, outcome for the attendee, similar to what happened to Odoacer, the king of Italy, and the Wallachian boyars. However, you can rest easy with me as your ally. I will not let anything untoward happen to you at the Queen's banquet."

"Your ancient anecdote isn't very convincing," Victoria said. "The Hongmen Banquet could be no more than an exaggerated folklore made up by Han historians to glorify their founder."

"Oh, you know about the sausage factory of history," Sting said with a chuckle. "Alright, to meet your standards, let me refer to an event backed by reliable records from multiple primary sources in recent history, even with photographs. A Hongmen Banquet happened during the Chinese Civil War. Chairman Mao attended such a banquet of death set up by his archrival, Generalissimo Chiang Kai-shek."

"Now, this is something I can relate to. It didn't happen too long ago, and I know a bit about this part of Chinese history."

"Excellent! So I can skip the background story. Right after Japan surrendered in 1945, Generalissimo Chiang Kai-shek invited Chairman Mao to visit Chongqing, or Chungking, China's wartime capital after the fall of Nanjing, to discuss, face to face, a political solution for preventing the recurrence of civil war. While the Americans had guaranteed Mao's safety, Chiang would have no qualms about surgically decapitating the Communist leader if he believed he would benefit from it. Chiang's military counsel was all for it. His secret service agents were itching to pounce. The Generalissimo certainly agonized over it during the forty-four days the Communist leader was within his grasp.

Realizing the mortal danger, Mao accepted the challenge because he knew the Chinese Revolution did not depend on one person, and his assassination by Chiang's treachery would help the Communist cause. Taking appropriate precautions, Mao went, drank and slipped through Chiang's fingers; the rest is history. Now, Victoria, it's your turn to be brave and visit the tiger's den."

(Mao Zedong and Chiang Kai-shek in Chongqing Aug. 28, 1945)

Chapter 33

The Amortal Foe

"I'll be brave," Victoria said, "but we need a plan. Tell me about Queen Lilith's strengths and weaknesses, and what will convince her to leave us alone. More importantly, how can I spring my parents and Charlie out of the Queen's prison?"

"The Catoptron can help if used properly," Sting said. "Queen Lilith will hide her hostages. However, the Magic Mirror should be able to open a portal leading to a safe location near them. Walls, locks and force fields will stand in your way, but you can easily walk through them. You have super strength and bones of steel. Personal weapons can't do much more than irritate you. At any rate, Queen Lilith will not harm you."

"What about the Watchers and Sephirahs? What are their weaknesses?"

"The Watchers were android agents built to serve DIAS, helping to manage the perpetual paradise on Shangria, my home planet. Powered by the divine fire, I developed the smarts to hack DIAS's digital hash signature. I stole DIAS's ID and masqueraded as the protector god of Shangria, tricking some Watchers to accompany me to Betel. Don't judge me. I have no choice.

"After the Queen got the Watchers, her engineers learned how to clone them. Their latest models are now female and are called Sephirahs. Churel, the intruder you met earlier, is a top-of-the-line upgrade. Despite their high IQ, the Amazons are unaware of the hash weakness. Therefore, once we enter the Qaanaaq, your job will be to rescue the hostages and create a diversion while I hack into the ship's computer to shut down all the androids. In the ensuing commotion, you can spring a surprise attack on the Queen and make her an offer she cannot refuse."

"What about the sand puppies? I would like to know what to do when a pack of growling, snarling three-headed hellhounds stand in my way."

"You can use the power of persuasion from your father's side of the family. Combined with the telepathic power from your mother's side, you should be able to work wonders. Most living creatures have trouble perceiving reality precisely. Indeed, a little delusion is sometimes necessary for surviving adversity. All you need to do is fool the sand puppies into thinking you're the Amazonian Queen, and they'll eat out of your hand. Moreover, the hideous creatures are voracious feeders. Keep some snacks handy, and your puppy problems will evaporate."

"Great! Thanks for the tip. Now, how do I neutralize Queen Lilith? Can I use mind tricks?"

"The Queen will be a tough nut to crack. First of all, she has all the powers you have and more. So you're not going to fool her or overpower her. Madonna Lilith's problem is her traumatization at a young age by war. Sometimes, you can't even blame her for what she has become, as she is a product of atrocities. She is the blowback. Queen Lilith suffers from serious emotional problems, making her unpredictable. For example, she is clinically and uncontrollably bipolar. So, be careful not to let on you are not exclusively devoted to her, as she might go off the rocker on you."

"Got that. By the way, you said Queen Lilith had taken four thousand years to build her new Gateway system. Do you mean she is at least four thousand years old?"

“Four thousand Earth years is about eighty Betel years,” Sting said. “And the average Haryan lifespan on Betel is thirty years, which their astronomers recalibrate as ninety cycles. Despite the Amazons having cellular recuperative powers, their genetic structure breaks down as they age, and they expire. Queen Lilith has lived far beyond the average because she is amortal. I had to give her the technology. It was the deal breaker.”

“You mean the Queen is immortal.”

“No, she is amortal. Our technology, developed by Lord Millistar, extends life almost indefinitely. Death can, however, occur as a result of mortal wounds. Since one does not die naturally but from trauma, the person is not immortal but amortal. As such, it is possible, if difficult, to end all your alien invasion problems with a lethal blow or deadly poison, preferably both.”

“I’d rather not use violence, if possible. What about Amazonian reproduction? Without the help of men, how do the Amazons have babies, or do they make all Amazons amortal to keep their population stable?”

“The entire Amazonian population has indeed infected themselves with the amortal gene. Nevertheless, people still die from accidents, negligence, suicide, and a slew of other reasons. Most Amazons eventually terminate themselves because endless life could be unbearably depressing. The average lifespan for the amortal Amazon is about three thousand Earth years. Even the loyal Leona left the Queen’s side at age four thousand after filling the vacancy with her clone. The Queen has lived for five thousand years because she wanted to lead the Amazons’ migration from the soon-to-explode Betelgeuse, but more importantly, to see you again, though she must pay a terrible price for defying Nature.

“In terms of replenishing the population, the Amazons have long ago perfected the means to manufacture zygotes with bespoke genes and simulate natural gestation by android surrogacy. Thus, the Amazons have truly achieved independence because they no longer need the male sex to propagate the species and are not hampered by the maternal role of pregnancy, childbirth and child-rearing. Excuse me for telling the truth about human females. As long as their gender's biological duties enslave them to carry babies and give birth, all talk of equality is smoke and mirrors."

"Perhaps the Amazon example will teach men not to oppress women. As for Queen Lilith having to pay a price for defying Nature, what side effect is she suffering from? It may be her Achilles' heel."

"The amortal gene, over time, changes the Queen's blood into pus. Her white vascular fluid, known as ichor, deprives her skin of colour and reduces her fulsome figure into a shrivelled spectre of her former self. Furthermore, it causes her to emit the putrid stench of death from every pore. Nowadays, the Queen cannot leave her bedchamber without heavy makeup and strong perfume. Everything the poor woman eats tastes of the bitterest bile. She cannot swallow food without smothering it in rare spices. She dreads sleep because of her recurring nightmares of being eaten alive by the slain. She wakes up screaming several times each night. Frost has snuffed out the fire in her heart and deprived her of the joys of life. She hates being alive, and yet she refuses to die."

"Poor Madonna Lilith, I feel sorry for her."

"Pity will not help your cause," Sting said. "The only way you can stop her is by violence, and you may be the only one with the power to succeed. Listen to my advice. To save Earth and humanity and to keep yourself on the path to the Great Reset, you must catch Queen Lilith unawares and strike at her heart with all your might. After I have shut down all the androids, you should approach her during the confusion and deliver the coup de main. When you supplant her on the throne, the Amazons will submit to you as their new Supremo."

Chapter 34

Enter the Qaanaaq

"our Majesty!" the Sentinel in charge cried in surprise as she scrambled to stand at attention. "It is well past the Witching Hour. You should be in bed."

The Amazonian Queen was strolling with Churel and Leona in a section of her flagship seldom graced by her presence. On duty at the guard station for guest quarters were a Sentinel and her assistant, each with a three-headed sand puppy on a triple leash.

"At ease," Queen Lilith said. "You know I like to perambulate when I suffer from insomnia. Since I'm here, I wish to inspect the earthlings. Lead the way."

"We have moved them to the Holo-lodges according to the asset rotation schedule," the Sentinel in charge said.

"Well, what are we waiting for?" Leona said. "Take us there."

Activities in the flagship had slowed to a crawl after the Witching Hour. Only a few janitor droids were at work, and they kept out of the way, minding their own business. The Queen and her coterie took a leisurely and undisturbed stroll along the Main Promenade, a wide passage lined with various themed bars, where off-duty Amazons relaxed and sought someone with whom to share their lonely evenings.

They soon arrived at an entrance guarded by a Warder.

"Here we are," the Sentinel said. "The Warder takes over from here. I have to return to my post. Your Majesty."

The Warder led the Queen and her companions through a passage into a spacious hall, in the centre of which squatted a grim throne bristling with eleven fearsome weapons. Seated upon the throne and surrounded by her guards was Queen Lilith herself.

"My dear Victoria," the enthroned Queen said. "You may do away with your pretense. We have been waiting for you. Come, introduce your friends to me."

Abiding by Sting's advice to use her powers of persuasion and telepathy, Victoria caused everyone in the Flagship Qaanaaq to see her as Queen Lilith, Emma as Churel and Jackie as Leona II, the young clone of the departed Leona. When Victoria told the girls about her quest to save her parents and Charlie, as well as humanity, they refused to let her face the enemy alone. She only relented after Sting agreed the Weird Sisters might be more effective working as a team. After all, failure meant the end of the human race. Jackie and Emma might as well help Victoria rather than wait helplessly to die.

As the three girls realized the Queen had exposed their disguise, they quickly stood back to back against each other, ensuring no one could sneak up from behind.

"They're my best friends, Jackie and Emma," Victoria said. "We're sisters bound to each other for life. It's almost Amazonian. Once upon a time, you said I was one of you. You shouldn't have taken my family and my friend Charlie as hostages."

"You are one of us, your family is my family, and your friends are my friends. Where did you get the crazy idea I have taken anyone hostage? I bet it's Sting, the cockroach. Never trust a bug. Charlie and all your parents are having a grand old time. It's good you've brought your best friends. Everyone will be safe here."

"Are all four of my parents here? When will I see them?"

"How I envy you," Madonna Lilith said. "Two sets of parents to love you and two sets of parents for you to care about. They're on an excursion and expected to return shortly. They're in bed now. Let's not wake them from their sweet dreams. You'll see they're safe and free to come and go. But all in good time."

"While we're waiting," Victoria said, "shall we be friends and catch up on old times?"

"I would love nothing more. Since the day you left without saying goodbye, I've been dreaming of this moment. Even power without limit and life without end cannot come close to the comfort you gave me. If I did not have this terrible pining to see you again, I would have given up this miserable life long ago."

Madonna Lilith clapped her hands and ordered, "Paladinas, set up the Honoured Guest couches for Victoria's friends at the outer ring and serve our rarest delicacies and ambrosial drinks. We must ensure Jackie and Emma feel at home. We will honour Victoria as our Most Precious and Serene Princess. She will sit beside me in the Curule Chair. Crone, record this. Notwithstanding the law forbidding anyone to approach me without my permission, I decree an exception for my dearest Victoria, who shall have unrestricted access to me. I am the law, and I have spoken."

After everyone had settled down and Victoria had stowed her LV knapsack under her chair, the Paladinas brought a small table for each of the guests, placing on each a fancifully decorated drink and a mound of colourful confections on an ornate silver plate. Victoria could hardly restrain herself from partaking of the enticing refreshments.

The Queen reached out and grabbed Victoria's hand. Almost instantly, the woman entered a state of rapture. Queen Lilith's eyes rolled back. She arched her chest forward and turned her face heavenward. She furrowed her brow, parting her lips to gasp for air and letting out tiny whining noises. The plaintive notes of Schubert's *Ave Maria* wafted into the room, demanding total submission to the mother goddess of love. An evil demon struggled in the Queen's heart, causing her body to convulse as if transverberated by the flaming spear of the Archangel Uriel. Finally, she went limp and passed out. The Sephirahs rushed over to attend to the Queen.

"What happened?" the shocked Victoria exclaimed. "Is Queen Lilith alright?"

"She'll be fine," Churel said. "You're a cruel girl, making the poor woman suffer all these years of yearning."

"I'm sorry. I have no idea."

After the Queen regained her senses, she struggled to open her eyes halfway while allowing a rare smile to emerge.

"A moment of rapture for a lifetime of suffering," she sighed. "I suppose it was all worth it."

"I did not know my touch had such an effect on you; otherwise, I would have stayed," Victoria said, exercising guile on her part. "Since we have reconnected, I wish to ask for a favour."

"Ask away, my precious. I'll be happy to oblige."

"I hope you will reconsider purging Earth of humans."

"Dear me, you must think we're genocidal killers trying to take over the bountiful Earth from humans," the Queen said as she sat up, helped by the Sephirahs. "It is very far from the truth. We are here to cure the planet of her blight. We have known about Earth for a long time. The planet had been getting on swimmingly until she became infested by a kind of virulent, blood-sucking, brain-dead parasite known by the pompous name of Homo sapiens. These infernal pests rape the land, befoul the waters and defile all flora and fauna. They cut and drill her without mercy, leaving deep scars. They eviscerate and poison her. Finally, they suck her blood dry, turning her into the living dead. Now, through their egregious greed, profound ignorance, criminal negligence and endless strife, they'll destroy Earth in a blood-dimmed tide of self-inflicted devastation. We intend to cure the planet of this pestilence."

"I'm sure humans deserve much of what they're getting from Mother Nature. But you don't have to pile on all those unnatural disasters. If you allow Nature to run its course, humans may learn their lessons and set things right. You don't have to kill them off. Earth is a big place. With your technologies, Amazons and humans can share the planet and thrive together."

"My precious princess, this is what I love about you. If curing the plague needs strong medicine, you'll worry about hurting the germs. You see, we have been studying this planet and its inhabitants ever since we discovered it. Our Plancket quantum device has, without fail, generated a nontrivial output indicating total devastation of the planet if we do not intervene. We have tested many permutations of variables and parameters only to arrive at the same conclusion. For Earth to survive, humans must die. The impending supernova of Betelgeuse is not the only reason we are here; it merely gives us the impetus to speed up our Project Gomoira of human extermination. After we have purged Earth of her pests, we will become her mistress and take much better care of her. I want you and your loved ones to be a part of our future."

"If you truly care about me, you should remember I can't stand violence. I will not be a party to your human extermination project. Besides, your Plancket quantum device does not predict with perfect accuracy. Everyone knows it's tough to make predictions, especially about the future. What if we explore new ideas to change the output? Will you reconsider?"

While Sting was taking much too long to hack into the ship's computer system, it gave Victoria time to engage in dialogue rather than violence. But an unexpected development threw a wrench into Victoria's plan. Jackie and Emma had unwisely consumed the Amazon's snacks and fallen into a slumber. The girls should have remembered the rule never to take food or drinks from strangers.

"I'm a reasonable ruler," the Queen said. "If you can tweak the parameters to generate a positive set of possible future quantum states for Earth, I'll be happy to reconsider. The ship's computer will handle the computations in real-time. Go ahead, my dear."

"As you may be aware, I am what is known as the Sibyl, and I command powerful divine instruments. Moreover, the mysterious *Book of Heavenly Secrets* is in my possession. I can use my power to reset Earth's path for a better future, provided the Amazons agree to spare the humans and share the planet with them."

"To change humanity's future, you need to activate the Great Reset. Your gadgets alone are not powerful enough. We'll need the Twirligig and the one true Grist. According to what I've learned from reliable sources, the Sibyl must chant the Incantation of Creation and Destruction while playing the harmonic chord of the eleventh key with the divine instrument," the Queen chuckled. "Seriously, my dear, you should propose something more viable. I'm afraid your robotic cockroach friend has been messing with your head, feeding you a bucket of *Quatsch* and *Kauderwelsch*."

The Queen tapped a medallion hanging from her necklace, inquiring, "Computer, what's your analytical output?"

"Too many perturbations and unknowns; does not compute."

"What if I prove to you humans are worth saving, and you shouldn't kill the good with the bad?"

Victoria had to keep talking, emulating Scheherazade in the *Tales of the Arabian Nights*, hoping to dissuade the Queen from wiping out humanity, failing which, she would have to resort to violence, an option she wanted to avoid by all means.

"Fine, oblige me with a good reason," Queen Lilith said. "All I need is a single unassailable and convincing example."

Victoria mused for a moment and decided to plead her case with positive human achievements. The current unipolar master of Planet Earth must have some redeeming qualities.

Chapter 35

Project Gomoira

"Humans have developed language, which sets them apart from animals," Victoria argued. "With verbal communications, humans can educate, organize and cooperate. Language also helps them make abstract concepts for both art and science. Humans have developed many different languages. It is a testament to their superior intelligence, very similar to yours. They don't deserve extermination."

"Language is indeed a great human achievement," the Queen rebutted with a sarcastic sneer. "Unfortunately, they also use it to insult, slander and incite, leading to tribalism, extremism and militarism. When we examine the language of the powerful and their institutions, we encounter mostly half-truths, false narratives and bald-faced lies, nefariously manipulating the masses to believe in absurdities and commit atrocities.

"Language, once a gift, is now a curse because humans have so sorely corrupted it. Their language has become a weapon for psychological warfare and a drug for self-delusion. It's impossible to read any human composition nowadays without finding a falsehood in every sentence. Their news reporting and political speeches have devolved into mud-slinging contests with liars calling each other liars. It is such a circus, the audience won't know whether to laugh or cry. The abuse of language is why humans must die."

“So, Shakespeare is not your cup of tea,” Victoria said, quickly switching to another topic. “However, you must admit the development of laws is a great human achievement. People cannot do whatever they please but must follow a set of rules. Laws enable people from different backgrounds to live harmoniously in society. Humans wouldn’t have been able to achieve the high civilization they enjoy today without the development of laws.”

“Yes, thanks to ‘an eye for an eye’ of good old Hammurabi’s Code,” Madonna Lilith riposted with her customary ironic tone. “But a poor man’s eye is cheaper than a rich man’s eye. A woman’s eye is certainly not equal to a man’s eye. I’m not saying we shouldn’t have laws. I enact quite a few every day. I even made one for your benefit a moment ago. The truth is, those with power create the laws, usually for keeping the rabble under control, so the lower classes can slave away for their masters and pay their tithes, tariffs and taxes for the right to exist.

“Laws are designed to protect the rich, allowing them to amass their ill-gotten gains while maintaining their power, privileges and slave-wage peons. I’m saying this because I know. I won’t lie to you. I didn’t suffer the wounds and risk my life to fight for half-measures and end up under someone else’s thumb. If you have any doubt, check out your great lawgiver. Of Hammurabi’s two hundred and eighty-two laws, only one pertains to his government, and none to the king. Laws are made by the powerful for the weak.

“Let me put it this way. The idea of the rule of law is not necessarily bad, but law enforcement often involves violence. Laws are also subject to interpretation by human judges and juries. Humans being human, those with the prerogative to exercise violence in the name of the law and those empowered to interpret the law in judgment of others are not infallible, nor are they saints. I have witnessed far too many examples of the rich and powerful wielding the law to plunder the poor and powerless. Too many elite earthlings demanding the rule of law from others are themselves lawless scofflaws.

"It's a travesty when whistleblowers who disclose high crimes of the powerful are prosecuted and judged by the criminals. The rewards for telling the truth are often incarceration, banishment, torture, financial ruin and dishonour. These heroes would end up being exiled or locked up in dungeon cells, with their few supporters reduced to begging the criminals for mercy. In our society, the miscreants thus exposed would be unceremoniously dragged out of their ivory towers by the people and festooned on trees. Quite frankly, we're unimpressed by human justice."

"Queen Lilith, you're a harsh critic," Victoria complained, but moved on. "I still believe humans are worth saving because, much as the Amazons and your ancestors, they are highly spiritual. Most humans are religious. Even those who do not believe in a higher existence hold their disbelief religiously. Religion gives humans a soul and sets them apart from animals."

"Except humans created religion for political purposes and financial gain," Madonna Lilith countered with an authoritative air. "It's not only my opinion but one shared by many prominent human sages since antiquity. For example, the Roman historian Titus Livius said so even when their rulers were considered gods. During peacetime, religion keeps hungry people from causing trouble. Whereas during wartime, it removes the fear of death from the soldiers' hearts and justifies bloody murder. From my study of human religions, I find most of them induce people to believe in some cockamamie human concoction, and people believe them because of their ignorance and fear of the unknown. None of these commonplace human religions can compare with the incomparable Amazonian religion, which worships the God of Creation, the one and only God With No Name."

"But all religions say the same of their god or gods."

"Not all religions ask the pertinent scientific questions we ask of our God. Our society does not brook superstition. Indeed, religion, for us, is a branch of science. We know our God, to the extent we know we don't know and will not know—*ignoramus et ignorabimus.* Our God is the Creator and the Destroyer. Our God is infinite in the past and in the future. Our God has no beginning and no end. Our God is the beginning and the end. Our God is infinitely large and infinitesimally small. Our God is everywhere and nowhere. Our God is the reason for the universe's existence. Our God is existence. Yet our God does not discriminate and never intervenes. We enjoy free rein to act as we wish and suffer the consequences. We do not pray to our God, and our God does not heed our prayers. Our God has uncountable forms; our God has no form. Our God is the only self-emergent existence. Our God is omnipotent, ubiquitous and inexorable. No mortal can understand or describe our God. I'm doing a poor job of it. Our God has countless names; our God has no name."

"What about religions with no gods?" Victoria challenged the Queen. "Pure Buddhism, for example, does not concern itself with the Creation or gods and is very much against superstition."

"What is pure Buddhism? Do you mean Hinayana? Buddhism did not burst out of a rock. It is a reform offshoot of Hinduism, incorporating many core Hindu beliefs such as reincarnation, Samsara, Karma and Dharma. These are axioms entirely born out of human imagination, unprovable one way or another. Didn't I tell you our society does not brook superstition? What is the eternal truth for enlightenment, and why achieve Nirvana? So we don't have to reincarnate? It forces me to believe in something neither based on logic nor supported by empirical data.

"People waste their lives talking about a human, and Gautama insisted he was human, who never heard of Pythagoras' Theorem or Newton's laws of motion, forget about Einstein's General

Relativity and Heisenberg's Uncertainty Principle, and didn't leave anything in writing. Yet they choose to believe this Homo ignoramus discovered the eternal truth. I have learned humans will believe what they want to believe, but as long as they neglect the omnipresence of the God With No Name, destruction is their lot."

"You can't blame humans when they have never heard of the God With No Name."

"The God With No Name has always lived among humans and manifests in all scientific equations of existence. Yet none of your great thinkers, philosophers and scientists has ever asked the question of this omnipresence. They are preoccupied with creating false gods and peddling blind faith to the public. Human religions have caused terrible bloodshed and horrific suffering with little redeeming value. This degenerate species does not deserve a seat in the congregation of higher beings. Humans must go."

"I was hoping to present a case for human achievements in science and technology, but Your Majesty, in one fell swoop, dissed our scientists and inventors together with our prophets."

"Science and technology could have counted as great human achievements if they had not used their knowledge to benefit the elites, serve the warmongers, slaughter the defenceless, intimidate the meek, destroy the environment and devastate the planet. In Amazonian society, the development of science and technology is a shared achievement intended to benefit everyone, as no scientist, inventor or engineer can succeed without help from others. After innumerable iterations of the Plancket quantum device, we have arrived at one inevitable conclusion: human science and technology will destroy the planet. Humans must go."

"But Your Majesty cannot ignore how modern human society has given individuals the most robust democracy, the greatest personal freedom, the largest share of political power, the highest level of equality, the most extensive human rights, immense wealth, global connectivity, highly dynamic social mobility and an unprecedented era of peace in human history. These are undeniable achievements. On the other hand, your government structure is a totalitarian and dictatorial monarchy, with supreme authority resting in the hands of a single ruler. How can you dismiss these human achievements without giving credit where it's due?"

"Ha, I'm well aware of their fantastic feats," the Queen sniffed in contempt, "and all those euphemistic phrases meant to stimulate the secretion of dopamine, block logical thinking and evoke hysteria. Contrary to what your Homo ignoramus population may think, we have been engaging in the business of governing before the word appeared in the human vocabulary. Betel's parent planet, Shangria, was a paradise with perfect governance. We happen to know a few things about governments. We know all human institutions are flawed because they're designed and run by flawed creatures with flawed logic. To assume delusional human blather based on a language of lies can demonstrate the positive result of superior governance is the most laughable flaw of all."

"I'm not saying we have a perfect government, but I dare say ours are better than yours by comparison."

"Your argument in favour of human institutions illustrates a cognitive defect known as the Dunning-Kruger effect. Ignorance is not necessarily a sin, but the ignorance of one's ignorance could be deadly. In contrast, we know our weaknesses and try to learn from our mistakes. We do not gauge the success of our government by mouthing mindless memes like 'vote for change' or 'make excuses great again.' We measure how well we have achieved our goals. We don't merely give everyone a ballot and call it democracy. We genuinely try to understand what everyone wants, decide on a course of action, and ensure it benefits individuals and society in a balancing act, closely monitoring the feedback to make timely adjustments. In this way, I've governed Betel for eighty Betel years with a 99% approval rating, not as an autocrat hogging up all the power but as a mother tending her flock.

"Conversely, what is the approval rating of Earth's best system with all its deceptive rhetoric? I have closely studied your so-called popular governments. Your election systems are a joke because of party politics, which puts the interests of the parties above those of the people. Furthermore, your democracy adopts a winner-takes-all approach, which means if one party wins by one vote, they get all the power of the office. How is it representative of the people? I haven't mentioned the influence of money, corporations and media, all designed to diminish the individual's voice.

"Your politicians also employ tactics such as gerrymandering to disenfranchise voters. Finally, consider the Electoral College, which, in addition to not being representative of the people's will, also plays a winner-takes-all game, sometimes resulting in the candidate with fewer votes winning the popular contest.

"For political systems which prefer proportional representation, they end up with many small parties, wasting time and resources on bickering, accomplishing nothing. The English Parliamentary system fares no better. Party politics, rather than the popular vote, elect the prime ministers. Yet the obliquity of human hypocrisy lets them wag their sanctimonious fingers at others.

"The entire charade of your so-called democracy is merely a complex game with convoluted rules to decide who seizes power in a reality television show, not about representing the people and certainly not about serving them. Since you use the words 'win' and 'lose' to describe the result of an election, your democracy may be nothing more than a competition to claim a prize."

"I can't argue with a supreme ruler who's always right," Victoria conceded and pivoted. "What about us having guaranteed inalienable human rights for everyone on Earth? I don't believe you even have such a concept on your planet."

Chapter 36

Plan B

"The only thing worse than a liar is a liar who is also a hypocrite," the Amazonian Queen declared, keeping up her relentless attack. "I am tired of hearing their ridiculous claims of caring for human rights. Please spare me the holy tirades unleashed by the slave masters against the forced labour they have created. These bloodsuckers have no qualms about denuding ancient lands of their native people by rapine and murder. They do not give a tinker's damn about millions of people, half of them children, suffering the horrendous conditions of a never-ending siege and being wantonly bombed within an open-air prison, all of which the lying hypocrites have empowered and inspired to happen. They forget about having directly caused the death of half a million children in a suffocating embargo. They are too busy casting aspersions and dropping explosives on people of faraway lands who refuse to echo their human rights lies.

"Humans deserve to perish by their hypocritical double standard. Notice the biggest plunderer of your planet is espousing rights they never intend to uphold while they're strangling millions in endless sanctions and butchering the defenceless with impunity, all with the support of the so-called free press and the indifferent electorate. By the same principle, we will exercise our right under the mandate of supreme power and its rationale of 'because I can' to rid the Earth of this virulent scourge of hypocrites. Call it karma or blowback. Hypocrisy is a two-headed snake; it bites the hand that feeds it. I have scrutinized all your empty claims about human rights and the government of the people and find most of them are vapours with no more substance than flatus. Humans must go."

"I respectfully disagree," Victoria contended. "Humans have ended slavery and have done much to improve the human condition. I believe no government, including yours, can grant as much freedom to its people. In our society, people are free to express themselves, travel, do business and make their own life choices. Freedom is the loftiest and noblest aspiration of the human spirit. For this reason alone, you must spare them."

"I believe I've seen that movie too," the Queen responded with a wry grin. "But I'm not so easily persuaded. Yes, the slaves gained freedom from their masters. But they also earned the freedom to be destitute, freedom to starve, freedom to live in hovels, freedom to be helpless when sick, freedom to spend their lives in hard labour, freedom to be illiterate, freedom to be treated as animals, freedom to be a target of discrimination, freedom to rot in jails, freedom to be terrorized, whipped and lynched and, of course, freedom to be deprived of all human rights and dignity, all within a land of light whose shameless politicians and free press purport to care for the human rights of forgotten tribes living on the other side of the planet, whom they're about to help with sanctions and bombs. These oft-repeated lies would be funny if they were not so sad.

"Do you know why, even after so many years, the children of freed slaves are still marching in the streets demanding equal treatment? Do you understand why the dream of your Dr. King of decades past is still a pipe dream?"

"I suppose some people are not as free as they can be," Victoria acknowledged, "but no one promised anyone a rose garden. Life is not always fair."

"I'm not here to pass judgment, my dear," the Queen said. "Flawed earthlings may not have a good solution. Sometimes, humans prefer to believe in lies because it is less discordant with the lies they've consumed all their lives, which permeate every cell in their body. Some humans are so infected with the disease a mere glimpse of the truth may kill them. Notice how the boy who cries wolf repeats the ruse twenty thousand times, yet the villagers repeatedly fall for it. You can't even fool a squirrel more than three times with the same trick. However, the self-appointed sons of God never fail to believe in the myriad lies continuously spewing from the lying machines, which everyone knows do nothing but lie.

"Therefore, let me expose the silly lie that people dying of hunger and thirst can be free unless you mean free from living. None are more hopelessly enslaved than those who falsely believe they're free. What's more, one shouldn't expect freedom, with the bonus of equality and brotherly love, to be free. The emancipated slaves did not have political power, and they never fought as an organized political and military group for that goal and won. They shouldn't expect respect or redress without putting up a good fight.

"At the same time, the proponents of a 'fair and free' capitalist society would have you believe the children of the freed slaves are poor competitors. These purveyors of prejudice are heinous hypocrites. Their 'fair and free' hundred-metre dash competition is a rigged game, which amounts to asking a five-year-old malnourished cripple to race against the fleet-footed, winged-sandalled Hermes, who starts the contest enjoying a fifty-metre lead and a five-second head start.

"For the underprivileged victims, they have no human rights, no justice and no freedom. For those suffering ill-treatment, it's all a pack of lies. But why wait for a miracle to happen? As your Dr. King so eloquently enunciated, 'A man can't ride you unless your back is bent.' People have to stand up for their rights. It was the same for us women on Betel. We tried to gain peacefully only a handful of rights, but were brutally attacked merely for daring to dream. It made us into who we are, the Amazons.

"I'll be the first to admit our Amazonian freedom is a chasm apart from human freedom. After establishing the Amazonian dynasty, we reformed our society based on our parent planet, Shangria. The Amazons enjoy freedom from want. Everyone is born with the right to food, shelter, clothing, healthcare, education, travel, free association and communication with others. Everyone is guaranteed dignity and love from the moment they're born with the same freedom of choice.

"The Amazons also cherish freedom from fear. Violent crimes are non-existent, and capital crimes are unheard of. No individual may lay a hand on another. Even verbal abuse and verbal assault are serious offences, freedom of speech be damned. Bigotry and perjury are punishable by exile. Ours is a high-trust society. Our justice system is simple, unambiguous and impartial, and law enforcement is swift and incorruptible. As a rule of thumb, we may only enjoy freedom when it does not infringe upon others' freedom. Of course, we must give up some freedoms, but it's a matter of choice and priority. We have had to execute all the male criminals and emasculate those who don't deserve to die. It's a small price to pay for a peaceful society free of crime and poverty.

"In our Amazonian society, the young must behave with respect and proper manners toward their elders, the same for students toward their teachers, subordinates toward their superiors, and vice versa. Mutual respect is a fundamental rule. When in doubt about how we should behave or what we should say, we remind ourselves of three simple guidelines, very similar to the ones you have on Earth, except earthlings ignore them. The first one is basically the Thumper principle, 'If you can't say something nice, don't say anything at all.' The second reminds one of something espoused by Twain: 'It's better to keep your mouth shut and appear stupid than to open it and remove all doubt.' And the third could very well be some ancient Chinese wisdom found in a fortune cookie: 'Trouble comes out of the mouth.'

"Liars, scammers, slanderers, equivocators, dissemblers, hypocrites, braggarts, demagogues and rumour-mongers are ostracized. By our standards, human politicians and purveyors of news would all receive a free one-way ticket to a remote island where they can eternally wallow in their own cesspool of lies.

"It is also our choice to ban pornography and the airing of intimate acts in public. Our culture draws a line when it comes to protecting the innocence of young children from exposure to the vulgar behaviour of adults. True, we do not have human freedom of expression, but it is our freedom of choice, and we respect the choice of anyone to be different. Unlike humans, who, by their semi-evolved reptilian brains, believe their freedom is the best and whosoever does not agree must be excoriated, vilified, sanctioned, embargoed and bunker-bombed with extreme prejudice. You may think highly of human freedoms, but we beg to differ."

"I think you're looking at Earth from a vantage point," Victoria said resignedly. "It's hard for humans to have a clear view of themselves. And I must say you are very persuasive. If I listen to you for another minute, I'll lose all faith in the human race. Before it happens, I believe I need to use the washroom. May I?"

Victoria knew she was getting nowhere confronting the Queen with diplomacy and debate. No news was forthcoming from Sting. The Sephirahs and Paladinas were still functioning. The boastful toy robot must be having trouble hacking the ship's computer. The Canadian girl who would be the world's saviour was running out of time and options. Asking to go to the washroom was Plan B. With the Queen's assent, Victoria rose from her chair with the fork from the fruit plate surreptitiously hidden by skillful palming.

Leona leapt up and fired a beam at the girl to forestall her assassination attempt, and poof, Victoria vanished without a trace.

"Now, why would you do such a stupid stunt?" the Queen chided Leona. "Do you have to use your new toy so soon after getting it from Sting? Now we'll need the cockroach to find the girl. Where is the pricklouse?"

"But my Queen," Leona said, "it's not wise to let the girl have her way with you. I'm responsible for your safety, and she had a hidden weapon. I have been monitoring her vital signs. She did not need to use the washroom. She had evil designs toward you."

"Victoria was no threat to me. She was probably more of a threat to you. I know about the 'Godfather washroom scheme.' She got it from the bugsplat, who got it from me."

Queen Lilith leaned back, tapped her medallion and said, "Sting, answer me. Do we have AlphaOmega?"

"Patience, my dear," Sting's voice emerged from the ship's communication system. "I have transferred AlphaOmega to your control. Now you have to fulfil your end of the bargain."

"You'll have the gateway control codes, the coordinates of the Isle of Exile and Victoria's knapsack. But before you leave, help us find the girl."

"Don't worry about Victoria," Sting said. "She'll find you. Without her gadgets, she will take longer than usual, but she may not return at the most opportune moment for you. So, watch out. Well, I guess this is it, my dear Madonna Lilith. Other than your indecorous references to me as a cockroach, bugsplat and pricklouse, it has been a pleasure doing business with you. Feel free to call if you need my services again. Good luck trying to win over Victoria, and best wishes on your colonization of Earth. Over and out."

Chapter 37

Dungeon of the Heart

Kingku reclined atop a grassless knoll, gazing at the universe above. The sun had dipped below the horizon, and the moons had not yet emerged. It was the Witching Hour, the best time to observe the glorious galaxy of two hundred billion twinkling stars measuring a hundred thousand light-years side to side. Kingku wondered if, somewhere out there, someone might be gazing back at him.

As the young man closed his eyes, the vision of a red-haired girl flooded his mind. Rolling his head to the right, Kingku lifted his eyelids to peek at Serah lying on her spot about two metres away. By coincidence, she also turned her head around to lock eyes with him, pursing her lips to manufacture a bittersweet smile.

The space between them belonged to Milu, who didn't show up.

"What's with Milu?" Kingku asked. "He never misses our special time together. Is he mad at me for not letting him join me in battle tomorrow?"

"He said he wanted to double-check all the equipment," Serah answered in her soft, sweet voice, "and to ensure the new features on the Aquila drones will not break down during battle. You know how Milu is meticulous to a fault. With the arrival of the long-awaited Final Showdown, we have no room for error."

"Do you know why I want you and Milu to stay behind?"

"You're a mystery, Kingku Orphius. No one can fathom what goes on in your precious head. I only know I should be at the front lines. Even without the Aquilas, my Pandiva bow and Pugu arrows will send every last Yarjuni to kingdom come. Now I'll have to stay in camp and wait for news. It's maddening."

"I need you to stay behind to execute a most crucial covert operation in our battle plan. Milu will brief you tomorrow. And if you let me take his spot, I'll let you in on a secret."

"I love secrets. Milu's not coming. His spot is all yours."

Kingku playfully rolled over to Serah's side as if he were the carefree boy before the firebombing of Petra, temporarily relinquishing his dignified airs as the Animorta's Supremo.

Their eyes met again. This time, they were so close an arc of electricity seemed to leap between them. Milu crafted a new eye to replace the Opticon. Kingku could see through everything with it except Serah's heart.

Technology helped Kingku forget his physical handicap. But Serah's perfect beauty reminded him of his imperfections, and his heart would be overwhelmed by grief and remorse.

Finally, Kingku realized the unsaid truth. He had always loved Serah. As a boy, Kingku acted distant because he did not recognize the unfamiliar wrench in his heart. He was ecstatic when Professor Stane asked him to look after Serah. He could hardly believe his luck nor disguise his joy. But circumstances changed their destinies. Serah and Milu grew up together and were inseparable. They always walked hand in hand while Kingku watched at a distance. Milu was intelligent and handsome. Serah was vivacious and angelic. The maimed Animorta Supremo, on the other hand, was less than half a man. He was a soulless creature, partly flesh, partly cold metal, haunted by the nightmares of the past, and his heart burned with the undying flames of rage and vitriol. Kingku feared he might have lost his chance with the love of his life.

"You already know," Kingku began, "Professor Stane, may he rest in peace, once entrusted you to me. Unfortunately, the bombs fell, and I couldn't look after anyone. In my absence, Milu has taken excellent care of you, hand-crafting the awesome Pandiva and Pugu arrows to keep you safe. I have not had the proper occasion to thank him. As for tomorrow's battle, we all know how dangerous it will be. We must breach the Great Wall of Sheol to launch a direct assault on Menda City, the Yarjunis' last bastion. I must face Lord Killem and Prince Cambi, and they wield the invincible Last Resort. No one knows if anyone can come out of it alive, let alone unscathed. If I do not emerge victorious, I need Milu to be the next Supremo to continue the struggle and to watch over you as part of my promise to Professor Stane."

Serah placed her hand over Kingku's mouth to prevent him from uttering an unintended curse.

"You will triumph over the Yarjunis," she declared with brave words. "The Sibyl has spoken, and it shall come to pass."

"Your cryptic verses are fanciful vaticinations, not ironclad certainties. The Plancket Uncertainty Principle is infallible on this assessment, the Mahashangria notwithstanding."

"You're right," Serah conceded. "I have no idea where those verses come from. Perhaps my mother taught me when I was young. Some people want to believe I'm the Sibyl. I'm merely going along with everyone's wishes."

"Yet the power of blind faith is real and potent," Kingku said, "which reminds me to thank you for teaching me the Incantation of Creation and Destruction. It transforms every Animorta soldier into a most fearless and fearsome warrior. However, battles are unpredictable. Lord Killem and Prince Cambi will be my biggest test. For the first time, I lack complete confidence in winning a clash of arms. I have a secret locked deep in my heart, which I have not revealed to a single soul. If I don't come back from this battle, I will regret not having disclosed it to you. But I'm not sure if I should. I fear it may bring me disgrace in your eyes."

"Nothing you say or do will ever lessen my regard for you. From the first moment you took up the Animorta's leadership, I have been a part of your relentless campaigns, conquering one Yarjuni vassal after another. You have always charged at the van of pitched battles, reckless of blood and pain. You have caused the fall of all Yarjuni cities and forts, even the impregnable Atro City, until only Menda City remains. You have given us reason to believe in the impossible. By the Final Showdown with Lord Killem, we will end the Endless War. You should know everyone loves and admires you, and you can trust me with your profoundest thoughts. Promise me you'll return safely, and I will also reveal a secret to you."

"Serah, I need to tell you," Kingku stammered in hesitation, "I-I-I … I love … I love … how well you and Milu get along. When you two decide to tie the knot, I wish to officiate your wedding."

At the last moment, Kingku changed his mind. He must never reveal his love for Serah. It would be unfair to her and Milu. Besides, the maimed Supremo did not forget he was half machine. Serah could never love him as she loved Milu. Kingku was ashamed of his selfishness and of being inconsiderate toward those dearest to him. He resolved to lock the secret in the dungeon of his heart and throw away the key.

Of course, Serah noticed what was not said. The pain on Kingku's face betrayed his innermost torment.

"Kiku," Serah said, deliberately using his childhood name, "you must open your heart to me. Release whatever is eating you up. You can confide anything in me, and I will keep your secret, even from Milu, if you want me to."

Kingku would reveal a secret but not the one Serah expected to hear.

"Alright, I'll be honest with you. I have a reason for this uncertainty plaguing me about the outcome of tomorrow's battle,"

Kingku said, following a measured pause. "I had sworn an unbreakable Bhishma Oath in the name of the nameless God I would never raise a weapon against Prince Cambi. I'll have to face him tomorrow, unarmed. The Yarjunis do not discriminate in the slaughtering of their enemies. I have a secret plan to survive our encounter. However, plans are but plans, fallible as the works of mice and men. I also have a Plan B, but not for all contingencies. If I do not return, I hope someone will organize a remembrance of my name. It's a childish and selfish wish, and I'm ashamed."

"Dear Kiku," Serah said. "We all love you and can never bear to lose you. So, you had better return to us in one piece, or we will expire in sadness and despair. You should have trusted us and told us about your friendship with Prince Cambi. No one understands how you can forge such a strong bond with a Yarjuni, not to mention the Crown Prince, but you shouldn't doubt we will always support you. We already guessed your secret some time ago. Why else did you avoid him as if he were the plague? So many times, you could have challenged him and settled the issue, but each time, you veered off to another front and left the matter until the end. Now, promise me you'll come home on your feet; otherwise, I'll throw myself into the Inferno and reduce myself to ashes."

It was Kingku's turn to put his hand over Serah's lips to prevent her from committing sacrilege.

"My dearest Seraphina, whatever happens to me, you must live life to the fullest. I'm comforted knowing Milu loves you very well and will care for you much better than I ever can. I do not want to die, but I have sworn upon the mutilated bodies of my parents and Una to avenge their deaths, come what may. I will pay any price to ensure they did not die in vain. I will come home, I promise you, on my shield if not my feet. In return, you will promise to live a long and joy-filled life, with or without me. If I'm not here to enjoy your sweet love, please give my share to Milu."

Kingku's melancholy words struck Serah's heartstrings, causing her eyes to well up with emotions, and she reached out for Kingku's hand.

It was the first time the one-eyed hero felt his lady's tender touch. All of a sudden, he realized why he had become a true brother to Prince Cambi. It had arisen out of his profound love for Serah. The secret he discovered about her from the Truth Portal was so ironic he dared not tell anyone until shortly before the passing of Professor Stane. Kingku, kneeling by the deathbed, whispered the forbidden words into the Professor's ear. The dying man sighed, let out his last breath and took the secret to his grave.

Serah's touch sent a shock wave through Kingku, who took it to be one of the side effects of his new skin, designed by Milu based on the indestructible hide of Abysso-mamba, the Great Worm of Shangria. The technical description of the artificial epidermis was "Transmutable nano-twinned amorphous Boron Nitride Proteus epidermis on self-healing 1.1□magic angle offset multi-layer molybdenum graphene-borophene bonded polymer substrate doped with Indium, Vanadium and Neodymium."

Serah also experienced a shockwave. In the blink of an eye, she realized she had always known her grim fate with Kingku. She remembered an oracle she had uttered long ago in a trance, cryptic words with no meaning at the time. The revelation cut her to the quick, crushing her tender soul. Serah wept pearly drops of blood, as tears were not allowed for her kind. She discreetly wiped them to hide her grief. How she wished she were not the Sibyl!

Chapter 38

Dies Irae

Travelling by hover chariot from his camp, Kingku reached the Great Wall of Sheol upon sunrise. The Animorta was already deployed before the Gate of Tartaros, poised to breach the wall by storm upon the Supremo's command. Once upon a time, the fortification surrounded the enemies of the Yarjunis, strangling them under a stifling siege. Kingku turned the tables and imprisoned the Yarjunis within their own walls.

Majestically arrayed in silver armour and black mantle, godlike Kingku led his elite guards to the front of the Animorta army. Purple banners displaying his motto, "*Recalcitrat Undique Tutus*," billowed and fluttered in the wind. Kingku raised Lituus, once his golden baton but now a blind man's cane, and commanded, "Transmigurate!" Thereupon, the stick manifested its magnificent form, a two-metre walking staff known as the Nephrustan.

Three black birds circled the sky, announcing their arrival with boisterous squawks. One of them landed on top of the Nephrustan, unfurling its wings to mimic the military standard of the Animorta. Kingku raised his left arm, allowing the second bird to land on his fist while the third settled on his helmet. These winged predators were drones known as Aquilas. The one on Kingku's fist was named Munin, meaning "memory," the one on his helmet was Hugin, meaning "thought," and the one on the Nephrustan was Augin, meaning "sight." Milu crafted these lifelike drones to help Kingku defeat Lord Killem in the Final Showdown.

"Animorta warriors," Kingku addressed his troops. "Today marks the day of reckoning for the Yarjunis. Beyond these walls lies Menda City, their capital and an impregnable bastion. Lord Killem and Prince Cambi will take their last stand before its front gate. We shall settle the score today. Some of us will fall, but we have no fear because of who we are. We are …"

"Animorta, the soul-dead. *Ave Supremo*! *Morituri te salutant*," roared the army of invalids in one voice as the Aquilas took flight into the golden amber sky.

The one-eyed rebel leader disembarked from his hover chariot and led the troops in a silent march toward the Great Wall of Sheol. Drummers held their sticks in check, trumpeters removed the mouthpieces from their instruments, and no one made a peep, not even a cough. The Animorta forged on with solemn resolve, shaking the ground with each step. As the Army of the Soul-Dead drew within range of Yarjuni weapons, a barrage of fiery slugs rained upon their ranks. The bullets, however, bounced off the soldiers, falling harmlessly at their feet.

Raising the Nephrustan, Kingku roared, "Halt," and the entire army came to a standstill. While the Yarjuni defenders were reloading for another volley, Kingku rammed the Staff of Power on the ground, drawing a hellish howl from the depths of the planet's bowels. He thrust the staff into the earth again, creating a terrible tremor. Cracks began to spread along the Great Wall of Sheol as the defenders on the ramparts fled for their lives. The Animorta Supremo raised the Nephrustan for the third time and drove it into the ground while bellowing the command of destruction, "Ashiverate," bringing down the Great Wall of Sheol and the Gate of Tartaros. Nothing stood between the Animorta and their final objective, Menda City, the Yarjunis' last bastion.

The march to Menda City would take half a day. The Yarjunis had expected the attack, having raised extensive defensive works before the city walls. They had positioned and aimed massive, cunningly wrought dealers of death at the approaching Animorta. The Yarjunis had prepared a bloodbath for their uninvited guests.

Midway through the Animorta's march of death, the Aquila Augin returned from reconnaissance, reporting the evidence of a minefield up front, where the Yarjunis had buried a prodigious amount of Erinysite. When ignited, the infernal flames would incinerate everyone to ashes. Erinysite was the source of the Yarjuni's wealth and power. It was as if they were prepared to burn all their money to win the war.

Kingku selected twenty "forlorn hopes" from the elite guards and bade them discard their arms. After conducting a detailed inspection of their armour and cloaks, he led them into the minefield while the rest of the army stayed behind.

Kingku, the cunning one-eyed leader of the Animorta, was famous for making unexpected moves, and the Yarjunis expected him to do the unexpected. But the amazed and perplexed Lord Killem and Prince Cambi, observing enemy movements through their telescopes, never expected to see the Animorta Supremo march defenceless and unarmed into an Erinysite minefield.

Much water had passed under the bridge since Kingku as Deskull decamped to join the Animorta at the Hellian March. Prince Cambi became the captain of the Revenants. Outfitted in black armour and nicknamed the Black Prince, he wielded a divine weapon known as the Flagellum Dia, the Scourge of God, which would pulverize its unfortunate victims into countless smithereens.

As Kingku and his "forlorn hopes" entered the Erinysite minefield, Lord Killem gestured for the ignition countdown.

"Cambi, you may bid farewell to your erstwhile brother," Lord Killem said. "This is the end of the story for the traitor."

Prince Cambi wished it did not have to come to this, but he could not stop Lord Killem. The Yarjuni's survival was at stake.

The flames of Erinysite rose with the violence of a volcanic eruption, engulfing Kingku and his men. The Yarjunis celebrated, believing they had vaporized their worst nightmare in the blink of an eye, but they believed wrong.

"I see something moving inside the blaze," Prince Cambi cried. "It's impossible! The flame of Erinysite melts even tungsten."

"Inconceivable!" Lord Killem remarked darkly. "We have underestimated the Animorta. Fie on Plancket. It can only be his work. I should've broken his neck when I had the chance."

According to myth, the Great Worm Abysso-mamba burrowed underground until it reached the Eternal Inferno. The flames did not harm it. After ingesting a bellyful of Erinysite, the Great Worm brought the treasure to Lord Abaddon. Milu developed Kingku's artificial epidermis from the moulted skin of Abysso-mamba, which could withstand extremely high temperatures. The "forlorn hopes" had received similar treatment for their armour and cloaks, rendering them fire-resistant and bulletproof.

Meanwhile, the flames sizzled all over and around Kingku, his ears ringing with the howling of the firestorm and the caterwauling of the lost souls offered to the gods by the holocaust. It reminded him of being barbecued by the Fire of Orc. Fortunately, for this occasion, he suffered neither heat nor pain. He could, however, succumb to suffocation. Kingku promptly raised the Nephrustan and uttered the Incantation of Creation and Destruction.

"Anil nathrach, ortha bhis is beatha, do chal danaimh."

At the same time, he smote the ground with his staff, creating a hypersonic seismic wave and, incredibly, extinguished the unquenchable flames of Erinysite, sending a massive mushroom cloud into the stratosphere.

Every Yarjuni warrior gawked at the prodigy with eyes wide opwn and mouth agape as Kingku and his "forlorn hopes" survived the Erinysite flames, emerging scatheless from the soupy fumes.

"Lord Killem, I extend my most humble thanks for your hospitality," Kingku thundered, his voice amplified and projected by the three Aquilas circling the sky above him. "As you can see, we are unarmed. We do not seek battle. Today, we seek a truce, allowing both sides of this conflict to enjoy a respite from the incessant killing. Hopefully, people could get used to peace."

"Ingrate, turncoat, guttersnipe, whippersnapper, lickspittle, vermin of Badlam, scum of Abyssum," Lord Killem vituperated with a litany of opprobria. "I dug you out of your early grave, plucked you from your lowest of the low dung pit and elevated you to our highest Yarjun Warrior caste. I spared no expense to mend your handicaps and empower you. I educated you in the art of war and made you a leader, even adopting you as my son. And how did you repay me? You ran off to join the Animorta."

The Yarjuni soldiers, to a man, spat in contempt.

"You led them to attack our vassals and protectorates," Lord Killem continued. "Now you lead your beggar army into my stronghold unarmed. What more can I say? You seek death."

"Lord Killem, I died the day you destroyed Petra and slaughtered my family. I was once Yarjuni, but only as a victim of your deception. I am now Animorta, the soul-dead, and the dead have no fear. I come, however, not to fight or dig up the past. For the sake of my brotherhood with Prince Cambi, I come to offer peace. And I offer life for the Yarjunis. I even offer forgiveness, though I cannot forget. Choose peace, and we shall live without fear of each other. Choose war, and you shall all perish, the Yarjun caste eradicated and the name purged from memory. The choice is yours. If you wish to discuss the offer with your counsellors, I'll be here until the Witching Hour, awaiting your answer."

"Ha, yes! Crown Prince Cambi, my flesh and blood, who will one day succeed me and become the Supremo Lord of the Yarjunis. He is indeed your brother. But it means less than nothing after you become a traitor. We need no counsel. Prince Cambi will personally demonstrate what we do to turncoats. He will cut your heart out and feast on it."

Upon his father's order, the Black Prince, accompanied by his personal guards, approached Kingku. The brothers commanded their men to stay behind as they met at the rendezvous point.

"Has life treated you well after our parting?" Kingku asked.

"Not as well as you, apparently," Cambi replied. "But here we are on the battlefield, fighting against each other in an existential struggle. Since you're unarmed, I'll let you turn around and walk away. Go now and do not show your face again. My Flagellum Dia holds no mercy for anyone."

"Cambi, listen to me," Kingku, taking grave risks to avert tragedy, had no choice but to reveal the truth. "Lord Killem is not your father. Not only did he deceive you about your identity, but he also murdered your father. Years ago, Lord Killem became mad with desire over a red-haired beauty and was enraged because she loved your true father instead, who was the opposite of Lord Killem in every way, despite sharing the same genes. Your true sire is Lord Strongarm, the identical twin brother of Lord Killem. Your parents ran off and lived among the rebels as Leelord and Leela until the Revenants captured your father and locked him up in the dungeons of Badlam, where they broke him upon the wheel. Unable to gain your mother's submission by guile or by threat, Lord Killem threw her into an oubliette, where she gave birth to your sister, while he raised you as his son. Tragically, your mother died in a prison escape, but your sister lives. She is with the Animorta. Join us, and we shall end the Endless War together."

"What plumbless piffle!" Prince Cambi cried. "Where, pray tell, did you gather this fabulous figment?"

"I've read your top-secret classified files, Cambi. Though it sounds crazy, it is, unfortunately, the plain truth."

Prince Cambi was troubled by what Kingku said. He had heard whisperings in backstairs and dark corridors about him having a sister, supposedly dead after a difficult childbirth, which also led to their mother's tragic demise, a topic forbidden for discussion.

"Take a hike back to your dung heap and never return," Prince Cambi cried. "If I see you again, I shall not hold back my Flagellum Dia."

Prince Cambi turned around and marched back to his post beside Lord Killem.

"Pepé Killem, I take no joy killing unarmed men. Besides, when we were young, Deskull swore an unbreakable Bhishma Oath never to fight me. As long as I'm here, he will not attack us because the day he raises a weapon against me is the day he cuts out his own heart."

"But he is in our face, threatening us with his peace offer. Should we ignore him? What do you think about his claim you're the son of my criminally insane renegade brother?"

Prince Cambi was surprised but not shocked his father had placed him under surveillance. Lord Killem did not trust anyone, not even his son. The Yarjunis lived in a highly distrustful society.

"It was a ploy to sow discord with deception," Prince Cambi said. "I have no reason to believe his lies. Tell him to take a walk or be bombed to oblivion."

"Treacherous scum," Lord Killem turned around and roared at Kingku. "Since the Prince excuses himself from staining his hands with your unclean and unholy blood, I will demonstrate what we do to traitors, the same way I gave my brother, Thomas the Strong of Arm, his due for betraying the caste and clan."

Without forewarning, the Yarjun Supremo unsheathed Prince Cambi's deadly dagger, Xiphos, and thrust the bodkin through a chink in the young man's armour into his heart, cruelly twisting the wavy blade as he plucked the cursèd steel away. The Black Prince was both surprised and shocked, staring at his own blood gushing forth from the gaping wound. Before he had time to say Taras Bulba, darkness shrouded the Prince's eyes as he succumbed to dolorous death.

"No-o-o-o-o-o!" Kingku cried, charging toward Lord Killem. To a man, the entire Animorta army followed and surged forward.

"Ha-ha-ha-ha!" Lord Killem laughed with maniacal giddiness. "The Animorta has a fond boy and a nincompoop for their leader, offering us life and peace indeed. Let us return the favour and offer the cretins a taste of our MOANs, the Mother Of All Nooks."

Lord Killem climbed to the top of the main watchtower and shouted at Kingku, "Dog-faced maggot, you have caused Cambi's death. Now, you will pay with your life."

Lord Killem stretched out his arms and gazed upward at the golden amber sky as if praying for supplication to the God of Retribution, roaring the command of death, "Expectorate!" Scores of MOAN missiles erupted from their silos and split the air with their ear-busting, skin-crawling, hair-raising, mind-numbing, soul-crushing screams of banshees toward Kingku and the Animorta army. Meanwhile, the Yarjuni defenders riddled the enemy's ranks with a hail of hot lead from their Exponential Blunderbusses.

The Yarjunis expected every Animorta attacker to perish in short order. But as the Sibyl prophesied, the one-eyed hero ended the Endless War instead, obliterating Menda City while disarming the Last Resort, all without firing a spitball. He erased the Yarjun caste from memory and started the New Golden Age of Shangria, becoming the One King to rule them all. As for how he achieved the impossible, it's a fantastical tale for another time.

Chapter 39

Story of the Stone

It had been three months since Victoria woke up in a farmer's hut, a bit dazed but none the worse for wear. She was lucky an old peasant found her in the fields, whose wife cleaned her up, dressed her, fed her and put together a half-decent bed for her to sleep in.

Victoria wondered why people possessing precious little would share whatever they had with a stranger. Indeed, it was a tradition for many ancient cultures to be hospitable to strangers, particularly if they needed help. Perhaps it was people hoping to add diversity to the local gene pool or believing karma would someday repay their kind act in an hour of need. It was a good policy until wars based on fear and deception destroyed trust.

Leona's ray gun combined the effects of a stun gun with quantum transport. It would have seriously damaged mere mortals. Fortunately, Victoria inherited exceptional recuperative powers, and she quickly recovered. But she found herself trapped in an unfamiliar world with no means to return to where and when she was supposed to be. Victoria did not understand the local language. Other than figuring out she was in ancient China, she had no idea of her exact location or year. She had left her LV knapsack containing the *Book of Heavenly Secrets*, the Magic Mirror, also known as the Celestial Catoptron, and her unicorn rings in the Qaanaaq. How could she return to Ultima Thule to stop Queen Lilith from exterminating the human race?

After acclimatizing herself to the free-range chickens, curious villagers and the persistent aroma of manure, Victoria decided to learn the language and integrate with the locals. Only through these efforts could she hope to find Shang descendants with the wherewithal to help her journey back to the future.

Endowed with her parents' high language aptitude, learning a spoken dialect for Victoria was a cakewalk. All it took was about a month of immersion for her to talk fluently to the villagers, while the writing took slightly longer. Since the simple folks around her were illiterate, she had to learn basic calligraphy and reading from the village teacher, Mister Liang, a failed scholar who had given up trying to pass the national exam. On the whole, it had been surprisingly easy for Victoria, a Canadian girl from a small town in Ontario, to adapt to this altogether weird time and place.

During this period of exploration and learning, Victoria established a few facts. Her village was about a day-long journey by foot from a major city on the Yangzi River named Jiangning, meaning "river peace." The villagers, however, referred to the city as Nanjing, "South Capital," which received the moniker after the Ming Dynasty's third emperor, one of its most influential, Yongle (1360–1424 CE), relocated the capital from this city to Beijing, "North Capital," which people referred to as Jingshi, or "Capital City." Emperor Yongle's favourite court eunuch, Zheng He (1371–1433 CE), a Muslim, was famous for having undertaken seven maritime expeditions, one of which reached eastern Africa.

Victoria learned she had landed in China during the Qing Dynasty. It was the twenty-fifth year of Emperor Qianlong's (1711–1799 CE) reign. Victoria finally appreciated the importance of learning history lessons about China from David Huang. Her Gamebox experience helped her understand where and when she was; otherwise, she would never find her way back.

Victoria remembered the Qing Dynasty of China lasted for two hundred and sixty-eight years, ending in early 1912, making its starting year 1644 CE.

The village teacher, Mister Liang, told Victoria the famous tale of China's first Manchu emperor, Shunzhi (1638–1661 CE), who died at the tender age of twenty-three. Many commoners believed he did not die but became a monk after his beloved consort met an untimely death. His reign was seventeen years. The next to sit on the throne, Kangxi (1654–1722 CE), was one of the longest-lived emperors of China, overseeing the blossoming of the Qing Dynasty. He ruled for sixty-one years and was succeeded by an illustrious though short-lived emperor, Yongzheng (1678–1735 CE), who was rumoured to have stolen his throne and died at the hands of an assassin. He ruled for thirteen years, followed by Qianlong. Victoria did some arithmetic and concluded the twenty-fifth year of Emperor Qianlong's reign was 1760 CE. Victoria had arrived early in the summer. She only built up enough confidence to start finding her way home around mid-autumn.

The old peasant couple had a son named Niu Dashi. His family name, Niu, means "cow," and his given name, Dashi, means "big stone." He was never home, a consequence of his employment as a lowly footman at the Jiangning Department of Textiles in Nanjing. Although the position paid a piddling stipend, it was a prestigious one for someone with a peasant background. Dashi got the job only because a distant relative had been a servant at the department since Emperor Kangxi's reign. Nevertheless, his poor father had to borrow from everyone he knew to pay the hefty employment fee.

While Dashi was a nameless grunt in the massive machinery of the government, he was clever enough to leverage the long service of his kinsman and the prestige of his employer to make something of himself. He slowly worked his way up to become a trusted courier, a job with many opportunities to glimpse the lives of the rich and powerful and, at the same time, earn a respectable income from gratuities, often paid by both ends of the delivery jobs he would perform from time to time.

The extensive premises of the Jiangning Department of Textiles used to be the home of Cao Yin (1658–1712 CE), the court official in charge of the department and a childhood friend and confidante of Emperor Kangxi, serving more as the Emperor's eyes and ears than a government official. Misfortune befell the Cao family when Kangxi's son, Emperor Yongzheng, evicted them and confiscated everything they owned during the fifth year of his short reign, leaving the Cao family destitute. Yongzheng's son, Emperor Qianlong, took over the manor as his travel palace. Historical records indicated Emperor Kangxi visited the south six times during his reign, five of which he had stayed at the Cao Manor. One could only imagine the grandeur of this palatial building complex during her glory years.

At first blush, none of these would get Victoria any closer to finding a quantum gateway until Niu Dashi came home for the Autumn Moon Festival. Tanned and muscular, the young man proudly displayed the characteristics of his peasantry stock. At the same time, he was square-jawed and round-browed, with dark, intelligent eyes darting here and there, always trying to figure things out. More importantly, he had a genial disposition and a knack for relating anecdotes without resorting to rumours, calumnies or hyperboles. He reinvented himself as a raconteur and fabulist, which contributed to his modest success working as a footman for the government.

The old folks were overjoyed to see their only son. They had many other children, but none survived past childhood. Such was life in the olden days, an admixture of deaths, lost dreams and broken hearts. All the hopes of the Niu family rested squarely on the shoulders of Dashi, and the young man did not disappoint, bringing home many presents and delicacies, such as brined ducks, moon cakes, printed fabrics and distilled liquors, from the big city for his parents, relatives and neighbours.

Dashi was thrilled to see a pretty girl living in his home. He thought his parents had found him a wife. While he was crestfallen to learn he had made a wrong assumption, he would not be discouraged from trying his best to achieve such an eventuality. Dashi spent the evening chatting up Victoria, hoping to learn all he could about the mysterious girl. He would not be successful. Victoria had, by this time, worked out a plausible amnesia story. She could tell nothing if she remembered nothing. She heeded Sting's warning to exercise caution regarding the dangers of causality paradoxes. Meanwhile, Dashi painted a pretty picture of his life in the big city, working for princes, dukes and governors.

"Niu Da'ge," Victoria said, using a disarming term meaning "big brother" to ensure Dashi kept his hands to himself while acceding to her wishes. "Will you stay long this time? When will you go back to Nanjing? Won't you take me along to visit?"

"I have a job to deliver something to Jingshi," Dashi replied. "I'm taking advantage of the Moon Festival to drop by and visit the old folks. Look what I found. The moon goddess Chang'e is staying at my home. I'll stay an extra day for the honour, but I must be on my way. If you are serious about visiting Nanjing, I'll have to organize proper lodgings, you'll need a chaperone, and it has to wait until I return from Jingshi."

"What an exciting life you have!" Victoria exclaimed. "How I wish I could travel and see the world! Can you tell me stories about your job and the high officials you work for?"

"My number one big boss is the Governor of Two Rivers," Dashi explained, getting all puffed up by identifying himself as the underling of a powerful aristocratic official, "in charge of the three provinces of Jiangsu, Jiangxi and Anhui, His Grace Yin Jishan

(1695−1771 CE). His office has asked me to deliver a package to a down-and-out wordsmith. I don't suppose you'd be interested."

"I'm all ears," Victoria purred as she poured more rice wine for Dashi. "I want to learn all about your exciting life."

"Well, okay. Listen up," Dashi, prone to be loquacious after several quaffs of the ambrosia, could not resist the temptation to extemporize. "I got this job mainly because I'm acquainted with the recipient of the package, who now lives in the western suburbs of Jingshi. His name is Cao Zhan (1715−1763 CE), courtesy name Xueqin, "Snow Celery." He claims to be a scion of the once illustrious Cao clan and once lived within the premises of the Jiangning Department of Textiles decades ago, relocating to Jingshi after Emperor Yongzheng evicted the Cao family. Of course, no one believed him until my relative, who worked for the Cao family, bumped into him and started reminiscing about the good old days. Those must have been poignant memories because Mr. Cao wept tears enough to fill a fish tank. And, by gum, the man was a sot. I lost count of the litres of liquor he guzzled. Thankfully, the pub owner was a friend and let me run a tab.

"Mr. Cao had not returned to his birthplace for decades. Governor Yin had retained him to work on a cultural project last autumn. So he took the opportunity to visit his old haunts and shed a few tears of nostalgia. By coincidence, Mr. Cao has been writing a novel about life in the Cao Manor. The book is a work in progress and still in manuscript form, but everyone at the Governor's office who read it loved it, including Governor Yin. When Mr. Cao had to return to Jingshi at the end of the project, the Governor borrowed the manuscript to make a copy for his private library. Though it took longer than expected, the scribe finally completed the job. The Governor has granted me the privilege of returning the manuscript and delivering a personal gift."

"What's the book's title? Can I flip through it?"

"Mr. Cao hasn't decided on a name yet. He did mention *The Story of the Stone* as the book's provisional title. I believe an older version was titled *The Treasure Mirror of the Wind and the Moon.* He also mentioned *Dream of the Red Chamber.* The book has too many names. As for letting you flip through the manuscript, I'm afraid I can't. Governor Yin's office has sealed the package. If you want to read it, you may have to ask the author himself."

Victoria remembered talking to her mom about the *Dream of the Red Chamber.* The book was titled *The Story of the Stone* because it was about a heavenly stone incarnated on Earth as the son of a powerful official. Was it coincidence her mom was reading the book, and did it have something to do with the mysterious one-eyed Stone Man? The story took place in Nanjing, which was nicknamed the City of Stone. Furthermore, the person telling Victoria about all this was named Dashi, "Big Stone."

The Canadian teenage time-traveller received a jolt when she heard the book was alternatively named *The Treasure Mirror of the Wind and the Moon.* It was too similar to one of the names of the Magic Mirror, the *Looking Glass of the Favonus Wind and Twin Moons.* As the saying goes, there is no coincidence, only the illusion of coincidence. Someone must know something about the dimension-tunnelling Catoptron. Its mention in the Chinese classic was a secret advertisement seeking a missing person lost in the vastness of time and an ocean of humanity, namely Victoria, which meant only one thing; she must meet Cao Xueqin, the author of *Dream of the Red Chamber.*

Chapter 40

The Grand Canal Cruise

"Niu Da'ge, will you be a big brother and take me along to Jingshi, pretty please?" Victoria pleaded, adding treacle to her request. "I have a hunch I'm from the Capital. If I see the city gates or the Drum Tower, my memories may come back. I promise I won't create any headaches for you."

"You are already giving me a headache," Dashi said, not swallowing Victoria's unconvincing story because of her local accent, but secretly pleased his chances of gaining the hand of this fairy goddess had suddenly improved. "I mean, I can take you, but you'll need a chaperone. Otherwise, you'll have to go as my wife, which is fine by me. So, what do you say?"

"I don't think it's appropriate," Victoria said, thinking, *Good try, but no cigars, dude.* Without missing a beat, she continued, "On the other hand, if you help me find my family, you'll have our eternal gratitude. Besides, I know how to solve the chaperone problem. I can travel as a man."

Dashi had reservations but found himself inexplicably acceding to every one of Victoria's capricious demands. He soon tasted a substantial sampling of Victoria's power of persuasion when they went to procure a man's outfit for her from the county tailor. Victoria bedazzled the dour dressmaker with her expert haggling delivered with honeyed words of unctuous praise. She dramatically slashed the price from four taels of silver down to eight maces, an eighty percent discount, which left Dashi, who had seen everything in the big city, absolutely gobsmacked. The mesmerized sempster, a notorious penny-pincher and a skinflint not known to be pliable on prices, had no idea what hit him. In addition to the discount, Victoria could pay whenever her financial situation permitted. Dashi was determined to learn Victoria's negotiation skills in case he failed in his pursuit of marriage.

When Victoria tried on the long robes, the riding jacket known as *Magua*, cotton pants, cloth shoes and a beanie on her head, carefully tucking her hair in while leaving a pigtail hanging down her back, she took on the appearance of a handsome young man from the Qing Dynasty.

Dashi had planned to deliver the package on horseback, which meant the trip would be dirty, bumpy, prone to accidents and dangerous, especially if one ran into bandits. However, the job would be short and profitable, though it would not be a desirable journey for a young girl from Canada, disguised or not.

Victoria again had her way, and they decided to take a more leisurely cruise along the Grand Canal, travelling by the same route the Jesuit priest Mateo Ricci took in 1600 CE. It would be a safe and comfortable arrangement, albeit bordering on extravagant. The Grand Canal is an ancient engineering wonder connecting Hangzhou in the south with Beijing. It was an infrastructure built about a thousand years before Ricci's time. By this watery belt, northern China and southern China became integrated into one China. The Grand Canal was also a courier route, giving Dashi the perfect excuse to take the cruise. As for the expenses, Dashi left it up to the mysterious girl to handle the negotiations.

Victoria, of course, made sure she had her private cabin and admonished Dashi to keep his fantasies to himself; otherwise, she would send him flying into the canal for a long, cold bath.

Before they set off, Papa Niu took Dashi aside and gave him a package, bidding him to deliver it to a relative living in the Capital.

For the first leg of the journey, their boat glided downstream on the Yangzi River to the city of Zhenjiang, nationally renowned for its dark vinegar, where they turned north onto the Grand Canal, passing through Jiangsu Province along the battlefields of the decisive Huai-Hai Campaign between the People's Liberation Army and the Nationalist Army in the future. They crossed Shandong Province, where General Su Yu's Eastern China Field Army would storm the impregnable fortress of the provincial capital, Jinan, and took it in only eight days, and finally entered Hebei Province, arriving at the port city of Tianjin after four weeks. From this bustling trade hub and port, they travelled the last leg of the journey to the end of the Grand Canal in Tongzhou, where Victoria witnessed, via David Huang's VR Gamebox, the Anglo-French soldiers rout the Qing defenders of Beijing in the Second Opium War a hundred years hence.

Victoria sated her senses with the sights and sounds along the way, enjoying being lavishly feted by Dashi with the various styles of local cuisine. During their conversations, Victoria discovered the secrets behind the Niu family. Nothing was as it seemed, and she likely did not end up where she was by accident.

"What are you delivering for Papa Niu?" Victoria pried.

"It's nothing," Dashi replied. "I'm taking an old book and a folding paper fan to a distant relative I've never met before."

"Can I have a look? Papa Niu didn't seal the package."

"You're a nosy one, aren't you?" Dashi said as he showed Victoria the book. "It's personal stuff, but I'll make an exception for you. This curious book has been collecting dust in the family for generations, but Pops says it belongs to the north, and some clan elders have asked him to send it to an important family member in Jingshi. The chore will not be as simple as it sounds. The man is supposed to be a top official, a renowned scholar and a wealthy collector of ancient scrolls. But he doesn't know me. I won't be able to get near him without spending a fortune. Maybe you can help me negotiate my way into his presence."

Victoria was speechless, staring at the *Book of Heavenly Secrets*. She realized she was on the right track for finding her way back to the future.

"I'll see what I can do," said the stunned girl when she finally found her tongue. "What is your relative's name?"

"Pops says his name is Zhu Yun (1729–1781 CE). I've never heard of this blood kin, probably because his branch survived by collaborating with the Manchu invaders. Those rats! He's supposed to be so famous in Jingshi I shouldn't have any trouble locating him."

"His family name is Zhu, and yours is Niu," Victoria said. "How are you two blood kin? Are you pulling my leg?"

"We have the same patrilineal ancestor. It's a convoluted tale, some of it fantastic and mostly unbelievable. I say no more."

"Don't be such a killjoy. Where did this book come from, and how did it end up in your family? Humour me. And explain why Zhu and Niu belong to the same lineage."

"Suppose I tell you what Pops told me. You won't believe a word of it, and you'll laugh me off the boat."

"Oh, Niu Da'ge, I would do no such thing. Pray tell."

"Alright, but don't you dare guffaw or chortle."

Victoria put her hands on her mouth and shook her head.

"According to Pops, our Niu (牛) family, which means 'cow,' originated from the Zhu (朱) family, which means 'red.' Notice the similarity between the words? As you know, it's not uncommon for people to change their names for many reasons. Now, the old man says this is not any common Zhu lineage," Dashi lowered his voice into a hush, "but the royal Zhu family of the Ming Dynasty."

"Oh, shut up!"

"See, you don't believe me. Okay, I'm done talking."

"I'm sorry, my bad," Victoria filled Dashi's cup with rice wine. "Keep talking, I'll shut up."

"Fine, but no more jeers. What I'm about to recount may seem to be a fabulous tale from the *Book of Mountains and Seas.* The first patriarch of my Niu branch, my great-great-grandfather, was a well-known painter and a Taoist monk named Niu Shihui (1628–1707 CE), 'stone wise.' Now you know why Pops named me Dashi, Big Stone. It comes from Wise Stone. Our Niu patriarch's older brother, a Buddhist monk and a painter, is famous to this day. Some of his paintings may be worth a king's ransom. I wish he had left me one. He is known as Bada Shanren (1626–1705 CE), literally 'eight great mountains man.' The brothers were ninth-generation descendants of Ming Taizu (1328–1398 CE), the mendicant monk who became king."

"With the help of the mysterious Stone Man With One Eye," Victoria thought. "Ming Taizu's wife was a secret Shang."

"The brothers grew up during the collapse of the Ming Dynasty," Dashi continued, "and nomads from the north were overrunning the country. Being of royal blood, they refused to submit to Manchurian rule, and one way to survive was to become monks. However, having the Zhu name of the Ming's royal house was dangerous. So they invented noms de guerre. Notice how when you put together Niu (牛), 'cow,' and Ba (八), 'eight,' you get Zhu (朱), 'red'? The two brothers' fake names combine to form their original family name.

"According to Pops, this book I'm taking to Zhu Yun is supposed to be full of esoteric arcana, and it was originally a gift bequeathed to Ming Taizu from his wizardlike strategist, Liu Ji (1311–1375 CE), better known as Liu Bowen. Since no one understood the book, people deemed it worthless and ignored it. After Taizu ascended to heaven, the book somehow passed into the hands of his seventeenth son, Zhu Quan (1378–1448 CE), my direct ancestor. It bounced around over the years until it ended up in my family, probably because no one wanted it."

"It's a wild yarn but not impossible, I'll grant you that. What about the fan? Can I have a peek?"

Dashi spread the folding fan to show Victoria a familiar sight. It would one day hang on the wall of her bedroom.

"Does the fan have a background story?" Victoria asked.

"Everything has a story. This fan is my family's only valuable possession. It fell onto our lap under unusual circumstances. But now I'll have to present it as a gift to Zhu Yun. Otherwise, he'll kick me out as an imposter."

Although the fan hung on her bedroom wall, Victoria did not know what the poem was about. Having taken Chinese lessons from Teacher Liang, she tried to decipher it with Dashi's help.

[昨夜星辰昨夜風]

Last night's starlight. Last night's breeze,

[畫樓西畔桂堂東]

West of the ornate tower. East of the Osmanthus Hall.

[身無彩鳳雙飛翼]

My body lacked the two wings of the colourful phoenix,

[心有靈犀一點通]

But the rhinoceros (one-horned creature, a unicorn) spirit in our hearts connected us by a wink.

[隔座送鉤春酒暖]

In alternate seats, we passed the tokens for warm spring wine,

[分曹射覆蠟燈紅]

Under the red candlelight, we guessed the drinking tokens.

[嗟余聽鼓應官去]

Alas, I heard the official's drums summoning me to work,

[走馬蘭台類轉蓬]

I raced horseback to the Orchid office as a reed in the wind.

***

[唐李商隱]
Tang Dynasty Li Shangyin
[無題]
Untitled

It was the first time Victoria realized the famous Tang Dynasty poet's name had a special meaning. The given name of Li Shangyin (813–858 CE) meant "hidden Shang." For some reason, this Shang descendant authored a nameless poem, alluding to the mythical mind-reading unicorn by referencing the rhinoceros.

"How did this treasure end up in your family?" Victoria asked.

"Pops said, when he was a kid, a neighbour gifted this fan to the family. People used to call this person Stonehead, which means 'stone idiot,' referring to his intellectually challenged nature. Apparently, Stonehead came over one evening and gave this fan to my grandpa without saying why or wherefore. The sheriff arrested the idiot the next morning and confiscated his property. Nobody knew what happened to him or ever saw him again.

"My grandpa said although Stonehead was destitute, he owned twenty rare and valuable fans. No one knew how he came to possess them, and only a few close friends, including Grandpa, had seen the precious collection after swearing themselves to secrecy. When one of them ratted out the fans to people at the Cao household of the Jiangning Department of Textiles, then the most powerful family in Nanjing, a Cao buyer showed up offering a phenomenal sum for the fans. It was a fortune for Stonehead but a rounding error for the Cao family's daily petty cash account.

"For whatever reason, the idiot refused to sell the fans. Next thing you know, an official, incidentally also a Cao, arrested Stonehead for delinquency in repayment of a nonexistent debt. Since the bumpkin had no money, the official took possession of his home and auctioned everything off. It was all conducted under the rule of law. Perhaps someone tipped off Stonehead the sheriff was coming for him, and he gave this fan to my grandpa rather than let the Cao people take everything. Poor Stonehead learned too late you don't own anything you cannot defend or hide."

"Do the rich and powerful always act this way?" Victoria asked, remembering Queen Lilith's excoriation of the human race.

"Pretty much. But sometimes, karma rides the whirlwind and lashes the wrongdoers. Emperor Yongzheng evicted the mighty Cao family from the magnificent Cao Manor and confiscated all their belongings. The Cao descendants do not possess even one of those precious fans for which their powerful patriarchs committed rapine and murder."

In any event, Niu Dashi's package reached Zhu Yun, who was pleasantly surprised to receive such a valuable gift from a stranger claiming to be a relative. Recognizing the "hidden Shang" on the paper fan, he stowed the *Book of Heavenly Secrets* in his library. Zhu Yun was a child prodigy, a Qing official and a renowned bibliophile with a library of thirty thousand books, the largest private collection in China at the time. It included works from the patriarch of the Cao household at Jiangning, Cao Yin, whose family would produce one of the greatest authors of all time.

Later, Zhu Yun would become an editor of the *Encyclopedia of the Four Libraries.* The *Book of Heavenly Secrets* would end up in one of the four libraries at the Old Summer Palace, which the Anglo-French soldiers would loot and burn after the last battle of the Second Opium War. Being constructed with the indestructible hide of Abysso-mamba, the *Book of Heavenly Secrets* survived the fire and was picked up by a one-eyed hobo. Through a blind fortune-teller, it would pass to Michael Solana outside of Guangzhou's White Swan Hotel, where foreign families adopting children in China usually stayed. And the book ended up in Victoria's knapsack to help her reset the universe one day.

Oh, what a tangled web we've spun!

Chapter 41

The Nuns' Story

It was a long trip from Tongzhou, even by mule carriage, going north around the Beijing city walls to the north-western suburbs known as Xiangshan, "Fragrant Hills." The neighbourhood was and still is known as Zheng Baiqi, or "Plain White Banner," a residential area taken over by the Manchurian tribes when they first occupied Beijing and started the Qing Dynasty. Today, it is outside Fifth Ring Road within the Haidian District, the technology hub of the modern capital city. Cao Xueqin belonged to the Zheng Baiqi tribe. Being a penniless writer, he returned to live in his tribe's old settlement area.

After making quick work of a light breakfast, Dashi and Victoria started their chilly and bumpy journey, stopping for lunch and washroom breaks along the way, and arriving late afternoon when the crepuscular light of the setting sun was at the cusp of fading away. Candles and oil lamps were lighting up the rows of simple brick houses. The driver asked around and finally took the worn-out passengers to a dwelling with three Scholar trees in front. The slanted tree on the east side marked Cao's humble abode.

Before setting out, Dashi had sent a rider to notify Cao of his arrival so the author could prepare for his guests' reception. As the Governor's gift-bearing courier, Dashi would enjoy the proper hospitality, which extended to his travel companion.

Victoria was surprised to see China's GOAT author in a wretched and decrepit state. Cao was prematurely grey, his face sallow, gaunt and stubbly, and his skin jaundiced from heavy drinking. He also reeked of rotgut. Cao Xueqin was only forty-five, but his health was in irretrievable decline because of his famously bibulous ways. He would have three more years to live, expiring before he completed his masterpiece, bequeathing a mountain of mysteries for future readers and scholars to decipher.

Cao led Dashi and Victoria through a small open courtyard into the main building. The first room on one side was his study, sporting a plaque with the words "Mourn Red Pavilion" affixed at the top of the door frame. In his opening chapter, Cao recorded he had spent ten years in this room writing and editing what would be titled *Dream of the Red Chamber.* Chinese calligraphy and paintings lined the walls of the room. Stacked on a desk were reams of paper filled with tiny Chinese characters written in black ink, embellished by emendations and insertions in red.

Dashi introduced his travel companion as Wenlong, or "Tattoo Dragon." Victoria borrowed the name from her biological father. Cao smiled knowingly and bowed with a namaste.

Cao's young wife brought tea. The author lovingly called her Fangqing, "Fragrant Lover." In most cases, the traditional wife would not show her face to strangers, but Dashi was almost kin. Besides, the host could not afford a servant. Cao said his ten-year-old son was spending the evening at the neighbours', affording the grown-ups the freedom to enjoy a Dionysian soirée. He had no idea his son's thread of life would be cut short by an illness. The tragedy so devastated Cao it would lead to his own early demise.

The author unsealed the package to find his manuscript in good order. Also present were a folding paper fan and a Silver Note for two hundred taels of silver, a sizable windfall. Cao promptly broke open his jug of *shaojiu,* or "burned alcohol," meaning distilled spirits, to celebrate his good fortunes, served together with a bowl of savoury snacks and a plate of lean donkey brisket.

Cao Xueqin insisted Dashi and Victoria stay for dinner and overnight if necessary. Dashi had no choice because he needed to have his receipt signed and sealed as well as receive a decent gratuity for his troubles. After dinner, Cao hired a carriage to pick up two nuns from a nearby nunnery. They were also from the Nanjing manor and shared much of the author's romantic nostalgia for the good old days.

Two middle-aged women dressed in nun habits arrived shortly. They retained their hair, indicating they were not full nuns. Cao introduced one as Zhiyan, "Rouge Inkwell," and the other as Jihu, "Weird Courtier-Tablet," both cultured ladies brought up in a privileged environment. Even without applying makeup, the half-nuns radiated grace and beauty. They had taken refuge in religion rather than entering into undesirable marriages and degrading themselves with the demeaning life of desperate housewives.

Victoria asked Cao for permission to read the manuscript. He agreed, provided she chugged a shot of *shaojiu* with him. Since Victoria was immune to alcohol, she gamely complied. Afterward, the happily vinomadefied author showed everyone the fan he received from Governor Yin. Victoria was familiar with it. Li Shangyin's poem "Spring Showers" was written in exquisite calligraphy on the fan. It would one day hang on her bedroom wall under her other fan titled "Untitled."

[悵臥新春白袷衣]
In early spring, I lie in bed dressed in my white robes,
[白門寥落意多違]
Feeling blue at the sight of the lonely white door.
[紅樓隔雨相望冷]
Through the rain, I watch your cold and empty red chamber,
[珠箔飄燈獨自歸]
I return alone to the lamp and pearl screen swaying in the wind.
[遠路應悲春晼晚]

Long-distance separation and dusk sadden me,
[殘宵猶得夢依稀]
Only as night passes will I faintly see you in my dream.
[玉璫緘劄何由達]
How can I deliver these jade earrings to you?
[萬里雲羅一雁飛]
May the wild goose send my love across ten thousand miles of cloud-cloaked sky.

"I remember this fan," Zhiyan said. "It used to belong to my father. He had quite a collection. I know how he got them. It's not something I can be proud of. Fate sends this one back to the Cao family. Xueqin, I'll tell you the true story to add to your book."

"Absolutely, but tomorrow," Cao said. "Tonight, my heart is filled with bittersweet memories. The evening is young and wine aplenty. Let us answer Bacchus' call and get plastered."

"Does this gift come with a message?" Jihu queried.

"The Governor asked me about possible titles for my book. Besides all the ideas we've bandied about, *Dream of the Red Chamber* came up. With this Li Shangyin poem on the fan, the Governor is hinting he likes the title. The poem has all three words, 'red,' 'chamber,' and 'dream.' Well, I like it too. So it is decided, *muchas gracias* to the Governor and Li Shangyin. Let us drink to *Dream of the Red Chamber*. Ganbei!"

While the Nanjing Cao Manor clique drank and prattled, Fangqing stuck her head into the room, asking if anyone wanted more snacks to go down with the *shaojiu*. Victoria raised her hand and said, "This morsel is truly scrumptious. May I have some for my return trip? By the way, if it's not a family secret, I'd like to have the recipe."

"I'm glad you like it," Fangqing said. "I'll put some in a box for you. It's Xueqin's favourite snack from an imperial kitchen recipe. He has included it in his book. The snack is called *qiexiang*, or 'aubergine umami.' Its original preparation was complicated, so I helped simplify it. First, prepare some Shiitake mushrooms, fresh white mushrooms, bamboo sprouts, five-spice dried bean curd and whatever nuts you have. Dice everything and set it aside. Next, prepare a fresh chicken. Boil it to make a broth and set it aside. Fillet the cooked chicken and cube the meat. Throw the whole kit and caboodle into a wok, pour the chicken broth to cover everything and reduce, finishing with a dash of sesame oil. Afterwards, prepare some aubergine, or, for some people, eggplant. Remove the skin, cube the flesh, and fry in chicken fat. Mix everything, and *qiexiang* is almost ready."

"Awesomesauce! I can totally do this."

"Yes, but the crucial last step needs a special ingredient. You'll have to soak everything in a bit of *zaoyou*, a sauce made from rice wine mash. It is a popular condiment in the Jiangsu and Zhejiang provinces, where people drink rice wine. Let the *qiexiang* sit for a few days in a sealed can. Toss in a handful of fried diced chicken and melon seeds, mix well, and it is ready to serve.

"Xueqin and I met last year when he was in Nanjing. He swept me off my feet, and before I knew what hit me, we got married. I brought a large jug of *zaoyou* when we came home to Jingshi. *Qiexiang* is savoury because of this secret sauce."

Victoria could not be a part of the Cao Manor clique's conversation, so she sat in the corner and started to read Cao Xueqin's masterpiece. Fangqing, being semi-literate, was also an outsider. She brought Victoria a box of *qiexiang* snacks in a small bag and sat beside her to embroider a handkerchief.

Chapter 42

Dream of the Red Chamber

Except for the many poems in the book, the language used in *Dream of the Red Chamber* was mainly in the vernacular. Although Victoria had trouble understanding some of the rare words, erudite terms and dialects, she had no trouble getting the gist of the story. In any case, she was looking for clues, not parsing the whole book word by word.

The story opens with the description of a mythical time when a fissure formed on the empyreal firmament, resulting in a heavenly downpour and a biblical deluge. The primeval goddess of China, Nüwa, a name used by the ancient Chinese Jews of Kaifeng to mean Noah, crafted thirty-six thousand five hundred and one divine stones to mend the fractured welkin. She used all the stones except one, which, over time, developed a spirit. Unemployed, the stone suffered low self-esteem and deemed itself useless. As the years passed, the stone gained the physical form of a man known as the Celestial Jade Servant of the Red Jade Speckles Palace. He spent his days roaming the timeless realm until he chanced upon an herb, the Scarlet-Red Bead Grass, struggling to survive by a rock. He felt pity for the plant and began to water it every day.

After the passage of unknown eons, the stone was discovered by a Taoist monk named Miao Miao, meaning "infinitesimal," and a Buddhist monk named Mang Mang, meaning "infinite." *Miao miao mang mang*, as a phrase, means "indefinite." Noticing how the gods had breathed life into the stone, the monks decided to incarnate him on Earth and record his life story for remembrance. Meanwhile, the Scarlet-Red Bead Grass gained the physical form of a girl and incarnated on Earth to repay the stone's kindness with her tears. By coincidence, if such a thing were possible, Dashi's ancestor, Niu Shihui, was a Taoist monk, whereas Niu Shihui's brother, Bada Shanren, was a Buddhist monk.

During their descent to Earth, the two monks, Miao Miao and Mang Mang, encountered the spirit of a man lost in a dream. He was Zhen Shiyin, phonetically identical to "true events hidden." The stone would be born into an aristocratic family as a spoiled son with a silver spoon in his mouth, figuratively speaking. He was literally born with a piece of jade in his mouth. His name, Jia Baoyu, is phonetically identical to "fake precious jade."

The story is about this great aristocratic family named Jia, a homophone of "fake." The Jia family has a very close relationship with a similarly powerful family named Zhen, a homophone of "true." The Zhen family has a son named Zhen Baoyu, which is phonetically identical to "true precious jade." Thus, the author reveals the characters in the book are fabricated based on real people. This form of novel is known as roman à clef in the West.

In the story, Jia Baoyu enters a dreamland where he peeks into a book of oracles titled *The Twelve Ladies of Jinling*. Jinling means "gold mound," a moniker for Nanjing. Thus, the "fake precious jade" learns the fates of the women in his life.

"Another secret book of oracles," Victoria thought. "We may have something here." And she started exploring through Fangqing. "Madam Cao, are you one of the *Twelve Ladies of Jinling*?"

"Oh no. I'm an ordinary girl of the servant class. Zhiyan and Jihu belong to the list. Zhiyan is crucial for telling Xueqin insider stories of the Cao Manor he could not otherwise have known."

Zhiyan was leaving the room to use the courtyard latrine. She overheard the question and interjected, "Xueqin built the character

Xichun, the fourth sister, based on me. She is a talented artist tasked with painting the Grandview Garden, yet she aspires to be a nun. She knows all the goings-on in the manor but does not get involved. Apart from the tragic Lin Daiyu, Baoyu's love interest, she's the only one out of the Twelve Ladies unsullied by men.

"Jihu is the inspiration behind the young half-nun Miaoyu in the story, who calls herself *Jiren*, a weirdo. Xueqin aptly describes Miaoyu as a nun but not a nun, a lay person but not a lay person, a woman but not a woman, a man but not a man. Miaoyu's background is a big mystery. She grew up in a temple at a location described in the book as Xuanmushan, or "mysterious tomb mountain," a real place Emperor Kangxi had visited several times, usually accompanied by his childhood best buddy, Cao Yin, my grandfather. No one knows why they went. It is not a coincidence the young half-nun Miaoyu, who owns so many rare treasures, ends up living in the Jia Manor's Grandview Garden with Jia Baoyu and the other girls.

"After the eviction order, the Sui family takes over the manor. One of the Sui sons, a brute and a notorious lecher, hurries over to check out the famous beauties of the Grandview Garden and runs into Miaoyu, promptly kidnapping her and making her his mistress. Poor Miaoyu almost loses the will to live. Not long after, it's the Sui family's turn to receive an eviction notice. Miaoyu's keeper, having led a dissipated life, dies from a combination of intemperance, idiocy and illness. The fortunate Miaoyu, living at the Grand Canal crossing on the Yangzi River, takes a cruise to Jingshi and finds Xichun. Now I have dear Jihu as my sister and lifelong companion at the nunnery."

"So we may assume," Victoria said, "the *hu*, or 'courtier tablet,' of Jihu, means she comes from an aristocratic family with some unspoken connections to Emperor Kangxi."

"Amitabha!" Zhiyan cried, invoking the name of the Amida Buddha as a popular form of exclamation. "You are clever. But in front of the Merciful Buddha, we're all equals."

"Is the Jia Baoyu character based on Mr. Cao?"

"Yes, but only in part and not by as much as you are who you say you are. Jia Baoyu is also partly based on my half-brother, who has decided to be a Buddhist monk. I haven't heard from him since he walked away from his wife and son. He was devastated by being forced into an unhappy marriage, especially when the girl with whom he had pledged a secret troth committed suicide by starving herself to death. It was a tragedy. Yet the cruelty he visited upon his family is unforgivable."

The Cao Manor clique took turns going to the washroom and returned to their bacchanalia.

Victoria soon reached the chapter mentioning the Treasure Mirror of the Wind and the Moon. A Taoist monk lends the divine instrument to a young man who is bedridden with a high fever because of his unrequited love for a married woman. The young man must seek the terrible truth from the back, but gives in to his desires by peeking at the front instead, causing his untimely death.

Suddenly, a barrage of boisterous banging rang from the front gates. It set off a chorus of barking from the dogs. Fangqing laid down her embroidery, muttering, "Who would be making such a ruckus at this ungodly hour?" She seized a lamp and asked Victoria to accompany her. When they opened the door, they found two men standing outside. One was a bald Buddhist monk holding a staff known as the Khatwanga. He had a patch over his left eye. The other was a Taoist monk. They asked with one voice, "Where are we and what are we doing here?"

Having read Cao's book, Victoria knew the answer. She responded, "This is a transit area, and we're only passing through."

"Well, what are we waiting for?" the monks said. "Let's go."

Cao Xueqin stuck his head out from the front door of the house and asked, "Who goes there? What's the buzz?"

"It's the monks, Miao Miao and Mang Mang," Victoria said. "I have to go with them."

"Oh, them. Where are you going? Are you coming back? What should I tell Mr. Niu? He is three sheets to the wind and won't notice you're gone."

"I'm going to where I'm going. I suppose I won't be back. Please thank Brother Niu for me. It's too bad I can't thank his parents in person. They took good care of me. And Mr. Cao, keep writing your book. It's a beautiful story."

Turning to Fangqing, Victoria said, "Thank you so much, Madam Cao, for your *qiexiang* snacks. Before I go, I have a question. What is the meaning behind the name, Mourn Red Pavilion?"

"Everyone asks this question," Fangqing said. "Xueqin told me all about his past when we married. He almost lost his mind after his first wife died of consumption at a young age. Her name was Lin Hongyu, 'Red Jade.' She was the real person behind the book's main character, Lin Daiyu, 'Black Jade.' In the story, Hongyu is the servant Xiao Hong, or 'Little Red,' who has a secret romance with Jia Yun and will, eventually, marry him. You can find a bit of Xueqin in Jia Yun and Jia Qin, 'fake mustard,' and 'fake celery,' both Jia Baoyu's relatives from minor branches. 'Mourn Red Pavilion' is where Xueqin mourns 'Little Red.'"

Cao Xueqin hid the secrets in the names. Both *qin*, "celery," and *yun*, "mustard," are plants with the "grass" radical. In the book, all names of sons with the "grass" radical belong to minor branches. Their survival depends on gaining employment at the Cao Manor, usually as glorified servants. The sons of the main branch have names with the "jade" radical. The self-assigned courtesy name Xueqin, "Snow Celery," reflected the author's struggles as a son of the minor branch to survive with high morals. Celery does not thrive in snow, and snow symbolizes a blameless character. Xueqin studied hard and was well-educated. He was the unemployed jade servant not given the chance to prove himself.

In the story, Jia Qin, "fake celery," is in charge of a group of young nuns, much as Xueqin, "Snow Celery," became close friends with two half-nuns from the Cao Manor. Zhiyan and Jihu contributed invaluable scholia to Xueqin's early manuscripts. In the same vein, Jia Yun, "fake mustard," is in charge of tending flowers in the Grandview Garden where Jia Baoyu and the girls live, whereas the stone man, as the Celestial Jade Servant of the Red Jade Speckles Palace, waters the Scarlet-Red Bead Grass. The word "bead" is itself made up of the "jade" radical and the word for "red." It is in the Grandview Garden where Jia Yun, "fake mustard," meets the servant girl, Xiao Hong, "Little Red," whose real name is Lin Hongyu, "Red Jade." But she can't use the name because of its similarity to the fictional Lin Daiyu, "Black Jade," Jia Baoyu's cousin and secret amour. Thus, all clues point to Hongyu, "Red Jade," as Xueqin's love interest.

Cao Xueqin left more clues. Jia Baoyu, "fake precious jade," lives in Yihong Yuan, or "Enjoy Red Court," in contrast to Xueqin's Mourn Red Pavilion. Jia Baoyu names his study Jiangyun Xuan, meaning "Scarlet-Red Mustard Pavilion," tying the Scarlet-Red Bead Grass with *yun*, mustard, connecting Xiao Hong, "Little Red," with Jia Yun, "fake mustard," and, at the same time, bringing together Hongyu and Xueqin. Finally, the heavenly Red Jade Speckles Palace suggests Hongyu was a servant and, therefore, not of the highest quality, as speckles are jade blemishes. Experts have conjured a thousand convoluted explanations for the secret meaning of "red chamber" in the book's title. Perhaps it refers to the bedchamber of Xueqin's beloved wife, Lin Hongyu, "Red Jade," also known as Xiao Hong, "Little Red."

Chapter 43

Tweedle Dee and Tweedle Dum

Victoria crossed the donut-shaped portal of the Celestial Catoptron with Miao Miao, the Taoist monk, and Mang Mang, the one-eyed Buddhist monk, into an unfamiliar countryside. It was the final moment of a peaceful midsummer night. Rosy-fingered Dawn was donning her saffron robes. A thick mist blanketed the flat landscape at the confluence of a wide river and a marshy tributary stream. Beneath the white shroud, a beast dark and foreboding crouched and crawled.

Victoria could barely make out four picturesque villages in the mist, each composed of several hundred stone houses and a church crowned by a tall spire, three of which peacefully reposed on the southern bank of the tributary trickling eastward through a shallow valley and debouching into the wide river. Out of these three, the westernmost village snuggled at the foot of trackless wooded hills. The next group of houses to the east congregated about one and a half kilometres from the western hills and four kilometres from the river. The easternmost village, Blindheim, Home of the Blind, sprang up almost flush against the confluence of the river and its tributary, with two water mills forming the gateway leading to the village's northern palisade. North of the rivulet was another settlement closer to the hills to the west. An orderly matrix of five thousand camps and bivouacs was arrayed less than two kilometres south of the tributary on the recently harvested fields. The villages were coming alive, but the camps remained in languorous sleep.

The three temporal travellers sat in a grove by the river to watch the reddening of the eastern sky, welcoming the arrival of a new day. Victoria learned she was enjoying the scenery along the storied Danube. She whistled the famous tune of the Waltz King, and an ensemble of robins and warblers immediately responded with their morning matins.

"Wow!" Victoria exclaimed. "Are we in a fairytale kingdom? Do we know exactly where and when we are?"

"We've gone back fifty-six years to an area about a hundred and twenty kilometres west of Munich," the one-eyed Buddhist monk said after checking his pocket watch. "We'll be stuck here for a while. First of all, we're both pleased to see you again."

"We have met before, haven't we?" Victoria said, "Hopefully, this time, you can explain who you are, how we're related, and why we keep running into each other?"

"I'm Tweedledee," the Buddhist monk Mang Mang said.

"And I'm Tweedledum," Miao Miao, the Taoist monk, said.

"We're going where we're going," Mang Mang chimed.

"And we're from where we're from," Miao Miao rhymed.

"The most important thing is," Mang Mang said, "you must understand the nature of your quest."

"Otherwise," Miao Miao concluded, "you'll never be able to save anyone."

"Frankly, I don't understand any of this," Victoria said, "especially the part about saving people. I know things aren't what they seem, and the world is full of lies. But I'm also having difficulties believing in you, Queen Lilith and the scorpion. I miss my little world where I know who I am and how things work."

"You can make all of us go away any time you want," the one-eyed monk Mang Mang said. "All you have to do is close your eyes, click your heels and repeat three times, 'There is no place like home.' You'll wake up and realize you've been daydreaming."

"But if you stay with us," Miao Miao said, "we'll tell you who you are, where you're from, and how you can reset the universe."

"Alright," Victoria said. "I'll let you guys have one more crack at it. Convince me."

"Good, let us begin," Mang Mang said. "First and foremost, we're not total strangers. Your parents have told you about us. I'm Mr. Hua, the One-eyed Apothecary. To David Huang, I'm his ancestor, Huang Yin. His father, Huang Shi, knows me as the One-eyed Fortune-teller and the Fablemonger. Madonna Lilith knows me as the One-eyed Soothsayer. Sting knows me as Pepé Kiku. Charlie knows me as Yashinsky. I financed David as Comte de Saint-Germain to help him fulfil his destiny. You and I have met at Tim Hortons and Truffle Pigs. I'm sorry to have frightened you. I was keeping an eye on you. No pun intended.

"You may have noticed the ring-maker was a fan of the *Back to the Future* trilogy. It's no coincidence the flux capacitor needs 1.21 gigawatts of electricity to work. It is 1.1 squared. Spielberg knows the secret of 'eleven,' but an ironclad NDA ensures he keeps it to himself. The same deal goes for the writers of *1899*, who use 1011, the binary form of eleven, for the portals into the mysteries of the series, the Duffer Brothers of *Stranger Things*, who name their protagonist Eleven, the Spierig Brothers of *Predestination*, whose time travel tale conjures a Temporal Bureau with eleven agents, and the Wachowski sisters, previously brothers, of the Matrix trilogy, who designate the number eleven for the Nebuchadnezzar hovercraft. Our vast network also includes the brains behind ElevenLabs and the Ellen DeGeneres-owned Eleveneleven record label, among many others. Keep your eyes on 'eleven' while my friend fills you in with the rest of the story."

"Let me introduce myself," Miao Miao said. "I am known to my friends as Sator, short for Satanu Sung. Being inorganic and having received the spark of divine fire, I am not afflicted with the flaws of evolution. We have already met long ago in a faraway land. I would not be here if you had not saved me. It is how your decision in the future can significantly change the past.

"Having followed the princely tribes that carried the 'ghost' genes known as Half-Keys to this planet, I befriended some humans. For example, I'm the model for the android Data Soong in *Star Trek: The Next Generation.* I disclosed the secret Shang background of the Soong to Roddenberry. I had also suggested Omicron Zeta as Data's home planet, but the script assistant mistakenly recorded Omicron Theta. She didn't realize Omicron Zeta meant Oz. I'm the prototypical model for the Tin Man. I don't have a heart. Frank Baum got his inspiration from me.

"Another buddy, Carlo Collodi, wrote *The Adventures of Pinocchio* based on me. I told him about the source of my life force, the Grist of Life, which he associated with the Pineal Body, considered the third eye by some. René Descartes even referred to it as the principal seat of the soul. In fact, the name Pinocchio comes from the words for 'pine' and 'eye.' Are you surprised?"

"I'm numb from surprises," Victoria said. "So why are you two going back and forth in time and space, wreaking havoc with people's lives?"

"A long, long time ago," the one-eyed Buddhist monk said, "I was an invincible warrior and the powerful ruler of a planet named Shangria. Despite having the intelligence to create a perpetual paradise, I was unschooled in matters of the heart. It proved to be my undoing and the unravelling of our universe's space-time fabric. For a long time, I have been trying to repair the damage with the help of my good friend, Sator. But no matter how hard we try, we cannot succeed. We can only postpone the inevitable. I thus mock myself with the vain hope I may one day lie in eternal rest with my sins absolved. As for resetting the universe to restore harmony, you are our last and only hope."

"Sting told me about Shangria, and I visited," Victoria said, "only now learning I had unintentionally changed the course of events. But the past is history, and you can't change it. What is this Great Reset everyone is referring to, and why does it concern me?"

"Ah, Shangria, our home from long ago and far away," the one-eyed monk sighed. "It was a planet blessed with inexhaustible energy and indescribable beauty. Yet its insensate inhabitants, the Haryas, destroyed everything in an endless war. Eventually, I ended the War according to a prophecy. Afterwards, Sator and my best friend, Milu, who became Lord Millistar, worked with me to usher in the New Golden Age, inventing technologies to maintain the paradise of Shangria in perpetuity.

"Our science and logic were impeccable. We built layers of fail-safe redundancies, implementing self-debug, auto-repair and unlimited upgrades. We removed all possibilities of Haryan tempering. We ensured the Haryas could enjoy peace and harmony on the planet until the End of Days. But the God With No Name refused to allow perfect happiness. Love made me mad and blind, and I caused the destruction of everyone and everything I loved. At the last moment, Sator pulled me back from the brink. We studied the Twirligig Almanac, known on Earth as the *Book of Heavenly Secrets*, and learned about the possibility of redemption.

"A passage in the book suggests by uniting the 'ghost' genes known as Half-Keys to form the complete Key, a new Sibyl would arise, who would locate the Grist of Truth. She must insert it into the Renifleur chamber of the Twirligig, chant the Incantation of Creation and Destruction and play the lost chord of the eleventh key to activate the Great Reset, by which our universe returns to a pivotal moment before the disaster, granting us a chance to right our wrongs. After tracking the Half-Keys across the galaxy to Earth, we believe you are the Sibyl with the complete Key destined to play the Twirligig. We're here to help you reach your destiny."

"Because of you, everyone else is here," Sator added. "If not, they're on the way."

"According to David, I'm the Oracle, but according to Delo and now you, I'm the Sibyl. I don't understand."

"They mean the same thing," the one-eyed monk said. "The Sibyl is blessed, or maybe cursed, with the memory of an epic known as the Mahashangria, which contains many oracles. She is an anomaly and extremely rare. We have studied your lineage, tested your genetics and witnessed your blossoming. Evidence confirms you are the Sibyl bearing the complete Key, who will moot all our scientific theories."

"Assuming I'm as important as you suggest and supposing I'm willing to play along, what crime of passion have you committed serious enough to destroy everything? I should know if I'm the one to remedy what you've done."

"I'm sorry, I can't divulge all my secrets to you because of causality rules," the one-eyed monk said. "This secret is a festering wound in my heart. I'm not even supposed to be talking to you because I'm neither here nor there. I exist in a quantum flux, which allows me to materialize for brief periods. Because of my sin, I suffer the punishment of the Ashwatthama Curse to languish in a personal hell for all time until a fool takes my place and releases me from my chains.

"My time here is limited, so listen carefully. Queen Lilith is but a diversion. People you trust have misled you. You'll have zero chance of defeating her. The Queen holds all the trump cards, whereas you have none. She has imprisoned everyone you love, keeping them as hostages, plus she is ready, willing and able to do whatever she deems necessary without compunction. Do not waste your time saving Earth. Armadas of similarly cold-blooded killers harbouring implacable hatred for each other are arriving from Gamma Crucis and Antares. It will be a bloody mess for the planet and its inhabitants. Our redemption relies on you finding the one true Grist of Truth, not fighting the Amazonian Queen. The end of the 'world as you know it' is a foregone conclusion."

"What about my parents and my best friends?" Victoria said, doubting her fantastic power to reverse the course of time. "I can't pretend I don't care what happens to them. Besides, I have to go back and retrieve my quantum devices."

"Earth and humans are not your concern," Sator said. "And you don't need your gadgets because we have the Catoptron in this timeline. If you insist on returning to the Queen, we'll have failed in our endeavour, and all will be lost. Nothing has any meaning unless you execute the Great Reset."

"I will not leave my parents and best friends in the hands of a psychopathic mass murderer. I'm also not prepared to give up on Earth and humans. If you want me to reset the universe, which I'm not so sure about, you had better first help me defeat the Queen."

"Thus, the fortune cookie crumbles," the one-eyed monk said resignedly. "If you return to Madonna Lilith at the Qaanaaq, you cannot take the Catoptron because it is a unique and non-local monopodial quantum gateway. Only one may exist in any instant across the universe. In your present timeline, one already exists in your LV knapsack, and the chance of you getting it is slim to none. Without the Catoptron, I don't see how you can ever find the Grist, and without the Grist, you won't be resetting anything."

"I have made up my mind," Victoria said. "Don't confuse me with your empty words. Nothing you say holds any meaning for me. How do I know you're not sending me on a wild goose chase, running a fool's errand for an impossible quest? If I fail to reset the universe, I will have given up everything for nothing. Why don't you save your breath and help me defeat the Queen instead? I can try the Great Reset afterwards."

"Well, it is what we expect from you," Sator said. "We're making a last-ditch effort. It's a long shot, but worth a try."

"We're disappointed," the one-eyed monk said. "But we'll help you as much as possible. First, let us face the facts. You're not going to defeat the Queen on her turf. So, what next? You should be aware the Queen has a weakness you can exploit. She will not harm you. She will, however, torture everyone you love within an inch of their lives unless you give in to her demands. She enjoys a commanding advantage over your weakness. You have a heart; she does not. Therefore, your best strategy may be to avoid the Queen, rescue the hostages, retrieve your Magic Mirror and transfer everyone back to Earth. As for how you can accomplish the feat, we have no idea. In any case, Earth has no defence against the alien armadas. It does not matter whether it'll be with a whimper or a bang, the human race will end."

"Words, words, words," Victoria complained, "I'm sick of words. I'm hoping you guys can lend me some material help. David taught me never to take a knife to a gunfight. Maybe you have a divine weapon or two I can borrow."

"Guns will not harm the Queen," Sator said. "But we do have a deadly dagger for you. It's presently on loan for an assassination in ancient China. You shall have it when our domain stabilizes."

"Because of the unpredictable nature of quantum flux," the one-eyed monk said, "we have arrived at this time and place beyond our control. We won't be able to leave until the Catoptron eliminates all the perturbations, which may take hours. Meanwhile, we can beguile the time and enjoy this brief sojourn, as long as we comply with the rules of causality. By coincidence, if such a thing were possible, a great battle would soon play out before our eyes. We might as well watch and learn. You may not like violence, but sometimes violence comes knocking. Sator, please explain to Victoria the background of the upcoming battle."

Chapter 44

The Unsinkable Mr. Freeman

"The impending battle is the first major clash in a world war between a global empire on the one side," Sator explained, "and on the other, a fragile alliance cobbled together by several fractious small states and weak sovereigns separated by long distances, all of which have divergent interests and *divers* internal problems. Any of these comrades of convenience is ready to jump ship whenever the wind of fortune changes, or worse, to plunge a knife into the heart of the grandiosely named Grand Alliance whenever it serves their immediate selfish purpose. Most of the states of this unwieldy coalition constantly fight among themselves, and the coming battle is the direct result of a major member defecting over to the enemy, threatening the complete collapse of the Alliance. It is a 4D chess game of crazy complexity.

"Surprisingly, this ramshackle Alliance agrees to let an old country gentleman from England lead its Coalition Army. This captain-general, nicknamed Mr. Freeman, has never commanded a large army or fought a large-scale battle. He is merely a servant of the royal family, a lifetime courtier and a convenient appointee with no independent authority. Mr. Freeman is neither the heir to a substantial family estate nor the beneficiary of an esteemed title passed down by an ancestor of renown. He has had to turn down exalted titles he could not afford to maintain. In the eyes of Mr. Freeman's aristocratic peers, he is but a popular subject of ridicule.

"To illustrate how challenging Mr. Freeman's job is, his hodgepodge Coalition Army is composed of soldiers from the allied states led by their own aristocrats or generals, most of whom have an inflated opinion of themselves. These haughty princes and officials may, at any time, refuse to cooperate with Mr. Freeman, openly obstruct his orders, apply dilatory tactics or splash a bucket of holy water, making solemn promises they never intend to keep. Meanwhile, they secretly deliver military secrets to their relatives working in the enemy camp. After all, this is Europe, and everyone is related to everyone else by blood or marriage.

"Mr. Freeman's nominally subordinate generals either display open disdain or nurse secret resentment at his command, and these homunculi constantly contrive to trammel their commander at every turn by holding interminable debates on the merits of an operation while the opportunity for action slips away. Thereupon, they would scatter posthaste in all directions to fabricate voluble venomous public letters vociferously vilipending their commander for not having won the greatest battle of all time to end the war. Mr. Freeman is subjected to all these insufferable hindrances because he is not of royal blood, and his generalship of the Coalition Army has come about as a compromise under complicated political considerations beyond his control."

"Yet," interjected the one-eyed monk, picking up the thread from Sator, "Mr. Freeman turns out to be the most outstanding military genius his country has ever produced. Such an efflorescence of genius may arise only once in the entire history of a nation or, more likely, never at all. Compared to him, King Henry V, Oliver Cromwell and Duke Wellington are but children playing in a sandbox; even Napoleon pales in comparison to Mr. Freeman, considering these famous historical figures commanded armies with unquestionable authority, and none had to contend with poisonous backstabbing at home and in the field.

"For this war, Mr. Freeman has been relegated to the role of an informal and ineffectual chairman of a discordant committee. The perpetually exasperated commander-in-chief cannot make a move without first gaining consensus and obtaining permission from all the allies, the most significant of which, the obsessively defensive-minded Dutch Republic, has installed two deputies in his camp, each with the veto power to forfend any offensive action.

"To baffle his enemy, Mr. Freeman must first deceive his allies. To defeat his foe, he must first conquer his friends, usually through endless cajoling, inveigling and finagling. After all, the heads of the so-called Grand Alliance hold the political power, the purse strings and the control of supplies necessary for waging war. Meanwhile, Mr. Freeman's government, the political factions and the monarch are playing treacherous games of intrigue back home, ready to undermine or betray their general at the drop of a hat, which would eventually transpire when they illegally negotiate a secret treaty to betray the Alliance behind his back."

"Why on earth would anyone want such a thankless job?" Victoria exclaimed. "Why doesn't Mr. Freeman quit?"

"Loyalty to his queen and colleagues? Duty to his country? Dedication to the Alliance? Faith in his religion?" Sator posited. "It could be any or all of the above. At any rate, his queen refuses to let him quit. Detractors brand him a warmonger. Others claim he's in it for the money. But it's a high-pressure job with no room for a single defeat, as Mr. Freeman's myriad enemies from home and abroad will have a field day. He'll certainly not survive the fallout. He can hardly survive his most magnificent victories.

"On today's battlefield, Mr. Freeman, in his mid-fifties, is the oldest general, if not the oldest soldier. He is on horseback all day, regularly risking life and limb riding into action with his redcoats, once nearly getting his head removed in a cavalry charge in Brabant, and another time narrowly escaping after being captured on the Meuse by accident. In another famous battle two years from today, Mr. Freeman would fall off his horse in a melee and miss a cannonball by a hair. Each time, he survives by the skin of his teeth. However, despite his consistent military successes, all the slandering, bickering and backstabbing against him would never abate. In private letters, he constantly swears he would resign rather than subject himself to another year of undignified mortifications. But when duty calls, he never fails to show up."

"I would rather jump into a lake," Victoria remarked. "I wonder how Mr. Freeman keeps up his spirit."

"We will soon see," the one-eyed monk said. "Mr. Freeman's adversary, Louis XIV, also known as the Sun King, is the most formidable supreme ruler of an empire on which the sun never sets. The Sun King has all the resources of this global empire at his beck and call. His marshals have long subdued all foes for his ambitious conquests, and he has a vast population from which he can draw a seemingly inexhaustible number of stout-hearted men for the fielding of superior and imposing armies on every front.

"On paper, this war is hardly a contest between equals. Yet, throughout ten years of continuous campaigns, Mr. Freeman would enjoy an incredible record of one hundred percent success on the battlefield, changing the course of history for Europe, America, Canada, Africa, India, China and the rest of the world.

"However, the English general must swallow the bitter fruit of his military might. After his most remarkable campaign, when the Sun King tearfully concedes, agreeing to pay any price for peace, the triumphant and hubristic politicians at home manage to conjure more war with their unreasonable maximalist demands. Mr. Freeman would win the battles, but the Grand Alliance would lose the peace. And they all blame the Englishman."

"People of your era have forgotten this peerless warrior and his exploits," Sator added. "He has seldom received fair treatment from his monarch masters, fellow countrymen or the nation's pen-wielders. Despite gaining power and glory for his country, Mr. Freeman would be thrown under the bus by the political party he belongs to, mercilessly mauled by the opposition, stabbed in the front by his son-in-law, betrayed by his wife's cousin whose entire family he has saved from ruin, double-crossed by the Secretary of State who owes his position to Mr. Freeman, stabbed in the back by his Secretary of War, whom he loves as a son, vilified by his own country, which would transform from a sickly island nation wrecked by internal strife, whose kings once took bribes from the Sun King, into a global empire born from the seeds of his victories and, finally, wronged by his queen whose ascendancy and glory he has helped bring about in a lifetime of loyal service.

"With grand irony, English ministers, armed with royal assent, would unknowingly appoint a French spy as their envoy to conduct illicit, covert negotiations with the Sun King in betrayal of Mr. Freeman and the Grand Alliance. It might be comical if it were not so sad. Mr. Freeman's reward is voluntary exile to be received everywhere he visits with the pageantry of a prince."

"If I were Mr. Freeman," Victoria said, "I would put a pox on those dingbats so they'll always get dummies to lead them."

"Mr. Freeman loves his country too much to wish ill of it," the one-eyed monk said with a mysterious smile. "The much-maligned hero would stand the test of time. He would return to the English court's favour upon the accession of the next king and hold the highest military post until shortly before his death.

"Since Mr. Freeman's last surviving son had fallen victim to smallpox at the age of seventeen, less than a year before this coming battle, his estate and title would pass to the son of one of his daughters who had married into a distinguished aristocratic family. Mr. Freeman's descendants from this lineage include a famous wartime prime minister, a widely beloved but tragic princess and a future king, to name a few. By coincidence, if such a thing were possible, Mr. Freeman is also Canadian."

"Are you messing with me?" Victoria cried. "Canada is good at producing comedians, not generals."

"Mr. Freeman is one of the earliest Englishmen," the one-eyed monk said, "to conduct trading in Canada under a royal charter. A portrait of Mr. Freeman once hung on the wall of an iconic Canadian institute. His name is honoured by a major Canadian river and a northern fort. While people may argue he is not Canadian in the modern sense, he is an early founder and should at least be considered an honorary Canadian. Search your Trivial Pursuit database for his identity. I'm sure you can figure it out."

"I need more clues. How did Mr. Freeman get his nickname?"

"It's a sobriquet used exclusively by the Queen of England," Sator said. "His soldiers call him Corporal John or the Old Corporal. Surely, you must know his name."

"Nope, I give up. Don't know any Corporal John. Mr. Freeman's story is quite intriguing, though. How does he overcome so much adversity? Where does he find his strength? Maybe I can learn something from a fellow Canadian."

"What better than to turn around and inspect the fields behind you," Sator said.

As brave Helios rose from the netherworld in his heavenly chariot, his warm rays began to lift the morning mist. Victoria realized the fields and meadows to the north of the tributary were teeming with columns of soldiers in red, blue and buff, their bristling bayonets flashing in the first rays of the golden sun.

"A great battle, indeed, one of the greatest battles of all time, is about to take place," the one-eyed monk said. "You will witness the iron will and genius of the English-Canadian commander, the leader of the Coalition Army, and learn the subtle lessons to help you face your future."

Chapter 45

Home of the Blind

The camps south of the tributary were finally coming alive. Messengers on horseback raced hither and thither. Bugles blared to recall the foragers. Soldiers in blue, red and buff uniforms spilled out of the camp and marched to occupy the three villages along the southern banks of the tributary stream. These men were the finest soldiers of the French Empire, fighting alongside their new Bavarian ally, the recent traitor and backstabber of the Alliance, together referred to herein as the Grand Army as opposed to Mr. Freeman's Coalition Army.

Two small hamlets north of the tributary stream were ablaze. They were the Grand Army's forward posts and had been set afire by the retreating pickets.

Pointing at the three idyllic villages on the south side of the tributary, the one-eyed monk and Sator took turns explaining the military situation to Victoria in layman's terms.

It was evident the Grand Army had entrenched themselves in an unassailable defensive position. A marshy stream, with banks covered by a thick growth of rush and marigolds, shielded its front. Mr. Freeman's troops would be hard-pressed trying to cross it in good order. It would be downright dangerous if the French cavalry were to attack during the crossing. The Danube to the right of the Grand Army and the trackless wooded hills on its left secured the flanks of their formidable battle line.

By fortifying the three villages, the Grand Army ensured Mr. Freeman could not attack the centre without marching into the teeth of withering fire while having to defend against flank attacks from the battalions posted at these village strongholds.

Mr. Freeman had another problem. He had fewer soldiers than his opponent. The hamstrung general had to divest a quarter of his army after hearing whispers about the Margrave in charge of those troops passing military secrets to the enemy camp while allowing the enemy to concentrate and dominate the field uncontested. It was a delicate situation for Mr. Freeman because the Margrave was the commander-in-chief of an ally known as the Holy Roman Empire, which was sadly neither holy, Roman, nor an empire.

The so-called empire was, in fact, on the verge of total collapse because of the rebellion of Hungary to its east and the betrayal of Bavaria to its west. The situation jeopardized the entire Alliance. Mr. Freeman had to mislead the other allies, notably the Dutch, disguising his objectives while marching his English redcoats and other Coalition soldiers across the breadth of the continent in the face of the Sun King's armies, risking everything in a test of arms to save this mortified ally, even though the ally's general could very well be a traitor.

Under these precarious circumstances, Mr. Freeman could not afford to be stabbed in the back by a suspected Judas during the heat of battle. To keep the Margrave and his troops away from the battlefield, Mr. Freeman sent them reinforcements to conduct a meaningless siege, further weakening himself, despite being fully aware he would soon be engaged in a mortal struggle with a stronger enemy led by two French marshals of the highest renown.

Thus, Mr. Freeman ended up with fifty-two thousand soldiers against the Grand Army's well-entrenched fifty-six thousand, and, in violation of the rules of combat, which gave the advantage to the defence, went on the offensive with a smaller army.

"The French marshals are surprised by this turn of events," the one-eyed monk said. "The Coalition Army unexpectedly shows up early in the morning, suggesting they have marched all night. The marshals are flabbergasted when Mr. Freeman makes preparations to attack. After all, his soldiers have marched four hundred kilometres across a hostile front in only three weeks. If they were mere mortals, they should be half-dead. They are also far from their home base, with major French armies blocking their return route. By all the arts of war understood by these experienced and heretofore invincible French marshals, Mr. Freeman must be making a demonstration and will turn away from the numerically superior Grand Army entrenched in an inexpugnable position."

"See the French horsemen dressed in blue, red and buff coats moving into the fields at the centre?" Sator said, gesticulating with a sweep of his hand across the fields south of the rivulet. "The Grand Army will deploy its cavalry at the centre, where the terrain is flat, and where they will be charging down a gentle slope at their foes. The Grand Army is confident of victory if the enemy is stupid enough to attack. Mr. Freeman, however, knows his troops enjoy significant tactical advantages while his opponent lives in a delusion created by years of unrivalled success. Mr. Freeman also has a sound plan relying on courage and a readiness for sacrifice. After demonstrating his intentions to seek battle, the English general will soon jolt his opponents out of their dreams."

"So, what may appear to be a hopeless situation," Victoria remarked, "could actually be the exact opposite."

"True … and vice versa," the one-eyed monk said. "Accurate perception of reality is paramount. Don't fall into the trap of fooling yourself with your own lies. It is Mr. Freeman's true advantage over his enemy. It is what you must learn if you wish to succeed in your quest and conquest. Human self-delusion may feed the ego or reinforce prejudices, but it won't change reality or help humans face the adversity reality sometimes delivers. The human flaw of Confirmation Bias, causing people to put their faith in lies rather than facts, will bring about their ultimate demise."

"People will learn if you give them a chance. Homo sapiens has overcome numerous adversities to become the dominant species of the planet. I would not give up on them so soon."

"Your faith in these defective creatures is admirable, but I'm afraid it may be misplaced. Most humans are maggots in a cesspool. They will insist feces are delicious. It's impossible to convince them otherwise. Do you know why humans spend all their time paying attention to bald-faced lies repeatedly told by professional and pathological liars? Do you know why they go to great lengths debating fatuous lies told by these known liars? Don't they understand they're imparting substance to flatus? Humans are a lost cause. If I were you, I would not waste my time on them."

"Listen, we've already agreed to disagree. I won't give up on my family, best friends and the human race. Don't waste your time trying to confuse me. Anyway, I'm really tired. My brain needs a break, not an argument. But first, I have to use the washroom."

Victoria slept through the cannonade with the help of earplugs magically produced out of thin air by Sator. The vibration of the ground hypnotized her into a deep sleep. During her ambrosial rest on a Buddhist prayer mat, Sator disappeared into the blinding flash of an Elitzur-Vaidman quantum blast, returning after an hour in possession of a dagger with a wavy blade in an ornate sheath, Prince Cambi's Xiphos, known in China as Yuchang, meaning "fish gut." An aristocrat from ancient China's Wu state during the Zhou Dynasty had borrowed it to assassinate his first cousin, the Duke of Wu. After accomplishing the bloody deed, Xiphos, the Kin-slayer, found its way back to the belt of the one-eyed monk. Victoria woke up as the stage was all set for the bloodletting.

A curtain of cannon smoke hung above the fields between the armies, masking the movement of Coalition troops over the trackless wooded hills on the western flank. They had marched all night by another route to join the battle according to plan. Mr. Freeman determined this was the time and place to do and die. He had a knack for accurate predictions, a talent shared by the Communist general Su Yu centuries later. The two generals also shared another trait; both suffered from debilitating headaches.

Along the marshy rivulet, Coalition pioneers began repairing a stone bridge and building several causeways with fascines and pontoons. These were essential for moving the soldiers, horses and cannons across the soggy *quag* to the fields where the Grand Army's cavalry patiently awaited the violent clash.

Dense columns of English redcoats had crossed the tributary near the confluence on the eastern flank, waiting for the signal to attack Blindheim, Home of the Blind. Amidst exploding grape shots and bounding cannonballs, the soldiers sat down for their midday meal. For many, it would be their last.

"What time is it?" Victoria, rubbing her eyes, asked the monks.

"You mean now?" Sator said with a crooked grin. "I'm a little confused myself with all this time-travelling. The shadow says it's about noon."

"You must've been exhausted," the one-eyed monk said. "The cannonade has been going on for three hours, and you slept through it like a newborn babe. The Coalition Army has already suffered casualties in the thousands. Mr. Freeman doesn't want to commence action until his ally, Prince Eugene of Savoy, the hero who had stopped the westward expansion of the Ottoman Empire, is deployed at his right wing. The warrior prince is late because his soldiers have been marching over trackless hills, but they're finally in position. You've awakened in time to witness the serious clash of arms in the next phase of the battle."

Sator passed a gourd bottle to Victoria.

"Take a sip of the fresh milk we borrowed from the neighbourhood," he said. "This is what real milk tastes like. We have *roujiamo*, Chinese burgers, which some people have jokingly nicknamed Roger Moore, for lunch. After you have tamed your belly and replenished your strength, you should change into modern clothing. We have retrieved your things from Dashi's home, including Queen Lilith's dessert fork. We must be careful with causality."

Victoria was glad to put on her comfortable, everyday togs. After finding a spot with an unobstructed view, the three temporal travellers settled down to watch the action unfold.

The Coalition soldiers finished their meal and went on their knees to pray. Each regiment and battalion from the various allied states, speaking different languages, held their separate holy service in a cacophony of prayers.

The bombardment slowed, though it did not stop. It was as if the Grim Reaper wanted to pay due respect to their universal God. "Yea, though I walk through the valley of the shadow of death, I will fear no evil: for thou art with me; thy rod and thy staff they comfort me." Another cannonball tore through the ranks and robbed some more young men of their lives and limbs. The Psalms continued uninterrupted amid the groans and the screams. No one stirred from their position. By a toss of the dice, the soldiers gave themselves up to Providence to decide whether they should live, die or lose a limb or two.

Chapter 46

Death by the Danube

Guided by the two monks, Victoria directed her gaze north toward a gentle rise behind one of the burnt-out hamlets, where a group of aides-de-camp, adjutants and officers surrounded a man outfitted with a scarlet coat astride a grey steed.

"Behold, a pale horse," quoth Sator, "and he that sat upon him, his name was Death, today also known as Mr. Freeman."

The old general had festooned a blue riband across his chest, indicating he was a Knight of the Garter, a member of an exclusive club of the royal family invested with the right to ask the English redcoats to do and die for the greater glory of God and country.

As Mr. Freeman was a conspicuous target for the enemy, a cannonball landed right next to him, instantly killing some of his adjutants and raising a general gasp among the Coalition soldiers. But the calm and composed Mr. Freeman was neither shaken nor stirred, having said his prayers and received the sacrament.

An aide-de-camp of Mr. Freeman galloped across the field from the western flank, announcing Prince Eugene's troops were deployed and ready for action. Mr. Freeman issued battle instructions to his officers and dispatched the men to their posts. All the soldiers praying on their knees hastily wrapped up their orisons, rose to their feet, dressed their ranks, fixed their bayonets, and marched forward to meet their fate against a hail of hot lead.

In short order, violent attacks engulfed all three villages, with the most savage at Blindheim, the Home of the Blind, where the

English officer leading the first wave of redcoats fell in the opening assault. The flying balls of lead did not discriminate between wealth and rank, punching gaping holes in heads or chests to lay men low and render them equal. The second wave followed at the heels of the first. The soldiers promptly fell upon a bed of their dead compatriots, joining them in the land of eternal dreams.

The carnage was so shocking the French defenders of Blindheim believed they were witnessing the approach of the Apocalypse. The Sun King's gallant soldiers at this village had no doubt they would bear the brunt of the Coalition assault. The Grand Army's reserves poured into Blindheim to ensure a bountiful harvest for the Reaper. Mr. Freeman, noting he had achieved his objective by the generous sacrifice of brave but unfortunate men, ordered his troops to stand down while continuing to pose a lethal threat.

Meanwhile, the Coalition's assault on the other two village strongholds ebbed and flowed. Prince Eugene, the renowned warrior who saved Europe, bravely led his soldiers at the van of the Coalition's right wing, stopping his fleeing men and turning them around to charge again into infernal fire. Another prince attacking the middle village was mortally wounded, creating an anxious moment when the Coalition line was in danger of rupture.

During this phase, Mr. Freeman led the troops at the centre in person, advancing by a steady and determined march across the marshy stream, covering the double lines of cavalry in the front and rear with his infantry. By this novel deployment, designed by Mr. Freeman himself, his horse and foot soldiers could defend each other as they conducted this perilous crossing. Noticing the difficulties encountered by the Coalition troops in the centre, the Grand Army's cavalry charged with the violence of a voracious beast. The thundering of the hoofs and the roaring of the muskets rang across the valley and over the fields. Fortunately, Mr.

Freeman was up to the task. With the prompt and selfless assistance offered by a hard-pressed Prince Eugene, the aged English gentleman successfully plugged the gaps and repelled the enemy's assault, stabilizing the Coalition's line.

At this juncture, the Grand Army believed victory was within reach. It had repulsed all of the Coalition Army's attacks. Since the enemy could not advance, its only option was to retreat, signalling defeat. Imagine what the headlines of the news would say the next day. The Sun King's grand marshals rubbed their hands in glee as they reflected upon the happy thought.

It was almost three o'clock, and the fighting had been raging from end to end along the front for two hours. For reasons unknown, an eerie lull descended upon the battlefield as if the Twirligig had induced everyone to suspend the senseless slaughter.

"Why do I have to watch all this killing?" Victoria complained. "I'm never going to get used to it."

"Here is an example of why humans are not worth saving," Sator remarked, "They will kill each other off even if the Amazons don't kill them all. And if you get mixed up in the Project Gomoira, you'll incur the wrath of every party soon to arrive in large numbers, armed to the teeth with weapons of mass destruction. Before you know it, you'll be spilling blood as well. Trust me."

"I'm not going to trust anyone who tells me to trust them," Victoria thought.

"Didn't you wish to borrow divine weapons from us?" the one-eyed monk said, passing Cambi's murderous blade to Victoria. "This is a deadly dagger named Xiphos. It will inflict a wound from which the Queen will not heal. If you want to save the human race, let the killing begin. But you'll have to draw first blood."

Victoria unsheathed the dagger, only to be almost struck blind by the green glint of gruesome death. She quickly returned the beast to its grim cage before her heart froze into a block of ice.

"To defeat Queen Lilith," the one-eyed monk continued, "you'll need courage. Mr. Freeman leads by courage and example. He would not ask his men to do anything he wouldn't do himself. As the supreme commander, Mr. Freeman braves bullets and cannonballs alongside the rank and file. He crosses swords and dodges sabres while charging with his cavalry. He places himself at the epicentre of the battle, gaining the best view of developing events so he can make timely adjustments when necessary.

"In contrast, the Sun King is eight hundred kilometres away, sprawled on a plush couch in the safety and comfort of Versailles, soused with Champagne and Burgundy, enjoying his royal prerogative in the bosoms of buxom and voluptuous ladies. Mr. Freeman's lethal strike would, once and for all, extinguish the Sun King's imperial ambitions. So, my dear Sibyl, when the time comes to do and die, you will need the courage to enter the tiger's den, fix your eyes on the target and thrust the deadly blade home."

Victoria tried to visualize herself in such a life-and-death struggle. She was not sure when she had the chance, whether she could harden her heart and plunge in the knife.

By four o'clock, Mr. Freeman's troops in the centre had completed the crossing of the tributary stream. He now had a fresh and numerically superior Coalition army before a tired enemy cavalry scantily supported by the infantry. Most of the Grand Army's reserves had joined the fight at Blindheim, where they packed the village streets tighter than sardines in a can and could hardly raise their weapons.

After half an hour of preparation, the Coalition Army under Mr. Freeman resumed the march, the cavalry pressing forward in a double-line formation across the three-kilometre front, the infantry marching behind in two lines, and the field artillery following at the same pace. The French cavalry tried to impede their advance, but in vain. The Coalition artillery fired grape shots into the Grand

Army's infantry squares, inflicting horrific casualties. By this relentless advance, the Coalition Army took an hour to come to grips with the enemy at the centre of the battlefield.

Positioning himself at the front of his cavalry, Mr. Freeman drew his sword, pointed it at the enemy and ordered the trumpet for the charge. The entire line surged forward at a trot, accelerating into a canter and finally a gallop, cold steel flashing, with a ruthless fixity of purpose to cut down everything standing in its way. The Grand Army's cavalry did not wait for the impact but turned and fled, leaving the infantry at the mercy of the attackers.

Setting the example for Napoleon's Old Guards a century later at Waterloo, the foot soldiers of the Grand Army refused to retreat or surrender. To a man, they died fighting where they stood.

Victoria turned her face away from the savage slaughter. She couldn't comprehend why people would rather die than live to fight another day. Did they believe they would enjoy the reward of an eternal afterlife languishing in a fool's paradise?

"If you're determined to face the Amazonian Queen," Sator said, "you better get used to the butchery. She's not known to wear kid gloves. There will be blood. Heed our advice and give up your fixation on Earth and humans. They're a dead end."

"All the more they need my help," Victoria said with resolve.

"If you must go down this path," the one-eyed monk said, "do not hesitate to wield your weapon and submit to its power. Mr. Freeman enters the battle knowing his army is more potent than the French. The Coalition infantry's highly disciplined platoon firing system far outclasses the Grand Army's battalion volleys. Their concentrated and nonstop firepower does not take long to demonstrate its telling effects on the French and Bavarian soldiers. Moreover, the Coalition infantry's bullets are fifty percent heavier and are, therefore, more destructive. Coalition infantry also employs the ring bayonet, allowing them to charge and fire at the same time.

"More importantly, Mr. Freeman's cavalry delivers shock by cold steel while the Grand Army's cavalry is no more than musketeers on horseback. Once the French horseman has discharged his firearm, he is defenceless against the sword. As such, Mr. Freeman ties up numerically superior defenders in the village strongholds while concentrating his cavalry at the centre to deliver the coup de main. Mr. Freeman's decisive breakthrough at the enemy's heart is what makes this battle immortal."

"Yes, but what's the point?" Victoria said. "At his age, he lives in a tent and spends hours on horseback for what? According to you, Mr. Freeman's countrymen do not appreciate him. He risks his life in return for ingratitude. And as you say, his generals disobey him. His allies obstruct him. When he wins, people slander him. What would happen if he ever loses? Besides, everyone intrigues against him. Why doesn't he quit? Doesn't he have a family he can better spend his time with?"

"Indeed, he does," replied the one-eyed monk. "And this is the secret sauce of his success. Moments after the collapse of the Grand Army, who do you think is the first person Mr. Freeman writes to? Not the allies, not the Queen of England, not his country's government and politicians, but his wife, whom he addresses in his numerous letters as 'my dearest soul,' and to whom he tirelessly professes undying love with lines such as 'my heart is entirely yours,' or 'I love you more than I can express.'"

The two monks had anticipated this conversation. Sator's excursion to retrieve Xiphos also took him on a detour to the British Museum, where he borrowed some of Mr. Freeman's well-known letters to his wife. The one-eyed monk started reading some of them. "I do this minute love you better than ever I did before …

I am going up into Germany … but love me as you now do, and no hurt can come to me."

He read from another letter. "God had blessed her majesty's arms with as great a victory as has ever been known … for never victory was so complete, notwithstanding they were stronger … and very advantageously posted … my dearest life, if we could have another such day as Wednesday last, I should then hope we might have such a peace as that I might enjoy the remaining part of my life with you."

Mr. Freeman would have other memorable victories at Ramillies and Oudenarde in the Spanish Netherlands, but he would not gain the peace or the retirement he hoped for. His enemies at home attacked him for not being a party to their political extremism. The allies immediately returned to their selfish jealousies and secret intrigues, casting to the wind all hopes of a fair and long-lasting peace, which had been made possible by Mr. Freeman's genius and the sacrifice of so many lives.

In utter desperation, with the weight of the world on his shoulders and a thousand vitriolic barbs from his detractors lodged in his heart, Mr. Freeman wrote to his wife, begging for a palliative word to salve his agonizing wounds. "But you may be assured that you are dearer to me than all the world besides … My dearest soul, pity me and love me."

"These private and intimate letters," said the one-eyed monk, his voice breaking up as if he were talking about his own experience, "seem not so much to convey the thoughts of a careworn man writing to his wife of thirty years but the passion of a young ardent lover in the heat of pursuit. Mr. Freeman's secret source of power stems from his having found someone whom he truly and deeply loves, and who loves him back with equal measure. And with true love in his heart, all the endless and insufferable tribulations and vexations would become bearable."

Chapter 47

Omnia Vincit Amor

The Grand Army lost all semblance of order. Thousands of French and Bavarian soldiers fled the battlefield in a pell-mell toward the Danube. Those who tried to cross the river in a panic drowned. Twenty-seven battalions of the Grand Army's finest foot soldiers defending Blindheim were hemmed in and cut off from anyone who could rescue them. The Coalition Army surrounding the village soon pounded the defenders into submission. Mr. Freeman did not merely round up a boatload of small fry; he netted the mother of big fish. Among the numerous generals, captains and officers he captured was one of the marshals of the Grand Army, Comte de Tallard, a man of the highest renown in both military and diplomatic circles, a favourite of the Sun King and a darling of the court at Versailles.

The battle went down in history as one of the greatest ever fought. The genius of Mr. Freeman was manifest for all to witness and study. His students included the likes of Napoleon and Wellington, Lee and Grant, Moltke and Pershing, et cetera. Less than forty years after Mr. Freeman's passing, General James Wolfe applied the same devastating platoon fire to win the Battle of Quebec, deciding the fate of Canada.

By this time, Victoria had guessed the true identity of Mr. Freeman. Was it a coincidence Charlie asked her those trivia questions? Churchill, the Polar Bear Capital, was not named after the famous Prime Minister but after John Churchill. The town was established at the mouth of Churchill River, also named after him, on the Hudson Bay. Besides his feats of war, John Churchill, the first Duke of Marlborough, was also the third Governor of the Hudson Bay Company. He took the job after his boss, the Duke of York, whose title gave New York its name, vacated the position to take the throne of England as King James II. John Churchill consistently generated considerable profits during his tenure. He might save the company if he were its CEO today.

A hundred years after the battle, Napoleon's historian said this about John Churchill: "Thenceforward the name of Marlborough became as it were a new power which entered into the confederacy and upheld it by a terror, the profound marks of which the passage of a century has not effaced." Napoleon practically copied the Duke's genius at Blindheim, anglicized as Blenheim, to record one of his most signal victories at Austerlitz. Lord Acton, who owned the famous quote, "Power tends to corrupt," commented thus about Marlborough's victory by the Danube: "The day had been won not by the persistent slaughter of brave soldiers but by an inspiration of genius executed under heavy fire with all the perfection of art."

The reputation of John Churchill among his peers before this battle had been rather dismal. He grew up in a family impoverished by the English Civil War. His detractors often besmirched him, calling him a money-grabber and a skinflint. Historical documents, however, indicate he had quietly given up princely sums and a lucrative governorship for the common good of the Alliance. Ever since he was a young lad, John Churchill had always found himself torn between two opposing factions, even within his family. In later life, despite his Tory background and his wife's overt support of the republican Whigs, he resolutely refused to subordinate the nation's interests to the virulent extremism of the political parties, making him a popular target of attack by both.

Beneath his urbane exterior, John Churchill inherited the warrior blood coursing through his veins and circulating among all the male members of his family. Indeed, his father was known as the Cavalier Colonel, who fought faithfully in a thankless civil war for the losing cause of God and King. The poor King was Charles I, who had the mortifying experience of having his head dislodged by his subjects. One of John's brothers, George, to whom the quote "Dead men tell no tales" was attributed, was a high officer of the navy, and the other brother, Charles, was a general of the infantry at the centre of this very battlefield by the Danube. One of the Sun King's most capable marshals, the Duke of Berwick, was John's nephew, with whom he had kept a secret correspondence through the years. Everyone was related to everyone in Europe.

The Duke of Marlborough would prove to be one of the greatest generals in the history of the world. His only weakness was in winning every military action as a leader of armies, contrary to the sage advice, "It's not the best policy to win every battle." John Churchill would lose his battles in some other arenas.

"Despite his martial genius," the one-eyed monk said, "Mr. Freeman, or as you know by now, John Churchill, was no match for his wife, Sarah, for she conquered his heart. When John first courted her, their love match was impossibly impractical because the teenage girl was barely half his age, and both were penniless. Rumours of John's dalliance with the King's mistress were running rampant from the palace backstairs to every eager ear seeking juicy gossip. To pluck John out of a royal pickle, his father had already set him up with a perfect match, a plain-faced but sharp-tongued heiress with a substantial estate. But the dashing Lieutenant-Colonel, said to be the most handsome man in the royal court, was smitten with the young and ravishing Sarah, who already had the reputation of being a spitfire and a termagant and, when crossed, exhibited the temper of a tigress.

"Sarah would triumph over the invincible warrior by a simple stratagem. Despite her disadvantages of having a father who died early and a mother drowning in gambling debt, she resolutely refused to be conquered, as an uncommonly attractive girl in her situation in those days could not aspire to be anything beyond being an object of conquest. Indeed, John Churchill's sister was a mistress of the Duke of York and the mother of four royal bastards, one of whom was the aforementioned Duke of Berwick.

"Faced with the terrifying prospect of losing the love of his life, John Churchill did something considered rare during the seventeenth century. He married for love. Sarah would turn out to be one of the most extraordinary women of her era. Her story is an epic in itself. Armed with Sarah's love, John Churchill went on to perform prodigies of conquest against all odds."

"Moreover, hidden in John's blood," Sator added, "is a secret strand of power inherited from his mother's side of the family. A maternal great-great-grandfather of his was a sheep farmer named George Villiers, whose son and grandson somehow became the primus inter pares as the favourites of kings, both titled the Duke of Buckingham. Although the farmer's daughters could not be princesses or queens, they became mistresses of kings and princes, commingling their blood with the powerful and privileged.

"The most notorious royal mistress at the time, who amused herself by twirling King Charles II around her little fingers, was John's maternal kin, a direct descendant of the Villiers, the sensual and voluptuous Countess of Castlemaine, later Duchess of Cleveland. Famous for her transcendent beauty and infamous for her lack of scruples, she was said to be John's lover until the arrival of a brilliant and headstrong girl at the royal court, who at once captured the young man's heart and never relinquished it.

"The branches of the Villiers prospered and spread. Besides bearing prominent fruits such as the Duke of Marlborough, their descendants included many powerful politicians and prime ministers, from the third Duke of Grafton and William Pitt to Winston Churchill and David Cameron. The lineage would entwine with others to great effect. One of the sheep farmer's daughters married into the Washington family from which the first President of the United States of America would emerge."

"What is most intriguing," the one-eyed monk picked up where he left off, "and what serves as the subject of my study on rare human anomalies is the long and unwavering love between John and Sarah. Even after decades of marriage, the aged Duke would still write poignant love letters to his wife about how he longed to be with her, describing how he had stayed at the side of his departing ship, straining to see her fading image by the pier. Although we have a trove of letters from the Duke, only a few from his wife survived. Fortunately, we have a note penned by Sarah by which we might capture a glimpse of her love for John.

"Shortly after the Duke's passing, the attractive widow was immediately courted by one of the wealthiest aristocrats in the country. Sarah's response, more deadly than Xiphos and typical of her outspoken ways, is legendary: 'If I were young and handsome as I was, instead of old and faded as I am, and you could lay the empire of the world at my feet, you should never share the heart and hand that once belonged to John.' She could have politely declined. Even Harlequin Romance cannot make up such an immortal love affair, which is a true story in history."

"The Churchills couldn't afford a home at the time of their marriage," Sator cut in again. "But Sarah would be the wealthiest woman in England after her husband's death. The Duke was famous for his frugality, always sacrificing his personal comfort to ensure neither his soldiers nor his family would ever suffer from want. His wealth had accumulated over the years from prudent investments since his youth and his official remuneration as the

Commander-in-Chief of the Coalition Army. More importantly, Sarah had the perspicacity to convince John to exit the market moments before the bursting of the South Sea Bubble, adding a hundred thousand pounds to the family fortune, an incredibly immense amount at the time. The political impeachment of the Duke for peculation was cynical, unsupported by fact and later proven to be without merit.

"Sarah would apply her wealth toward completing the Blenheim Palace, cementing her husband's legacy. She would also financially support the people's prerogative in government, for which she had been a vociferous exponent all her life, at times to her own detriment as Queen Anne's childhood friend and personal favourite. She had the far-sightedness during her youth to be the patron of Robert Walpole and, in her old age, of William Pitt, both young Whigs rising to become the most prominent prime ministers in England's history, building the foundation of the island nation's democratic government, warts and all."

"John Churchill, the lucky Mr. Freeman, is the envy of us all," the one-eyed monk said wistfully. "He found the true love sadly missing in my life and the lives of so many others. As an invincible warrior myself, I once ruled a planet and could have anything my heart desired. Yet I'd gladly give it all up to be Mr. Freeman for one day, only to experience how it feels to love and be loved."

"Mr. Freeman is truly a wonderful story," Victoria said. "I hope you can see why humans have some redeeming values."

"It's out of our hands now," Sator said. "You have Xiphos, and it is up to you to save the human race."

The one-eyed monk checked his Patek Phillippe Sky Moon Tourbillon watch and exclaimed, "Oh dear! We're late."

"Now is the time for us to part, Victoria," Sator said. "The Celestial Catoptron has worked out the locations of all the hostages, but it can only take you to one of them. You'll have to locate and rescue the rest on your own. We cannot predict what will happen. Our Plancket quantum computations have failed to generate unique answers. You're truly an anomaly of Nature. We'll have to let the chips fall where they may."

"Sator and I are heading for the Isle of Avalon," the one-eyed monk said. "I don't know if you'll succeed in your battle against the Queen, but if you do, seek out the God With No Name to learn the whereabouts of the one true Grist of Truth. Join us at the blessed isle on the eleventh day for the Great Reset. Don't be late."

Sator sought the one-eyed monk's approval with an enigmatic question, "Should we or shouldn't we?"

His companion nodded.

Turning to Victoria, Sator offered a cryptic couplet, "'Upon the rendezvous of the tiger and the hare, 'tis consummation of the dream extraordinaire.' It is an oracle from the Mahashangria about the fate of the universe, but we don't understand what it means. Maybe when the time comes, it will all make sense."

"It sounds familiar. Where have I heard it before?"

"You may have encountered it in *Dream of the Red Chamber*," the one-eyed monk said. "Cao Xueqin overheard us trying to decipher this oracle and inserted it in his book as the oracle for Yuanchun, the eldest sister, in *The Twelve Ladies of Jinling*. It has become an enduring mystery in his story."

"We're out of time, Victoria," Sator said. "Instruct the Catoptron on the first person you wish to rescue. You will have to figure out the rest. Good luck and godspeed."

Victoria figured Charlie was the least valuable of the hostages; therefore, the Queen would likely post fewer guards or maybe none at all. Furthermore, Charlie should not be involved in all this. Victoria might have other considerations, but she had no time to weigh the pros and cons. She would break Charlie out of his cell first and save the others with his help.

Chapter 48

In Extremis

Victoria crossed the portal into a room identical to the one at Emperor Inn, where she stayed after meeting Charlie and Viola in Shanghai's Tianzifang. The Queen's attention to detail was impressive. She wanted Charlie to feel at home while being held hostage. She did not even post a guard. Charlie had put on his earbuds and was in bed listening to music with his eyes shut. He did not notice Victoria was in the room.

"Charlie, get out of bed," Victoria said, shoving the young man gently. "We have to go."

Charlie did not seem surprised. He spent much of his time during incarceration figuring out how Victoria would show up.

"Hi, Vic, I knew you'd find me," said Charlie as he hopped out of bed and hugged his rescuer. He took off the earbuds and placed them in Victoria's hand. "You should try these. They're fantastic."

"Later," Victoria said, casually stuffing the earbuds in her pocket. "Right now, we'll have to get out of here and rescue the others ASAP. We have no time."

"But we may not have a home to go back to. I've met Queen Lilith of the Amazons. She has been ranting and raving about giving Earth a makeover. She's deranged. We've got to stop her."

"I know. I'll deal with the Queen. But first, I need to get you and the others as far away from here as possible."

"Do you have any idea where the others are?" Charlie said. "Come to think of it, I don't even know where we are."

“We’re inside the Qaanaaq, the Queen’s flagship, 6.6 billion kilometres from Earth, anchored to a Kuiper Belt planetesimal known as Ultima Thule, nicknamed Eleven. The Amazonian armada will soon journey towards Earth. Humans have no defence against them. I’ll have to get you guys out of here and figure out a way to stop the Queen.”

“It is hopeless, Vic. How do we leave the ship and return to Earth without magic or alien technologies?” Charlie sighed, “In case I don’t get a chance to say this, Vic, I … eh … eh … *luacke* you very much.”

“Is that a word? What does it mean? I guess I *luacke* you too.”

Victoria tried the doorknob, swinging the door open to find Queen Lilith standing in front of her with Kerbera, the three-headed sand puppy, growling and baring her teeth.

“Are you going somewhere, children?” the Queen said, trying to sound maternal. “Victoria, my dear, you’re so predictable. But your weakness is also your strength, and I love you for it.”

Victoria telegraphed a message to Charlie with a wink, produced a handful of *qiexiang* snacks by sleight of hand and tossed them to one side, temporarily removing the Kerbera threat. Being voracious gluttons, sand puppies could not resist savoury morsels strewn before them. Their three heads would vie violently with each other for every scrap and lose their effectiveness.

With the slavering abomination out of the way, Charlie lunged forward and wrapped his arms around the Queen.

“Run, Vic, run,” he cried.

Victoria did not run. She unsheathed Xiphos and brought its point against the Amazonian Queen’s chest.

“Release all the hostages and leave Earth alone,” Victoria demanded. “Otherwise, my dagger Xiphos will end your life.”

Queen Lilith did not struggle or react. She smiled as if she were toying with her kittens.

"And all this time, I thought you disliked violence," the Queen said in her lily-like voice. "If you think killing me will change anything, you should go ahead. You'll be doing me a favour. It is my wish to terminate by the hand of someone I love."

"Don't listen to her," Charlie said. "She can lure birds to fly into a cage."

"Now, what have I done to deserve this, Charles?" the Queen protested. "Have I not treated you with the utmost respect and catered to your every whim? When you wanted to binge-watch television, I indulged you with every show on your list, including those hard-to-find cult classics *The Hidden*, *The Invaders* and *The Prisoner*. You wanted music, and I placed the entire iTunes library at your fingertips. We had such fun listening to bands you've never heard of. Don't tell me you don't like Badfinger or Genesis. You were enjoying 'Without You' and 'Undertow' a moment ago. You said you wished Victoria could be here, and voila, here she is."

"Ignore her, Vic," Charlie said. "Push in the blade to save the world from this psycho."

"I can't do it," Victoria cried as she dropped the dagger. She learned too late she had no stomach for slaughter.

Meanwhile, Leona and Churel had arrived to unhook Charlie from the Queen, dragging the kicking and cursing young man away. Victoria shouted, "Charlie, I'm sorry. I can't commit murder, but I'll save you if it's the last thing I do."

Victoria could barely make out Charlie's reply, "Too blave leber ties," as the guards threw him down a chute.

"How cute," Queen Lilith chuckled. "I wish I were young and innocent so I might enjoy the thrill of puppy love."

She tapped her medallion and ordered, "AlphaOmega, exit holo-hotel."

The illusion of the hotel room dissolved, revealing the spacious hall of the Queen's Court.

Victoria finally realized she had been duped and double-crossed by a disreputable robotic cockroach.

"What took you so long, my dear Victoria?" asked Queen Lilith as she sat on her grim throne. "We've been expecting you. But I must say your timing is impeccable. We're about to launch our first wave towards Earth. Don't worry about Charlie. He'll be fine. However, you must take a stand. Are you with me or against me? Is it going to be war or peace between us?"

Victoria thought about everyone she loved. They were all aboard and would be safe if she answered "peace." But the compromise would spell the end of Homo sapiens.

Although ignorance, prejudice and self-deception afflicted the human race, Victoria knew some individuals were clear-thinking truth-seekers. Although it was human nature to be greedy, selfish and cruel, she knew many examples of generosity, selflessness and kindness. Although humans had allowed themselves to be ruled and ruined by liars, hypocrites and murderers, she knew some humans were trying their best to serve the people.

Victoria could not blame most humans for being maggots because they have lived their entire lives in a cesspool. If all maggots say poop tastes good, why would you believe otherwise? Not only are humans their own worst enemies, but they are also their own victims. They do not deserve to die. They need to wake up from their stupor.

Despite the Queen's less-than-rosy assessment of the human race, Victoria thought they did not deserve to be extinct. She did not know what came over her when she answered "war," as if war were the only salvation for Earth and its inhabitants.

Thus, the conclusion of Victoria's saga arrives at the beginning, when the Queen warned, "Surely, one who fights with immortals is not long-lived."

Having escaped from the Queen's Court, Victoria ended up trapped inside a jetsam chute, pondering whether to press the Exit or Eject button. Victoria knew she did not enjoy the luxury of Hamlet's melancholy choice to die, to sleep, no more. She needed to survive to keep alive whatever flicker of hope not yet extinguished. Besides, our heroine had promised to save Charlie, come what may. Victoria recalled the lessons she learned from Mr. Freeman and David. Sometimes, surrendering brings unexpected results. She sighed resignedly, "I have to submit to the Queen. I have no choice," and pressed the Exit button.

Unfortunately, frequent time travel messes with one's cognitive functions. What Victoria assumed to be the Exit button was, in fact, the Eject. It was unbelievably bad timing for her to make such a monumental mistake. In the blink of an eye, Victoria found herself hurtling headlong at the speed of light to infinity and beyond, to be lost forever as jetsam among the numberless stars. For the moments before being devoured by the eternal void, Victoria panicked at first but became strangely calm and peaceful. Having no means to change her inevitable fate, the only thing she could do was accept the impending doom. Before letting out her last breath, Victoria watched the skull-shaped Qaanaaq receding at blinding speed. She could hear Phil Collins singing "Undertow."

"If this were the last day of your life, my friend, tell me, what do you think you would do then? Stand up to the blow that life has struck upon you. Make the most of all you still have coming to you. Lay down on the ground, and let the tears run from you, crying to the grass and trees and heaven finally on your knees …"

And darkness reigned.

The End

Is death the end?

Learn the universe's fate in Book 3: Augenblick

Why you should write Reviews

Authors and their books need reviews for readers to discover them. Readers need reviews to find the books they want to read. Without reviews, great works of art will be buried in obscurity. Without reviews, the lions of literature will wither away into oblivion. Reviews, therefore, sustain creative writing, an art form which defines human civilization and the meaning of our very existence. Your review is of paramount importance, whether it is a one-liner or a dissertation, and whether your rating of the book is good, mediocre or bad. We welcome and appreciate your opinion.

Book Website: https://www.petermanauthor.com/

Join the mailing list to learn secrets disclosed only to members.

Many Thanks!

Privacy policy: your email address will not be disclosed or distributed to any third parties without your expressed written consent. You may remove yourself from the Mailing List at any time and at your sole discretion by sending an email to the author with your expressed written instructions.

Image licenses and acknowledgment

Cover created using Copilot.ai, touch-up by author

Chapter 32 Banquet at the Wild Goose Gate photo public domain

www.ingramcontent.com/pod-product-compliance
Lightning Source LLC
Chambersburg PA
CBHW020447030826
49196CB00026B/65
9781999401986